GOOD MORNING, MADAM . . .

I made it to Melanie's service door at eight-thirty on the nose, just the way the bitch always told me to. I rang the doorbell and waited. And waited. Still no answer. Oh great. Melanie was playing dominatrix again. What was it this time? Was I three and a half seconds early? Or late? I pushed open the door and peeked inside the kitchen, then went into the maid's room, changed into my uniform, and headed for the office.

I knocked softly; no answer. "Hi, Ms. Moloney," I called out. "Just wanted you to know I've been here since eight-thirty on the dot. And thanks for leaving the back door open for me this morning. I really appreciate it."

She flat-out ignored me, so I turned the knob and opened the door slowly. Then I let out a scream to rival Faye Wray's in *King Kong*.

She was slumped in her chair, her head resting on her desk, her back to me. Oh, God. She's dead, I realized when I touched her body and found it stiff as a board.

What should I do? I had fantasized her death so many times, but now that she had actually bought the farm, I was paralyzed. What if people thought *I* was the murderer? What if I had to go to jail? What if my picture were splashed all over the tabloids with the caption "Mad Maid Murders Melanie"? What if the state of Connecticut had a death penalty and I got it?

And I'd been worrying about people finding out I was a *maid* . . .

CHA CHA CHA

Jane Heller

ZEBRA BOOKS
KENSINGTON PUBLISHING CORP.

Grateful acknowledgment is made for permission to reprint material from HOW TO REMEMBER AND TELL JOKES by Jim Pietsch, Avon Books, a division of the Hearst Corporation. Copyright © 1992 by Jim Pietsch.

ZEBRA BOOKS are published by

Kensington Publishing Corp.
850 Third Avenue
New York, NY 10022

First Kensington Hardcover Printing: July, 1994
First Zebra Paperback Printing: June, 1995

Printed in the United States of America

For Godie Forester

Acknowledgments

I'd like to thank the following people for their part in my becoming a published novelist: Ruth Harris, who loved *Cha Cha Cha* so much she actually bought it; Ann LaFarge, whose enthusiasm and intelligence propelled me to finish the book in record time; Jane Dystel, whose Thanksgiving phone call got the ball rolling a few years ago; Judy Fisher and Peggy Van Vlack, whose astonishing predictions boosted my morale; all my friends, who said, "We always knew you'd do something like this" and meant it as a compliment; and my parents, Joyce and Mort Reznick, who root for me no matter what I do. A very special thanks to Detective Michael Barrett of the Westport Police Department, who can plot a novel a whole lot better than the rest of us can catch a criminal.

Truth is mighty and will prevail. There is nothing the matter with this, except that it ain't so.

—*Mark Twain*

Everybody loves to cha cha cha.

—*Sam Cooke*

Prologue

"Everybody is in shock that something like this could happen in Layton," said Lisbeth Tolliver of 231 Dogwood Path, echoing the sentiments of many Layton residents, who were shaken by the death on Tuesday of celebrity biographer Melanie Moloney. The 55-year-old Moloney, who resided at 7 Bluefish Cove, had penned a half-dozen exposés of America's most famous stars. Her most recent title, Reluctant Hero: The Unauthorized Biography of Charlton Heston, *spent 27 weeks on* The New York Times *bestseller list and was optioned for a TV movie. A tireless researcher, Moloney, a native of Illinois, moved to Connecticut in 1988 in order to be closer to the subject of her latest unauthorized biography, retired actor and former United States Senator Alistair P. Downs, 75, current owner of* The Layton Community Times. *Lieutenant Raymond Graves of the Layton Police Department acknowledged that no arrests have been made in the case, but said he expects a break soon. Lieutenant Graves added that the Moloney homicide is only the twelfth murder to be committed in Layton in the past 40 years. He declined further comment. Moloney, who lived alone, was reportedly killed by a blow to the head sometime during the evening of Tuesday, February 20th. Her body was discovered the next afternoon by her housekeeper . . .*

—The Layton Community Times, *February 23, 1990*

Part One

Chapter 1

On October 19, 1987, while I was sitting in Monsieur Mark's Beauty Salon having my legs waxed, my nails polished, and my hair blown dry, the stock market crashed.

Of course, I didn't find out about it until later in the day, when my husband, Sandy, appeared in my bathroom, just as I was stepping into a nice hot Jacuzzi, and delivered the bulletin that we were broke. Just like that. Monday morning we had money, Monday night we did not. Monday morning I was a suburban princess on her way to a manicure, Monday night I was a desperate woman on her way to losing her husband, her home, and her job—and to becoming a murder suspect, of all things. What a difference a day makes.

I remember Black Monday as if it were last Monday. Black Monday. Stock Market Crash Monday. Say Goodbye to the Good Life Monday. Sandy had been speculating in the market on margin and had left himself exposed to potentially big losses if the market were to crash, which, of course, it did on that fateful October day.

"It's gone!" Sandy had yelled, grabbing me by my bare shoulders as I stood knee-deep in swirling hot water.

"What's gone?" I asked, looking down over my nakedness to make sure I hadn't lost one of my body parts.

"Everything." He sat on the edge of the tub with his head in his hands and mumbled something.

"I can't hear you," I said. The motor of the Jacuzzi was drowning him out.

"Our money's gone," he said and began to sob.

I had never seen Sandy cry, so I was more than a bit alarmed. "What do you mean, 'Our money's gone'? Tell me what happened."

"The stock market crashed, that's what happened. We lost it. There's nothing left."

"How can that be?"

"It just is. And what is, is." Sandy had taken a course in est in the mid-seventies and resorted to est-speak whenever he was under stress.

"But Sandy, all our money isn't in the stock market. We have Money Market Funds and Treasury Bills and IRA accounts."

"Not anymore. I converted all of that to stocks months ago."

"You what?" Suddenly, I thought I might hurl my lunch right into the Jacuzzi. All our money was in the stock market? The stock market crashed? We were broke? It was too much to bear. Quick! A joke! A joke! When in pain, make a joke, Alison. That's always been your credo. Think of something amusing to make it all go away. Crack yourself up so you won't have to feel anything. "Sandy," I ventured. "What's the definition of an economic advisor?" My husband gave me a disbelieving stare. "Someone who wanted to get into accounting, but didn't have the personality." I waited for him to get the joke. He didn't; he looked at me as if I'd lost my mind. But I hadn't lost my mind, just my money. Sandy's money. The very money I'd married him for.

"Alison," he said as patiently as possible, realizing how traumatized I must be to tell a joke at a time like this. "It's true. All our money *was* in the market, and the market crashed today. Try to deal with it. Like I am."

I took a few slow, deep breaths. "Okay. Okay. I'm calm.

I'm rational. So tell me: why on earth did you put all our money in the stock market?"

"You never complained about the way I managed our money in the past."

"And I'm not complaining now. I'm just trying to 'deal with it,' as you say. So tell me why you put everything we had in the stock market."

"Because I was doing well in the market. I was making money for us—so much money that I decided to put our assets where I could really keep an eye on them."

"But Sandy, you're not an investment banker. You're a retailer. You sell clothes and shoes and underwear." My husband ran Koff's, our town's biggest and oldest department store.

"Yeah, but all the guys are in the market now, Alison. Look at Bert Gorman and Alan Lutz. Bert may be a dermatologist but he calls his own trades. So does Alan and he's a dentist. It's not that big a deal."

"Not that big a deal? You tell me you've lost all our money and it's not that big a deal?" My face was flushed and my legs were numb from standing in the hot Jacuzzi water for so long. I climbed out of the tub and wrapped myself in one of the Adrienne Vitadini bath towels I'd bought at Bloomingdale's. Then I waited for Sandy to say something psychological, something est-like, the way he usually did when there was trouble.

"All right. I fucked up," he said finally. "But I'm owning up to it. I'm getting in touch with my pain, my guilt, and my shame. In fact, I'm getting so in touch with my shame that I've decided we should leave town. I can't face people whispering about me in restaurants."

"Leave Layton? You must be kidding." A rural yet sophisticated Connecticut town nestled along the shores of the Long Island Sound, about an hour and fifteen minutes from Manhattan, Layton had been my home all my life. "We can't leave Layton, Sandy. We live here. Our parents live here. And what about your job at Koff's? The store's a

Layton institution. A gold mine. So don't worry. You'll make our money back in no time."

"Haven't you heard a word I said, Alison? The stock market went under! You think the store won't go under next? You think people will have money to spend on designer clothes now? Come on, kid. Get real."

I *was* real, kid. That was the problem. Try as I might, I couldn't escape the awful reality that our "abundant life," as my favorite magazine *Town & Country* called it, was about to be over.

Of course, Sandy was right when he predicted that the stock market crash would turn Koff's business to shit. Thanks to a skittish economy and an even more skittish consumer, his income from Koff's fell off dramatically. So did his spirits. He became utterly despondent over the downturn his finances had taken, and his despondency sent him back into therapy with Dr. Weinblatt, the psychologist he'd consulted when his first marriage broke up.

Apparently, Dr. Weinblatt made Sandy nostalgic for the good old days of that first marriage, because ten months after Black Monday stripped me of whatever sense of security I had, Sandy announced he was leaving me for his first wife.

It happened on a Tuesday night in August, an evening I came to call Black Tuesday. Sandy and I were having Chinese take-out food for dinner. We always had Chinese take-out food for dinner on Tuesday nights because Tuesday was Sandy's therapy night. Some husbands have their bowling night; my husband had his therapy night.

Sandy preferred eating at home after therapy. He said he felt too "exposed" after his sessions with Dr. Weinblatt to go to a restaurant where people would be scrutinizing his every move. Sandy suffered not only from an aversion to being scrutinized, but from a delusion that people in restaurants found him interesting enough to scrutinize.

There was a decent Chinese restaurant right next door to Dr. Weinblatt's office, so our routine on Tuesday nights was for Sandy to stop at the Golden Lotus before his session, place our order, pick up the food after his fifty minutes with Dr. Weinblatt, and bring it home.

"Home" was an 18-room, 7,200-square-foot brick Georgian colonial. No, the house didn't have water views, but it was considered one of Layton's prime properties because of its four-plus acres and numerous outbuildings—"dependencies," the realtors called them. They consisted of a guest cottage, staff apartment, and party barn, none of which we had used in months, as we no longer had any guests, staff, or parties.

When we bought the house in 1984, Sandy suggested we name it. "All estates have names," he assured me. I was skeptical. I thought it was pretentious for a nouveau riche Jewish couple named Alison and Sandy Koff to try and act like old-money WASPs, who routinely gave their houses names like "The Hedges," "Harmony Hill," or "Tranquility." But we kicked around some possibilities one night and I started to get into the whole thing. Eventually, we settled on "Maplebark Manor," a name that gave the century-old maple trees on the property the respect and recognition they deserved.

Maplebark Manor was decorated in Greed-Is-Good Eighties style. In other words, we spent an obscene amount of money on a well-known New York decorator, who made us feel so insecure about our taste in furnishings that we allowed him to transform our home into the chintz capital of the United States. Nancy Reagan created the slogan "Just Say No" for people who are tempted by drug pushers, but I think it's equally appropriate for clients who are intimidated by their decorators.

Despite all the chintz, the house had many wonderful features—spacious bedrooms, each with its own bathroom and fireplace; baronial, high-ceilinged "public" rooms; and an enormous, eat-in kitchen, which, after our $50,000 renovation, boasted sparkling new floors, cabinets, counter tops, and state-of-the-art appliances but was supposed to look

like it had been that way for generations. The room I loved
most was on the second floor. It had once been used as a
children's wing, but we converted it into a large office for
me. We had decided to postpone having children until we
were older. I was thirty-four when we bought the house and
Sandy had just turned forty—old enough, you're probably
thinking, but the trend among driven, I-want-what-I-want-
when-I-want-it couples of the eighties was to wait until their
child-bearing years were just about over, then try their over-
achieving hardest to get pregnant, become incensed when
they couldn't, divert the thousands of dollars they'd been
spending on their houses, clothes, and cars to in vitro fertil-
ization and fertility drugs (don't let anyone tell you the drug
of the eighties was cocaine—it was Clomid), and then, when
nothing worked, drive themselves even crazier trying to
decide what to do next: adopt, join a Big Brother/Big Sister
program, forget about children altogether or take a soothing trip to the Caribbean to think about all of the above.

The room that was now my office faced south, was
flooded with sunshine most of the day, and overlooked our
swimming pool, tennis court, and gardens. It was in this
room that I wrote articles about celebrities. I was a freelance
writer whose work appeared in the *Layton Community
Times,* a twice-weekly newspaper serving the residents of
Layton and neighboring towns.

Big deal, you're probably thinking. So she writes for a
dinky local paper. What kind of celebrities could she possibly get to interview?

Plenty, I promise you. First of all, Layton has its very
own community playhouse that does revivals of the best
Broadway shows, and I was the reporter who covered all the
openings and interviewed all the stars. Second of all, Layton
is home to dozens of famous people—movie stars, TV personalities, writers, rock stars, you name it—most of whom
are only too happy to plug their latest ventures.

It was in my capacity as celebrity reporter for *The Layton
Community Times* that I met Sandy Koff—Sanford Joshua

Koff, the son of the Koff behind Koff's Department Store, a retailer who was around long before the Gaps and Benettons came to town. The occasion for my interview with Sandy was the announcement in March of 1983 that his father was retiring and turning over complete control of the store to Sandy.

I looked forward to our meeting because I'd heard Sandy was newly divorced. I was newly divorced myself and living in the two-bedroom condo I had shared with my first husband, Roger, who had left me and his medical practice to become a G.O. at Club Med. Roger's father owned a button business in Long Island and was very rich. As a result, Roger was very rich, which was why he could afford to become a doctor and then decide not to.

The day I met Sandy was a good hair day; my shoulder-length, brown locks, which have a tendency to frizz, had not done so. I remember looking at myself in the mirror that morning and thinking, Not too shabby, Alison.

Actually, I'm not bad-looking. I'm thin (size 6) but not profoundly flat-chested (size 34B), am of average height (5'5"), and have remarkably even features for a Jewish person (no hook nose). I have a raspy voice, big brown eyes, and freckles across my nose. People say I look like the actress Karen Allen, which means that I also look like the actresses Brooke Adams and Margot Kidder, because Karen Allen, Brooke Adams, and Margot Kidder look the same.

My interview with Sandy took place in his office on the second floor of Koff's Department Store.

"Nice to meet you," he said, getting up from his chair and stepping around his big desk to greet me. I could tell he was checking out my outfit and wondering if I'd bought it at Koff's.

I explained the nature of my article to Sandy and we chatted about his plans for the store. I sensed that he was a very sincere person because of all the psychological things he said during our first forty-five minutes together. Psychological things like: "I've been struggling to get in touch with my conflicts about surpassing my father." And: "I have a primal urge to succeed as well as a subconscious wish to sabotage my success." Not having had much exposure to psychology, I assumed that people who spoke in psychological terms were more open and trustworthy than people who didn't. And, God knows, after having been raised by a mother whose idea of openness was never telling people her real age, and after having been married to a man whose idea of trust was leaving it to his secretary to tell me he was divorcing me, I was in the market for an open and trustworthy person.

I responded positively to Sandy's appearance, too. He had a nice smile, with big white teeth that positively shone—a smile that broke up his long, thin, somber, Stan Laurel face and gave it some warmth. He also had a long, thin nose, long, thin fingers that had little black hairs growing around the knuckles and were manicured, and a long, thin body. As a matter of fact, everything about Sandy Koff was long and thin, except his very dark hair, which was short and thin, and his penis, which was long and fat. (More on that later.) He wasn't your basic leading man, but I found him attractive in a Tony-Perkins-with-a-receding-hairline sort of way. I was particularly taken with his Adam's apple, which bobbed up and down with such ferocity that I couldn't take my eyes off it.

The other thing I noticed about Sandy that first day was how tan he was for the middle of March. He told me that he had just come back from Malliouhana, the resort in the Caribbean that used to be a little-known hideaway for sleek and sophisticated Europeans but was now, after being featured on "Lifestyles of the Rich and Famous," the vacation-spot-of-the-moment for the Rolex set, i.e. suburban doctors, lawyers, and garmentos. If you were on the beach at Malliouhana and yelled, "Is anyone here named Irving?," every man in the place would say yes.

Sandy and I started dating right after that meeting in his

office. He took me to lunch. He took me to dinner. He took me to sporting events. He took me to romantic little inns in Vermont. He introduced me to his friends. He introduced me to his parents. He even introduced me to his "physical catalyst," which is what he called his personal trainer, who came to his house three mornings a week and showed him how to pump iron. Before I knew it, we had memorized each other's phone number and given each other intimate little nicknames (my name for Sandy was Basset, because he reminded me of a basset hound; his name for me was Allergy, because the word sounded like Alison and because I apparently got under his skin like a pesky rash). Before I knew it, we had told each other juicy and disgusting things about our first spouses. Before I knew it, we had grown comfortable with each other, especially in bed: I no longer slept in the nude, he no longer asked me to sleep in the nude; I no longer acted as if I enjoyed giving him a blow job, he no longer acted as if he didn't notice that I didn't enjoy giving him a blow job. Before we knew it, we were an eighties couple in love.

What about passion, you ask? I wasn't looking for passion then. I just wanted some certainty in my life—some guarantee that the man I married was loaded. This I learned from my mother, who told me over and over that a man wasn't to be trusted unless he had money; that he wasn't worthy of respect unless he had money; that he certainly wasn't marriage material unless he had money—preferably inherited *and* earned. After years of such brainwashing, the best I could deduce about men was that it was okay to harbor a secret sexual attraction for a gas station attendant as long as the guy you married owned the pumps.

So I married Sandy Koff, who had money, in 1984. He seemed very happy. So did my mother. Two out of three was pretty good, I thought, which tells you something about my level of expectation.

We sold my condo and lived briefly in Sandy's six-bedroom house on the water, which he had rented after his first wife kicked him out of their five-bedroom house on the water. Then we bought Maplebark Manor and moved in there. Life was sweet. Sandy ran Koff's Department Store, I wrote newspaper articles about the famous and nearly famous. We wore expensive clothes, drove expensive cars, ate in expensive restaurants, and indulged in just enough lovemaking to keep our sex organs from atrophying. I discovered the joys of gardening, Sandy discovered the thrill of speculating in the stock market. I bought all of Martha Stewart's books so I could learn how to throw parties, Sandy bought a computer so he could keep track of his stock transactions. We had friends, we had staff, we had money—until Black Monday, the day we lost it all. Oh, well, we still have each other, I consoled myself during the next few months. Then came Black Tuesday, the day Sandy came home from Dr. Weinblatt's office with more than Chinese take-out food on his mind.

"I'm home," he'd called through the intercom in the kitchen. We had installed intercoms on every floor of Maplebark Manor so that we never had to raise our voices.

"I'll be right down," I said through the intercom in my office on the second floor. It was seven-thirty, and I'd spent the past few hours working on an article about June Allyson, who had come to Layton not only to promote Depend Undergarments, but also to star in *South Pacific,* currently in production at the Layton Community Playhouse.

I hurried down the back staircase and entered the kitchen, where Sandy was unpacking little white boxes of Chinese food and spooning their contents into the pretty Depression glass bowls I'd picked up at an auction at Sotheby's. He had already changed into his robe and slippers, and he appeared to be smiling, which is something I hadn't seen him do in months.

"You're in a good mood," I said cheerfully as we carried the food, placemats, napkins, and silverware into the glass-enclosed breakfast room off the kitchen. We sat down across from each other at the round butcher-block table and started to dig in.

"Egg roll?" Sandy asked, offering me one of the items from the Pu Pu Platter.

"No thanks," I answered, content with my sesame noodles for the time being. "So tell me why you're in such a good mood. Is business up at the store?"

"No," Sandy said with a mouth full of egg roll. "It has nothing to do with the store. It has to do with Soozie."

"Soozie?" I asked sweetly, making a real effort not to let bitchiness creep into my voice. Soozie was Sandy's ex-wife. She was also a caterer who, unlike my idol, Martha Stewart, didn't have much of a head for business. Yes, she knew how to cook, as Sandy never ceased to remind me every time I tried to make anything in puff pastry and failed. But she didn't have a clue how to market herself. Consequently, she was a caterer with few parties to cater. She had divorced Sandy because she had wanted to "spread her wings and soar." From what I heard, she'd been doing plenty of spreading, all right, but it had nothing to do with her wings. Not that I cared how Sandy's ex-wife spent her free time, mind you, just as long as it wasn't with Sandy.

"I was going to wait until we finished dinner," Sandy said, setting his fork down on his plate, reaching across the table to take my fork out of my hand and wrapping both my hands in his. I knew something big was coming, but I honestly had no idea what. "Allergy, I feel really good about myself now that I have an awareness of where I was coming from in terms of my feelings for you."

He paused. I stared. Had he always talked like that? Had I never noticed how ridiculous he sounded?

"Allergy," he continued. "I feel so close to you, now that I can put a label on your role in my life." Another pause, then a deep breath, then a big smile. "You were my transitional woman."

I stopped chewing. The sesame noodles that had tasted so good seconds before suddenly turned to cardboard. My heart began to beat faster as I waited for Sandy to finish his speech. I knew there was more. There always is.

"The thing is," Sandy went on, getting up from his chair to put his arm around me, "Soozie still loves me and wants me back, and I still love her and want her back."

Quick! Think of a joke! I thought as I struggled to comprehend what my husband was telling me.

What *was* he telling me? That he'd been seeing Soozie behind my back? That the two of them were lovers again? That he'd loved her all along and only married me out of loneliness or boredom? That I was a failure as a wife, as a woman, as a cook? That he was leaving me forever? That I was going to be alone again?

I was tempted to heave my plate of Chinese food at Sandy, I really was. The image of that thick, tan sauce dripping down his fluffy white Ralph Lauren terry-cloth robe, the one with the "family crest" on the front pocket, was mighty appealing. But I was too distraught to clean up the mess, and I was much too compulsive to leave it for Maria, our Peruvian housekeeper, who never found a speck of dirt when she arrived each morning because I always cleaned the house before she got there.

Quick! A joke! A joke! My eyes burned with hurt and anger, but I willed myself not to cry. Never let 'em see you sweat. Isn't that what the commercial says?

Sandy, my husband. Just look at him, I thought. What a pitiful sight. He graduated with honors from Columbia University and was at the top of his class at NYU Business School, so he can't be a complete idiot, and yet listen to how he talks. Look at how he looks. He combs his three remaining hairs clear across his prematurely balding head and he thinks he's fooling everybody. We all know you're going bald, asshole. And Soozie, the caterer-whore. Of all the women to be left for. Soozie, whose real first name is the perfectly acceptable Diane but who insists that everyone call her Soozie.

"I know you must be devastated," Sandy said, getting up from the table and wrapping me in his arms.

Devastated? Devastated? I thought, trying desperately to conceal my panic. Don't let your husband think you're dependent on him, my mother always said. Never let him know how much you care. Always make him guess. Keep your real feelings to yourself. Never wear your heart on your sleeve. Quick! A joke! A joke!

"Allergy? Are you all right? Say something," Sandy said, looking genuinely concerned about me.

I took a deep breath and said two things to my faithless second husband. One was: "Sandy, I think it's good that you're going back to Soozie, because I've been wanting to see other men for some time. You know my motto—'Never put all your eggs in one bastard.' "

I waited for him to get the joke before proceeding with the second thing I said, which was: "And Sandy, if you ever call me Allergy again, I'll tell everyone in Layton the truth about Soozie—that the secret ingredient in her 'all natural' chicken salad is MSG and that her 'homemade' cakes aren't from scratch, they're from a mix."

Sandy scowled at me, shook his head, and walked out of the room. "You're in denial," he said. "Big-time denial."

"Deny this," I yelled as I gave him the finger. Then I wondered which was worse—losing your man or losing your meal ticket. I had just lost both, which was nothing to joke about.

Chapter 2

As you might imagine, I didn't sleep at all the night Sandy left me for Soozie. Every time I closed my eyes, I thought about the two of them together—the stock market big-shot and the caterer-whore.

One of the images that kept drifting in and out of my mind was their dopey reunion. I imagined that after Sandy left Maplebark Manor (he'd packed his Louis Vuitton bags, jumped into his Mercedes, and sped off to Soozie's, leaving me with a dining room table full of Chinese take-out food), he'd arrived at the caterer-whore's, barely able to contain his joy at having successfully removed the one obstacle— me—that was standing in the way of their happiness. Can't you just picture them? He'd pull into her driveway and there she'd be, standing at the front door, waving a potholder at him. He'd leap out of his Mercedes and rush into her arms, in slow motion, like in those shampoo commercials. She'd run her fingers through his three hairs. He'd bury his hands under her apron. Then they'd go inside and make mad, passionate love on the kitchen floor. They would be so nauseatingly ecstatic about being back together again that they'd forget to bring Sandy's bags in from the car and somebody would steal them—and the car.

I'd throw in that last part every time I started to feel overwhelmingly panicked about Sandy leaving me. It would serve Sandy right to have his precious Mercedes stolen right from under his long, skinny nose. God, did I hate him. How could he abandon me and Maplebark Manor? What if that recession all the talk shows were talking about sent the country into a *depression?* How would I cope without my husband at a time like that?

I wouldn't. That was the conclusion I reached at about 5 A.M., the morning after Black Tuesday. I simply would not let Sandy go. I would not go through this economic downturn alone. I would win him back. I would convince him that the stock market crash and the problems at Koff's had made him understandably nostalgic for the good old days with Soozie, but that if he really thought about it, it was I who could make him happy, I who had helped him build a rich, abundant life. After all, it wasn't as if Sandy and I didn't have property together: we had Maplebark Manor. Some couples stay together for the sake of the children. We would stay together for the sake of the house. I would go to Sandy's office first thing in the morning and show him photographs of Maplebark Manor. He would smile at me and say, "Forgive me, Allergy. It was the recession that made me do it. I'm leaving Soozie and coming home to you. To Maplebark Manor."

I was just getting out of bed and thinking about what I'd wear to Sandy's office when the phone rang at about 9:15. It was Adam Greene, a lawyer who'd been a friend of Sandy's since high school.

"Sandy isn't here," I said, assuming that Adam was looking for my prodigal husband, who was probably still at Soozie's, resting up after a night of unbridled passion. Actually, all jealousy and bitterness aside, it was hard to imagine Sandy engaging in a night of unbridled passion. Sure, he had an enormous cock, but what good was owning a Ferrari if you couldn't drive a stick shift? Not only that, Sandy was the quietest lovemaker since Marcel Marceau. He never moaned. He never groaned. He never said, "Oh, baby. Do it to me. Give it to me." He never said anything at all—not a word. When we had sex, you could hear a pin drop, which meant, of course, that I wasn't doing any moaning and groaning either. It wasn't that I didn't have it in me to moan and groan. It was just that it was next to impossible to scream with pleasure when (A) I wasn't having any, and (B) my partner was like an actor in a porno movie for the hearing impaired.

All right. So our sex life wasn't exactly the stuff of romance novels. I didn't care. I was not about to go through the turbulent nineties alone. I was going to get Sandy back, and that was that.

"I know Sandy's not there, Alison," Adam Greene said to me over the phone. "He's here in my office. We've been discussing your divorce."

"Divorce?" Here I was, planning to win back my husband, and he couldn't wait twenty-four hours to dump me.

"Have you retained an attorney yet, Alison?" Adam asked with not nearly enough concern in his voice to suit me. Adam Greene was supposed to be *my* friend as well as Sandy's. He and his wife, Robin, had been to Maplebark Manor dozens of times, just as we had been over to Belvedere, the 23,000-square-foot mansion they called home. Belvedere had only four bedrooms, but it had an indoor squash court, which Adam and Sandy had used quite a bit until they gave up squash for golf. The last I'd heard, the Greenes were planning to convert the squash court into a movie theatre that could show two movies simultaneously, just like the Loews Twin Theatre in Layton.

"No, Adam. I haven't hired a lawyer yet. I wasn't aware Sandy wanted a divorce until just this minute. The body's not even cold."

"What's that?"

"Nothing. Tell Sandy he can have his divorce, but he's going to feel it in his wallet."

"I don't think so, Alison. You'll be on your own from now on."

"What are you talking about?"

"You signed a prenuptial agreement in 1984, before you and Sandy bought Maplebark Manor. Remember?"

Shit. I had forgotten all about that. Sandy had insisted that we have it drawn up, seeing as he was the one with the big money, and I, not wanting to appear dependent—or worse, gold digging—signed the thing, which said that if we ever broke up, I would get what I came to the marriage with and he would get what he came to the marriage with, which, of course, was a hell of a lot more than what I came to the marriage with. As for Maplebark Manor, the agreement stipulated that one of us could buy the other out. If neither of us wanted the house, we could sell it and split the profits, seventy-five twenty-five. Guess who got the twenty-five.

"Sandy asked me to tell you he doesn't want the house, since he and Soozie plan to live at her place. You can stay on at Maplebark Manor, provided you come up with the money to buy Sandy out."

"Oh, right," I said, wondering how much worse things could get. "Sandy knows damn well I don't have that kind of money."

"In that case, you'll have to put Maplebark Manor on the market," Adam said.

"You mean sell it? Our beautiful house that we poured every dime we had into? The real estate market is dead these days, in case you and Sandy haven't noticed. We'll have to *give* the house away."

"I'm not your attorney, Alison, but if I were, I'd tell you that you really don't have any choice. Sandy's finances aren't what they were, as you know, and he won't be able to make the mortgage payments any longer. If he has to file for bankruptcy and your beautiful house goes into foreclosure, you won't walk away with anything but a lawsuit and a lousy credit rating."

"That's it? That's all Sandy has to say to me after five years of marriage? That if I don't sell the house fast, the bank will take it and I'll be broke?"

Adam put his hand over the mouthpiece of the phone and

whispered something to Sandy. Then he came back on and
said, "Sandy asked me to tell you something, Alison. He
says, 'Life is a mountain. Go climb it.' "

"Gee thanks, Adam. Now I'd like you to tell Sandy something: 'Life is a cliff. Jump off it.' "

I hung up on Adam, ran downstairs to the kitchen, and
made myself a Bloody Mary. It was only 9:30 in the morning, but I needed fortification: I was about to call my mother
and break the news that Sandy, her favorite of my two
husbands, had left me. If I didn't tell her soon, she'd hear
about it at the hairdresser or the dry cleaner or, God forbid,
at the gourmet produce market, where people had as much
fun trading local gossip as they did buying designer lettuce.
I decided to get dressed before I called my mother. I
always got dressed before I called my mother. I trudged
upstairs and walked into my walk-in closet off the master
bedroom, pulled out a navy blue Fila warm-up suit, and put
it on. Then I sat down on my bed and glared at the phone
on the night table, gulped down the rest of my Bloody
Mary, and dialed my mother's number.

"Hi, Mom. It's me," I said breezily after my mother,
Doris Waxman, answered the phone.

"It's *I*," she corrected me in That Tone. My mother was
a vigilante when it came to the English language—a verita-
ble Guardian Angel of Grammar. If you were foolish
enough to say something like "between you and I" in her
presence, there would be hell to pay. She also had a voice
like Suzanne Pleshette's—an extremely low, husky,
smoker's voice that people often mistook for a man's. When
she put you down with That Tone and That Voice, you
could consider yourself put down. "As a writer, Alison, you
should pay more attention to your words," she added for
good measure.

"To tell you the truth, Mom, I've got more pressing

problems to deal with—sorry—more pressing problems with which to deal." Oh, God.

"That's a good girl. What pressing problems. Is business still bad at Sandy's store?"

"Yes. But that's not the most pressing problem right now."

"Oh? Then what is it?"

"It's something else." It was perverse of me, I know, but I loved making my mother pull information out of me. After years of being manipulated by her, it was my way of turning the tables.

"It's not your health, is it?"

"No."

"Your job at the newspaper?"

"No."

"Something to do with the house?"

"In a way." I figured I'd back into the subject of divorce. My mother felt the same way about divorce as she did about dangling participles. She and my father had been ecstatically happy during their short-but-sweet marriage, which came to an abrupt and tragic end in August of 1960, when I was ten. It happened during the annual Mixed Member Guest Tennis Tournament at Grassy Glen, the country club my parents and all their friends belonged to. My father, Seymour (everybody called him Sy) Waxman, was an "A" player and the hands-down favorite to win the tournament, especially since his doubles partner was the formidable Jack Goldfarb, the men's champion over at Rolling Rocks, another club in Layton. But on match point—just as my father and Mr. Goldfarb were about to secure their victory—my father wound up to serve and then suddenly grabbed his chest, fell to the red clay surface, and died. Just like that. Game, set, match. Fortunately, my mother and I were not there when it happened. She was at Neiman Marcus buying Christmas presents (yes, it was summer, but she liked to plan ahead, and yes, we were Jewish, but we still bought Christmas presents). I was at sleepaway camp in Maine, learning how to excel at archery, synchronized swimming, and other activities that would prove completely irrelevant to my life as a grown-up. When I found out my father had died, I went into shock. Sy Waxman, the Mattress King, had always been my security, my stability. I couldn't believe he was gone. I couldn't believe he would no longer be there to hug me, kiss me, love me. I couldn't believe he would leave me alone to deal with my mother for the rest of my life—my mother, who handled his death by becoming an impossibly angry, lonely woman. The first thing she did after he died was to turn their bedroom into a shrine, hanging photographs of him wherever there was wall space. The second thing she did was to refuse to give his clothes away. The third thing she did was to boycott the country club where he'd met his untimely end. For months, she just sat around the house, chain-smoking her Winstons and watching "As The World Turns," the one constant, besides me, in her life. Never a barrel of laughs, my mother became The Grouchiest Widow in Connecticut, maybe even in the Tri-State Area. Consequently, I became The Daughter Who Was Forever Trying to Cheer Her Up, which is another way of saying I was always trying to please her. I cleaned my room. I combed my hair. I did my homework. I spoke in grammatically correct sentences. And I told jokes—lots of grammatically correct jokes. Here's a sample:

"Knock, knock."

"Who's there?"

"Marmalade."

"Marmalade who?"

"Mama laid me. By whom were you laid?"

As I grew older, my eagerness to please my mother manifested itself in a new, more disturbing way: I began dating, and eventually marrying, rich men. She was thrilled when I got married to Roger, but you should have seen her face when I told her I was going to marry Sandy! This woman who smiled only on rare occasions was so happy she broke out into a grin the size of Imelda Marcos's shoe closet.

I never knew where her reverence for rich men had come from. I supposed it stemmed from her humble beginnings in Queens. I knew there'd been a man in her life before she met my father—a man who'd made it big and then left her in the dust. Whatever the reason, her obsession with rich men was hard to take, try as I did to take it.

"I know this is going to disappoint you, Mom," I began, "but Sandy and I are calling it quits."

Dead silence. Then a big inhale and exhale. I could practically smell the cigarette smoke through the phone.

"What did you do?" my mother asked. It *had* to be my fault.

"Sandy has gone back to his first wife, Soozie." An enormous lump formed in my throat.

"He picked that woman over *my* daughter?" My mother was taking Sandy's defection personally. "She's a nobody. A person who cooks for people. And isn't her father a gentile?" My mother's attitude toward Christians was that they had low IQs and zero taste in clothes.

"Yes, Mom. He went back to Soozie," I said.

"Your father would never have understood all this . . . this . . . casual marrying and divorcing. I know I don't. Why can't children today finish anything they start? Why can't my only daughter finish anything *she* starts?"

"I have finished things," I said weakly. "For eleven years I've worked at a newspaper owned by Alistair Downs, former Hollywood star and U.S. Senator from Connecticut. I may not be buddy-buddy with the man, but I've been his loyal employee. That's something to be proud of, isn't it?"

"Something of which to be proud. But what about your personal life, Alison? It's an embarrassment."

"An embarrassment? To whom?" I knew to whom: my mother's friends at Grassy Glen, where, except for her brief boycott following my father's death, she'd been playing canasta three times a week for years.

"I'm sorry about you and Sandy, dear," she conceded. "But these divorces of yours are wearing on me."

"On you?"

"Of course, on me. I've been waiting a long time for you to settle down with the right man, and I'm not getting any younger."

"None of us are," I said.

"Is, Alison. None of us *is."*

"I've got to go, Mom. Someone's at the door." Someone wasn't at the door, but I used this ruse frequently when I wanted to get off the phone with my mother. It never occurred to her to ask who was ringing my doorbell at all hours of the day and night, and it certainly never occurred to me to be honest with her—i.e. tell her to fuck off.

My next call was to Janet Claiborne, the broker at Prestige Properties who had sold us our house.

"Mrs. Koff. I've been expecting your call," she said.

"You have?"

"Yes. So soddy about the divorce," she said in her Connecticut lockjaw voice.

"How did you know my husband and I were getting a divorce?" Did everyone in Layton know I'd been dumped, or was it just that real estate agents made it their business to know everybody else's?

"I attended a Junior League luncheon the other day, and Soozie Koff of Soozie's Delectable Edibles was dishing up the most divine chicken salad."

Obviously, Soozie had been dishing up more than chicken salad. Small-town life was such fun. "Well, about the house . . ."

"So soddy you have to sell," Janet Claiborne said, barely able to conceal her joy at capturing our three-million-dollar listing yet again. "The market is a bit depressed right now," she added, covering her ass, "but properties like Maplebark Manor—isn't that the charming name you gave the place?—are absolutely recession-proof."

Janet promised to send someone over with papers for me

to sign, and pledged that Prestige Properties would not only advertise Maplebark Manor in *Town & Country* and *Unique Homes,* but produce full-color brochures showcasing the house and mail them to Japanese businessmen who, she felt, would be our best customers.

Having dispensed with my duty calls, I debated what to do next: hide in the house so I wouldn't have to face everybody in Layton gossiping about me, or go out in public and start dealing with the two harsh realities of my new life—poverty and singlehood. What a choice. If I stayed in the house, I'd probably end up watching hours and hours of Phil, Oprah, Sally, Joan, and Geraldo, and learning more than I ever wanted to know about cross-dressers, mud wrestlers, and women who were born without clitorises. If I went out in public, I'd probably end up bumping into someone I knew and having to respond to questions like, "So, Alison. Where will you live after the bank forecloses on your house? How will you support yourself? How will you ever find another man to love you?"

The thought of staying home and becoming an agoraphobe didn't appeal to me. I was supposed to hand in my feature article about June Allyson anyway, so I changed my clothes and went over to the newspaper.

As I drove into the parking lot, I narrowly missed rear-ending the gleaming white Rolls-Royce Corniche driven by Layton's most illustrious citizen (and my boss) Alistair P. Downs, owner of *The Layton Community Times.* He was backing his car out as I was pulling mine in, and we would surely have collided had I not slammed on my brakes and sent my neck whiplashing all over the place. Just what I needed.

"Oh, I'm so sorry, Senator Downs. Please forgive me," I called out through my open window. The mishap was clearly Alistair's fault, but a little groveling was in order.

"Don't you worry, little lady," Alistair chuckled. "My

chauffeur's off today, and I haven't driven in a while. Guess I'm a little rusty. Ho ho."

"Are you okay?" I asked. The man was seventy-five, after all. He looked robust, but once you hit seventy, you could go at any time. At least that's the bit my mother used when she wanted me to feel guilty that I didn't call her every day.

"I'm splendid. Just splendid, dear," said Alistair as he maneuvered his Corniche around my Porsche and sailed out of the parking lot, giving me a little wave in his rearview mirror.

"Yeah, I'm splendid too. Thanks for asking," I muttered. What an egomaniac, I thought, as I parked my car and climbed the steps to the brick building that housed *The Layton Community Times* offices. Alistair Downs didn't seem to give two shits about my well-being, although he was always very cordial in social settings. Whenever he'd throw an office party at the Sachem Point Yacht Club, the 100-year-old sailing club where he was the commodore, he'd glide right over to me, smooth as you please, look me straight in the eye, shake both my hands, and say, "Lovely to see you again, dear. You're doing a splendid job at the paper. Splendid." Then he'd vanish, leaving me in a cloud of Old Spice.

What a character, I thought, as I considered Alistair Downs's stature, not just in Layton but nationwide. Larger than life. That's what he was. Here was a man who had parlayed his way with the latest dance steps, first into a Hollywood movie career, later into the United States Senate. Never mind that he came into the world as Al Downey, a handsome Irish kid from Queens. Never mind that he began his professional life as a dance instructor in an Arthur Murray Studio. Never mind that if a talent scout hadn't stopped by the studio that fateful day and seen what a favorite of the ladies Al Downey was, there might not have been an Alistair Downs at all.

But then the story of how Al Downey reinvented himself wasn't a story Alistair Downs liked to tell. Unlike Kirk

Douglas, who wrote a book about his humble beginnings as Issur Danielovitch, the ragman's son, Alistair Downs preferred to deny his past. No one ever pressed him about it—until Melanie Moloney, the queen of the sleaze celebrity bio, came to town. The author of bestselling exposés of the lives of Dean Martin, Ann-Margret and other well-known entertainers, Melanie Moloney had received a reported $5.5 million to write a book about Alistair Downs, who told the media, "I plan to pay no attention to Miss Moloney or her so-called biography." Personally, I couldn't wait to read Melanie Moloney's book, which, according to *USA Today,* was due to be delivered to her publisher in just a few short months.

The first person I ran into at the newspaper was the last person I wanted to run into: Bethany Downs, Alistair's daughter and the paper's managing editor. Former cheerleader, debutante, and homecoming queen, Bethany was arrogant and dumb, a lethal combination if ever there was one. The popular rumor was that her father had bought the *Community Times* as a toy for his only child, to keep her out of trouble. Forty-two years old, Bethany had never been married. She preferred sleeping with other women's husbands, coaxing them just to the point of leaving their wives and then dumping them and moving on to some other chump. Blond and pretty, if you like the type (she had the face of a horse if you ask me), she was that dangerous sort of girl who had the notion that anything and anybody was hers for the taking.

"You don't look well, Alison," were Bethany's first words to me. We were standing in the third-floor lounge. Hoping to steady my nerves after nearly putting a dent in Alistair Downs's high-priced fender, I had gone there for a cup of coffee. Bethany had gone there to grab a few jelly donuts. Bethany had an addiction to sweets, but never seemed to gain weight, which, in addition to being a husband stealer, was another reason why most women hated her.

"I've had a tough twenty-four hours," I replied.

"Domestic problems?"

"As a matter of fact, yes. My husband and I are splitting up."

I waited for a response, but Bethany just chomped on her jelly donut. Then she said, "See? That's what I keep telling people. There's no point in getting married. Marriage only leads to divorce."

"That's pretty defeatist, Bethany. Don't you ever yearn for the company of one man, a man who'll be there to love and protect you always?"

"I already have that man. His name is spelled D-A-D-D-Y."

"Right. How could I forget?"

"Speaking of Dad," Bethany continued, "there's a meeting in my office in ten minutes. It's about that bitch who's writing a book about him. I suggest you be there."

"I wouldn't miss it for the world," I said.

Ten or twelve of us gathered in Bethany's corner office. I waved to my best friend at the paper, Julia Applebaum, and motioned for her to sit next to me on the sofa.

"How're you doin', Koff?" she whispered. She always called me by my last name. "You don't look so great."

"I don't feel so great but I'll tell you about it later," I said, wondering if I should have come to work with a paper bag over my head.

Ever since we'd met at the paper, where I covered celebrities and she covered civic news like Planning and Zoning Commission meetings and school budget proposals, Julia and I had been close pals. Sandy had never liked Julia, maybe because she refused to take shit from men. She'd been married briefly, to Layton's current mayor, but divorced him when she realized that his idea of partnership was letting her drive his Lexus. Maybe Sandy didn't like Julia because she spoke passionately about saving the environment and reducing the deficit—issues that made Sandy extremely nervous. Or maybe he didn't like her because she was a Democrat. Who knows. I admired Julia tremendously, even though she often ridiculed my lifestyle and made me feel about as shallow as the water in my Jacuzzi.

"Everybody here?" Bethany said, calling the meeting to order. "My father asked me to talk to you today about Melanie Moloney. As you've heard, she's writing a book about him." Julia and I stole a look at each other. "As you may also have heard, this woman has bought a house right here in Layton." I had heard that, all right. Liz Smith had written about it in her column. She'd said Moloney had moved from Chicago to Layton to be closer to her latest subject and that she and her research assistant would be interviewing dozens of Alistair's friends and confidantes in our quaint little village. "My father is requesting that those of you who are approached by Melanie Moloney tell her in no uncertain terms that you will have no comment. My father would also like you to know," Alistair's Stepford Daughter continued, "that while he has a high regard for people who remain loyal to him, he has little use for those who don't. In other words, if you speak to Melanie Moloney, you do so at your own risk."

"What's the Senator going to do if we talk to this Melanie Moloney?" I asked Julia as the meeting broke up. "Fire us? Break our kneecaps?"

She shrugged. "Let's go eat," she said. "Melanie Moloney is Alistair's problem, not yours."

Chapter 3

"So the bastard went back to his first wife," Julia mused as we ate grilled tuna with sun-dried tomatoes at Belinda's Grille, a trendy local restaurant owned by an ex–Victoria's Secret model. "Don't you dare pine for him, Koff," she warned, shaking her finger at me.

"You never cared much for Sandy, did you?"

"You got that right. The guy's an ass and a fraud and a fool, and you're better off without him."

"Oh come on, Julia. Tell me how you *really* feel about him," I laughed.

"I'm serious, Koff. He's all show, no substance."

"Well, he had plenty of substance when I married him—a huge bank account, a money-making department store, a gigantic stock portfolio . . ."

"Yeah, but what about a soul? Did he have one of those?" Julia scowled. A tall, big-boned woman of forty with dark hair worn in a long braid, dark eyes, and an appearance that could best be described as "handsome," she was a no-nonsense type who could spot a phony a mile away. "As much of a toad as he was, he wasn't your biggest problem."

"Oh? What was my biggest problem?"

"You. You never thought you could depend on yourself. You thought you needed Sandy to support you. Now you'll see you were wrong."

"What are you talking about? I *do* need Sandy to support me. I can't pay for Maplebark Manor on my own."

"Sandy can't pay for it either. Isn't that what you told me? And he shouldn't pay for a place like that. It's an obscenely big house for two people. Obscene. Just unload it and find something more modest."

"I'm trying. I put it on the market this morning. But how will I keep the place going in the meantime? The pittance I make from the newspaper won't even pay the electricity, oil, cable TV, and garbage pickup bills every month. I'm in deep shit, Julia. I really am."

"So quit living like a princess."

"I have," I said, trying not to be defensive. "I've stopped having my groceries delivered."

"Yeah, what else?"

"I'm buying my gasoline at the self-serve pumps now, and I'm doing my own nails."

"No shit," said Julia.

"And I let my housekeeper go."

"How do you expect to sell your house if you don't keep it clean?" Julia asked, exasperated.

"Who said it won't be clean? I've been cleaning it myself."

"Yeah, sure."

"It's true. Keeping a house clean is something I actually know how to do. I was raised by a mother who was so compulsive about neatness that whenever she made a sandwich, she cut the lettuce leaves with a scissor so they fit perfectly inside the bread."

"So your mother didn't have a cleaning lady?" Julia asked.

"Oh, sure she did—and does." My mother had hired and fired dozens of cleaning ladies over the years. She kept help the way George Steinbrenner kept managers. "But she made *me* clean the house on their days off."

"Okay. So you're going to save money by cleaning your big house yourself. The next question is, how are you going to earn more money and be able to support yourself for a change?"

"Good question. I don't have a clue."

"For Christ' sake, Koff. You're good with celebrity interviews. Why the hell don't you get a job with one of those national magazines, like *People?*"

"I wouldn't know where to start."

"Just do it," said no-nonsense Julia. "You know how to talk to people. If you can write for our little paper, why can't you do it for big-time publications?"

Julia was right. Why couldn't I? I'd interviewed more than just local businessmen and fading actresses for the *Community Times;* I'd talked to major-league baseball players and Oscar-winning movie actors and bestselling novelists. Maybe I *was* ready to hit the big time. I sure could use some big-time money.

"You have options, Koff. But until things improve, why don't you get your mother to help out with the bills?"

"No way," I said, knocking over my glass and spilling what was left of my wine. "My mother makes me feel like a complete failure because I haven't been able to sustain a marriage. I'm going to pull myself out of this mess without her, I promise you."

"Are there any men on the horizon?" Julia asked, arching an eyebrow. "You're not the type to go cold turkey. You've got some guy waiting in the wings, don't you, Koff?"

"I wish. I'm so out of practice I wouldn't know how to find a man, let alone flirt with one."

"Well, when you're ready, there are plenty of them around."

"How do you know? You haven't had a date since your divorce two years ago."

"I'm telling you. They're around." Julia was being mysterious, but I decided not to press her. If she had a secret lover, good for her. "What you need, Koff, is a guy who'll introduce you to reality in these tough economic times."

"You don't think I'm in touch with reality?" I asked, a little wounded.

"Do you?" Julia said, motioning for the waiter to bring the check.

I considered the question, then became distracted when the waiter arrived. "Let's just split it," I said, as Julia grabbed the check and started to verify its accuracy.

"Fine with me. With tip and tax, your share comes to $52.50."

"Are you sure?" I said, not believing that a piece of fish could cost so much.

"What did you expect? That they'd throw in the wine for free? The Beaujolais was your idea, remember?"

"But I can't keep spending money like this," I wailed. "I just don't have it to spend anymore."

"Welcome to reality, Koff. It's all the rage and everybody's doing it."

That night, I took a long, painful look at my finances. I really was in deep shit. I didn't have enough money to keep the lights on at Maplebark Manor, let alone the heat. Fortunately, it was still August, and I wouldn't be needing the heat for a couple of months. What I needed in the meantime was some quick cash. But from where?

I sat down on my bed, flipped on the TV, and what did I see? A commercial for the Ritz Thrift Shop on Fifty-seventh Street in Manhattan, where they sold used fur coats at bargain prices. That was it! I'd take my fur coats down to the Ritz Thrift Shop and pawn them! Well, maybe just the raccoon and the Persian lamb. I'd keep the mink for old times' sake. After all, Sandy bought me the coat for our first anniversary. On second thought, I'd sell the mink too. Fuck old times' sake.

The next morning I stuffed the coats into garment bags, packed them into the tiny trunk of my Porsche, and drove down to Manhattan. I had considered wearing a disguise:

what if someone from Layton saw me pawning my fur coats? What if someone found out that I, Alison Waxman Koff of Maplebark Manor, couldn't pay my utility bills? Don't be ridiculous, I told myself. Why would you see anyone you know at the Ritz Thrift Shop?

I found a garage on Fifty-sixth Street, parked the car, and carried the bundle of coats one block to the store.

"May I help you, madam?" said a middle-aged man with pasty white skin and hair that had been dyed shoe-polish brown.

"Yes. I understand that you buy used furs."

"Right you are, madam. Are those the furs in question?" he said, pointing to the garment bags in my arms. I nodded. "Very good. Let's have a look at them."

He pointed to a nearby rack. I was about to unpack the coats and hang them on the rack when he excused himself, saying he had to finish up with another client and would be back to me shortly.

I shook out the coats, fluffed the skins, and hung them on the rack. Goodbye, raccoon. Goodbye, lamb. Goodbye— gulp—mink. Goodbye, old life.

"Thank you so much for your patronage, madam," I heard the salesman say to his client as she walked past me to get to the door. What was this "madam" shit? This was the Ritz Thrift Shop, not Bergdorf Goodman.

"Alison? Is that you?"

I spun around to face the woman who'd just finished her transaction and was on her way out of the store, and who should it be but Robin Greene, the wife of Sandy's divorce lawyer! I'd been caught! Now everyone in town would know I was poor and desperate—so poor and desperate I was forced to sell my furs! I was tongue-tied. "Robin!" I finally managed.

"Are you here buying or selling?" she asked.

I didn't know which was the right answer. "Selling," I admitted.

"Me, too. Terrible, isn't it?"

"Robin, don't tell me *you* have to sell your coats too?" She nodded. "But I don't understand. You and Adam have Belvedere, plus your dude ranch in Wyoming, your ski lodge in Aspen, and your beach condo in Boca Raton. Why would someone like you have to sell her fur coats?"

"Same reason you do, honey. Times are tough. Between the stock market crash, the real estate slump, and the fact that we're in debt up to our ears, money's real tight. We've got all our houses on the market and can't unload any of 'em. The banks are about to take everything."

I was shocked. I thought *I* was the only one in Layton in financial trouble. "What are you and Adam going to do?" I asked Robin.

"Probably move our primary residence to Florida. They call it 'the debtor's state' down there. You put all your assets in Florida and your creditors can't touch 'em."

"Wow. How did you find out about that?"

"I'm married to a lawyer, remember? He knows lots of creative ways to dodge the banks. Guess what we're doin' next weekend?"

"What?" I asked.

"Goin' to Atlantic City. Adam says another way to hide your assets is to go to Atlantic City or Vegas, buy a bunch of chips, do a little gambling, bring the rest of the chips home, and keep 'em in the house. How's the bank gonna grab your assets when they're all in gambling chips?"

"Really? How ingenious," I said. Yeah, ingenious and illegal. I decided I'd stick with my own plan to get out of my financial mess: sell my house and get a better-paying job.

"Sorry about your trouble, Alison. I hear Sandy's gone back to Soozie and you're trying to unload Maplebark Manor. Lotsaluck."

"Thanks. You too."

Luck. That's what I needed. As the weeks went by, things got worse, not better. For starters, I hardly got any assign-

ments from the newspaper anymore. Advertising was way
down and so were the number of pages in each issue, and the
first section to be shrunk was the Arts & Features section—
my section.

For another thing, Sandy and I had hammered out a
separation agreement and would be divorced any day. I felt
panicky and alone. I missed his companionship. I missed
hearing his footsteps as he entered the house at the end of
the workday. There was no longer a structure to my days.
They just melted, one into the other. I was depressed, in a
rut.

Then there was Maplebark Manor, the house I could no
longer afford. The money I made from the sale of my fur
coats only went so far toward maintaining the house. Eventually, I had to sell more of my possessions—the Wedge-
wood china my mother had given me, the big diamond
engagement ring from my first husband, Roger, the even
bigger diamond ring from Sandy. The only thing I absolutely refused to pawn was the gold locket my father gave
me on my sixth birthday. It was all I had of him, and I
vowed not to surrender it, even in the face of the scary
letters I kept getting from the Layton Bank & Trust Company, which threatened to foreclose on Maplebark Manor
if we missed one more month of mortgage payments. In a
weak moment, I called Sandy at the store to ask him what
we should do.

"Mr. Koff's office. This is Michelle speaking."

"Is he there?" I asked Michelle, who was new.

"And you are . . . ?"

"Alison."

"From . . . ?"

"A past life."

"That's the name of your company?"

"No, that's not the name of my company. I'm Alison
Koff, Sandy's about-to-be-ex-wife."

"Will Mr. Koff know what this is in reference to?"

"Yes. Well, not exactly."

"Is there anything I can help you with?"

"Would you like to buy my house?" I said, my patience wearing thin.

"I beg your pardon?"

"Would you like to buy my house?"

"I don't think so, Mrs. Koff. I already own a condo."

"Then there's nothing you can help me with," I told Michelle. "Please get Mr. Koff on the line."

"I'll see if he's available," she said, putting me on hold and forcing me to listen to "Feelings" as performed by the AT&T orchestra.

"Alison?" Sandy said finally.

"The bank is starting foreclosure proceedings," I snapped. "What are we going to do?"

"I don't know what you're going to do, Alison, but I'm not going to do anything."

"Why not?"

"Because there's nothing I can do. I can't make the mortgage payments anymore. Can you?"

"Of course not. But we can't just sit back and watch them take Maplebark Manor."

"We're not sitting back. We're trying to sell the house, aren't we?"

"I guess so." Janet Claiborne still hadn't produced a buyer, and she'd had the listing for months.

"Maybe you should think about getting a real job," Sandy said.

"What kind of a job?"

"I don't know. Be a salesgirl or something."

A salesgirl, he said. Not a salesperson. Not a saleswoman. A salesgirl. And I was married to this man?

"I'll be just fine," I told Sandy. "It's not your problem anymore."

"Remember one thing, Allergy. Life is about allowing yourself to feel fear . . . about taking risks and risking change and changing gears. It's about growing and stretching and having the courage to—"

Click. Yes, I hung up on Sandy. It was either that or go mad.

Sandy and I were divorced on November fourth. Whoop-peedo. Julia and I celebrated with burgers and fries at McGavin's, the local hangout for *Layton Community Times* staffers. She paid.

The next day I decided it was time to snap out of my doldrums. I had unloaded Sandy; the next order of business was unloading Maplebark Manor. The problem was that no one wanted to buy it.

"The market is slow," Janet Claiborne explained when I asked why she hadn't shown the house once since we'd listed it back in August. And when I asked why she hadn't sent a photographer to shoot the house for the brochure and why she hadn't run a single ad, her response was: "I'm waiting for the trees and flowers to bloom." "But that won't be till spring," I said. "Yes, but leave it to me, dear. I know my business," she said.

I would have loved to leave it to Janet to sell my house but she never seemed to have the time. A week later she called to tell me she finally had a customer but was too busy to bring the couple over. "I have a veddy important appointment with my masseur that I can't possibly break," she said, then asked if I wouldn't mind showing Maplebark Manor to a Mr. and Mrs. Fink from Manhattan. "No problem," I told her. I was beginning to understand why the real estate market was in the toilet.

The showing was scheduled for three-thirty the next afternoon. It was snowing and I worried that the Finks might not be able to make it up from the city. But they arrived on time in their fire-engine red Range Rover which, they later explained, was their "country car."

"Hello. Come right in," I said cordially, opening my front door to people who might very well buy my house and save my financial life but also force me to confront my future as a thirty-nine-year-old, two-time divorcée who had a better chance of getting killed by a terrorist than of marrying again.

"Hi. I'm Ira Fink," said the man, extending his hand. He was short, fat, and fiftysomething, and wore Guess jeans that were so tight they pushed his love handles up to his ears, which, by the way, were both pierced.

"And I'm Susan Franklin-Fink," said the woman, who was a fraction of her husband's size and age.

"Welcome to Maplebark Manor," I said to the couple standing in my foyer. For the next twenty-five minutes, I did my best imitation of a real estate broker. I guided the Franklin-Finks from room to room and pointed out things like crown moldings, air-conditioning ducts, and linen closets. I showed them Maplebark Manor's seven bedrooms and baths, the laundry and sewing rooms, the living room, the library, the dining room, the kitchen, the butler's pantry, the wine cellar, the billiard room, the music room, the solarium, the media room, the exercise room, and my office. Then I took them outside and showed them the swimming pool, the tennis court, the guest cottage, the party barn, and the staff apartment over the three-car garage. When we got back to the main house, we stood in the foyer and I asked them if they had any questions.

"There's no family room," Mr. Fink said, looking genuinely pissed off.

"No family room?" I said. "How large is your family?"

"Right now, it's just the two of us, but we're planning to have children," said Mrs. Franklin-Fink, who then confided that Mr. Fink was estranged from his five grown children from prior marriages but that he was looking forward to being a "quality father" this time around.

"What exactly would you want from a family room?" I asked, trying to be as patient as I assumed Janet Claiborne would be if she were showing the house instead of having a massage.

"You know—a *family* room," said Mr. Fink, not believ-

ing my ignorance. "It's a big room off the kitchen that has
a fireplace. It's where the whole *family* can watch TV together."

"Obviously, you don't have children," Mrs. Franklin-
Fink said accusingly. "People with children have family
rooms."

"And you couldn't turn one of the other rooms into a
family room?" I asked as politely as I could under the
circumstances.

"Mrs. Koff," said Mr. Fink, "for the amount of money
you're asking for this house, I don't think we should have
to 'turn' any of the other rooms into anything."

At that very moment, the telephone rang. "Excuse me,"
I said as I went to grab the phone in the kitchen. It was my
mother. "I can't talk now, Mom. There's someone at the
door." It was the first time I'd said that to my mother
without lying. I hurried back to the Franklin-Finks but they
had already left without so much as a "Thanks for taking
the time to show us your lovely home." Some lovely home.
It didn't even have a family room.

The next day Janet Claiborne called to say she was sending over another couple and hoped I wouldn't mind showing the people around myself. Janet, it seemed, had a riding
lesson she couldn't cancel. Her cantering, she said, was in
shambles.

But it was my spirits that were in shambles a few hours
after Janet's "buyers" left; it seems they were more interested in *taking* than buying. While I led the woman on a
tour of the second-floor bedrooms, the man, who had excused himself by saying he had to go out to his car to make
a phone call, made off with all my silver! To think I spent
forty-five minutes exposing my home and its contents to
thieves!

"Please get me some *real* customers," I screamed at Janet
Claiborne a day or two after I'd finished dealing with the

police and the insurance company. "I don't care if it's winter. I don't care if the trees and flowers aren't in bloom. Just
send the photographer."

"There's no need to get upset, dear," Janet said. "If you
want the photographer, you'll have the photographer. It *is*
your house, after all."

My house. My beautiful house. My beautiful house that
was fast becoming a symbol of my utter gluttony. Julia was
right. Why did Sandy and I need a 7,200-square-foot house?
So we'd never have to run into each other? So we could
impress our friends? What friends? Where'd they all go?
What ever happened to all those people who were only too
happy to come for Super Bowl Sunday and Academy
Award Night Monday and were similarly only too happy to
invite us for Election Night Tuesday? Where were the couples who ate with us and traveled with us and complained
with us about taxes, gasoline prices, and the dearth of good
domestic help? Gone, that's where. The minute Sandy lost
his shirt in the stock market crash, they got "busy"—they
stopped calling us, we stopped calling them. Then when
Sandy and I split up, they got "blind"—I waved to them in
the street, they pretended not to see me. And when word
spread that Sandy and I were about to lose the house, they
got Alzheimer's—someone mentioned my name, they said,
"Alison who?"

Just send that photographer over, Janet baby, and let's
get this house sold. I want off this Titanic before it sinks.

Chapter 4

"Coming," I called as I ran to answer the front door. It was a bright and sunny late-November morning. Janet Claiborne had finally arranged for a photographer to take pictures of Maplebark Manor, and he was a few minutes early.

"Morning," said the man standing outside. "I'm Cullie Harrington, the photographer for Prestige Properties. Is it all right to come in?"

"Not through here," I said, observing his snowy boots and dusty cases of equipment. "You'll have to use the service entrance. And please remove your shoes before coming into the house." Now that I was cleaning the place myself, I couldn't bear to have anyone traipse dirt and grime onto my floors.

Cullie Harrington shot me a scowl before lugging himself and his equipment back down my front steps and around the driveway to the service entrance. He's probably got some kind of attitude, I thought, hoping his photographic skills were better than his manners.

I met him at the kitchen door and let him in. "Don't forget to take off those boots," I cautioned him.

"How about my hat and coat? Would you mind if I took them off?" he asked sarcastically.

"Oh, sorry. You can put your things in there," I said, pointing to the recently vacated maid's room.

Cullie flashed me another fuck-you face and disappeared

into the maid's room. A few minutes later he emerged, carrying two black bags and a tripod. I had a good look at him for the first time. He was a lanky six feet tall, with a perfect swimmer's physique—broad shoulders tapering to slim hips and long, muscular legs. He wore a navy-blue-and-white ski sweater and faded blue jeans with holes at the knees. He had hair the color of wheat—wispy, soft, and worn medium-long, curling up the middle of his neck. His beard and his mustache, though, were dark brown, flecked with gray. His eyes were pale blue, framed by tortoise-shell glasses. His face was etched with little lines that made him look slightly older than the mid-forties I assumed he was. He had the look of an Ivy League professor, the demeanor of a craggy sea captain, and the body of a sinewy athlete. The whole package was not unappealing, but the man was hardly my type.

"Now I'd like to show you the rooms I think should be showcased in the brochure," I said, motioning for Cullie to follow me through the house.

I went into the living room and began to describe the renovations Sandy and I had done and point out what I thought were noteworthy decorating details—the matching carpet and window treatments, the antique brass sconces and the original Picasso sketch that hung over the marble fireplace mantel. "I'd like you to include all of these things in the shot," I said, turning around to face Cullie, who was nowhere to be found. Apparently, I'd made my little speech to an empty room. "Hello?" I called out, wondering if he had made off with what was left of my valuables.

"In here," he said.

I followed the voice and found Cullie at the other end of the first floor, in the dining room, where he had set up his equipment and was now rearranging my flowers.

"May I ask what you're doing?" I said, crossing my arms over my chest.

"Getting ready to take the shot," he said, not looking up.

"But I thought we'd start in the living room."

"Light's better in here at this time of day," he said, walking over to his camera and sticking his head under a black cloth.

"But in the living room the carpet matches the curtains, and the Picasso is perfect over the marble mantel," I sputtered. The dining room was lovely, of course, but I was particularly proud of the living room. Sandy and I had spent a fortune on it.

"Look, Mrs. . . ."

"Koff."

"Look, Mrs. Koff. I'll be shooting the interior of your house for a brochure, a brochure that's supposed to give prospective buyers an idea of the size and layout of the rooms, the feel of the property, that sort of thing. It's not supposed to be a monument to your decorator."

"If you really think so," I conceded. I figured this Cullie Harrington must know his business. Janet said he photographed all the important houses in town. "Are you planning to shoot every room in the house?" I asked.

"Look, lady. Mrs. Koff. This is for a brochure, not a book. I'll be shooting four to six of your primary rooms. Not your closets. Not your bathrooms. Just your main rooms—probably the dining room, living room, kitchen, master bedroom, and family room."

The man's manners were appalling. "Maplebark Manor doesn't have a family room," I snapped. "That's why *you're* here—to do a brochure showing people that a house doesn't necessarily have to have a family room to work. Sort of the way a photographer doesn't necessarily have to have manners to *get* work."

"Hey, that's pretty good," Cullie said, then smiled at me for the first time. "I didn't know you people had a sense of humor."

What was this "you people" stuff? Did Cullie Harrington have a major-league attitude or what? I thought it best to say what I had to say and get out of his way. "Since you'll only be photographing my primary rooms, can you manage to do your work, clean up after yourself, and be out of here in an hour?"

"Why? Got to rush off to a manicure?" he snickered before ducking back under his black cloth and refocusing his attention on the shot of my dining room. Then, his voice muffled by the cloth, he said, "Yeah, it'll take me an hour all right—to do this one room. I plan on being here all day. That okay with you?"

God, no, I thought, but nodded that it would be all right. I needed to sell my house, and if this pain-in-the-ass's pictures were going to bring me a buyer, I could hardly kick him out. "I'll be upstairs in my office if you need me," I said. Bethany had actually given me a new assignment for the newspaper. I was to interview Bill Medley, the tall half of the sixties' singing duo the Righteous Brothers, who had recently bought a house in Layton. The story was only going to run a half-page (Bethany wasn't sure if the readers of the *Community Times* knew the Righteous Brothers from the Ringling Brothers), but I was thrilled to have the work.

"Your office? You have a job?" Cullie pulled his head out from underneath the black cloth and smirked at me.

Oh, spare me. "Yes, I have a job."

"What do you do?"

"I'm a journalist." I rarely had the nerve to call myself that. I mean, I wasn't exactly Bob Woodward. But Cullie Harrington's infuriating manner made me want to inflate my job description just a tad.

"A journalist? I'm surprised," he said with new respect for me.

"Why are you surprised?"

"I just didn't take you for a woman who did anything except look down on the little guy."

This person was unbelievable. I turned on my heel and walked out of the room.

* * *

I didn't see much of Cullie that day. I stayed away from
him and he stayed away from me. And thank God. The
more I thought about the gargantuan chip on his shoulder,
the angrier and more resentful I became. How dare he come
into my house and treat me with disrespect, like I was some
superficial rich bitch from a Judith Krantz novel? Who was
he to look down his nose at me, especially since he had
accused me of looking down *my* nose at *him?*

A few days later, Janet Claiborne called to tell me Cullie
had stopped by her office to drop off several transparencies
of Maplebark Manor. "They look absolutely divine," she
said.

"I'd love to see them," I said, dying to know if this guy
who'd gotten under my skin like a case of ringworm had any
talent.

"The brochure will be ready in a couple of weeks, just in
time for the holidays," Janet said.

Oh, great, I thought. Nobody's out buying houses during
the holidays.

Since I couldn't do anything to control the real estate
market, I decided to concentrate on something I thought I
could control: my job situation. It was time to dust off my
résumé, pick out my best interviews, and send them to
editors at the big-time magazines.

I chose a cold, snowy Saturday night to get down to
business, because I had nothing better to do on Saturday
nights these days. Julia had been busy with her mystery
man, and the only other option would have been to spend
the evening with my mother, who kept inviting me for dinner so she could lecture me about my inability to hold on to
a man. Anyone for root canal?

I ate some scrambled eggs, drank some Almaden (I really

was trying to economize), and wrote letters to magazine editors—thirty-five of them.

The next morning I mailed the letters. A few days later I followed up with phone calls, not one of which was returned. If I was lucky, I'd make contact with some editor's assistant, only to get the brush-off. Oh, they'd admit they received my mailing all right, but when I'd ask if I could come in and discuss a possible position, they'd act as if I had a contagious disease. I did: it was called desperation. "We'll keep your material on file and let you know if anything opens up" was the stock response.

"Koff, what you need is a reference, a recommendation from someone with clout when it comes to the media," Julia suggested when I stopped in at the newspaper and reported my lack of progress on the job front.

"Yeah, and who do I know with clout when it comes to the media? Bethany Downs?"

Julia laughed. "Have you noticed her mustache?"

"Her what?"

"Her mustache. I'm not kidding. She's always got this white stuff stuck on her upper lip."

"It's powdered sugar."

"Are you sure?"

"Sure I'm sure. She has a thing for jelly donuts. She eats them by the dozen."

"You see, Koff? You'd be great at *People* magazine. Nobody knows all that intimate stuff like you do."

When I got home, I thought about what Julia had said. Maybe the magazine editors would return my calls if I had a reference. But who?

I was flipping through the latest issue of the *Community Times* when it came to me: Alistair Downs knew everybody in the media. Maybe he'd call one of his cronies and say, "Ho ho. This gal Alison does a splendid job at my paper.

Splendid. How about doing your old pal Alistair a favor and giving her a job?"

The idea didn't seem that farfetched. No idea seemed that farfetched, now that I was poor and desperate.

The next morning, I summoned up my nerve and called Alistair's secretary at the newspaper. Although he only came into the office once a week, he checked in with his secretary several times a day from his home, a twenty-room stone manor on Layton Harbor called Evermore. I explained to his secretary, a thin-lipped, blue-haired woman named Martha Hives, that I wanted to speak with Senator Downs about a personal matter. She called me back later in the day to say that the Senator would see me two days later at four o'clock at Evermore. I was thrilled to get an audience with Sir Alistair before he left for his annual trip to Lyford Cay in the Bahamas, where he and Bethany had been spending the Christmas and New Year's holidays for twenty years. Maybe my luck was changing. Just maybe.

At three forty-five on the appointed day, I pulled myself and my portfolio together and drove over to Layton Harbor, taking a little time to marvel at the number of sailboats anchored there, despite the time of year. Settled in the seventeenth century, the snug harbor on the Long Island Sound was once a major shipping port. Now it was one of the most prestigious addresses in the state.

Overlooking Layton Harbor, midway between Layton's historic village district and the Sachem Point Yacht Club, Evermore, Alistair Downs's six-acre estate, was sequestered behind a fortress of mature evergreens. Stone pillars with wrought-iron gates flanked the entrance to the property, which consisted of a 15,000-square-foot, 65-year-old manor house, two stone carriage houses, and a swimming pool and cabana. Approached by a long banked driveway, the estate was surrounded by park-like grounds with specimen plantings, rock and rose gardens, and a pool and tennis court. Everything about Evermore suggested substance, influence, permanence. I suddenly thought of Cullie Harrington and

wondered if he had ever photographed Evermore. Then I
wondered why I bothered thinking about Cullie Harrington. I was sure he wasn't thinking about me.

I navigated my Porsche up Evermore's winding driveway
and parked in the motor court to the right of the arched
front door. My palms got clammy as I was hit with a wave
of insecurity. What was I doing here? I was Miss Middle
Class, Alison Waxman, daughter of the late Sy "The Mattress King" Waxman and his wife Doris who, despite her
pretensions, was just a nice Jewish girl from Queens. What
right did I have calling on a bona fide American icon?

I was shown inside the house by a butler, who said Senator Downs would be detained for a few minutes and I
should wait in the library, a dark green room with bookcases, plaid carpeting, a desk, several leather chairs, and a
stone fireplace over which hung an oil painting of The Great
One himself. I deposited myself in one of the chairs and
studied the room: it was a shrine to the master of the house.
Everywhere I looked there were clusters of sterling silver
frames showcasing Alistair Downs in all his glory. There
were photos of him making his screen debut as a gladiator
in the 1950 Victor Mature movie *The Defiant Warriors*
. . . playing a boxing champ in the 1952 film *Kid O'Reilly*
. . . starring opposite Virginia Mayo in the 1953 World War
II adventure *The Bold Battalion* . . . romancing Susan Hay-
ward in the 1957 frontier drama *The Plains of Passion*
. . . and rescuing Doris Day in the 1959 detective thriller
Around Any Corner. There were photos of his post-Holly-
wood years, when he became a powerful presence within the
Republican party, ran for the United States Senate, won by
a landslide, and served two terms in Washington. There
were photos of him linking arms with Barry Goldwater
. . . shaking hands with Richard Nixon . . . playing golf with
Gerry Ford . . . and praying next to Billy Graham. There
were photos documenting his charity work and public service accomplishments, photos of him standing outside the
new Alistair P. Downs Hip Replacement Center at the

county hospital . . . visiting a school for handicapped children . . . congratulating local servicemen who had defended
our country in Grenada . . . and signing the papers that
bought him ownership in *The Layton Community Times,* his
retirement toy. And finally, there were photos showing the
personal side of Alistair Downs, photos of him embracing
his late wife, the former showgirl Annette Dowling, who
died tragically while still in her early forties . . . sailing in the
Bahamas with Bethany aboard his 65-foot yacht *Aristocrat*
. . . wrestling on the grounds of Evermore with Murphy, his
prize-winning Irish setter . . . and blowing out the candles at
his recent seventy-fifth birthday party at the Sachem Point
Yacht Club.

Such a rich life, I sighed enviously. My own life seemed
barren by comparison. I mean, what were *my* biggest
achievements? Marrying men with money? Being dumped
by men with money? Buying a house I couldn't afford?
Watching the house I couldn't afford be taken over by a
bank?

I wondered how my mother would react to my visit to
Alistair's house. She'd croak, that's how she'd react. Her
daughter at Evermore? Getting an audience with a legend—
and a rich bachelor yet?

"The Senator is on his way," the butler heralded, interrupting my little reverie.

"Thank you," I replied.

"Not at all, miss," he said before turning to leave. I loved
him. Nobody had called me "Miss" since high school.

A few minutes later I was standing in front of Alistair's
bookcases, about to pull out a leather-bound edition of *War
and Peace,* when I caught a whiff of Old Spice and heard a
voice bellow, "Hello, dear. Ho ho. Delightful to see you."
I turned around and saw Alistair P. Downs striding toward
me. He looked every bit the retired movie star in his navy
blue velvet smoking jacket, white shirt, navy blue and red
striped silk ascot, gray flannel slacks, and brown Bally loafers. Six feet tall, with broad shoulders and only a hint of a

paunch, he had a remarkable head of hair for his age—
thick, wavy, and reddish brown. His green eyes held the
mischief of a teenager, and his face was relatively free of sun
marks and broken capillaries. Only the skin on his neck,
which was badly wrinkled and hung lifelessly over his ascot,
and his hands, which were dotted with liver spots, suggested
he was no longer the Don Juan of the Arthur Murray dance
studios, the ambitious young buck who had charmed the
ladies to distraction while he taught them how to cha cha
cha. In every other way, he was the very image of a handsome Hollywood movie star who had parlayed his screen
popularity into a career in politics and, though retired from
public life for the past several years, was still in there parlay-
ing.

"It's nice to see you again too, Senator Downs," I said as
Alistair shook both my hands.

"What brings you here, dear?" he said as he sat back in
a leather wing chair and crossed his legs. He didn't invite me
to sit down, but I did anyway.

"Well," I began, "I'm thinking of making a job change,
and I thought you might be able to help me with it."

"What is it you do now, dear?"

"You mean, what do I do at the newspaper?" How could
he have forgotten? He'd always acted as if he knew me.

"The newspaper. Yes, of course."

"I interview celebrities such as yourself. Well, not celebrities of your caliber, of course, but famous people who—"

"That's all right. I understand what you mean."

"You see, Mr. Downs. Sorry. *Senator* Downs. While I
truly enjoy my work at the *Community Times,* I feel it's time
for me to move on. I've had some financial problems lately
and my marriage has recently broken up, and I find myself
needing to look for a full-time and, frankly, better-paying
job. Since you seemed to be so supportive of my work—"

"I'm supportive of all my people, yes," Alistair said dis-
tractedly, then checked the time on his watch.

"—I thought perhaps you might recommend me for a job

at one of the national magazines. I hope to interview celebrities for *People* magazine, for example, just as I've done for your newspaper, which, may I add, is an absolutely top-notch paper, thanks to your very capable daughter Bethany, who's a true professional and a pleasure to work with." Shovel, shovel. Grovel, grovel.

"Delightful of you to say so, dear."

"So as I was telling you, I'd like very much to work for a national magazine like *People,* but I feel I need a really good reference, just to get my foot in the door, a recommendation from someone who has influence with the media. Someone such as yourself."

"I've been on the cover of *People* magazine three times, and they tell me my covers sold the most issues in the magazine's history, not including the Elizabeth Taylor and Jackie Onassis covers, of course. But then those two are Democrats, so what do you expect? Ho ho."

"That's very interesting, Senator. Really it is. But getting back to my situation, which has become somewhat dire . . ."

"I've been interviewed by every magazine in the world," said Alistair, pulling a white linen handkerchief out of his smoking jacket pocket and giving his nose a loud honk.

"Yes, Senator, I know. You're quite an interesting man." And an egomaniac too.

"Yes. Ho ho. I enjoy being interviewed. Always have. Come to think of it, why haven't you interviewed me for our little newspaper?" Alistair said with a chuckle.

"I'm sure Bethany thought you'd be far too busy," I said. Now can we get back to *me* and the fact that I need a job?

"Nonsense, dear. I'm never too busy to help a member of my team—especially such an attractive member." Oh, save it. "You want to interview me sometime? Is that it? Don't be shy. Just give my secretary a call."

"Well, thank you, Senator Downs. I'll do that. But to get back to my job situation . . ."

"As a matter of fact, I'll be back in Layton the end of

January unless, of course, the weather at Lyford is too glorious to give up. You just tell Mrs. Hives over at the newspaper that I said it's okay."

"That's super, Senator. Really. Now if I could just—"

"An interview with me will help you get that big job you're after, dear. You'll see."

"I'm beginning to."

"And now, if you'll excuse me, dear. I must get going or Mrs. Hives will have my head. She's got me so overcommitted I'm apt to forget my own name."

Fat chance. If there was one thing Alistair Downs would never forget, it was his name.

"Daddy, I'm leaving to go back to the paper and I—Alison! What are you doing here?"

Alistair was about to dismiss me when Bethany marched into the library munching on a jelly donut and sprinkling powdered sugar on the dark plaid carpeting. Julia was right. She did have a white mustache. Judging by the look on her face, I was the last person she expected to find in her father's house.

"Hi, Bethany," I said. "I just stopped by to—"

"She came to interview your old dad," Alistair said.

"Well, if she wanted to interview you, she should have come to me first," Bethany told her father.

"She must not have known that," said Alistair. They were talking about me as if I weren't even there. "I'm sure she'll go through the proper channels the next time."

"I'm sure she will," Bethany said, eyeing me suspiciously. "Everyone tries to get to my father, so I have to be very protective of him," she explained. "Especially now that Melanie Moloney, that low-class, low-life—"

"Now, now, Bethany honey," Alistair comforted her. "Let's not get all upset about *Ms.* Moloney. She may be a little too curious about my life for my taste, but we all know that it was curiosity that killed the cat, don't we?"

Bethany nodded, then gave her father a peck on the cheek as he put his arm around her.

I'd had it with the Downses. I said goodbye and got the hell out of Evermore. No wonder Alistair Downs had found stardom as a dance instructor. That bastard could dance his way out of any situation. He had no intention of helping me get a magazine job. He had no intention of hearing what I had to say. He had no idea who I was!

You'll be okay, you'll be okay, I told myself, as tears of anger and frustration stung my eyes. You don't need a rich man to save your life anymore, Alison. Not this time.

Chapter 5

By the middle of January, Janet Claiborne still hadn't produced a real buyer for Maplebark Manor. The last person I showed the house to wasn't even sure she wanted to live on the East Coast, much less in Layton. Of course, if Janet had showed the house herself, maybe things would have gone differently. But she was busy having a new car phone installed in her Jaguar and couldn't possibly cancel her appointment. A good car phone installer, she said, was as rare as someone who could make a good martini.

I finally got to see the brochure on the house, though. Cullie had left a handful of copies in my mailbox with his business card, on which he had scribbled, "Here's the finished product. I do nice work, eh?" He was right; the photographs were spectacular. Maplebark Manor looked grand. I do nice work, too, I thought, remembering all the time, energy, and money that had gone into the renovation of the house. Now if someone would only buy the place, I'd be in business.

I called the number on Cullie's business card so I could thank him for taking such beautiful pictures, but I got his answering machine and hung up. Let's face it, the man intimidated me. He was handsome and talented and called his own shots. What's more, he seemed to have confidence in himself and his abilities, which was something I certainly didn't.

It was hard to have confidence in myself and my abilities when the bank had begun foreclosure proceedings on my house and I couldn't find a job. Day after day, I called magazine editors in New York, and day after day I got nowhere. I decided what I needed short-term was some local, part-time work to supplement my meager income from the newspaper while I waited for one of the big-time magazines to hire me. But where would I find local, part-time work? The only things I knew how to do were interview famous people and clean house. Maybe I could clean house for famous people, I laughed. But seriously, what was I going to do?

I pulled out the latest edition of the *Community Times* and flipped to the classified section, where there were Help Wanted ads for a legal secretary (not qualified), a dental hygienist (not qualified), a computer programmer (not qualified), and a fitness trainer at a gym (not qualified—my idea of "going for the burn" was ordering the Hot 'n' Spicy Buffalo Chicken Wings at McGavin's). Then I turned the page and saw the following ad:

HOUSEKEEPER WANTED

Honest, reliable, discreet, English-speaking person needed to clean house, do laundry. Must be well organized, have excellent references, drive own car, and have superb cleaning skills. $25/hr. Tuesday thru Friday. Call 555-7562.

I surveyed the other ads on the page—for a short-order cook, a bilingual bank teller, a manicurist, a stenographer, and a lane assigner at a bowling alley. There was also a big ad that read: THE GAP IS OPENING ANOTHER STORE IN LAYTON. SALES HELP NEEDED. Finally, a job for which I was qualified!

I called The Gap and arranged for an interview. When I showed up, I was told by the store's sixteen-year-old manager (or so she looked) that I wasn't quite right for the position, which was another way of saying I was too old. According to this manager, the kids who shopped at The Gap would feel mothered by a woman my age, and if there was anything kids didn't need when they were buying a new pair of jeans, it was a mother. Back to the drawing board.

My next attempt at part-time employment was equally humiliating. Since retailing was familiar to me (I'd done my share of shopping over the years), I interviewed for a position as a salesperson at a shop that sold maternity clothes and related accessories. The interview was going along nicely until the manager of the store asked me if I knew how to operate a breast pump.

I did not get the job.

As the winter wore on, the newspaper's classified section got slimmer and slimmer. The recession had settled on top of Layton like a dense fog; there were no jobs—at least none that I was capable of performing. Each week, I scanned the paper for possibilities, and each week my eyes rested on the same ad:

HOUSEKEEPER WANTED

Honest, reliable, discreet, English-speaking person needed to clean house, do laundry. Must be well organized, have excellent references, drive own car, and have superb cleaning skills. $25/hr. Tuesday thru Friday. Call 555-7562.

Boy, this lady must be hard to please, I thought as I re-read the ad for the umpteenth time. There were plenty of housekeepers out of work. It was hard to believe the job hadn't been filled.

What if *I* called the number and applied for the job? Twenty-five dollars an hour for eight hours a day, four days a week, came to $800 a week! That would keep the heat and lights on at Maplebark Manor until a buyer came along. But could I, Alison Waxman Koff, mistress of Maplebark

Manor, be a housekeeper? It was bad enough that I had to scrub my *own* toilets, but *somebody else's?* What would people who knew me say if they found out? What would people who didn't know me say if they found out? It would be the hottest gossip in Layton since the socialite up the street was arrested for running an escort service out of her house.

But why would anyone have to know that I was a housekeeper? Why couldn't I just gather up my Windex, my Fantastik, and my Pledge, hop into my Porsche, drive over to the woman's house, do the work, collect my money, and leave? Who would be the wiser? Nobody, that's who. Not Sandy. Not my mother. Nobody. If anybody asked where I went on Tuesdays through Fridays, I'd say I was in New York City meeting with magazine editors. If Bethany wanted me to do a story for the newspaper, I'd tell her I was free on Mondays or weekends.

I picked up the ad and read it again. HOUSEKEEPER WANTED. HONEST, RELIABLE, DISCREET, ENGLISH-SPEAKING PERSON NEEDED. I was honest, reliable and discreet, most of the time, and I spoke English well enough to communicate with everyone but my mother. MUST BE WELL ORGANIZED, HAVE EXCELLENT REFERENCES, DRIVE OWN CAR, AND HAVE SUPERB CLEANING SKILLS. I was very well organized (anal retentive, Sandy used to say), drove my own car, and had, maybe not superb, but certainly above-average cleaning skills. What I lacked were the excellent references. The only people who knew how well I could dust a table, scour a sink, and mop a floor were my mother and Sandy, and I wasn't about to ask them for a reference. Cross that bridge when you come to it, I told myself.

I ran my finger over the ad and felt my heart race. Call the number, call the number, a little voice whispered. Follow your instincts. Show everybody you can take care of yourself. Don't be a wimp.

I took a deep breath and dialed the number. I was about

to speak when I realized I had reached an answering machine.

"This is 555-7562," a woman's voice said. "If you're calling about the ad in the paper, don't even think about leaving a message after the beep unless you're absolutely sure you're qualified for the job. Beep."

I gulped and hung up. Who was this bitch? More to the point, was I absolutely sure I was qualified for the job? Of course not. The only thing I was absolutely sure of was that I could practically taste that $800 a week. I waited a few minutes and called again.

"This is 555-7562," the machine said. "If you're calling about the ad in the paper, don't even think about leaving a message after the beep unless you're absolutely sure you're qualified for the job. Beep."

"Good afternoon," I said, trying to sound perky and efficient. "I'm calling about your ad and I'm absolutely sure I'm qualified for the job. My name is Alison and my number is 555-8184. I look forward to hearing from you."

The die was cast. Now what would I do if the woman called back? I went downstairs and poured myself a glass of Almaden. What if she turned out to be someone I knew? Calm down, I told myself. If she calls you back, you can always say you've already taken another job, or that you dialed her number by mistake, or that you suffer from multiple personality disorder and one of your other personalities placed the call.

At four-thirty that afternoon my phone rang. I jumped. I considered letting my answering machine pick it up, but decided to be a big girl.

"Hello?" I said cautiously.

"Is this Alison?" a female voice demanded.

"Yes, this is she," I said.

"You responded to my ad in the paper. Tell me about yourself," the voice challenged.

"Well, I have superb cleaning skills," I began, as little

beads of sweat formed above my top lip. "And I'm used to working in luxury homes."

"Really? Where are you working now?"

"At a Georgian mansion on Woodland Way."

"Woodland Way. Nice address. Been there long?"

"About five years," I said, recalling the day Sandy and I closed on Maplebark Manor.

"Why are you leaving? Did you have a run-in with your employer?"

"Not at all. The couple who own the house are in financial trouble."

"It's happening all over. Did they get killed in the market?"

"I have no idea. My job is to keep their house clean, not ask questions." I remembered that the ad had said something about being discreet.

"I like that. I'll see you tomorrow afternoon at three-thirty. Number 7 Bluefish Cove. What's your last name?"

"Er . . . um . . . Koff." Everything was moving so fast.

"Fine. Tomorrow at three-thirty."

"But wait . . . I . . . I'm not sure I can—"

"Oh, right. I forgot. My name's Melanie. Melanie Moloney. Perhaps you've heard of me. See you tomorrow." Click.

Melanie Moloney? *That's* who wanted a housekeeper? Oh, baby. Now what was I going to do? If Bethany Downs ever found out I was going to see Melanie Moloney, it would be the end of my career at the newspaper, maybe the end of me! Well, fuck her and her father. I needed to earn Melanie's $800 a week a lot more than I needed to worry about incurring the wrath of the Downses.

Of course, there was no guarantee I'd even get the job. There was the pesky problem of those excellent references I didn't have. But I figured I'd deal with that matter when the time came. Meanwhile, I concentrated on the positives of being Melanie Moloney's housekeeper. First, there was the money. Second, there was the fact that I wouldn't have to give up my work at the newspaper or discontinue my search for a magazine job in New York. Third, I'd be working in virtual anonymity; no one except Melanie would ever have to know I was cleaning toilets instead of furthering my career in journalism. Since Melanie was an outsider in town, I'd be able to keep my secret from everyone who mattered. And finally, I'd be working for an author of bestselling celebrity biographies—a woman who wrote about famous people, just like I did, only for millions of dollars instead of pennies. Maybe Melanie was my ticket to stardom. You've heard of those Hollywood moguls who started out in the mailroom of ICM or William Morris? Well, what about starting out as some famous person's housekeeper? Maybe by cleaning Melanie's kitchen, dusting her office, and ironing her camisoles, I'd be able to get close to her, study her technique, find out how she got people to tell her things, learn how she rose from newspaper reporter to mega-author. Maybe she'd see how efficient and capable I was and make me her assistant, then her associate, then her co-author. Anything was possible, wasn't it?

My fantasy was interrupted by the phone ringing. It was Julia suggesting we have dinner.

"I can't afford to eat out. I'm into reality now, remember?"

"I'm proud of you, Koff—so proud I'll treat. See you at McGavin's in an hour."

I hadn't been to McGavin's in months, and I was shocked to see how much the clientele had changed. A ramshackle hamburger joint that used to cater to Layton's "underclass" (i.e., people on a budget) as well as to the *Community Times* staffers who worked next door, McGavin's had evidently gone trendy. Instead of seeing the usual array of four-by-fours and pickup trucks in the parking lot, all I saw were BMWs and Mercedes. Inside, the place was jam-packed with tanned and trim bodies sporting Carolyn Roehms, Donna Karans, and Ralph Laurens.

"What's going on?" I asked Julia as I spotted three couples who used to be my friends when I was married to Sandy but who now pretended not to see me.

"This is their way of downscaling," Julia replied. "They can't afford the fancy Italian restaurants anymore, so they come here. God forbid they should stay home."

"They're lucky if they have a home," I said mournfully.

"What's happening with your house? Any action?"

"None. Not one offer. Nobody wants it except the bank."

"That's tough, Koff. How are you handling it?"

"Okay, I guess." I was dying to tell Julia about my interview with Melanie Moloney, but there was no way I was going to tell *anybody* about that. Sure, Julia was a good friend, but she was also a longtime and very loyal employee of the *Community Times,* which meant that she had a strong allegiance to Alistair Downs. One little slip and I'd be out of the newspaper in a heartbeat. Another reason I couldn't tell Julia was that I had no idea how she'd react to my being somebody's housekeeper. She might be appalled that I wasn't supporting myself in a more politically correct manner. Better not to tell her anything, I decided.

As we ate cheeseburgers and French fries, I listened to Julia expound on everything from the Planning and Zoning Board's recent decision not to grant the refurbished Layton Delicatessen a liquor license to details of the town's controversial new recycling program (controversial because many Layton residents thought the little blue recycling baskets they were asked to leave outside their homes once a week were so unsightly they might contribute to the depreciation of their property values). Over coffee I asked Julia how her mystery man was.

"What mystery man?" she asked nonchalantly.

"Oh, come on. You've been seeing someone. I know you have."

"What makes you say that, Koff?"

"Because you're busy every night. I almost fainted when you wanted to have dinner tonight."

"Just because I'm busy doesn't mean there's a man involved. Life doesn't have to revolve around a man, Koff."

"Okay. So you don't want to tell me. Case closed."

The waiter brought the check, and as Julia grabbed it, I reached into my purse for a mirror, checked my mouth for telltale crumbs, and began to apply a fresh coat of lipstick. Suddenly, a familiar face materialized next to my reflection.

"Mrs. Koff, isn't it?"

It was Cullie Harrington, photographer extraordinaire. I was so flustered I couldn't think of anything to say, a rarity.

"You don't recognize me? I shot your house last month," Cullie reminded me. "You wouldn't let me in the front door, remember?"

Oh, man. This guy's attitude was everything I remembered it was. Well, I was not about to give him the satisfaction of saying one nice thing about his photographs. Meanwhile, for some bizarre reason, my heart raced at the sight of him. Never show a man he's gotten the better of you, my mother always said. Never wear your heart on your sleeve. Never let him know how much you care about him. "Shot my house?" I said, looking as if I were genuinely perplexed and couldn't place this man for the life of me.

"Yeah, I shot your house all right," Cullie smirked. "Maplebarf—er, bark—Manor."

"That's the name of my house, yes. And your name is Corny—sorry—Cullie Harrington?"

Cullie laughed. He had a great smile, damn it. With his wavy blond hair, his salt-and-pepper beard and mustache, his sinewy swimmer's body, and that great smile, he was a sight for sore eyes, if you liked the type.

"I'm Cullie Harrington," he said to Julia, extending his hand.

"Julia Applebaum. Glad to meet you," she said as they shook hands. "Would you like to join us?"

"We were just leaving," I said quickly. "Maybe some other time."

"Or maybe not. I only came by to see if you ever got those brochures I dropped in your mailbox. You *do* remember the brochures, don't you?"

"Of course I remember the brochures," I snapped. Would this man ever stop treating me like pond scum?

"A second ago you didn't remember that I shot your house."

"Well, I got the brochures. Thank you."

"And?"

"And what?"

"And did you like the way the house came out?"

"Actually, they were just fine," I said, stifling a sneeze and rummaging around in my purse for a Kleenex. I was probably allergic to this man.

"Just fine? Nice of you to say so," Cullie said, sounding surprised at my lack of enthusiasm and a little hurt by my response. Well, I wasn't going to fall all over myself raving about his pictures. I knew I was being rude, but I couldn't help it. The photographs were gorgeous, and Cullie was obviously very talented. So why couldn't I tell him so? Why did I have to high-hat him? Just because I was raised to be a snob didn't mean I had to be one.

I cleared my throat, looked Cullie right in his bespeckled blue eyes, and said, "The truth is, I thought the photographs were—"

"Hi, hon. I'm back."

I was about to admit that I really did like the photographs and that I was grateful to Cullie for helping me sell the place, when a young woman with long, blond hair and very large breasts slid her arm through his.

"Sorry I took so long in there," she said, pointing toward the ladies' room. "There was a line."

"No problem," said Cullie, obviously happy to see her.

"Hadley, this is Julia Applebaum and her friend, Mrs. Koff. Ladies, this is Hadley Kittredge."

Hadley Kittredge. Give me a break. And what was this Mrs. Koff bullshit? Cullie knew perfectly well my first name was Alison.

Hadley Kittredge smiled at Julia and me. She had perfect hair, skin, and teeth and I hated her. "Pleasure to meet you, Julia," she said. "You, too, Mrs. . . ."

"Koff," I said. "Like the thing you do when you have a chest cold." Hadley Kittredge probably never got chest colds.

"Let's go, Hadley," Cullie said to her. "The movie's starting in ten minutes."

"What are you seeing?" Julia asked the lovebirds.

"Moby Dick with Gregory Peck," Hadley said. "It's playing at that revival house in town. Cullie just adores sea stories."

"Have a whale of a good time," I muttered sourly.

"Hey, that's a real coincidence," Hadley said excitedly, slapping her thigh. "Did you get it, Cullie? Mrs. Koff told us to have a whale of a good time, and we're going to see a movie about a whale!"

God had a sense of fair play after all. He gave this girl a great body but no brain.

"Yeah, I got it," Cullie scowled. "Mrs. Koff has a lightning wit. The trouble is, nobody likes to get hit by lightning. Nice meeting you, Julia."

Cullie and Hadley walked out of McGavin's arm in arm, while Julia paid the check and I sulked.

"What was all that about, Koff?" Julia asked finally. "Why did you treat that nice man like you were Leona Helmsley and he was one of the little people? He was trying to be friendly and you had a bug up your ass."

"I know, and I'm ashamed of myself," I admitted. "I act crazy when I'm around that guy. He makes me nervous—so nervous my heart has palpitations, my hands shake, and my stomach gets the dry heaves."

"Then you'd better do something about it."

"Like what? Take Prozac?"

"No. See him again. Sounds to me like a case of true love."

Chapter 6

At three o'clock the next afternoon, I left Maplebark Manor for my three-thirty interview with Melanie Moloney. Not knowing what to wear—should I dress like the housekeeper or the lady of the house?—I finally chose a simple skirt and sweater outfit, made even simpler by the removal of all my jewelry.

Bluefish Cove, where Melanie lived, was about ten minutes from my house. A private, gated community that occupied a narrow strip of waterfront on the other end of town from Layton Harbor, Bluefish Cove was known as "Connecticuthampton" because of all the New Yorkers who had bought weekend houses there after having previously owned homes in Westhampton, Sag Harbor, and the like. The commute was better, many of them said.

Unlike the understated-but-nevertheless-million-dollar manor houses of Layton Harbor, the homes in Bluefish Cove were, for the most part, splashy contemporary residences that offered floor-to-ceiling expanses of glass, lots of marble, pickled wood cabinetry, and state-of-the-art bathrooms that were described as "spas." Old-money Laytonites dismissed the residents of Bluefish Cove as "climbers." Bluefish Cove-ers considered people who lived in Layton Harbor to be "boring old farts."

As I drove over to Melanie's house I tried to imagine how the interview would go. Then I tried to imagine how my life would go if I got the job. Then I tried to imagine how my life would go if I didn't get the job. Neither prospect thrilled me.

At three-twelve I pulled up to the Bluefish Cove gatehouse, where a uniformed security guard stopped me.

"Your name?" he barked.

"Alison Koff," I said, after opening my car window. "I'm here to see Melanie Moloney."

"Koff. Koff. I don't see any Koffs on the list. I'll have to call Miss Moloney. Wait here."

Oh, great, I thought. She's either forgotten about our appointment or hired somebody else already.

"Go on in," the guard said finally, opening the gate and waving me through.

I maneuvered my car past a parade of hedges, stone walls, and wrought-iron gates until I arrived at 7 Bluefish Cove. I pulled into the pink-graveled driveway, which was bordered by Belgian block and dozens of little white spotlights, and parked in the area to the left of the front door.

The exterior of the house was constructed of naturally weathered cedar shingles, and there appeared to be several decks and balconies protruding from all sides. Most striking at first glance were the number and size of the glass doors and windows. I panicked as I imagined myself Windexing all 6,000 square feet of them.

I walked briskly to the front of the house, rang the doorbell, and waited. Nobody came. After a minute or so, I rang again. Still nobody. It was a cold, blustery mid-January day, and the windchill factor made it feel like zero degrees. I pulled my cloth coat around me, wishing I hadn't pawned my mink. Where is she? I thought. Doesn't she care that I'm freezing my ass off out here? How rude can you get?

I pressed the doorbell again, this time giving it a couple of extra-long rings. The tip of my nose was starting to hurt, and my fingers and toes were going numb. Where on earth was Melanie? She had to know I was coming, because the guard had just telephoned her. Maybe she's in the "spa," I figured. Or maybe she's on an important long-distance call.

I waited another few minutes before ringing again. No one answered. Then, thinking the bell might be out of order, I knocked on the door several times. Still no answer. Was I too early for our appointment? Or too late? Had I showed up on the wrong day? Did I have the right house? The right town?

I was beginning to wonder if I had hallucinated the entire conversation with Melanie. Chilled to the bone, I decided to walk back to my car, turn on the heat, and sit there until I got some feeling back in my limbs. At three thirty-five I went back to the front of the house and rang the bell once more.

"You're late," said the woman who opened the door. She was wearing a black-and-mauve velour warm-up suit and black high-heeled shoes accented with little gold bows. She was short, painfully thin, and had shoulder-length, platinum-blond hair of a sheen and texture that could best be described as synthetic. Her pasty white face had been stretched and reshaped so many times that it reminded me of the vanilla Turkish taffy my mother used to bring me from Atlantic City. The only color on her face came from her heavily mascara-ed blue eyes and her thin-lipped mouth, which was overpainted with dark red lipstick. How old was she? There was absolutely no way to tell. All I knew was that she was standing inside her front door, her hands on her little hips, wearing the same expression my mother always wore whenever I'd commit some grammatical atrocity.

"Our appointment was for three-thirty," she said in a Betty Boop voice.

"I was here at three fifteen," I protested, shivering as a gust of wind nearly knocked me off Melanie's front step.

"Yes, but our appointment was for three-thirty. Not three-fifteen. Not three thirty-five. Three-thirty. I'm a woman who demands punctuality. That's why *my* housekeeper gets twenty-five dollars an hour and the rest of them get fifteen."

I nodded, too cold to speak.

"Come in," she said finally.

I was about to enter Melanie's house when she raised her hand and blocked me.

"Not this way. Through the service entrance," she said, pointing to the back of the house.

I gathered my coat around me, braced myself for yet another few minutes of bone-chilling air, and walked around to the back of the house, cursing all the way. I cursed Melanie for playing her little head game. I cursed Sandy for leaving me for Soozie. I cursed the economy for making it so hard to earn a living. I cursed my mother for not being the kind of parent I could go to for a loan. I cursed my father for dying and screwing up my life. I cursed Janet Claiborne for not selling my house. I even cursed the state of Connecticut for having such lousy weather. As I neared Melanie's back door, I suddenly thought of Cullie Harrington and how I'd made him use *my* service entrance. Then I cursed myself for acting so pretentious. What goes around comes around, I muttered.

Melanie showed me into her kitchen, a gleaming, high-tech affair with pickled pink Allmilmo wood cabinets, white Corian counters, white tile flooring, state-of-the-art appliances, and a center island, one side of which featured a Jenn-Air Grill, the other side a butcher block cutting board. In the corner was a small round table and four chrome-and-cane chairs. "Sit there," Melanie said, pointing to one of the chairs. She did not invite me to take off my hat and coat, so I kept them on, wishing I could use my hat to cover my nose. Melanie's perfume (I instantly recognized it as Giorgio, the fragrance everyone was wearing that year) was so strong it nearly choked me.

"As you can see, I like my house kept sparkling clean," she said, admiring the spotless white floor under our feet. "My previous girl mopped this floor twice a day."

My previous girl. How would I endure working for this

woman? "That won't be a problem," I said. I had come this far and I wasn't about to back out now.

"Tell me about yourself," she insisted. "Are you a local person or do you live in Jessup?"

Jessup was the blue-collar town that bordered Layton to the northwest. Most of the people who "serviced" Layton residents lived there. "I'm from Layton," I said, trying to sound matter-of-fact. "I've lived here all my life."

"Really? How long have you been cleaning houses?" she asked.

"Since I was a child." My mother used to rate the cleanliness of my room on a scale of one to ten. If I earned a ten, she'd take me out to Schrafft's for a hot fudge sundae. As clean as I kept my room, it was a miracle I wasn't the fattest kid in town.

"You said on the phone that you were most recently employed by a couple on Woodland Way?"

"That's right."

"And you're leaving because they can no longer afford you?"

"Yes."

"I'll want their names, of course, so I can check your references."

"Of course." Now what was I going to do?

"But first, I'll walk you through the house so you'll have an idea of the work involved."

"Would it be all right if I took off my coat? It's a little warm in here." I was beginning to defrost.

Melanie instructed me to leave my things on the chair. Then she led me on a tour of the house, which was decorated in early Maurice Villency. Practically everything in the place was white, just like Melanie's face and hair. The white wall-to-wall-carpeted living room was furnished with a white leather sectional sofa, white track lightning, and assorted glass tables. The room's only color came from the Italian verde marble fireplace, which looked as if it had never been used. The dining room, also carpeted in white, contained an enormous rectangular glass table and twelve chairs, upholstered in a white silk fabric. One of the dining room walls was mirrored, with glass shelving and a wet bar. Both the living room and dining room had sliding glass doors that opened up to the pool deck and offered spectacular views of the Sound. Adjacent to the kitchen was a small maid's room, a laundry room/mud room that had a laundry chute from the master dressing room upstairs and a dumbwaiter shaft to the garage down below, a 300-bottle wine cellar carved into a rock ledge to ensure perfect temperature, a combination TV room/exercise room (it had a large-screen television as well as a NordicTrack), and Melanie's office, which she said was off-limits until I became a member of her household. The second floor of the house, also carpeted in white, consisted of a spacious master suite: a cathedral-ceilinged master bedroom that enjoyed views of the water through sliding glass doors on both sides of a raised Italian verde marble fireplace; and a dressing room/bath featuring a Jacuzzi, sauna, and stall shower, a "vanity room" with mirrored walls and 24-karat-gold fixtures, and two walk-in closets. Down the hall from the master suite were two guest bedrooms, each with its own "spa."

No wonder Melanie's paying the big bucks, I thought. Never mind her crabby personality. With all the glass doors, mirrored walls, and white carpeting, the place was a housekeeper's nightmare.

"So, that's the house," Melanie said when we returned to the kitchen. "You think you can do the job?"

I took a deep breath and nodded.

"Good. Now let's talk about your references," she said. "Give me the phone number of that couple you worked for."

The moment of truth. Should I stall and say the couple was away on a trip and couldn't be reached? Should I give her a wrong number? Melanie was no dope; she was a journalist, after all, and she was bound to find out I was lying. I had no choice but to tell her everything. Well, almost everything.

"I'm the couple," I said, looking her straight in the eye.

"What do you mean you're the couple?"

"The house I've been cleaning on Woodland Way is my own."

"Look, what is this anyway? Who are you and what are you doing in my house? Are you from one of the tabloids or maybe from the 'Geraldo' show? Or do you work for Alistair Downs or something? He sent you here to steal my manuscript, didn't he?"

Melanie's face was so taut that when she spoke, nothing moved but her lips. The rest of her face remained perfectly still.

"No, I'm not from the tabloids or Geraldo. And I'm not a spy sent by Alistair Downs," I assured her, knowing she'd freak out if she found out I did indeed work for Alistair. "My name is Alison Koff and I live on Woodland Way. My husband and I are divorced, and due to his financial reversals, I've been cleaning Maplebark Manor myself."

"Maplebark Manor?"

"That's our house's name," I explained when Melanie looked puzzled. "But just because I've never been a professional housekeeper doesn't mean I can't clean like one."

Melanie remained skeptical. "I don't think so," she said, handing me my hat and coat.

I wasn't giving up so fast. "Your ad in the newspaper said you were looking for someone with superb cleaning skills, which I happen to have. It also said you wanted someone who was honest, which I obviously am since I've admitted the truth about myself. You said you wanted someone who was reliable. Well, I showed up for this interview fifteen minutes early. You wanted someone who was discreet, and I haven't told a soul I was coming here. And you wanted someone who spoke English. Think how handy it will be to have a housekeeper who speaks real, honest-to-goodness English. Think how confident you'll feel every time you ask me to answer the phone or communicate with your friends and business associates."

Melanie appeared to be considering my logic.

"I still don't like the idea," she said. "You don't have any experience taking care of someone else's house. How do I know you can really clean?"

There was only one way to prove to Melanie that I knew my way around a tidy toilet bowl. "If I had a good reference, you'd hire me, wouldn't you?"

"Probably. The other people I interviewed for this job acted like they'd never seen a nice house, let alone cleaned one. At least you didn't faint when I showed you around."

"I didn't faint when I saw your house because I live in a big house myself, a house I also *clean* myself. I promise you, I'll treat your beautiful things as if they were my own."

"I don't know . . ."

"Do you have twenty minutes?" I asked Melanie as I played my last hand.

"Why?"

"So I can give you that reference you wanted."

"I thought you said you didn't have one."

"I do. It's my house. Come with me."

After a few minutes of arm-twisting, I managed to persuade Melanie to take a ride over to Maplebark Manor.

"How do I know you don't have a housekeeper to do all this?" she asked after inspecting the place.

"Now that's a reference I *can* give you. Here's the number of the Peruvian housekeeper who used to work for me." I wrote Maria's phone number on a piece of paper and handed it to Melanie. "She'll confirm that I had to let her go and that I've been cleaning my own house ever since."

"This Maria's had professional cleaning experience. Maybe I should hire her instead of you," Melanie said.

"I thought you wanted someone who could speak English."

Melanie pursed her lips and tapped her tiny foot on the floor. "I'll try it," she said finally.

"You mean I'm hired?"

"You'll start next week," she said. "Tuesday through Friday, eight-thirty to four-thirty. I'll have the guard at the gatehouse issue you a pass."

"You won't be sorry," I said, grabbing Melanie's little hand and pumping it enthusiastically as I walked her to the door. I could see it now: Alison Koff and Melanie Moloney, interviewing the world's most illustrious celebrities, collaborating on bestseller after bestseller, fielding offers from television networks and movie studios . . .

"Oh, I almost forgot," Melanie said, stopping at my front door. "What size are you?"

"What size what?"

"What size dress. I'll need to order your maid's uniform."

"My maid's uniform?" The ad never said anything about a maid's uniform. I was mortified.

"Is there a problem?" Melanie said, her top lip curling into a nasty smile. No doubt about it: this woman had a sadistic streak. I had a feeling she was going to love making me bow and scrape.

"No problem at all," I managed, trying so hard to be a good sport. Up to that point, I'd been one. I'd stood outside Melanie's front door, nearly freezing to death while she took her sweet time letting me in. I'd used the service entrance, just as she'd insisted. I'd invited her over to my spanking clean house so she could see for herself that I was qualified for the job. But all of a sudden, the idea of my being a housekeeper—no, maid—seemed totally implausible. What was I trying to prove anyway? That I could succeed at being somebody's servant? Hell, I'd already proven that. I'd been my mother's little doormat for years. Wait a minute, this wasn't about being somebody's servant, I reminded myself. This was about supporting myself instead of living off a man's money. This was about solving my own problems, pulling myself out of my own messes. This was about surviving. "I'm a size six," I told Melanie as I walked her out my front door.

* * *

My mood wavered as I spent the weekend preparing for my new job as Melanie Moloney's maid. On one hand, I was excited about having a place to go every day, after eleven years of working at home. On the other hand, I couldn't stop obsessing about having to wear a maid's uniform. That little piece of cloth seemed to symbolize how dramatically my life had plunged from the glory days of the eighties. I kept having nightmares about being "found out"—dreams in which I'd be out shopping when suddenly all the people I used to know would start pointing at me and laughing; then I'd look down to find that I wasn't wearing the black gabardine Versace dress I'd put on that morning—I was wearing a black polyester maid's uniform with nothing underneath! Not a bra, not panties, nothing! No matter how often I told myself I didn't care what people thought of me, I couldn't get past the fear that *somebody might find out I was Melanie Moloney's maid!*

I especially couldn't stop thinking about my mother and what she would say if she knew I was going to work as a housekeeper. I felt as if I were betraying her, as if I were no longer the good daughter I had painstakingly tried to be. My guilt was so oppressive I could hardly breathe.

By the time Tuesday morning rolled around, I was exhausted from all the worrying. Bleary-eyed, I drove over to Bluefish Cove at eight-ten, hoping to make it to Melanie's service entrance at exactly eight-thirty.

The security guard at the gatehouse remembered me from the previous week and said, "Hello, Alison. Here's the pass Miss Moloney asked me to give you." At least Melanie hadn't changed her mind.

I arrived at 7 Bluefish Cove right on time and knocked on the back door of the house. Melanie let me in, wearing the same black-and-mauve outfit she'd worn the week before and the same nauseating perfume.

"Here's your uniform," she said before I'd even greeted

her or taken off my hat and coat. "You can change in there," she added, pointing to the maid's room off the kitchen.

My uniform turned out to be the very one from my nightmares—a black polyester number over which I was to wear a starched white apron. I was also given a pair of orthopedic-looking black shoes and a pair of white pantyhose. "I took a guess on your shoe size," Melanie said.

When I'd finished changing into my housekeeper's costume, I took a good look at myself in the narrow full-length mirror that hung on the back of the maid's room door. You look like Hazel, I thought glumly, reminding myself of the Shirley Booth character from the popular sixties' sit-com. God, don't let anyone find out about this, I prayed.

During my first half-hour on the job, Melanie ("Ms. Moloney," she said to call her) showed me where the cleaning supplies were and explained the order in which she expected me to clean the rooms. I was to begin upstairs in the master bedroom and bath, then do the guest rooms and baths, regardless of whether there had been any guests. Then I was to clean the kitchen, dining room, living room, and exercise room. At that point, Melanie would break for lunch and I was to clean her office. After that, I was to clean the kitchen and dining room all over again, whether she made a mess of them or not. Along the way, I was to take care of any laundry that had found its way into the laundry chute. I was to change the sheets on Melanie's bed every Tuesday morning. I was instructed not to answer the phone unless Melanie specifically asked me to, nor was I permitted to use the phone except for emergencies. I was to be paid in cash at the end of each workday. And I would not be given either my own key to the premises or the code to the burglar alarm. "It's not that I don't trust you," Melanie said without apology. "It's just that there's a very confidential manuscript in this house. Very confidential and very valuable."

Right, but what I really wanted to know was would I get

a lunch break at this job? My stomach was growling and it was only eight forty-five.

"If you think you'll have time," Melanie responded when I posed the question. "My previous girls didn't have a minute to eat. They barely finished their work by four-thirty."

Swell. Maybe I'd lose so much weight working for Melanie that I'd no longer fit into my uniform and she'd have to let me wear something else.

Before I started my chores, Melanie took me into her office, which, she explained, was kept locked when she wasn't using it. It was a large, impeccably organized room containing basic office furniture—desk, chairs, files, etc.— plus a long table on which sat dozens of boxes of index cards, cards I assumed contained every bit of dirt that could possibly be dug up on Alistair P. Downs. Conspicuously absent from the room was a computer; Melanie, as everyone who followed her career knew, was computer-phobic and produced all her manuscripts on a good old-fashioned Smith Corona.

There was a short, pudgy, middle-aged man sitting at the long table in the room, but Melanie didn't bother to introduce him. How rude, I thought. Then I remembered I was The Help, and nobody talked to The Help, at least not in Layton.

"You're the new maid," said the man finally, as I was turning to leave Melanie's office.

No shit, Sherlock. "Yes, I am," I smiled. "My name is Alison."

"This is Todd Bennett," Melanie explained. "He's my research associate and he'll be here most days."

"Nice to meet you," I said to Todd, who had pock-marked skin and curly brown hair and weighed close to 250 pounds. I'll bet old Todd gets a lunch break, I thought enviously.

"Nyth to meet you, too," Todd lisped, but he didn't go out of his way to be friendly. Oh well, who needed new friends? I did, but that was beside the point.

I carried my bucket of cleaning supplies upstairs and set it down on the floor of the master bedroom. Then I walked over to Melanie's king-size bed and began to strip off the mauve-and-gray bed linens. I was about to pull off the bottom sheet when I noticed several crusty yellow spots on the sheet. I thought a minute until it dawned on me: Melanie's got a boyfriend. It had been so long since I'd been with a man, let alone have sex with one, that I'd almost forgotten what semen-stained sheets looked like. Was Melanie getting it on with Todd? She was so frail and he was so chubby that I couldn't picture them Doing It for the life of me. But you never could tell what attracted people to each other. She did say he was in the house a lot.

While I finished stripping the bed I had to laugh at myself. Was this what maids did? Examine people's bed linens and speculate about their sex lives? Was that what Maria did when she worked for me and Sandy? If so, she must have been disappointed; Sandy and I were way too busy acquiring antiques, clothes, and cars to have anything so purposeless as sex.

I rolled up the sheets and tossed them down the laundry chute. Then I picked up the bucket of cleaning supplies and began to clean the room. Every few minutes Melanie would stick her platinum-blond head in. "Don't use wax on the dresser." "Don't use that abrasive on the sink." "Don't leave streaks on the mirror." She was making me a nervous wreck. If she kept interrupting my work every five minutes I'd never get out of there by four-thirty.

As it turned out, I didn't finish cleaning Melanie's house until seven-thirty that night, and she refused to pay me for the extra three hours of work. "You'll be paid for the work you do, not for the amount of time you do it in. If you want to be out of here earlier, you'll just have to work faster," she said.

I fell asleep the minute I got home. No eating dinner. No watching TV. No returning my mother's three messages. The first one said: "Hello, Alison. This is your mother. It's

Jane Heller

one-thirty in the afternoon. You haven't called me in a week." The second one said: "Hello, Alison. This is your mother. It's two-thirty in the afternoon and my friends at the club say their daughters call them every day." The third one said: "Hello, Alison. This is your mother. It's three-thirty in the afternoon and your lack of attentiveness is something about which I am very angry." So my mother was angry. What else was new? I couldn't remember ever being so tired, physically and mentally. But before I drifted off to unconsciousness, I took one more look at the crisp green bills that rested on my night table—all $200 of them. Sweet dreams, I wished myself as I turned out the light.

Chapter 7

If I thought life as Melanie Moloney's housekeeper would get easier as the weeks went by, I was wrong. Melanie turned out to be more than just an exacting boss: she was The Boss from Hell. If I cleaned the toilet bowl in the master bathroom first thing in the morning, she'd tell me to clean it again before I left in the afternoon. If she wanted me to polish her silver, she'd wait until I was just about to leave for the day and then tell me. She'd make me get on my hands and knees to scrub the kitchen floor, instead of letting me use a sponge mop; then she'd eat lunch at the kitchen table, leave a stack of dirty dishes in the sink, and make me scrub the kitchen floor yet again. Worst of all was what I came to call her "Carpet Torture." After I'd finish dusting the furniture in every room, I'd vacuum the white wall-to-wall carpeting that covered the floors throughout most of the house. I'd just be putting the vacuum cleaner away when she'd tap me on the shoulder, point to some invisible spot on the carpet, and say, "It's going the wrong way." "What do you mean?" I asked when the problem arose for the first time. "The nap of the carpet should go in one direction. I don't like it to look crisscrossed," she explained.

You'd think, with such a "hands-on" approach to running her household, Melanie wouldn't have time to write and research her books. Well, let me tell you a dirty little secret: Melanie Moloney didn't have time to write and re-

search her books—Todd Bennett did. One of the first revelations I uncovered during my stint as Melanie's housekeeper was that Todd Bennett did most of the work on the
books—and got none of the credit. He was the one who
toiled away at 7 Bluefish Cove, while Melanie basked in the
literary spotlight.

Sometimes, when she was out being interviewed, taking a
business meeting, or having her hair done, Todd and I
would sit in her office and chew the fat. He wasn't nearly as
standoffish as he'd seemed that first day, just overworked
and underappreciated.

"We were both at the *Chicago Thun-Times,*" he explained
when I asked how he came to work for Melanie. "She told
me she was writing a biography of Dean Martin and asked
if I'd like to help her. I've been her collaborator ever thince.
Or should I say *ghostwriter.*" That last word was said with
unabashed bitterness.

"So you're the one who actually writes the books. I'm
really impressed, Todd," I gushed. I had an idea that by
flattering Todd I'd get him to tell me things. He struck me
as someone who'd never been flattered as a child. He still
had the look of the fat, pimply kid who was always the last
one picked for the baseball team and never really got over
it.

"Yeth, I'm the one who actually writes the books and gets
zero credit," he admitted. "Anyway, everything's going to
change with the next book. I'll be getting my due with this
one."

"You mean the Alistair Downs book?"

"Yeth."

"Your name will be on the cover along with Melanie's?"

"You got that right. My name will be on the cover—and
up there on the bestseller list, right next to hers. She and I
have a deal."

"Hey, that's great," I said, thinking of my own literary
aspirations. If Todd Bennett could move from newspaper

reporter to bestselling biographer, why couldn't I? "By the way, how is the book coming along?"

"It's just about finished. We expect to deliver it to our publisher in a couple of weeks."

"Wow. That's really exciting. Is it going to be a shocker like the last ones Melanie—sorry, *you* and Melanie— wrote?"

"Let's just say people all over the world will view Alistair P. Downs in a new light."

A new and not very flattering light, I was sure. "Any chance I could sneak a look at the manuscript?" I asked Todd.

"No way," he said.

"Is that it over there?" I said, pointing to a carton containing what appeared to be over a thousand typewritten pages. It was sitting on the floor next to Melanie's desk and probably weighed a ton.

"Yeth, but don't get any ideas. Melanie would have a fit if you went near it."

I stared at the manuscript longingly. "Then how about giving me one little tidbit from the book, Todd? Tell me something really juicy about Alistair, please? I promise not to tell a soul."

"Not on your life," he scolded me. "We've got a big first serial sale to *People* magazine. Nothing about the book breaks until they break it."

"Aw, come on, Todd. Just one little morsel."

"Well, I guess I could tell you about the time Alistair threatened to—"

Just as Todd was about to share what I assumed was an eye-opener from the book, Melanie walked into the office. "What's going on here?" she demanded. It was amazing how much mileage she got out of that little Betty Boop voice.

Todd and I flinched like two little schoolchildren who'd been caught after writing dirty words on the blackboard.

"We weren't doing anything," I said, sounding like a five-year-old.

"You're damn right you weren't doing anything," Melanie sneered. "You were supposed to be working. Both of you!"

I gathered my bucket of cleaning supplies and scurried out of the office, leaving Todd to pacify Melanie. If they were indeed lovers, which I still hadn't determined, he'd find a way to calm her down.

To punish me for gossiping with Todd instead of doing my housework, Melanie made me wash all the sliding glass doors in the house, inside and out, which, on a frigid February day, was no picnic. She could be downright cruel at times. Even vicious. Yes, she was paying me very well. And yes, if I didn't like it I could always quit. But I'd made a deal with myself: I would continue to work for Melanie, no matter how awful she was, until I'd made enough money to pay the Layton Bank & Trust Company a nice chunk of the mortgage payments I owed them, and maybe even stave off the foreclosure on Maplebark Manor. I would stick it out no matter how battered and broken I felt at the end of each day. I would hang on until something happened to change my fortunes.

One of the ways I kept my spirits up during my days at Bluefish Cove was to fantasize about murdering Melanie. Bizarre as it must sound, my homicidal daydreams helped me perform even the most menial tasks with gusto. For example, I'd be making Melanie's bed and suddenly picture myself suffocating her with a pillow. Or I'd be scrubbing the bathroom sink and imagine holding her head under a sinkful of water. I wasn't proud of these thoughts, believe me. But they did help me pass the time.

The other way I kept my spirits up was even more shameful: I fantasized about making love to Cullie Harrington. There I'd be, folding Melanie's laundry, when all of a sudden I'd see Cullie's face close to mine, his beard and mustache tickling my cheek, his lips murmuring, "My sweet

Mrs. Koff. I'm sorry I acted like a jerk the last time I saw you. I don't know what came over me. And I don't love Hadley Kittredge. I love you. Marry me." Pathetic, huh? I was so middle class, even my romantic fantasies were middle class: they always ended in marriage.

What are you doing thinking about Cullie Harrington? I'd berate myself. You hate him and he hates you. I was much more comfortable fantasizing about murdering Melanie than lusting after Cullie. But I couldn't control my thoughts any more than I could control the number of glass doors in Melanie's house.

Other distractions from my housekeeping job were the periodic newspaper assignments I got from Bethany. I'd been able to do my interviews for the paper on Mondays, my day off. One Monday I did a story on a professional surrogate mother who had come to Layton to speak to the women's rights group that Julia had organized. Two weeks later, I interviewed a local woman who'd won a trip to Italy by entering a contest sponsored by the Ragu spaghetti sauce people. When I went to the newspaper to hand in my copy, Julia remarked how poorly I looked. "You lose weight, Koff?" she asked. "A little," I said. "Let me take you to McGavin's some night this week," she offered. I thanked her but said I was busy. Go out for dinner? By the time I got home from a day of cleaning Melanie Moloney's house, I had about as much energy as a dish rag. Besides, I'd managed to keep my secret from Julia, Bethany, and everyone else at the newspaper and didn't want to blow it. I'd also managed to keep my work at the paper a secret from Melanie and I certainly didn't want to blow that.

I did have a close call, though. One morning Melanie informed me that she was having a small buffet luncheon for some media types from Manhattan. "You'll serve," she said, indicating that I'd be standing behind the buffet table and dishing out whatever was on the menu. At first, I welcomed the assignment; it meant a break from my normal routine of dusting, scrubbing, and vacuuming. It also meant

I'd be interacting with some real, honest-to-goodness New York media types, maybe even the editor-in-chief of *People* magazine! But when Melanie told me the name of the catering company that was doing the luncheon, I nearly died. It was Soozie's Delectable Edibles! Yes, Sandy's first-and-soon-to-be-third-wife, Soozie the caterer-whore, was on her way over to Melanie's house with her infamous Lite 'n' Healthy Chicken Salad!

I broke out in a sweat. What if Soozie found out I was a housekeeper? She'd tell everybody in Layton. Hell, everybody in the whole world. "You'll never guess who's working as a maid," she'd say. "Alison, Sandy's second wife. Isn't that a trip?" That's how Soozie talked—in Sixties-Speak. She had never gotten over the fact that her parents didn't let her go to Woodstock, so to compensate she often used words like "trip" and "far out."

I had to do something to avert this catastrophe. But what? I couldn't let Soozie see me in my Hazel costume, I just couldn't. Think of something! Think!

"Alison, stop daydreaming. The caterer will be here any minute," Melanie snapped. "Dust the furniture in the dining room and get the buffet table ready."

"I dusted the dining room furniture this morning," I said.

"Dust it again."

"Yes, Ms. Moloney."

I was spraying the dining room table with lemon Pledge when the back doorbell rang.

"What are you waiting for, Alison. Get the door!" Melanie said.

How could I get the door? Soozie would see me. "But Ms. Moloney. I have to finish dusting in here before your guests arrive," I said.

"Oh, all right," Melanie said, obviously disgusted with my inability to perform two tasks at once.

Melanie went into the kitchen and opened the service door for Soozie. I strained to hear them talking.

"Hi, Miss Moloney. I'm from Delectable Edibles," a

chirpy voice said. "Where would you like me to put all the food?" Up your adulterous ass, I thought. Now what was I going to do?

"Just leave everything here on the counter until my maid finishes up in the dining room," I heard Melanie tell Soozie. "She should be through in a minute."

"Will you need me to stay for the luncheon?" Soozie asked.

"No, my maid will serve the guests. Alison? Aren't you done in there yet?" Melanie yelled.

God, Melanie had used my name. I wondered if Soozie had a clue it was me. Why should she? There were probably plenty of maids named Alison, right? "Coming," I said hoarsely, trying to disguise my voice. Soozie would know my voice. Over the years we'd seen each other at parties and run into each other at the beauty parlor and even talked to each other on the phone once or twice. Layton was a small town, after all, and you had to act like you could stand your husband's ex-wife, even if you couldn't.

"May I use your bathroom?" I heard Soozie ask Melanie. "I'm pregnant and I seem to have to pee every hour on the hour."

Pregnant?

"Congratulations," Melanie said.

"Thank you," Soozie replied. "The child's father and I are getting married very soon. We were just waiting for his divorce to go through before we told people about the baby. The whole thing is absolutely groovy, don't you think?"

I wanted to die. Sandy had never been interested in having children when he was married to me. Now he and Soozie were parents-to-be, and I was left out in the cold. Barren. Alone. Unloved. Tears sprang to my eyes. I tried to wipe them away with my dust rag, but that only made me sneeze. And sneeze. And sneeze.

"What's going on in there, Alison?" Melanie called out to me after six or seven of my sneezes.

"I seem to have caught a cold," I answered, wiping my eyes and blowing my nose.

"Come into the kitchen anyway. I need you here," Melanie commanded. The woman was all heart.

What could I do? I had to go. My cover was about to be blown.

I gathered myself up, took a deep breath, and walked into the kitchen with my head held high. When I got there, Soozie was still in the bathroom "peeing." I was safe, for the moment.

"Take the food and set it up in the dining room," Melanie instructed me.

I carried serving dishes of chicken salad and other cold entrées into the dining room. When I heard Soozie emerge from the bathroom, I froze.

"Before I go, I just want to check on the food," Soozie told Melanie in the kitchen.

I heard their footsteps as they set out for the dining room together. They were coming. They were coming. They were here!

Okay, I'm not proud of it, but here's what I did when Melanie and Soozie entered the dining room: I hid in the china closet. Yes, as they looked over the "Delectable Edibles" on the buffet table, sampled a few forkfuls of chicken salad, and discussed the merits of potato salad made with vinaigrette as opposed to potato salad made with mayonnaise, I, Alison Waxman Koff, mistress of Maplebark Manor, squatted on the floor of the china closet and remained there, huddled under the bottom shelf in a tiny ball, wondering how my life had taken such a bizarre turn.

"Everything looks great," I heard Soozie say.

"Yes, but the tortellini with pesto needs a serving spoon. I'll have my maid bring one. Alison?" Melanie yelled. "Where is she?"

I'm right here in the room with you, crouched and miserable at the bottom of this china closet, that's where I am. I figured if I stayed in the closet long enough, eventually

Soozie and Melanie would get bored with each other and go on with their day. Then I could go on with mine. All I had to do was stay perfectly still and perfectly silent.

"Alison?" Melanie yelled again.

"Maybe she's upstairs," Soozie volunteered.

"Who knows. Good help is more than hard to find—it's impossible to find," said Melanie, my dear sweet employer.

My legs were cramping and my back was in spasm, but I was almost out of the woods. Just a few seconds longer, then you can come out of the closet, I told myself. Suddenly, I had an overwhelming urge to sneeze. Oh, please. No. Not that. I pinched my nostrils. I counted to five. I prayed to God. Anything to stop the dreaded sneeze from ruining my life. Nothing worked. I sneezed—into my hands, if you must know. Fortunately, the technique muffled the sound. Unfortunately, the sheer force of the sneeze rattled the china on the shelf above my head.

"What was that?" Soozie asked.

"It sounded like it was coming from the china closet," Melanie said.

"Must be mice," Soozie offered. "Everybody in Layton has a mice problem."

"If there are mice in that closet, I'm certainly not going in there. I'll let my maid handle it. It'll give that girl something to do," said Melanie, who deserved much worse than mice.

Soozie left. Melanie went back to her office. And I emerged from the china closet with snot on my hands and muscle cramps in my calves and thighs.

I managed to carry on my duties as Melanie's luncheon helper, but my hopes of networking with her high-powered media friends from New York were dashed when she never bothered to introduce me to a single one of them. The only exchanges I had with them were: "Can I get you another napkin?" Or: "Would you like another helping of chicken salad?" Not the stuff of major career opportunities.

I was so wired when I got home that night that I couldn't

fall asleep. Instead of lying in bed, tossing and turning, I flipped on the light and decided to catch up on my magazine reading. I reached over to the night table and grabbed a handful of magazines I hadn't had time to look at. I was about to dip into *Vanity Fair* when a cover blurb caught my attention: "Melanie Moloney Exposed—A Closer Look at the Queen of the Celebrity Exposé." I found the article as fast as my fingers could turn the pages and spent the next half-hour digesting it. I couldn't get enough. It seems I wasn't the only one who found Melanie a trifle difficult. Every single person quoted in the gloriously mean-spirited article had a major gripe against her. Her fellow *Chicago Sun-Times* reporters complained that she couldn't write worth a damn and didn't deserve her success. Her friends from her pre-bestselling author days said she dropped them like a hot potato the minute she got famous. Her two ex-husbands reported that she was much too self-involved to make any man a good wife. A former secretary stated unequivocally that Melanie was the bitchiest woman she'd ever worked for. Among the bitterest of those named in the article was Melanie's former agent, Mel Suskind. The president of his own small literary agency, Suskind & Associates, Mel had been with Melanie since the early days, when she was writing biographies of celebrities for five-figure advances. He recounted how, as soon as Melanie's fourth book, *Ann-Margret: Diary of a Sex Symbol,* hit *The New York Times* hardcover bestseller list, she threw him over for a big-shot agent at ICM. "Someday she'll get hers," he said simply. Equally bitter was Roberta Carr, Melanie's editor at Sachs & Singleton. One of America's largest book publishers, Sachs & Singleton had forked over $3 million for the rights to publish Melanie's last book, *Reluctant Hero: The Unauthorized Biography of Charlton Heston,* and had put another half-million dollars into promoting the book, which spent twenty-seven weeks on the *Times* list. Then Carr and her colleagues watched Melanie move to Davis House, a rival publisher, for a whopping $5.5 million advance for the

Alistair Downs book. "There's very little author-publisher loyalty these days," Carr told *Vanity Fair,* "and Melanie Moloney is typical of the problem. It's customary for publishers to wish departing authors well. But it's hard to wish Melanie anything but her just deserts."

So I wasn't the only person who fantasized about Melanie getting hers. She seemed to inspire vengeful thoughts in everybody.

I was feeling relatively perky as I drove over to Bluefish Cove the next morning, probably because I was relieved that I had escaped running into Soozie and, therefore, managed to keep my life as a maid a secret.

When I got to the house, Todd informed me that Melanie had gone into Manhattan for a meeting with her agent and wouldn't be back until late afternoon. He also told me he was expecting a package from Federal Express and that I should bring it to him as soon as it arrived.

I was upstairs mopping the floor in one of the guest bathrooms when I heard the doorbell ring. I put down my mop and hurried downstairs to answer the door. As I ran, I passed the hall mirror and caught a quick glimpse of myself. What a mess. My uniform was all twisted, my apron was falling down around my waist, and my hair, the ends of which had fallen into my bucket of Mr. Clean, was hanging limply in my face. Who cares, I figured. So the FedEx man sees me like this.

I was almost at the front door when the bell rang again. "Hold your horses. I'm coming," I yelled, a little winded. Couldn't this guy wait two seconds?

"All right. All right. I'm here," I said, opening the door to find, not the FedEx man, but Cullie Harrington.

I was so shocked to see him standing there—this man I'd been fantasizing about, this man whose imaginary words of love had gotten me through many a long workday—that I couldn't do anything but gasp.

There he was, the man I'd been desperately hoping to see again, and what was I wearing for the big reunion? A maid's uniform! Now he would know I was a housekeeper. And once he knew, everybody would know. The whole charade would be finished, and so would my reputation in Layton.

After an eternity of the most uncomfortable silence I'd ever endured, Cullie finally spoke. "Well, if it isn't Mrs. Koff. Is it Halloween or are you and your friends dressing up for one of those charity affairs where the rich trade places with the poor for an evening?"

I was still too stunned to speak. Quick! A joke! A joke! Don't let him see how humiliated you are. Don't let him know how much you care what he thinks of you. Quick! A joke!

My mind searched for something witty and offhand to say, but nothing surfaced. Not a joke. Not a wisecrack. Nothing.

"What? No snappy comeback?" Cullie teased. "Will the real Mrs. Koff please stand up, or at least step out of her little costume?"

"It's not a costume," I said, looking down at my black maid's shoes. Anything was better than meeting Cullie's eyes.

"Let's see then," he said, stroking his beard. "If it's not a costume, it must be some new fashion statement: 'the servant look,' the designers are probably calling it. You people love those new fashion statements, don't you?"

"There you go again with that 'you people' stuff. What is your problem anyway?"

"Problem? I don't have a problem. I'm not the one who's answering somebody's door wearing a maid's uniform. Are you going to tell me what you're doing here?"

"First, tell me what *you're* doing here."

"I came to photograph Melanie Moloney's house. Since she's almost finished with her book, she's putting the house on the market," Cullie explained. "Okay, now it's your turn."

"I didn't know Melanie was selling the house," I said.

"Let's get back to *you*, Mrs. Koff."

"My name is Alison. You can stop calling me Mrs. Koff."

"Right, *Alison.* So are you a friend of Melanie Moloney's, *Alison?*"

I thought for a second, then said with a straight face, "Yes, I am. Melanie and I go way back, ever since we went to journalism school together." Never mind that Melanie was a good twenty years older than I was.

"You don't say," Cullie said skeptically.

"Yes," I pushed on. "Melanie and I have stayed friendly through the years, drawn as we both are to the art of reportage."

"I'll bet," Cullie said. "What made you come over to your good friend Melanie's house and put on a maid's uniform? Was it reportage or are you two into something kinky?"

I rolled my eyes and gave Cullie my most disgusted look. "It just so happens I'm wearing this uniform because Melanie is giving a costume party next week, and I wanted to show her what I'd be wearing. The theme of the party is sixties sit-com characters. I'll be coming as Hazel." Yeah, yeah, that's the ticket.

"You people sure know how to have a good time," Cullie smirked. "What's Melanie going to dress up as? Mr. Ed?"

"She hasn't decided yet. We're going to have dinner together tonight and discuss her—"

I was just about to pile on the bullshit when Todd Bennett rolled his tubby body into the foyer and spoiled everything. "Is that my Federal Expreth package?" he interrupted us.

"Uh, no, Todd. It's someone to see Melanie," I said. Now what was I going to do? My act was about to bomb.

"Melanie's not here," Todd told Cullie, who didn't want to leave his name but said he'd come back another time. "Oh, and Alithon," Todd lisped before going back to his office, "I thpilled coffee on the rug. When you're finished here, would you come in and clean it up?"

That was it. I'd been found out. There was nothing more

to do but be honest with Cullie. "Sure, Todd. I'll be there in a minute," I said.

Todd went back to the office and Cullie and I were alone, face-to-face at Melanie's front door.

"What's really going on here?" he asked.

Just say it, Alison. Spit it out. Give somebody a straight answer for once. It'll be a relief to tell the truth after leading a double life all these weeks.

I took a deep breath and plunged in. "My husband left me for his first wife. My house was about to go into foreclosure. I couldn't pay my bills. I couldn't make enough money writing articles for *The Layton Community Times* and I couldn't get a writing job anywhere else. So I answered an ad in the paper and took a job as Melanie Moloney's housekeeper." There, I said it.

Cullie stared at me for a few seconds and shook his head. "Are you giving me another cha cha cha?" he asked finally.

"Another what?"

"Another cha cha cha. You know, handing me a line of bull. Trying to make me believe you're something you're not. That's what my dad called it—giving someone the old cha cha cha."

"I'm telling you the truth. And I'd really appreciate it if you'd keep it to yourself. Nobody in town knows I'm scrubbing toilets for a living."

"I'm sorry but I don't believe a word you're saying, Mrs. Koff. *Alison.*" Cullie laughed and turned to leave. "The woman who ordered me around Maplebarf Manor would never be caught scrubbing toilets for a living."

"I wasn't caught—until today," I said to Cullie's back as he walked down Melanie's front steps.

He stopped, turned to face me, shot me a long, questioning look, then shook his head again. "I don't buy it," he said. "You're no housekeeper. Not my Mrs. Koff. You're giving me the old cha cha cha, just like I said."

I watched Cullie climb into his black Jeep and drive away. *My* Mrs. Koff, he'd said. That had a nice ring to it. Too bad he didn't give two shits about me. Too bad he had such an attitude. Too bad I had finally revealed my big secret to someone and the someone didn't even believe me.

Thoroughly dejected, I trudged down the hall to the laundry room and found the rug cleaner Melanie insisted I use. Then I went to her office and set about removing all traces of Todd's spilled coffee. As I got down on all fours to scrub the carpet, I began to replay the conversation with Cullie. If only I'd said this. If only he'd said that. If only Todd hadn't walked in on us. If only Melanie had been home to answer the door herself. Suddenly, I wondered why the security guard at the gatehouse hadn't called to announce Cullie's arrival the way he always did when a Bluefish Cove resident had a visitor. I'd just have to ask Layton's answer to Ansel Adams the next time I ran into him, which, to my absolute amazement, turned out to be the next evening—at *his* initiation.

I had just gotten home from work when my phone rang. Assuming the caller was either my mother or a loan officer from Layton Bank & Trust, I let the answering machine in my office pick up. As I screened the call, I heard a vaguely familiar male voice speak after the beep.

"Hey, Mrs. Koff. *Alison*. I'm taking you to dinner tomorrow night. Waterside table. Good food. Good company. Whaddayasay? Call me. 555-9080. Oh—this is Cullie Harrington. Bye."

Cullie asking me out on a date? I nearly fainted. I didn't believe it until I had replayed his message ten times. He had called to ask me out! I couldn't get over it! It had been so long since I'd been out with a man that the very idea of it both thrilled and terrified me. But what about that Hadley person Cullie'd been with at McGavin's that night? And what about his derisive attitude toward me?

Oh, call him back already, I reprimanded myself. So what if he spends the entire evening goofing on you. You'll get a free meal out of the deal.

At seven-thirty, I dialed Cullie's number.

"Hello?" he answered.

"This is Alison," I said matter-of-factly, trying to sound as if I called Cullie Harrington on a regular basis.

"Good, you got my message. Are we on for tomorrow night? Or do you work for Melanie on Saturday nights?"

"I thought you didn't believe I was Melanie's house-keeper," I tested him.

"Yeah, and I'm sorry about that. I believe you now."

"How come?"

"I called Janet Claiborne at Prestige Properties this after-noon."

"You told *her* I was Melanie's maid?" Telling Janet Claiborne was like telling "A Current Affair."

"Relax. She doesn't know a thing. I called her to check out the rest of your story—about your husband leaving you for his first wife and your problems with your house. She confirmed all that, so I figured you must be telling the truth about the maid part, too."

"Gee. Cullie Harrington thinks I'm telling the truth. I can finally sleep at night," I muttered.

"Hey, let's call a truce. I called you because I wanted to apologize for not believing you. How about letting me take you to dinner?"

"Your message said something about a waterfront res-taurant. Which one did you have in mind?"

"It's a surprise," Cullie said. "I'll pick you up at seven tomorrow night."

"What's the dress?" Most of the really nice restaurants in Layton had a dress code.

"Casual. You *do* own casual clothes, don't you?"

"Don't you ever quit?"

"Sorry. See you tomorrow night."

"Right."

"Alison?"

"Yes?"

"Chin up. I promise not to make fun of the name of your house or anything else about you."

"It's about time."

"Pick you up tomorrow night. Seven o'clock. Maplebarf Manor." Click.

Chapter 8

At precisely seven o'clock, Cullie rang my doorbell. "Nice to see you again," I said, determined to get the evening off to a good start. "Would you like to come in for a drink?" I, for one, could have used a drink. I was so nervous you'd think I was a high school girl instead of a two-time divorcée.

"No, thanks. We've got a seven-thirty reservation and I don't want to be late."

Boy, this waterfront restaurant must be a popular spot. Which one was it? Chez Pascal was on Layton Harbor, but the dress code there was jacket-and-tie, not casual. Les Fruits de Mer was on the Harbor, too, but it was closed during the winter season. Where could Cullie Harrington be taking me? I wondered as I let him help me on with my jacket. He didn't strike me as a cognoscente of the hottest places in town. But then, I didn't know much about him, did I? I only knew that he took terrific pictures, had a major attitude, and looked as appealing in reality as he did in my fantasies. His blue eyes sparkled behind his tortoise-shell glasses, his complexion was ruddy from exposure to the brisk outdoors, and his trim, athletic body was shown off by the same faded jeans and navy-blue-and-white ski sweater he'd worn the first day I'd seen him. The only new wrinkle to his appearance was the hint of lime-scented after-shave that made him smell like a Caribbean sea breeze.

"Ready?" he asked.

I nodded.

"Then let's go."

As he held my elbow to guide me out the front door, I felt a surge of warmth flood my body. Probably a hot flash, I told myself. I was only thirty-nine and had never experienced a single menopausal symptom, but I wasn't ready to accept my overwhelming desire for Cullie. I had never felt an overwhelming desire for any man, and I didn't quite know what to make of it.

As we drove through town in Cullie's black Jeep Cherokee, he pointed out the estates he'd photographed. I asked him how he came to shoot luxury properties for a living.

"I used to shoot boats for brokers and charter companies," he explained. "Boats are my passion. But when the yachting business started to go down the tubes, one of the brokers suggested I move into corporate jets. So I shot Lears and Gulfstreams for a while, then moved on to houses. Now I do real estate exclusively. That's where the money is. Not the kind of money *you* people consider money, but enough to keep me in cheeseburgers."

"I thought we had a truce," I scolded him.

"Right. Sorry. So how about you? How did you come to clean luxury properties for a living? It can't be easy to go from owning an estate to cleaning one."

"No, it isn't easy. But it's not the actual cleaning part that bothers me. In a weird way, I enjoy housework. Dirt is just about the only thing in life I have some control over. If the floor is dirty, I mop it. If the sink is dirty, I scrub it. My other problems should be so easy to solve."

"Then what is it about your job at Melanie Moloney's that's so tough?"

"Melanie herself. She doesn't treat me like a person; she treats me like a servant. It's devastating to be treated like a servant, believe me."

"Tell me about it. Last December I went to shoot a big house in Layton. It was below zero outside, and this lady made me use the service entrance, which meant that I had to lug my equipment all the way around the property to the back of the house. I almost broke my neck—and froze my ass off. Then she made me work without shoes so I wouldn't get her floors dirty."

I was about to commiserate with Cullie when I realized that *I* was the lady he was complaining about. "I don't blame you for resenting me."

"Hey, I don't resent you. I'm taking you to dinner, remember? I'm just glad you're getting the picture."

"I'm beginning to."

What I wasn't getting was any sense of where Cullie's fancy waterfront restaurant was. He seems to be heading out of Layton, I thought, as we passed through the outskirts of town. Then I saw an "Entering Jessup" sign on the side of the road. Jessup? There weren't any good restaurants in Jessup, waterfront or otherwise. There wasn't anything in Jessup except a trailer park, a 7-Eleven store, and a Kmart. So what did people in Jessup do for entertainment? Rumor had it, they had fun the old-fashioned way: they got laid. There were no gourmet food shops, no BMW dealers, and no second homes in Jessup, although the recently laid-off Wall Streeters who could no longer afford their high-ticket weekend places in Layton were starting to "discover" Jessup. My guess was that it wouldn't be long before the town became the scene du jour.

"Still won't tell me where we're going?" I asked Cullie.

"Nope. But we're almost there."

We were heading toward the water. That much I knew. But what could we . . . oh, God. I suddenly realized where Cullie was taking me: Arnie's All Clammed Up at the Jessup Marina. He'd said boats were his passion, but Arnie's All Clammed Up? Oh, please, no. Not there. People actually *died* from eating that food. I'd never been there, of course, but everybody said it was absolutely dreadful . . . a hangout for the county's seamier element . . . a beer-soaked dive filled with men who had lots of tattoos but no teeth . . . a dockside clam bar that smelled more like low tide than haute cuisine.

Sure enough, a few minutes later, Cullie pulled his Jeep into the marina parking lot. Just keep your mouth shut, I told myself. If this man's nice enough to invite you to dinner, the least you can do is act grateful. So you won't touch the food. You can eat when you get home.

"Here we are," Cullie said proudly as he came around to my side of the car and opened my door.

"Yes," I managed.

"Have you ever been here before?" he asked as we climbed onto the dock and walked toward the restaurant, which was a big, dilapidated white clapboard building in desperate need of a paint job, a new roof, and a new neon sign (it currently read: "A nie's All Cl m ed Up").

"No, this is my first time." I tried to sound enthusiastic.

When we got to the restaurant's front deck, I started to climb the steps to the entrance, but Cullie grabbed my arm. "Hey, where are you going?" he said. "That's not the waterfront restaurant I'm taking you to. I'm taking you to *my* place." He smiled broadly and his eyes twinkled.

Now I was mystified. There were no other restaurants at the marina, just dozens of boats of all shapes and sizes, tied up along the pier waiting for springtime.

I let Cullie lead me through a maze of docks until we stopped at the end of one of them. "Here we are," he beamed.

"Here? But this is somebody's boat." I was confused. I was standing in front of what appeared to be a forty-foot sailboat, the rear of which bore the name *"Marlowe.* Jessup, CT." I knew nothing about boats, but anyone could tell this one was a beauty. It was all wood—hunter green with teak decks and varnished trim—and it glistened on the water under the evening stars.

"Come aboard," Cullie said, helping me onto *Marlowe*'s gently rocking deck.

"But this is somebody's boat," I said again, hoping we wouldn't get arrested.

"No kidding, Mrs. Koff. Whatsamatter, you've never been on a sailboat?"

"Me?"

"What? No sense of adventure?"

"Are you nuts? My idea of adventure is taking my Porsche to a carwash that isn't brushless."

Cullie laughed as he unfastened a hook that resembled a pelican's beak and motioned for me to step down into the boat's cockpit. Then he unbolted a pair of teak louvered doors. "I'll just slide open the hatch and down we'll go," he said cheerfully. *"Voilà!"*

I peeked into the cabin below and was surprised to find a cozy, romantically lit refuge from the outside world. "What's that?" I said, as the aroma of garlic and herbs drifted languorously into my nostrils. "It smells absolutely divine."

"Come with me." Cullie helped me down the narrow steps into the cabin. "There. What do you think?" he said, holding out his hand as he surveyed the interior of the boat. "Welcome to Chez Cullie, my humble abode which, on special occasions, doubles as a waterside restaurant-for-two."

"Your humble abode? You live here?"

"Every day of the year. I'm what they call a 'live-aboard.' "

Cullie Harrington was full of surprises. His boat was fabulous, from the fully equipped galley on the port side of the main salon featuring a stove/oven, double sink, small refrigerator, and teak louvered cabinets, to the salon it-self—a stunning combination den/dining room/bedroom, complete with green-and-white-plaid upholstered berths, teak shelves for books and audiotapes, a propane heater, kerosene lanterns, and a mahogany table that could be folded up and stored on the wall when not in use but was now set with linen mats and napkins, a bud vase filled with

yellow mums, and a brass ice bucket in which a bottle of
white wine was chilling.

Just as I was about to tell Cullie how wonderful everything looked, his phone rang. I pointed to the mobile phone
that hung on a bracket over the navigation station where he
kept his charts, radio, and depth sounder, and said, "Aren't
you going to get that?"

"It's Saturday night," he smiled. "I'm entertaining."

I smiled back and continued to explore the cabin.

"How about a drink? Then I'll give you the tour," he said.

"What have you got?"

"White wine and Mount Gay Rum."

"I'll take the white wine, thanks." I'd never heard of
Mount Gay Rum, but I was sure it was something that
would make me lose my inhibitions; I needed them to keep
me from jumping Cullie's bones and making a complete fool
of myself.

He brought me an ice-cold glass of Pinot Grigio, made
himself a rum-and-tonic, and flipped on the stereo that had
been built into a shelf over one of the berths.

"You like the Everly Brothers?" I asked as sounds of
"Bye Bye Love" floated through the cabin. The Everlys
were my favorite singers when I was a kid.

"They're the best," he answered. "I'm a purist, and their
harmony is as pure as it gets. So's this sailboat. It's a John
Alden schooner built in 1932 by the finest wooden boat
craftsmen in Maine."

"Show me," I said eagerly, utterly fascinated by Cullie's
unusual mode of habitation.

"First, a toast," he said, raising his glass. "To *Marlowe*'s
new guest."

"I'll drink to that. And to *Marlowe*'s host." Cullie and I
clinked glasses. "How did *Marlowe* gets its name, anyway?"

"From the Joseph Conrad character," he explained.
"Conrad's sea stories are favorites of mine."

"I'm not surprised. But wasn't Marlowe more of a com-
mentator than an adventurer?"

"Maybe that's why I relate to him. I don't live the kind of emotionally empty life that a lot of the people in Layton do, but I sure know the horror of it when I see it."

"I don't want to shatter the relative calm we've established thus far tonight, but why on earth are you so bitter toward people with money?"

"I'll tell you when we get to be better friends," Cullie said, dancing around the question. "I'd rather tell you about *Marlowe.*"

"Fair enough. You said the boat was built in the 1930s. How did you come to be its owner?"

"My ex-wife and I used to spend the month of August sailing the coast of Maine. Preston's family summered in Northeast Harbor, which wasn't far from where I found *Marlowe.*"

"Ex-wife? You're divorced?"

"Yeah, for nine years. Preston didn't go for the idea of rebuilding a derelict boat from the keel up and then living on it."

"Preston? Cullie? Hadley? What ever happened to normal first names?"

"I have a normal first name. It's Charles. My full name is Charles Cullver Harrington, but I've always gone by Cullie. Haven't you ever had a nickname? Ally, or maybe Sonny?"

"My second husband used to call me Allergy, but I don't think that's what you mean. No, I've always been just plain Alison."

Cullie smiled. "There's nothing 'just plain' about you, Mrs. Koff. Would you like me to call you Sonny?"

I nodded. The nickname appealed to me. "So tell me more about the boat. You rebuilt this baby from scratch?"

"You better believe it. It broke up my marriage and cost me every penny I had, but it was worth it, wouldn't you say?"

I nodded again, although I wasn't buying that it was Cullie's passion for his sailboat that had broken up his marriage. I had recently come to understand that when two people marry for love, not money or status or security, the marriage isn't easily broken up, not by a boat or anything else.

"I saw an ad for the boat in *Soundings,* a monthly boating newspaper with lots of classifieds. The ad read: '43-Foot Alden Schooner 1932. Needs Rebuilding.' Since John Alden was one of this century's great designers, I jumped at the chance of owning one of his boats. And since this Alden boat was a schooner, I *really* jumped."

"What's so special about a schooner?"

"As I told you before, I'm a purist. And there's nothing a sailing purist loves more than a schooner. It's a totally impractical rig, but it sure is beautiful to look at." Cullie paused and sipped his rum-and-tonic. "So I went up to Maine to take a look at her," he continued. "Even though half of her ribs were broken, her keel was filled with dry rot, and she needed to be replanked, it was love at first sight."

"Love at first sight? I can see why Preston resented *Marlowe.* She was probably jealous." Neither of my husbands had ever spoken as lovingly about me as Cullie had about his boat.

"Preston jealous? I doubt it. But I do love this boat. We've been together for the last ten years. After I brought her back from Maine to the Jessup Marina, I began the long task of rebuilding her."

"Where were you living at the time?"

"In a beach cottage in Layton. Preston's family had money." Cullie scowled.

"Was that really such a bad thing—that they had money? You wouldn't have been able to live by the water if they hadn't."

"True, but the money vanished the day Preston did. So who needed it?" Cullie took another sip of his drink and continued the story of how he rebuilt *Marlowe* from stem to stern. I didn't understand much of what he told me—there were enough sailing terms to fill a dictionary—but I was able to deduce that Cullie Harrington was a man who had dreams, pursued his dreams, and didn't quit until he realized them.

"Time to eat," Cullie said suddenly after checking his watch. I checked my Rolex and it was nine o'clock. Where had the evening gone? I felt pleasantly lightheaded as I sipped my wine and allowed my body to roll with the gentle waves that lapped against the dock. All thoughts of Sandy, Soozie, Melanie, and Maplebark Manor evaporated in the sea air, as I found myself surrendering to the womb-like coziness of the boat. The fact that I was wildly attracted to my host didn't exactly detract from the situation.

"What can I do to help?" I asked as I followed Cullie into the galley.

"Not a thing. It's your night off, remember?" he said, flashing me a big grin.

"Okay with me," I said. "Whatever you're cooking, it smells wonderful."

"It'll be ready in about twenty minutes. I just have to do the rice, throw in the shellfish, and heat the bread. I started everything else before I left to pick you up."

The man could cook, too. Aside from the fact that he wasn't rich and didn't want to be, Cullie was starting to look like a mighty good catch.

I went back to the main salon, sat down on one of the berths that was about to double as a dining room chair, and listened to the Everly Brothers croon "All I Have to Do Is Dream." I felt like I was in dreamland myself.

"I want to hear all about Melanie Moloney," Cullie called out, breaking the spell.

"You said it was my night off."

"Yeah, but I'm curious about her. How's she doing with that book about Alistair Downs?"

"Todd, the guy she works with, said the book's almost done. He said it's going to be a real shocker, like her other celebrity biographies."

"Did he say what's in it?"

"He almost slipped me a juicy tidbit the other day, but

Melanie walked in and scolded us. I don't know what Todd's punishment was, but mine was Windexing all the sliding glass doors in the house."

"Sounds like fun. So you never got to hear the juicy tidbit about Senator Downs?" Cullie sneered when he invoked the name of Layton's most illustrious citizen.

"No, but I'm not giving up. I'll get Todd to talk one day soon. I'm dying to know what skeletons Alistair has in his closet. After all, he's my boss. My *other* boss."

"I forgot that you wrote for his paper. What's everybody down there saying about the book?"

"Not much. Melanie's done a great job keeping the manuscript under wraps. She won't let me near it, I can tell you that."

"Isn't it all on computer?"

"No. Melanie uses a plain old typewriter—and plain old index cards for the sources."

"Sources?"

"You know. People Melanie and Todd talked to about Alistair. People who have dirt on the guy."

Cullie was silent for a few minutes. I assumed he was putting the finishing touches on his meal.

"Voilà!" he said finally, carrying two plates of steaming hot food to the table, then sitting down next to me. "More wine?"

"Please."

Cullie poured us both some wine, then lifted his glass in a toast. "To Sonny's two bosses: Alistair Downs and Melanie Moloney. May they get what they deserve."

"Here, here," I said as Cullie and I clinked glasses yet again. "I know *I* have an ax to grind against Melanie and Alistair, but what's your problem with them?"

"Melanie writes books that invade people's privacy."

"Okay. And how about Alistair? What have you got against him, other than the fact that he's a very rich man, which, we all know, is tantamount in your mind to being a serial killer?"

"No, a serial killer has a code of morality, twisted though it may be. Alistair Downs is completely immoral."

"He may be a bit of a pompous ass but immoral? That's a pretty strong word, isn't it?"

"He's immoral. I'm telling you. But hey, our dinner's getting cold. Cullie's seafood stew, the specialité of the maison. *Bon appetit.*"

Cullie's stew was an aromatic potpourri of clams, shrimp, and calamari in a rich tomato-based, garlic and herb-infused sauce. Accompanying the stew were a nutty tasting wild rice pilaf and piping hot garlic bread.

"Dinner is absolutely delicious, Cullie," I told my host. "Where did you learn to cook like this?" Sandy's idea of cooking was reheating the little white boxes of Chinese food from the Golden Lotus.

"My dad was a good cook."

"Was? He's no longer with us?"

"Nope. He died about nine years ago."

"Right around the time your marriage broke up, if I remember correctly. That must have been a tough year for you."

"It was, but rebuilding *Marlowe* was great therapy."

"What about your mother?" I asked. "Is she alive?" Mine would have died if she saw me dining at the Jessup Marina, which was a far cry from Grassy Glen Country Club.

"She died when I was born. I never knew her."

"And your father never remarried?"

"He wanted to, but your friend Alistair Downs had other ideas."

"Did they know each other?"

"Paddy Harrington knew everyone connected with the sailing world."

"Paddy? That's your father?"

"Yup. He was from Isle of Wight off the coast of England. When he was in his late twenties, he crewed in the Fastnet Race, which is part of the Admiral's Cup series. You have to sail from Isle of Wight around Fastnet Rock off the coast of Ireland and back. Anyhow, after the race that year, my father met a rich American who suggested there were good-paying sailing jobs over in the States. He gave Paddy a couple of names and addresses, and a year later, my father was the sailing instructor at Layton's own Sachem Point Yacht Club, where your friend Alistair Downs is the commodore."

"So you were born in Layton?"

"Yup. My dad met my mom the year he got here. She was a waitress at the yacht club. They got married, lived at the club, and had me. She died in childbirth, so my dad raised me alone."

"He sounds like an interesting man. And it must have been wonderful living at the yacht club."

"Wonderful? It was hell. Paddy Harrington was the sailing instructor—The Help—and I was his kid. We lived in the servants' quarters."

"Is that how you met your wife? At the yacht club?"

"What else? Preston's family was big stuff there. They were appalled when she said she wanted to marry the sailing instructor's kid."

"I still don't understand how Alistair Downs fits in."

"Let's leave all that for another time," Cullie said. "How about some more wine."

I nodded, slipping into a deeper state of mellow.

"Tell me more about Melanie and her work. How does she keep the contents of her books such a secret?"

"For one thing, she doesn't let anybody into her house who isn't authorized to be there. And if you do get in, she watches you like a hawk. When I first interviewed with her, she thought I was from one of the tabloids, can you imagine?" Cullie smirked. "The security at Bluefish Cove is pretty tight, so someone would have a tough time getting into Melanie's house and sneaking a look at her book. Hey, that reminds me. How did you get through yesterday? The security guard never called to say you were at the gatehouse."

"That guy knows me. I've shot a lot of houses down at Bluefish Cove. More wine?"

"Oh, no. I've had plenty. Thanks." I had cleaned my plate, finished my wine, and felt only like stretching out on the berth and rubbing up next to Cullie. "How about some more music?" I suggested. The Everly Brothers tape had long since played out.

Cullie got up and put on a James Taylor tape. Then he sat down right next to me, slipped his arm around my shoulder, and pulled my face close to his. "When you're not barking orders at me, you're nice to be with, Sonny Koff," he whispered in my ear, his beard and mustache tickling my skin. "I think *Marlowe* likes you."

"I like *Marlowe* too," I whispered back, inhaling his scent, a heady mixture of aftershave lotion and sea air.

"Do you, Sonny?" he asked softly, nuzzling me.

"Oh, yeah." And I wasn't talking about *Marlowe*. Cullie's body was smack up against mine and old *Marlowe* was the last thing on my mind. I was dying to kiss Cullie, I really was. I had fantasized so often about what it would be like to suck on that soft upper lip hidden underneath his prickly mustache that I could practically taste it. Oh, please kiss me, I begged him silently, wishing I were the kind of woman who felt comfortable initiating lovemaking instead of waiting passively for it to descend on her. Oh, come on, Cullie. Take my face in your hands and kiss me. Press your lips on mine. Stick your tongue in my mouth. Bite my ear. Lick my eyes. Do it all. Do it. Do it. Say you want to make love to me, please?

"I completely forgot. I made a key lime pie. Let's have some dessert," he said instead, breaking away from me and heading toward the galley.

Dessert? I was crushed. I must be some hot number, I thought glumly. Or maybe it wasn't me at all. Maybe Cullie only had eyes for Hadley Kittredge. But if they were an item, why did he invite me to dinner on a Saturday night? Because he felt sorry for me when he found out I'd been dumped for my second husband's first wife? Because he heard I was poor and, therefore, a more appropriate dinner companion? Because he was a media groupie and wanted the inside scoop on Melanie Moloney's new book? He *was* asking an awful lot of questions about Melanie. But no, it had to be because of that Hadley person, who probably knew how to sail like a pro, in addition to having big tits. "Where's Hadley tonight?" I blurted out.

"Hadley? Why?"

"Isn't she your girlfriend?"

"My girlfriend? She's just the dockmaster's daughter. She and her dad have been great to me since I've lived at the Marina. It's pretty lonely here in the winter."

Great, so it wasn't Hadley that made Cullie pull away from me. It was probably me. He wasn't interested in me. Well, fuck him. "About that dessert. I think I'll pass," I said coldly, getting up from the table and stretching. I checked my watch and saw that it was ten-thirty. I faked a yawn, hoping Cullie would think I was bored. I was up to my old tricks, acting one way and feeling another, giving Cullie the old cha cha cha, as he would say. If he didn't want me, I sure as hell didn't want him to think I wanted him. Never wear your heart on your sleeve, my mother taught me. Never let a man see your insides.

"Tired?" Cullie asked.

"Yes. Must be all that sea air."

"Better get you home, then."

See? He didn't even protest a little or ask me to stay for a nightcap or offer to share a berth with me. "Are you sure I can't help you wash the dishes?" I asked. "Washing dishes is in my line of work these days."

"No, thanks. I'll take you home." He looked at me and shook his head. Then he cleared the table without a word. When he had finished his chores, he handed me my coat but did not help me put it on.

The mood on the boat had definitely soured. I threw my coat over my shoulders and waited for Cullie to open the doors to the cabin and help me up the hatch. As I stuck my head out, I felt the cold air hit my face like a blast of cruel reality. My cozy, romantic dinner on a sailboat in the dead of winter was over. It was back to civilization. Back to the land of foreclosures and bankruptcies. Back to scrubbing toilets for a living.

We rode back to Layton in near silence, and pulled into the driveway at Maplebark Manor at about eleven o'clock. Cullie came around to my side of the car and opened the door for me. Then he walked me up my front steps. He did not take my arm. I was tempted to invite him in for a drink, but I was sure he'd decline.

"Thanks for a nice evening," I said, as we stood awkwardly in front of my door.

"You're welcome. I enjoyed it, I think." Cullie looked as if he were waiting for me to confirm whether he had a good time or not.

"You *think* you enjoyed the evening? You're not sure?"

"No, I'm not. I thought I was enjoying myself, but something went wrong. Didn't you feel it?" He stepped a little closer and planted a quick kiss on the tip of my nose.

"Yes, I felt it. Is there any chance we could try it again?" How bold, for me. But what did I have to lose? "I'd love to see *Marlowe* again."

"How about me? Would you love to see me again?" This time he kissed my right cheek.

"Yes, I would." I closed my eyes and waited for Cullie to kiss my left cheek, or better still, my mouth. This was it, I just knew it.

"Let's hug on it," he said cheerfully.

Hug? *Hug?* Who did this guy think he was anyway, Leo Buscaglia? I was positive he was finally going to grab me and kiss me silly. Instead, he wanted to *hug* me. "Sure, let's hug on it," I said wryly, then gave him a tepid hug. We broke apart quickly and Cullie turned and walked down my front steps. We waved goodbye to each other as he drove away.

Confused and frustrated, I put my key in the door and let myself into my big, empty house. Too wound up to sleep, I cleaned the kitchen, then the living room, then the dining room, then the rest of the rooms on the first floor. Before I knew it, it was three o'clock in the morning and I was exhausted. When I finally crawled into bed at three-thirty, I still had trouble falling asleep, so I closed my eyes and pretended I was with Cullie aboard the *Marlowe,* rocking back and forth in our berth as if it were a cradle. Within minutes, I was dead to the world.

Chapter 9

At nine-thirty on Sunday morning, I was awakened by the ringing of the telephone. I was not amused. Sunday was my day to sleep late and I relished the opportunity. Whoever it was would just have to talk to my answering machine, I thought, and turned over in bed. Minutes later, the phone rang again. I let the machine pick up again. When it rang a third time, I could no longer ignore it, and leaned over to grab the phone off the night table.

"Hullo," I mumbled.

"Hi, Sonny. You sound sleepy."

"Cullie?" I bolted up in bed.

"Yup. I've been trying to reach you. I have a proposition for you."

"You do?" I was wide awake now.

"Yup. It's a crisp and sunny February morning. How about taking a walk on the beach and then having brunch on *Marlowe?*"

"The beach? It's freezing out."

"Naw. We'll bundle you up and you'll feel like you're at one of your fancy Caribbean resorts. Come on, you'll see."

How was I going to bundle up? I had sold all my fur coats. All I had left was a moth-eaten wool coat that would hardly keep me warm on a blustery day at the beach.

"I've got an extra down jacket you could wear," said

Cullie as if reading my mind. "And a ski hat and gloves. You'll look adorable."

"Well, when you put it that way . . ."

"I'll pick you up in a half hour."

"A half hour? I'm still in bed!"

"Then you'd better get out of bed. I'm on my way. Bye." Click.

I raced over to the mirror and gasped. I looked like hell. All that scrubbing and vacuuming till three o'clock in the morning hadn't done a thing for my complexion.

I showered, dressed, and was downstairs and ready when Cullie rang my doorbell. I was so excited I could hardly stand it. He was giving me another chance and I wasn't about to blow it.

"Boy. You look beautiful," he said as I opened the door.

"Oh, right. I don't have a stitch of makeup on. You didn't give me time."

"I'm glad. You look better this way. More relaxed, less . . . less . . . I don't know . . . less uptight."

"Thanks, I guess. You look pretty relaxed yourself." In fact, Cullie's spontaneous, laid-back manner was one of the qualities I liked best about him. I couldn't imagine him getting all agitated because someone stared at him in a restaurant, the way Sandy did. But then Charles Cullver Harrington and Sanford Joshua Koff were about as different as two men could be. And was I ever glad.

We drove to the Jessup Public Beach in Cullie's beat-up Jeep singing songs and playing a little Name That Tune. "Okay. What's this one?" Cullie would say, then hum a few bars of a rock 'n' roll song. " 'The Lion Sleeps Tonight,' " I'd shout. "How about this one?" I'd challenge, then hum a few bars of another song. "That's easy. It's 'See You in September,' " he'd guess. "Right," I'd scream, and we'd break out into simultaneous laughter. There was no mention of the previous evening, when we'd both acted stiff and uncomfortable every time things got remotely intimate.

We arrived at the beach and were not, to my surprise, the

only ones there. There were a handful of people walking along the sand, picking up an occasional shell, tossing crumbs at hungry seagulls and reveling in the fresh sea air.

"Shall we?" said Cullie as he handed me a ski jacket, hat, and mittens.

I braced myself for a blast of cold air, but when I followed Cullie down to the water's edge, I found the temperature curiously moderate.

Cullie reached for my hand and then patted it as we strolled along the shore. I was so grateful for the gesture that tears welled up in my eyes. I wasn't accustomed to such tenderness. But then this was a man who liked to hug and be hugged. Why had I trivialized that display of affection the night before? Probably because my two husbands had never hugged me; their idea of showing affection was to buy me things.

"Look! Mergansers," Cullie said excitedly, pointing toward the water.

I had no idea what he was talking about. I had been to summer camp and participated in the occasional nature walk and canoe trip, but was not exactly Sheena, Queen of the Jungle. "What's a merganser?" I asked Cullie.

"A type of duck. Look at their heads." Cullie released my hand and pointed to the ducks paddling peacefully in the water. "See how their heads have a fan-like crown or crest?" I nodded. "They're wonderful, aren't they?"

"They're fascinating, regal almost," I said, meaning it. Nobody had ever introduced me to a merganser before.

"And look over there! I see some mallards and some surf scoters!"

"What on earth is a surf scoter?" I asked, feeling like I was watching an episode of "Wild Kingdom."

"Another species of duck. Can you see their heads? The top is black and the sides are white."

I followed Cullie's line of vision. What fun, I thought. I'd lived near Connecticut beaches all my life and nobody had ever shown me their beauty—their true and natural beauty.

All I'd been told was that beachfront was prime property for development and that development meant big money.

Cullie took my hand again and led me down the seemingly endless stretch of curving coastline. I couldn't remember ever feeling so safe and warm, despite the winter cold. Mostly we'd walk in silence, listening only to the gentle waves, the cries of the seagulls and the quiet of the February morning. Occasionally, we'd stop dead in our tracks, face each other, and smile, for no reason other than because we couldn't help it.

At one point, Cullie turned me toward him and cupped my chin in his two hands. "This is nice," he said softly, then rested his lips on mine.

Automatically, without even a trace of my usual conflicts, I threw my arms around Cullie's neck and kissed him back, melting into him.

"Our noses are cold," he laughed. "How about letting me take you home."

"Home?" I must have looked alarmed. Was Cullie pulling back? Changing his mind? Would we have to play our silly games again?

"To *Marlowe*," he said, then put his arm around me and watched the relief spread across my face. "You're a big surprise, do you know that? I never expected this to happen."

I had no intention of spoiling the moment by asking Cullie what "this" meant. I kept silent. I felt happy. I wanted "this" never to end.

He led me back down the beach, to the parking lot, and into his Jeep. We did not speak during the five-minute drive to the marina. We stole glances at each other, just to make sure the day was not a hallucination. When we reached the marina, we climbed aboard *Marlowe,* hurried into the main cabin, and threw our jackets onto the settee.

"You probably want to have brunch now," I said, remembering the night before, when Cullie had killed our clinch by suggesting we have dessert.

"Food can wait," he said. "All I'd really like to do is kiss you."

He wrapped me in his arms and kissed me, first gently, then more ardently, his tongue darting in and around my mouth. Before I knew it, we were lying on top of each other on the settee, breathing heavily, kissing feverishly. I longed to feel his touch on my naked body, but I wasn't raised to initiate sex. He'd have to do it. Fortunately, he did.

He reached under my sweater and massaged my breasts. I moaned. I moaned? Did you hear that, Sandy? I moaned!

"Let's go in there," Cullie whispered, leading me into the V-berth at the bow of the boat. At that point I would have followed him into the Long Island Sound.

We undressed and admired each other's naked bodies. "You're beautiful," Cullie said, gazing at me through the sunlight filtering through the cabin's porthole.

"You're beautiful," I told him. And he was. His shoulders were broad, his stomach flat but rippled with muscle. His chest was covered in golden blond hair, flecked with gray. His hips were narrow, his butt high and tight. And then there was his cock. In truth, I had never seen such a perfect penis, not that I was such a connoisseur. But in my limited experience, I had never come across an organ so rod-straight, so shiny and pink, so . . . beckoning. I slid my hand over it. I couldn't help myself. I, who usually avoided genital contact like a trip to the periodontist.

"That feels so good," Cullie moaned. I continued to stroke him as we stood in front of the berth. "Let's lie down. What do you think?"

"I think it's a good idea," I said softly, refusing to let go of him. He was so smooth in my hand, like a piece of sculpture, so appealing I wanted to envelop him with my mouth. My mouth? Suddenly, I was overcome by an urge I'd never experienced in my thirty-nine years of life . . . a burning desire that I never would have attributed to myself—the desire to give a man head!

I moved down his body with my mouth, practically inhaling him as I went, stopping only when I arrived at his cock, which was so big and hard it looked like it might explode. I took it in my mouth, marveling at my lack of inhibition. Could this woman who was performing fellatio on a man she barely knew be Alison Waxman Koff, the same woman who'd rather scrub her kitchen floor than give a guy a blow job? Could this woman who was parading around naked on a sailboat in the middle of February be the same woman who was so modest she slept in her bra and panties, even when she was by herself? Yes, she was I, and I was having the time of my life.

"Oh, God. That feels incredible, but don't let me come, Sonny. I want to be inside you."

I practically had to tear my mouth away from his throbbing cock. So much to suck, so little time.

"Now," he said, laying me gently on my back. "Now."

By noon, I had registered seven orgasms on the Richter scale; Cullie had registered two.

"Do you want brunch?" Cullie asked as we rocked back and forth in the berth, in perfect sync with the gentle rolling of the waves against the boat.

"You mean I get eggs and bacon with the deal? Eggs and bacon *and* sex? This cruise ship has more activities than the *QE2*," I smiled, then entwined my naked leg around Cullie's and tickled him under his chin.

"I just wanted you to have whatever you needed, right here on the boat," Cullie said shyly.

"I do," I said, then threw my arms around him and kissed him.

I whistled to work on Tuesday morning, yes I truly did. After my heavenly weekend on the *Marlowe* with Cullie, a day at Melanie's didn't seem that daunting. Oh, I still allowed myself a few murderous fantasies about her. On my way over to Bluefish Cove, I imagined myself running her over with my Porsche as she stood helplessly in her driveway. Then I pictured myself spiking her Evian water with ammonia and counting the seconds until the poison took effect. I even pictured myself inserting one of her little fingers into an electrical socket and watching her Dynell hair stand out like Don King's. I was profoundly ashamed of myself for indulging in such fantasies, sort of the way I felt when I finished an entire package of Reese's Peanut Butter Cups, but Melanie seemed to inspire angry, vindictive thoughts.

I arrived at the entrance to Bluefish Cove, waved my pass at the security guard, and drove through the gate to Melanie's house. When I got there, she was in the kitchen waiting for me with her hands on her tiny hips and her overpainted mouth in a pout. Don't tell me, let me guess, I said to myself: she found some seagull shit on one of her sliding glass doors and she wants me to lick it off.

"Good morning, Ms. Moloney," I said cheerfully, determined not to let the Queen of the Sleaze Bio bring me down from my high.

"There's a problem," she said, not bothering to wish me a good morning.

"I apologize in advance," I smiled.

"No, not with you. With Todd."

"What's the problem with Todd?"

"He hasn't shown up in days. He was supposed to come in this weekend and didn't. And he didn't come in yesterday or today."

"Have you tried to reach him?" I asked. Dumb question, Alison. The woman was an investigative journalist. Did she need her maid to tell her to call the guy?

"Of course I've tried to reach him. I keep getting his answering machine."

"You must be terribly worried about him. He told me you two have been partners for years."

"Partners? He told you that? That's very funny," Melanie scoffed. Her tightly stretched face nearly cracked when she tried to smile. "I wouldn't call us partners. Todd works for me. And as far as being worried about him, I'm not. He does these little disappearing acts from time to time, whenever he's in a snit."

"Did you two have an argument of some kind?" I asked.

"Nothing out of the ordinary. But that's not your concern, Alison." Then why are you talking to me about it, bitch? "The reason I brought the subject up is that there's something you can do for me. It has to do with my book."

"The Alistair Downs book?" I was all ears.

"That's right. I wondered if you would help me with it, since it appears that Todd has abandoned his responsibilities."

"Me? You want me to help you with the book?" My dreams were coming true. My luck was finally changing. My life was turning around. I would be rich. I would be famous. I wouldn't have to declare bankruptcy. I wouldn't have to clean toilet bowls for a living. "Oh, Ms. Moloney. I'd be honored to help you with the book. As a matter of fact, I have some experience in journalism in that I've—"

"No time for that now," Melanie cut me off. "There's a lot of work to be done."

I followed her down the hall to her office. I could see it now: Melanie Moloney and Alison Koff writing bestseller after bestseller, earning millions upon millions. Maybe I should change my name back to "Waxman," I thought. Why keep "Koff" and give Sandy and Soozie an opportunity to ride on my coattails?

When we got to Melanie's office, she sat me down at her desk and asked me if I was ready. I said I was.

"Now," she said. "How's your handwriting?"

"Fine, I guess." Oh, boy. She wanted me to write a few pages of the book.

"Good. Here's a piece of paper and a pen. I'll dictate and you write down everything I say."

Okay, so I wouldn't exactly be writing portions of the book. But I'd be contributing in a meaningful way. And I'd be getting the inside scoop on the life and times of old

Alistair Downs. I couldn't wait to call Cullie and tell him.

"Ready, Alison?"

"Yes, Ms. Moloney."

"Four Smith Corona typewriter ribbons . . . two bottles of Liquid Paper . . . one ream of eight-and-a-half-by-eleven Xerox paper . . . two boxes of three by five index cards . . . one box of black Flair felt-tip pens . . . three packages of yellow lined legal pads . . . one Canon cartridge for the PC-20 copier . . . six packages of double-A batteries . . . and four blank sixty-minute audio cassettes. Have you got all that down, Alison?"

The only things that were "down" were my spirits—right down the toilet I'd be cleaning for the rest of my life. "Yes, Ms. Moloney. It's all right here." I handed her the shopping list. Was this the kind of task she made Todd perform? No wonder he was in a snit. No wonder he hadn't shown up for work. I was so disappointed I almost cried.

"What's the matter, Alison? You look ill."

"No, Ms. Moloney. It's just that when you said I'd be helping you with the book, I thought you meant that I . . ."

"That you what? That you'd be writing it with me? That I'd be sharing the contents of a very confidential manuscript with you? Give us both a break, Alison. You're my maid."

"You've made that very clear, Ms. Moloney. Will that be all?"

"All for right now. Just resume your usual duties."

"Yes, Ms. Moloney." And my usual fantasies about killing you.

I spent the evening on the *Marlowe*, regaling Cullie with stories about my awful day. He seemed more disappointed about my not getting a look at the Alistair Downs manuscript than I was. But we consoled each other with some good old-fashioned lovemaking, and felt much better by the time he brought me home at about eleven-thirty. I know *my* mood had lifted considerably.

I got up the next morning, hopped into my car, and drove over to Bluefish Cove, arriving at the gatehouse at eight twenty-five. I flashed my pass at the security guard, and he waved and let me through. I made it to Melanie's service door at eight-thirty on the nose, just the way the bitch always told me to. When I didn't see her in the window, I rang the back doorbell and waited. And waited. I let another minute or two pass and rang again. Still no answer. Oh, great. Melanie was playing dominatrix again. What was it this time? Was I three and a half seconds early? Or late? Did I ring the bell too meekly or did I press it too hard? I heaved a big sigh and rang again. Still no answer. Maybe Melanie was still asleep. And miss an opportunity to torture me? Never. I rang one more time and waited. Still no answer. Then, feeling a sneeze coming on, I rummaged around in my purse for a tissue, accidentally knocking my elbow against the back door. To my surprise, the door opened.

I pushed it open further and peeked inside the kitchen. The lights were on, but there was no sign of Melanie's tiny body and no scent either of her morning coffee or her Giorgio perfume. She's probably on the phone in her office, digging up more dirt on Alistair Downs, I figured.

There was no sign of Todd either, but then maybe they still hadn't resolved their little tiff.

Maybe Melanie was actually being thoughtful for a change by leaving the back door open for me instead of making me wait outside in the cold. Gee thanks, Mel.

I went into the maid's room and changed into my uniform. Then I got my cleaning supplies from the laundry room and headed for the master bedroom, as per my usual routine. When I reached the bedroom door, I stopped dead in my tracks: Melanie's bed had been made. That's weird, I said to myself. The woman never—I mean never—made her own bed, even on my days off. She had to have slept somewhere else, I decided, maybe at some guy's. Good for her. A night of torrid sex would mellow her out.

I spent the next twenty minutes dusting and vacuuming the master bedroom. I was just about to vacuum under the bed when I lifted up the dust ruffle and gasped: there were two boxes hidden under the bed frame, each containing half of the Alistair Downs manuscript! What on earth were they doing under Melanie's bed? I wondered. Why would she have hidden the manuscript there instead of leaving it in her office? To keep it from me? Not likely. She had to know I'd be vacuuming under the bed—she insisted I vacuum under all the beds and sofas in the house. So why would she leave something so valuable and confidential right where I could find it? Just to test my capacity for obeying the rules of the house? Was this another one of Melanie's head games—to see if I'd take the bait and read what she'd specifically forbidden me to read?

I'd better let her know I've seen the manuscript, I thought suddenly. If I don't, she'll accuse me of lying. Or else she'll accuse me of not vacuuming under the bed. Either way, I'll catch hell.

I scurried downstairs to the office. The door was closed, so I knocked softly. No answer. I knew Melanie was in there because I could see a light under the door and hear the faint hum of the all-talk radio station she liked. I pressed my ear against the door and listened more closely. She wasn't on the telephone, that was clear; I would have recognized her unmistakable, little-girl voice. I decided to risk disturbing her and spoke to her through the closed door.

"Hi, Ms. Moloney. Just wanted you to know I've been here since eight-thirty on the dot," I called out. "And thanks for leaving the back door open for me this morning. I really appreciate it."

She flat-out ignored me. Figures. She was probably too busy conjuring up new ways to play Torture the House-keeper.

Fuck her, I thought, and went on with my chores. If I

hurried, I might be able to clean the rest of the house, collect my money, get out of there at a reasonable hour, and spend the evening with Cullie.

I cleaned the rooms on the second floor, then went downstairs to do the kitchen and dining room. When I checked my watch I saw it was nearly one o'clock and Melanie hadn't taken her customary lunch break. How was I supposed to clean her office?

I knocked on the office door again, this time with more authority. When Melanie still didn't answer, it occurred to me to check the garage to see if her car was there. It was. I went back to the office and knocked again. "Ms. Moloney, may I come in?" I called. There was no answer.

The time had come to face the fact that something was going on in Melanie's house. Something I hoped I wouldn't be blamed for.

I turned the knob and opened the door slowly. Then I let out a scream to rival Faye Wray's in *King Kong*. The office was in complete disarray. Papers had been strewn everywhere. The long table that carried boxes of index cards had been overturned, sending the cards onto the floor in a huge heap. Hardcover books, some of them Melanie's own bestsellers, had been thrown from the shelves that lined the walls. The once meticulously ordered room looked as if it had been struck either by a tornado or a very angry person.

"Melanie!" I shouted when I finally focused on the fact that she was slumped in her chair, her head resting on her desk, her back to me.

I ran to her yelling, "Melanie. Can you hear me?" Oh, God. She's dead, I realized instantly when I touched her body and found it stiff as a board. She was wearing the same black-and-mauve velour warm-up suit she'd worn the day we met—the same outfit she often wore when she worked at home. There was a large bump on the back of her head and a bloody gash on her forehead. Her face was whiter than I'd ever seen it, and her hands and wrists were purple.

"Melanie, get up!" I yelled at her lifeless body as I tried

not to gag. I moved away from her and began to pace back and forth across the room, stepping over the debris on the floor. What should I do? What should I do? I asked the doll-like, curiously-still Melanie. I had fantasized her death so many times, but now that she had actually bought the farm, I was paralyzed! Melanie dead? How? For how long? By whose hand?

Whose hand? Oh my God. Melanie had been murdered! Quick! A joke! A joke! When in pain, make a joke! It was bad enough that Melanie was dead, but murdered? Oh, God. My fingerprints were all over the place. And I'd been alone with the body for hours. What if people thought *I* was the murderer? What if they thought I was some disgruntled employee who went berserk, bopped her boss on the head, and then continued to clean the house? You hear about nut cases like that all the time, only they're usually disgruntled postal workers, not disgruntled maids. But what if people thought I did it? What if I had to go to jail? What if my picture were splashed all over the tabloids with the caption: "Mad Maid Murders Melanie"? What if I were tried, convicted, sentenced to life imprisonment, and raped repeatedly by a band of crazed lesbians? What if the state of Connecticut had a death penalty and I got it? And I worried about people finding out I was a maid!

Quick! A joke! A joke! Don't let all this get to you. Don't let your imagination run wild. Don't panic. Quick! A joke! Okay. Okay. Here's one:

Why did the Mafia murder Einstein?

Because he knew too much.

Ha ha ha ha ha.

Okay, sport. Now what? Stop with the jokes and do something, I scolded myself. Dial 911, dial 911. My hand shook as I punched in the numbers on Melanie's Panasonic three-liner.

"Nine-one-one emergency," a male voice answered.

"Help! Help! Somebody's been murdered!" was how I described the problem.

"Address?"

"Seven Bluefish Cove."

"Name?"

"My name or the name of the person who was murdered?"

"The complainant's name."

"Complainant?"

"Yeah, the one who's calling in the homicide."

"Oh. That would be me. Alison Koff." God, now I was a complainant.

"And the name of the deceased?"

"Melanie Moloney. She's a famous author." I didn't know if the people who worked at 911 kept up with the bestseller list, so I thought I'd tell them Melanie was famous to make sure we got VIP treatment.

"We'll be right there," said 911. "Try to stay calm. Oh, and Miss Koff?"

"Yes?"

"Don't leave the crime scene and don't touch anything."

I hung up the phone and stared at Melanie's body. Suddenly, my mind flashed back to the manuscript hidden under her bed. Was it possible that the person who killed her had come looking for the manuscript? Was there some revelation in the book that the killer desperately didn't want revealed?

Something told me that I'd better get my hot little hands on that manuscript before the police did. Maybe it held the key to Melanie's murder. At the very least, it would make juicy bedtime reading.

I ran upstairs at full speed, charged into the master bedroom, crawled under the bed, and retrieved both boxes. I lugged them downstairs, stopping in the kitchen to catch my breath. I looked out the window to see if the cops had arrived. They hadn't. I pulled open the kitchen door, raced out to my car, and stuffed the boxes under the front seats of my Porsche. Then I ran back inside the house, waited by the front door, and tried not to look guilty. Seconds later, a police car and an ambulance tore into the driveway.

"Alison Koff?" two officers asked simultaneously as I opened the front door to let them and two EMS technicians in. Melanie probably would have made them all go around to the service entrance.

"Yes, I'm Alison Koff," I said, trying not to sound winded.

"I'm Patrolman Murphy and this is Patrolman DeRosa," one of the cops said.

"Ms. Moloney's down the hall," I said, leading them to Melanie's office.

The EMS guys gave poor Melanie the once-over, while the patrolmen bolted for the rest of the house, searching for "perpetrators" and waving their guns in the air.

Satisfied that there was no one in the house but the six of us (including Melanie), the patrolmen returned to Melanie's office and took a quick look at the body. "There's lividity," Patrolman Murphy said, eyeing my former employer's purple hands and wrists.

"She was always livid about something," I said. When in pain, make a joke.

Both officers shot me a bewildered glance, shrugged their shoulders, and got back to business. "You guys can forget it," Patrolman Murphy said to one of the ambulance operators. "This one doesn't need CPR. She needs the mortician."

Everybody nodded in agreement. "I'll go call," said Patrolman DeRosa as he walked the ambulance crew outside. When he returned, he informed his partner that their car radio was on the blink. He was carrying a huge roll of plastic yellow paper that read, POLICE CRIME SCENE—DO NOT CROSS. He erected a little yellow fort around Melanie's office. Then he went back outside to seal off the perimeter of the house.

Meanwhile, Patrolman Murphy and I stood together in

Melanie's office. I made nervous small talk while he made notes in his little spiral-bound pad.

"This phone work?" he asked, pointing to the Panasonic three-liner on Melanie's desk.

"It should. I just called 911 on it."

Patrolman Murphy nearly sent Melanie's stiff corpse flying as he reached over her to grab the phone, planting his fingerprints all over the handset and, presumably, obscuring everybody else's—including the murderer's. He punched in a few numbers and said to whomever answered, "Looks like a homicide. Send the technicians and have somebody get a Mincey Warrant."

"What's a Mincey Warrant?" I asked after he hung up. I was gaining a whole new vocabulary.

"The thing we gotta get before we can search the place."

Several minutes passed. Patrolman Murphy was in the midst of asking me about my position as domestic in the Moloney household when four or five more police officers stormed into Melanie's house.

"Whadda we got here, Murphy?" said a man in jeans and a T-shirt.

"Homicide," said Patrolman Murphy. "Famous author."

"A celebrity? Whoah. We've never had one of those. Corsini's gonna love it." The man looked at me and then asked, "Who's this one?"

"The maid," said Patrolman Murphy.

"What's her name?" the man asked.

"Hazel," I said. I knew I was behaving bizarrely, even for me, but the only way I could get through this ordeal was to make a joke.

"Says her name is Alison Koff," Patrolman Murphy offered, as if I wasn't there.

"My name *is* Alison Koff. Who are you and these other men?"

"I'm Detective Michaels. That's Detective Origi. Over

there is Sergeant Brown. And next to him is Sergeant Petrovich."

"Pleasure to meet you all," I said, although no one heard me. They were too busy greeting each other.

"Hey, Dr. Chen. Good to see ya," said Patrolman DeRosa as he waved to an Oriental man wearing a dark gray suit.

"Who's he?" I asked the room at large.

"Coroner," said Detective Michaels. "Now, why don't we go over here and talk." He steered me to a corner of Melanie's office.

How can I concentrate with all this activity around me? I wondered, as I watched police officers photographing the scene, barking at each other in TV police talk, and then greeting the six technicians who entered the room carrying medical instruments and little plastic bags.

"What's your exact relationship to the deceased?" asked Detective Michaels as he started writing in a small notebook.

"I'm her housekeeper," I said. "No, *was* her housekeeper." God, now that Melanie was dead I didn't have my maid's job anymore. And when Alistair and Bethany found out I'd worked for Melanie, I wouldn't have my newspaper job either. "Will I have to stay here awhile?" I asked the detective.

"Yeah. I gotta get your story. Then I'm gonna take you down to headquarters so my partner can interview you."

"Your partner?"

"Yeah, Detective Corsini. He'll take your statement, too."

"I understand," I said, understanding nothing that had happened to me in the past three years.

"You seem pretty cool about this whole thing, huh?" Detective Michaels said suspiciously.

"Cool? Me? No, I'm terribly upset. I worked for Ms. Moloney for nearly a month and enjoyed cleaning her house tremendously." Well, what did you expect me to do? Admit

I despised Melanie and spent my days fantasizing about killing her?

"I'm gonna ask you about your work here, how you discovered the body, all that. Okay?"

"Of course. I have nothing to hide," I said, wiping my clammy hands on my maid's uniform.

"Before we get started, I gotta ask you: Is everything just like it was when you found the body?" said Detective Michaels. "You didn't remove anything from the house, right?"

"Not a thing," I said. Well, not from *this* room.

"Why don't you tell me what happened, Miss Koff," said the detective. "And don't leave anything out."

Part Two

Chapter 10

"Sit there, Miss Koff," said Detective Joseph Corsini, the Layton Police Department's answer to John Travolta, as he pointed to the chair opposite his desk. Tall, dark, and handsome in the manner of a person who frequents discos at Holiday Inns, Detective Corsini was easily the most fidgety man I'd ever met. When he wasn't running his hands through his curly black hair, he was buffing his fingernails on his skin-tight pant leg or smoothing his tie so it lay flat against his shirt. At first, I thought his incessant preening was a tactic, meant to distract and unnerve suspects so they'd blurt out a full confession and beg for mercy. Later, I came to understand that the Detective was what Sandy would have called "appearance-driven." In other words, he was more intent on showing off his looks than on stamping out crime.

"Don't I get to make a phone call?" I asked him. We were in his office at the station house, two short blocks from Koff's Department Store.

"Why? You want to call a lawyer or something?"

"A lawyer? Of course not. I didn't do anything wrong."

"Nobody said you did, Miss Koff."

"Right." If I didn't stop acting so defensive, the detective might think I murdered Melanie. Stay calm, I coached myself. Pretend this interrogation is just a nice little chat with a local cop. No big deal. "I thought I'd call a friend, if that's okay with you."

"Be my guest."

"Thanks." Great, but who would I call? Oddly enough, the first person that came to mind was Sandy. Sandy, who used to take care of me. Sandy, who used to solve all our problems by writing a check or flashing his Gold Card. Sandy, who was probably so busy taking Soozie to Lamaze classes that he wouldn't even remember my name, let alone trek down to the police station to support me in my time of need. No, Sandy wouldn't do at all. Then there was my mother. No, she wouldn't do either. The thought of having to tell her that I was a suspect in a murder case—*and* that I was the murder victim's maid—was more than I could endure. What about Cullie? Yes, Cullie would help me, I was sure.

I walked down the corridor to the pay phone, fished around in my purse for Cullie's business card and a quarter, and dialed his number. Unfortunately, I got his answering machine. I gulped, then said, "Cullie, it's me. Alison. If you get this message soon, could you please come down to the Layton Police Station? I'll tell you why when you get here. I need—" I cut myself off and hung up. I was starting to cry.

"All set?" Detective Corsini asked when I returned to his office.

I nodded.

"Good. Let's get your interview now, okay?"

"Okay." I took a deep breath and said, "Exactly what do you want to know?"

"I'll just ask you some questions about your relationship with Miss Moloney, how you came to work for her, how you liked the job, where you were on the night of the murder, and the rest of it."

"But I already answered those questions for Detective Michaels."

"Yeah, I know. But you're gonna have to answer them again. For me."

"No problem."

I went through the whole sorry saga yet again—that I had been employed as Melanie Moloney's maid for nearly a month, that I had gone to work on the day of the murder and had found Melanie stone cold dead in her office, that I had spent the previous evening with Charles Cullver Harrington on his boat, which was anchored at the Jessup Marina, that Mr. Harrington had brought me home close to eleven o'clock that night, and that I neither saw nor spoke to anyone from that time until the police arrived at Melanie's the next afternoon. As I talked, Detective Corsini took notes. When he ran out of questions to ask me, he typed up the notes and handed them to me.

"Read this over. If everything's okay, we'll take your statement."

In nearly incomprehensible police-speak, his notes rehashed everything I had told him. "Seems fine," I said. "Now what?"

"I'll take your statement. Raise your right hand and repeat after me: I, Alison Koff . . ."

"I, Alison Koff . . ."

". . . do solemnly swear . . ."

". . . do solemnly swear . . ."

". . . that the statement contained herein . . ."

". . . that the statement contained herein . . ."

". . . is true to the best of my knowledge."

". . . is true to the best of my knowledge." All except for the parts about how much I enjoyed working for Melanie and how sorry I was that she was dead. Oh, and the part that said I didn't take anything from the crime scene.

"Now I'll take your John Hancock. Need a pen?"

"No. I've got one." I rummaged around in my purse and pulled out the sterling silver Tiffany pen Sandy had bought me as a gesture of thanks for interviewing him for the *Community Times* six years before. Six years before. Life had seemed so much simpler then, but maybe God was only resting me up for all the bullshit ahead.

148   *Jane Heller*

I signed the document and handed it to the detective.

"Now I'll just get the Sergeant to notarize it and you can go."

Thank God.

The notarizing ritual took a few more minutes. When everything was done, I rose from my chair. "Okay to go now?" I asked.

"Not just yet. There's something else I gotta know."

"Oh?"

"Yeah, what was it like?"

"What was what like?"

"Working for a celebrity like Melanie Moloney. Did she have movie stars over all the time? Did you get to meet anybody big? Anybody *important?*"

"You mean, important in the sense that the person had a motive for murdering her?"

"Naw, I mean anybody big, important. You know, anybody who's been interviewed on a Barbara Walters special." Detective Corsini winked at me, then buffed his nails on his pant leg.

"So you're looking for suspects from among the entertainment community," I volunteered. I was still under the delusion that Joseph Corsini was a police detective, not a media groupie.

"Fuck that," he laughed. "I'm looking for some good dirt. The kind of stuff that's in the *National Enquirer*. You know, 'inquiring minds' and all that."

The man was a fool, but I felt obliged to play along. If I gave him some "dirt," maybe he'd let me go home. "Actually, there was this one time when Melanie gave a luncheon for magazine editors."

"Yeah?" Corsini's tongue was hanging out of his mouth and he was panting.

"Yes. There were editors from *People* and *Entertainment Weekly.* There was also someone from the *Star.*"

"The *Star?* Wow, my favorite newspaper. Did they talk about anyone big at this lunch? You know, any celebrities?"

"Not that I recall. Most of the discussion centered around Alistair Downs and the book Ms. Moloney was writing about him." Damn, why did I say that? Now Corsini would ask about the manuscript.

"Oh, sure. Yeah. I almost forgot about him. I'm not one for books though. Not much of a reader, you could say. I'm one of those guys that likes a good tabloid TV show. Give me a half-hour of 'Hard Copy' and I'm as happy as a pig in shit."

"How nice for you."

"Yeah, well. Listen, before I forget, if anybody asks you about this case, send him to me."

"What do you mean?"

"The press. TV reporters. Anybody. They'll be swarming the area as soon as they find out that Melanie Moloney was murdered. Layton'll be a zoo."

"When will that happen?" Things were happening entirely too fast for my taste.

"My boss, Lieutenant Graves, will be holding a press conference later this afternoon. After that, this town will become Media City." Detective Corsini straightened his tie.

"Will this Lieutenant Graves be telling the media about me?" I asked.

"What about you?"

"That I was the one who found Melanie's body?"

"Sure. That's in my report."

"But does he have to use my name?"

"Naw, not at this point."

"I'm very relieved to hear you say that. What's the next step in your investigation?"

"Our forensic technicians will be going over the crime scene with a fine-toothed comb. Today's homicides are all about forensics. You know, testing of hair fibers, that sort of thing. We may be a local police department but we're just as up to date as the federal boys."

"I'll bet." I squelched a smile as I remembered how the Layton Police Department's crack officers had trampled the crime scene and the corpse, and very probably obscured whatever forensic evidence there was. Besides, *I* was in possession of the Alistair Downs manuscript which, I was certain, held more clues to Melanie's murder than all the hair fibers in Layton combined. I couldn't wait to pore over every page.

"You can go now," Detective Corsini said.

"You won't be needing me for anything else?" I was dying to go home. In all the excitement, the skin on my neck and stomach had erupted into a raging case of hives, and I longed to soak in a cool oatmeal bath.

"Oh, I'll be needing you all right. You don't have an alibi for the night Melanie Moloney was murdered. In other words, you can't account for the hours between 11:30 P.M. and 2:30 A.M. What's more, you admitted that your fingerprints are all over the deceased. I wouldn't leave town if I were you, Miss Koff."

"So you're saying I'm a suspect? You're telling me you actually think *I* killed Melanie Moloney?" My heart pounded and my rash raged on.

"Suspect or not, you're key to cracking this homicide. Maids are always key to cracking homicides. Didn't you see the interview with Sonny von Bulow's maid on 'A Current Affair?' I don't care what anybody says, that woman knows more than she's telling, and so do you."

"I'm sorry you feel that way. I've tried to cooperate with your department in every way possible."

"It's nothing personal, Miss Koff. But I'm a detective. It's my business to know when someone's hiding something. A thorough sweep of the crime scene by our boys in forensics and I'm betting we'll find out exactly what it is. You maids may think you know how to clean, but you can't clean up hair fibers. No way."

"Fibers, shmibers," I mumbled as I got up to leave.

"What was that?"

"I said, 'Tell Lieutenant Graves to break a leg at his press conference.' "

*   *   *

I was planning to drive straight home to Maplebark Manor, honest I was, but Detective Corsini's parting words—that I didn't have an alibi, that I shouldn't leave town, that I was key to cracking the case—reverberated in my mind and made me far too nervous to go home and soak in a cool oatmeal bath. I had to *do* something, take some sort of action. The hell with my hives.

It occurred to me that there was one person who could confirm my innocence, one person who knew positively that I arrived for work at Bluefish Cove at eight-thirty Tuesday morning, left Melanie's house at four-thirty Tuesday afternoon, and didn't return to Bluefish Cove until eight-thirty this morning. The police may have thought I killed Melanie somewhere between eleven-thirty and two-thirty on Tuesday night, but how could I have killed her? I wasn't there, and one person knew it: the security guard at the Bluefish Cove gatehouse. He saw me arrive yesterday morning, leave yesterday afternoon, and return this morning. I would go to see him and ask him to vouch for me. I would appeal to his sense of humanity, one humble servant going to bat for another.

I drove over to Bluefish Cove and pulled up to the gatehouse. The security guard, whose name I had never made a point to learn but now wished I had, came out of his little house and bent down to my car window to talk to me.

"Horrible business about Miss Moloney, isn't it?" he said. I had never really heard him speak before. I supposed that the touch of a British accent was feigned, as stipulated by the residents of Bluefish Cove, who did their share of cha cha cha-ing just like the rest of us.

"Yes, horrible. That's why I'm here."

"You won't be able to get into her house, I'm sorry to tell you. The police say it's off limits."

"Oh, that's all right. I'm here to speak to you."

"Me?"

"Yes. I was wondering if you keep a log of some kind, a record of who comes in and out of here and what time they come in and out."

"Only visitors."

"You keep a log of visitors?"

"That's right."

"So that means you have a record of my trips in and out of Ms. Moloney's house, right?"

"No, you weren't a visitor. You were her maid. That's different."

Out of the mouths of security guards. "Okay, but you have a *mental* record of my visits, right? I mean, you remember seeing me come to work yesterday morning and leaving yesterday afternoon, right?"

"Certainly, I do."

"Really? Oh, that's wonderful," I exclaimed. "I'm so glad to hear you say that, Mr. . . . ."

"Gordon."

"Mr. Gordon."

"No, Gordon's my first name. You can call me Gordy."

"Thank you, Gordy. You'll never know how much it means to me that you can confirm what I've already told the police. You see—"

"I didn't say I could confirm that you didn't come back last night and kill her."

"Excuse me?"

"They say she was killed last night. I go off duty at seven-thirty. The gatehouse is closed until seven-thirty the next morning."

"But you saw me leave here at four-thirty yesterday afternoon. Can't you at least tell them that?" My voice was more shrill than I wanted it to be, but I was panic-stricken.

"I told them that I had no idea who came to her house last night and killed her. I don't work nights. A man's got to have some sort of private life, doesn't he?"

"Yes, of course. But I—"

"I'm not complaining about my job, you understand.

With this recession going on, a man's lucky to have a job, if you know what I mean. Why just the other day my friend Rocky, the security guard at the Casa Marina condominium complex down the street, got laid off. The bank took the whole place and fired all the help. Rotten world, isn't it?"

"Yeah, it's rotten all right."

"Take yourself, for instance. You had a job as a maid. Now you don't have a job as a maid. You're what the newspapers are calling 'a casualty of the economic downturn.' "

No, Melanie was the casualty. I was just a maid out of a job.

At least I still had my freelance work at the *Community Times,* I consoled myself, as I drove home to Maplebark Manor, tormented by my itching, burning hives and the wretched state of my life. I flipped on the radio and worked the dial until I located WANE, Layton's only classical music station. I was hoping for a nice, soothing piano concerto; what I got was a news bulletin.

". . . That about wraps it up from the Layton Police Station. To recap, Lieutenant Raymond Graves, in his twenty-five-minute press conference this afternoon, confirmed the death of superstar celebrity biographer Melanie Moloney in her Layton home. Lieutenant Graves said the death has officially been ruled a homicide, which Graves believes to have occurred between the hours of 11:30 P.M. and 2:30 A.M. The author's body was found by her housekeeper early this afternoon. Graves stated that the housekeeper, who has been identified as Layton resident Alison Koff, will be questioned along with other members of the Moloney household. This is Rick O'Casey, WANE Radio, reporting. . . ."

That rat bastard Corsini! He said Graves wouldn't give

out my name! If you couldn't trust the men in blue, who the hell could you trust?

As I made the turn onto Woodland Way, I spotted a row of cars and trucks parked across the street from Maplebark Manor. The neighbors must be having a party, I guessed, wondering who would be so profligate in these difficult economic times as to throw a party. Who had the money? Who had the friends?

I pulled into my driveway and stopped the car at the mailbox. I opened the car door and had just jumped out to retrieve the mail when at least three dozen reporters shoved tape recorders and notepads in my face and another two dozen photographers and video cameramen nearly knocked me to the ground.

"Miss Koff?" "Hey, Alison?" "Hey, honey?" they yelled. "What do you know about Melanie Moloney's death?" "You were her maid, right?" "Did you kill her?" "Do you know who did?" "Talk to us, Alison!" "Give us an exclusive!" "We'll pay you!"

I tried to get back into my car, but the swarms of media vultures wouldn't let me. They swooped down on me. They surrounded me. I couldn't move. I couldn't breathe. I felt like Tippi Hedren in *The Birds.*

"Just give us a comment!" "Tell us what you know!" "Did you hate her?" "Did you kill her?" "If you're a maid, why do you have such a big house?" "Whose house is this anyway?"

They would not let me alone. They kept yelling at me and snapping my picture. Oh, God. My picture. Before the day was out, various images of me in my maid's uniform would be transmitted all over the country. I'd be a cover girl. Millions of supermarket shoppers would stare at my photograph as they waited in America's check-out lines. Millions more would read about me on trains, buses, and airplanes, in beauty parlors, in doctors' waiting rooms. My photograph would line bird cages, serve as kindling in fireplaces, become the stuff of papier-mâché dolls.

"How about an interview, Alison?" "Just one comment!" "Did you have a grudge against Melanie Moloney?" "Did she fire you or something?"

Just when I thought I couldn't tolerate one more second of this media onslaught, I spotted Sandy's Mercedes creeping up the driveway.

"Sandy!" I screamed. "Help me, please!"

The vultures were distracted. They turned away from me and focused their attention on Sandy. "Who are you, buddy?" "Are you a friend of Alison's?" "What do you know about Melanie Moloney's murder?"

Sandy parked his car next to mine and jumped out. "Leave her alone this minute!" he barked at the media as he tried to bat them away with his long, skinny arms.

I hadn't seen Sandy in months and, boy, was he a sight for sore eyes. I noticed that he was tan, and I felt a flicker of resentment as I wondered how he could afford a trip to Malliouhana when he claimed he didn't have a penny. But here he was, rescuing me from this nightmare, and I was so glad to see him I started to cry—a moment that was sure to be captured on videotape for airing on the eleven o'clock news.

"Let's go, Allergy," Sandy whispered in my ear. "Down the driveway. Right now. You go first in your car, I'll follow in mine. Once we're in the garage, we'll run into the house. Nobody will bother us then."

"Thank you," I said to him.

"It's okay. Just go. I'll be right behind you."

Sandy's Mercedes followed my Porsche down Maplebark Manor's long driveway and into our three-car garage. I disarmed the burglar alarm and opened the door into the house. We ran inside and locked the door behind us.

"We're safe," Sandy sighed. Then he hugged me.

I felt so faint I allowed it.

"Let's go upstairs and sit down," he suggested. "I'll make you a drink. Got any chilled Puligny Montrachet?"

"Fat chance. I drink Almaden now, Sandy. I'm watching my pennies."

"Good move. So are we."

"You and Soozie?"

"Sure. We've got to watch our pennies now that we've got a baby on the way."

"I guess I should congratulate you. You must be very happy." I was dying to know how he got his tan if he was so penny-pinching, but I held my tongue. There were more serious matters to discuss.

"Actually, the baby is one of the reasons I came by to see you," Sandy said, herding me into the living room and guiding me onto one of the chintz sofas. It was nice to have Sandy back at Maplebark Manor herding me and guiding me again. Maybe he wasn't such a bad guy after all.

He disappeared into the kitchen and returned with a cold glass of wine. I held it against my neck, hoping it would soothe my hives. Then I took a sip. Then another.

"You came over because of the baby?" I said finally. "I thought you came because you heard about Melanie's death—that I was her housekeeper."

"Well, to be honest, that housekeeper bit was quite a shock, Allergy. What possessed you to take a job as a maid?"

"What possessed me? Poverty. That's what possessed me."

"But there must have been other, less subordinate positions available."

"No, actually there weren't."

"I'm sorry about that, kid. But you know what I always say, 'Adversity builds character.' When I'm struck down by adversity and my inner child is wounded, I just close my eyes and visualize all the tiny cells in my body lifting weights and getting stronger."

"Cells lifting weights?" I stifled a laugh.

"I know it sounds funny but it works. A few minutes a day and your mind can become a tower of strength. Whenever adversity strikes, visualize those cells pumping iron. One two. One two. One two." Sandy began to huff and puff, as if to indicate the strenuous workout he was putting his cells through.

"Getting back to your visit . . ." I began.

"Well, I was in my office this afternoon when my secretary told me that Melanie Moloney was dead and that you were implicated in some way. Have you talked to a lawyer?"

"No. Everything happened so fast. I didn't have time. Besides, I can't afford a lawyer. That's why I took a job as a maid."

"I understand. But you really should seek legal counsel. Especially if this police detective they quoted on the news tries to pin the murder on you."

"Corsini? You know him?"

"I've seen him around. Hopelessly out of touch with himself, in my opinion."

"Sandy, what does all this have to do with your baby?" I asked, draining my wineglass.

"Remember I mentioned my inner child a few minutes ago?"

"Vaguely."

"Soozie and I feel very strongly that all adults carry around the hurts of their childhood, that these childhood hurts scar us. Of course, there's no way that we adults can avoid this 'emotional baggage,' if you will. But babies are another story. They get a fresh start, a clean slate. They come into the world with absolutely no emotional baggage, no childhood hurts and scars."

"I'm glad you and Soozie are taking parenting so seriously. But I don't see what this has to do—"

"As I said, babies should be given every opportunity to stay free of hurt, free of pain. Now, this unfortunate situation you've gotten us all into . . ."

"Us all?"

"Yes. Soozie, the baby, and me."

My rash took an immediate turn for the worse. "Melanie's murder has nothing to do with you or Soozie or your love child." My voice was rising almost as fast as my blood pressure.

"That's great. I appreciate that. So will Soozie. You see, we don't want our baby tainted by this sordid story or scarred by local gossip and innuendo."

"Sandy, you're hopeless," I said, peeling myself off the chintz sofa. "You're a silly, selfish man. Now go."

"So you'll agree to our request?"

"What request?"

"That from now on, you'll use your maiden name? That you'll refer to yourself in the media, in court, wherever, as Alison Waxman? That you'll drop the 'Koff' and give my baby a chance to let his inner child grow—free of pain, free of hurt, free of people talking about him in restaurants?"

"If you don't get yourself and your inner child out of here by the time I count to ten, I'll call the police and have them arrest both of you. *That* will give people in restaurants something to talk about, won't it?"

Chapter 11

After Sandy left, I went upstairs, took off my maid's uniform, and changed into my robe and slippers. Then I padded down the hall to my office and checked my answering machine for messages. The poor machine was overloaded. There were several frantic calls from my mother, several more from Julia, one from Bethany informing me I would never be writing for the newspaper again, one from Janet Claiborne advising me that people were suddenly very eager to see my house now that I'd been discovered by the media, and one from Cullie saying he was sorry he couldn't get over to the police station but was available for future hand-holding. There were also calls from television and radio shows, as well as from newspapers and magazines. There was even a call from a movie producer who wanted to buy the rights to my story. My story? I didn't have a story . . . or did I?

Too weak to respond to my callers, I took a bath. The hives on my stomach, neck, and face felt much better afterward, but as a precaution, I dotted them with calamine lotion. I looked like a pink polka-dotted rag doll, but who cared? I didn't plan on leaving the house anytime soon, so who would see me?

At about seven-thirty, I considered popping a Lean Cuisine into the microwave, but I didn't even have the energy to do that. Instead, I deposited my pink polka-dotted self into one of the wing chairs that framed my bedroom fire-place and stared up at the ceiling. I must have been sitting there for a half hour when I heard the doorbell ring. Assuming it was Detective Corsini, my mother, or one of the tabloid TV reporters camped outside on my front lawn, I stayed right where I was and ignored the bell. Whoever was at the door would get the hint eventually and go away, I figured.

I figured wrong. I let the bell ring and ring and ring, until I got so fed up I went downstairs to scream at the person who was being such a nuisance.

"Dinner is served," said the nuisance when I opened the door.

"Cullie!" I was delighted and mortified at the same time. Delighted to see this man I found so appealing. Mortified that I was covered with calamine-lotioned hives. "What are you doing here?" I asked, pulling my robe tighter around me. "And how did you get past those sharks out there?"

"It wasn't easy," he laughed. "But I'm a sailor, remember? I'm used to navigating through shark-infested waters. I came as soon as I heard about the whole horrible mess."

"But you should have called first. I mean, just look at me."

"You look beautiful."

"Yeah, right."

"You do. Now may I come in? This stuff's getting cold."

"What have you got there?"

"Dinner. I thought you might be hungry for a little food and friendship. The past few hours couldn't have been a picnic for you, Sonny, from what I heard on the radio."

"No, not a picnic at all," I said softly. I was so touched by Cullie's show of concern that I threw my arms around his neck and kissed him, calamine lotion and all. He didn't seem to mind. "You're really something special. I'll never forget this, Cullie. I mean it."

"You're very welcome. Now take me to your kitchen, woman. I'm famished."

Cullie followed me into the kitchen and set a large pot on the stove. "It'll just be a minute to heat this up," he said, taking off his ski jacket.

He was wearing a forest green sweater, a white turtleneck, and his customary blue jeans and hiking boots. His cheeks and nose were rosy from standing outside in the February night air.

I could love this man, I thought suddenly, then felt my own cheeks flush. The past few weeks had produced a flood of new feelings, feelings I'd never felt so intensely, feelings of fear, loss, and rage. But love? That was a bit premature, wasn't it? I had taken an instant dislike to Cullie when I met him. How could that dislike have turned to love? The idea made me tremendously uncomfortable and I didn't know what to make of it, but I was determined not to run away from it either.

"Smells good. What is it?" I asked, wrapping my arms around Cullie's slim hips as he stirred the pot on the stove.

"Catch of the day: chicken catch-a-tore. Get it?"

"Very funny."

"Whattasamatter? You think you're the only one who can make jokes?" Cullie kissed the tip of my nose.

"When on earth did you have time to make chicken cacciatore? You were gone all afternoon."

"I didn't make it. I bought it."

"Where?"

"At Arnie's All Clammed Up. You know, at the marina."

I gagged. The food there was poison, or so everybody said. Still, the chicken did smell good, and it was sweet of Cullie to take the trouble to buy it, transfer it to one of his pots, and bring it over. The least I could do was try it.

"To Maplebark Manor and her lovely mistress," Cullie toasted me as we sat at the very same butcher-block table where, six months before, Sandy and I had eaten Chinese take-out food and then ended our marriage.

Sensing my need to relax, Cullie didn't push me for information about Melanie's murder or try to engage me in idle chitchat. We ate quietly, murmuring an occasional "This chicken is *wonderful*" and commenting on how nice it was to be together. When I finished my dinner, he spoke to me.

"Do you want to tell me what happened?" he asked gently, then reached for my hand and squeezed it.

I recounted as much of the story of Melanie's murder as I could bare to retell, and expressed my anxiety about the police's investigation. "I think I'm a suspect," I confessed. "Detective Corsini seems very interested in the fact that I have no alibi for Tuesday night, that after you brought me back from the marina at eleven o'clock I was home alone for the rest of the night and have no way to prove it. But as soon as I'm feeling stronger, I'm going to fight back."

"How?"

"I'm not sure yet. I just know I will." I grinned as I thought of the Alistair Downs manuscript that was stashed under the seats of my Porsche. In all the excitement, I had completely forgotten to bring the boxes in from the garage. Oh, well. They'll still be there in the morning, I thought.

By ten o'clock my eyelids were heavy. I tried to stifle a yawn, but Cullie caught me.

"Off to bed with you," he said. "I'll do the dishes and tiptoe out of the house and you'll never hear a thing."

"Oh, please don't," I said, touching his arm.

"Don't do the dishes or don't leave?"

"Don't do the dishes *and* don't leave. I'll do the dishes in the morning. I've got to have *something* to clean, now that I'm out of my maid's job. And as for your leaving, I really wish you wouldn't."

"Then I won't," Cullie said, hugging me. "Which way's the bedroom? I've never slept in a house this big, I might get lost!"

"You won't get lost," I said, linking my arm through Cullie's and leading him up Maplebark Manor's front staircase.

When we entered the master bedroom, Cullie took my hand and walked me to the bed.

"I'm so tired," I said, resting my head on his shoulder.

Cullie scooped me up in his arms and laid me down across the bed. "Under the covers, woman," he instructed me.

I obeyed gladly, pulling the down quilt over me and turning on my side with my knees pulled up to my stomach, womb-style. "What about you? Aren't you coming in?" I asked sleepily.

"Right now," he whispered.

I heard him undress and lay his clothes on the bench at the foot of the bed. Then I felt him crawl under the covers and curl up next to me. "Ummm," I murmured as he spooned me from behind. "Tell me a bedtime story, would you, Cullie? Tell me all about the *Marlowe,* all about sailing trips and faraway places and species of ducks. Tell me all about . . ."

Before I knew it I was fast asleep, enclosed in Cullie's strong, sailor's arms, warmed by his soft sweet breath on my cheek . . .

The next morning, it was Cullie who lay fast asleep under the covers while I was downstairs in the kitchen washing our dinner dishes. I was just finishing up when he entered the room, grabbed me from behind, and kissed me.

"How'd you sleep?" he asked.

"Pretty well, under the circumstances. You?"

"I slept just fine. I had you next to me, didn't I?"

The guy was too good to be true, which worried me. My mother, ever the imparter of doom and gloom when it came to men, always said that if a man seemed too good to be true, he probably was. "Now, how about some coffee?"

"I'd love some."

I poured us both a cup and suggested we sit down.

"Can't," Cullie said, taking a sip of his coffee, then checking the time on his watch. "Gotta go do a shot of a house."

"So early?" I was disappointed.

"Yeah. The house faces north, so the light's only good in

the morning. How about getting together later? I could come back, if you want."

"Oh, I want," I said. "But I'm going over to the paper to see Bethany Downs. I want to explain why I took a job with Melanie."

"What about dinner? We could eat leftover chicken cacciatore together."

"Thanks, but I should have dinner with my mother. I really owe it to her to tell her what's happened. She must be in quite a state over all this." I shuddered to think how her canasta-playing friends at the Club were treating her, now that they knew her daughter was a maid.

"Want me to go with you?"

"What a chivalrous offer. But no, I'd better talk to her alone. She's . . . well, let's just say she's difficult to get to know." And I'd been trying for years.

"Will you be all right? I mean, it's okay to leave you?"

"Why are you being so nice to me?" I asked Cullie. "I acted like a jerk when we met."

"You were just giving me the old cha cha cha," he chuckled.

Cullie placed his coffee mug on the kitchen counter and wrapped me in his arms. He lowered his head and kissed my mouth, slowly, deeply, longingly. When we broke apart after several seconds, I took a breath, enhaling his musky morning scent.

"I'll call you later," he whispered, then kissed the tip of my nose.

"Please do," I whispered back.

At two o'clock I pulled my car out of the garage and headed down the driveway, wondering if the media vultures were still hovering. They were, complete with video cameras, tape recorders, and other tools of their trade. Determined not to be fazed by the fact that they were trespassing on my property, I gave them all a little finger wave as they ran toward the car. Then I gunned the accelerator and whizzed past them. Recession or no recession, a Porsche is one fine piece of machinery.

While I drove over to the newspaper to look for Bethany, I checked my rearview mirror and realized that I was being followed. The driver of the car behind me looked suspiciously like Detective Joseph Corsini of the Layton Police Department. Either he was out cruising for celebrities or making sure I didn't try to blow town.

I entered *The Layton Community Times* building and made my way to Bethany's office. She was not there. I took off my coat and gloves, sat down on her sofa, and gazed up at the in-your-face oil painting that hung over her desk. It was a painting of—guess who?—Daddy Alistair and his beloved only daughter, capturing in glorious full color the two of them sailing aboard Alistair's yacht, the *Aristocrat.* They appeared years younger and so damn full of themselves I almost puked. He wore a navy blue Lacoste shirt, white slacks, Topsiders, and a white captain's hat. She wore a red-and-white-striped boat-neck sweater, skimpy little white shorts, Topsiders, and a red America's Cup visor. They stood in the cockpit of the *Aristocrat,* one hand on each other's waist, the other hand on the boat's varnished teak steering wheel. They were tanned. They were smiling. They had the whitest teeth since Lena Horne. They looked like honeymooners, off on a joy ride, oblivious to everything except their good time. Weird, I thought. Just plain weird.

"What are *you* doing here?" a voice cried.

It was Bethany, Alistair's first mate. She was munching on a jelly donut and shedding powdered sugar all over the floor. "I wanted to talk to you about the message you left on my answering machine yesterday," I said.

"What's there to talk about? You betrayed my father," said Bethany, her blue eyes blazing.

"But I didn't, Bethany. Honest. You know my husband walked out on me. I *had* to find a way to earn extra money.

The stock market crashed. The country's in a recession. When I saw Melanie Moloney's ad in the—"

"Don't you dare mention that woman's name in this office," Bethany snapped. "She was trying to ruin my father. Now she's dead and I'm glad."

"But *I* wasn't trying to ruin your father. I was trying to stay out of bankruptcy. Can you really blame me for that?"

"There were other jobs. You didn't have to work for that woman. What did you tell her about my father? Did you give her some good gossip? Did you, Alison? Did you?"

"Bethany, try to calm down." She was overwrought. It must be all that sugar. "Why don't we go to the lounge and have a cup of coffee. Or maybe herbal tea would be better."

"I'm not going to the lounge or anyplace else with you. Not until you tell me what you told Melanie Moloney about Daddy."

"Melanie and I never discussed your father, Bethany. Really. I wasn't even allowed to see the book."

"I don't believe you. How could you clean her house without getting a look at that manuscript?"

"Trust me. I was too busy Windexing."

"Look, I'll make a deal with you, Alison. I'll do anything to get my hands on that manuscript, or at least find out what's in it. You worked in that house. You know where the woman put things. You know that guy Todd Bennett, the one who worked with her. Help me protect Daddy. He's seventy-five years old and he doesn't deserve people dissecting every aspect of his life. Once the book is published, there's nothing I can do to stop it. But if you help me now, if you help me get that manuscript, I'll let you come back to the paper. And I'll pay you double for every article."

Now what was I supposed to do? If I gave Bethany the manuscript, I'd get my job back. But if I held on to the manuscript, I'd find out who killed Melanie and get the cops off my back. How did I get myself into this mess? I wondered. How did I get myself into everybody else's mess?

"I can't help you, Bethany," I said, gathering my coat and gloves off her sofa.

"Then we have nothing more to say to each other," she said, then turned on her heel and stormed out of the office, probably down to the lounge for another jelly donut.

I took a last look at the father-daughter oil painting above Bethany's desk and sighed. Where was *my* daddy when I needed him? Where was Seymour Waxman, the sweet, unsophisticated man who built Sleep Rite, his successful mattress business, without lying or cheating or stepping on people? Where was the man who couldn't afford to go to college but worked his ass off so I could? Where was the man who put up with my mother's pretensions because he knew they made her happy? Gone, but not forgotten. Never forgotten. I laughed when I imagined an oil painting of my father and me. There we'd be—Sy "the Mattress King" Waxman, the Queens boy who made good, and Alison Waxman Koff, the princess who became a maid. But instead of standing next to each other with a fancy yacht in the background, we'd be posing in front of an extra-firm Simmons Beauty Rest propped against a warehouse wall, over which would hang a large sign emblazoned with the company's slogan, "Sleep Rite. Sleep Tight." I felt a lump in my throat as I realized that, for all Senator Alistair Downs's power and prestige, I'd rather have Sy "the Mattress King" Waxman for a father any old day.

It was snowing at six o'clock when I arrived at 89 Pink Cloud Lane—home, for the past fifteen years, to my mother, the widow Waxman. A five-bedroom Tudor set on two acres of impeccably manicured Layton property, my mother's house was located in what was referred to as the "Jewish section" of Layton, presumably because the neighborhood boasted the town's only synagogue as well as its only delicatessen.

I gathered my black wool coat around me, missing my

mink terribly, walked briskly to the front door of the house, and rang the bell. My mother's current maid, a Jamaican woman named Nora Small who was anything but, let me in.

"Mrs. Waxman is watching her stories," said Nora as she led me into the den where my mother was camped out on the sofa watching a videotaped episode of "As the World Turns." My mother often taped her favorite soap opera when a canasta game at the club or a beauty parlor appointment at Monsieur Mark's conflicted with the show's afternoon airing.

"Hi, Mom," I said, then began to cough. As usual, my mother was chain smoking, and the den was so thick with smoke I could barely see her, let alone breathe. But despite the haze in the room, I could tell she was impeccably dressed, looking every bit the trim-figured, suburban matron in her black wool Albert Nippon dress and black Ferragamo pumps. Her long, thin neck was draped in a gold chain-link necklace that matched the bracelet she wore on her left wrist. Her left ring finger still sported the diamond and gold wedding band my father had given her. Her nails were freshly manicured in their trademark Peach Melba, the color she also wore on her lips. Her graying, chin-length ash-blond hair, which Monsieur Mark touched up every four weeks, was in its customary page-boy, as well as its customary net of hair spray—a net that rendered it so rigid that gale-force winds couldn't disturb it. She's in costume, I thought. Her I-may-be-getting-old-but-at-least-I-have-money costume. Oh well, I sighed. We all have our costumes.

"Just a minute, Alison," she shushed me. "They're about to explain why she has amnesia and can't remember anything her husband asks her."

My own husband lost his money, then left me for his first wife, whom he later impregnated. Then my employer was murdered, and I became a suspect. What's more, my double life as a maid was exposed on national television, as was the desperate state of my finances. Sounded like a soap opera to me. But apparently my real-life saga wasn't juicy enough to tear my mother away from "As the World Turns."

I sat down next to her on the sofa and, ever the Good Daughter, waited for the program to be over. When it was, my mother turned to look at me.

"You look thin, Alison," she said, then drew on her Winston.

"I am thin, Mom. I've always been thin."

"No, it's this maid business. I nearly had a heart attack when I heard. Can you imagine? A mother finding out her daughter has been scrubbing toilets? Your father would have died."

"He did die."

"Don't be smart."

"I'm sorry you had to hear about it on the radio and not from me."

"Who heard about it on the radio? I heard about it from Edith Eisner at the club. Edith Eisner, of all people. You'd think her daughter was so special. A stewardess, for God's sake. A maid with wings. That's what those girls are."

"Yes, well, I'm sorry you had to hear about it from Edith Eisner, but I took the maid's job because I needed money. Can't you understand the fear of losing your house, of not having a home to go home to?"

"A home to which to go home."

"Right."

"Why didn't you ask me to help you, Alison? I have a little money saved. Of course, it's not that much, and I do have to be careful at my age not to overspend."

"That's why I didn't ask you to help me." That and the fact that I wanted to break free of you and feel independent for the first time in my life.

"Oh, my. It's after six," my mother said after glancing at her watch. "The reservation is for six-thirty."

"We're going out for dinner? I would have thought you'd prefer to talk about all this in private."

"It *will* be in private. We're going to the club. It's Maine

Lobster Night, and I haven't missed one of those in thirty years."

We drove over to Grassy Glen in my car—a tortuous ten-minute trip during which my mother berated me for dishonoring my father's memory, not only by taking a job as a domestic after he had worked so hard at his mattress business so I could afford domestics of my own, but by working for the likes of Melanie Moloney, whom my mother described as "trash." Apparently, my mother had very strong feelings about Melanie, as well as about Alistair Downs—feelings I'd never heard her express before. "A woman who deliberately sets out to ruin the life of an important man like Alistair Downs deserves whatever harm comes to her," she said.

As we pulled up in front of the ivy-covered brick clubhouse which had once been a convent and later a rehab clinic for wealthy substance abusers, the valet parking attendant sped over to my mother's side of the car, opened her door and said, "Good evening, Mrs. Waxman. How are you this evening?"

When we entered the huge main dining room with its heavy silk drapes and crystal chandeliers, a dark-haired, tuxedo-clad man with the unctuousness of a game-show host sashayed over to us and kissed my mother's hand, which had actually been extended in preparation for his display of servitude. "Marvelous to see you again, Mrs. Waxman," he said. "You're looking wonderful this evening."

"You're looking well yourself, Marvin," my mother replied without smiling, narrowing her eyes as she scanned the room for people she knew.

"And here's your lovely daughter," Marvin said.

"Yes, Marvin," my mother beamed. My mother rarely beamed.

"Right this way, ladies," Marvin said, leading us to a

table next to a big picture window which, when it wasn't dark outside, overlooked the club's eighteen-hole, Jack Nicklaus–designed golf course and driving range.

As we walked across the ballroom-size dining room, I was shocked to see so many empty tables. The club was hardly playing to a packed house. "Where is everybody?" I asked my mother. "I thought Maine Lobster Night was the hottest night of the week here."

"It's that recession," she hissed. "Some of the members couldn't pay the seventy-five-hundred-dollar yearly dues and had to drop out. Can you imagine?" Oh, I could imagine, all right.

Marvin seated us at our table and placed white linen napkins on our laps. "Would you care for your usual cocktail, Mrs. Waxman? Dubonnet Rouge over one ice cube, twist of lemon?"

"That would be lovely, Marvin," my mother answered, lighting up a Winston.

"And how about your beautiful daughter? Would she like a cocktail?" Marvin said, looking at me.

"I'll have a glass of white wine," I said. Then I flashed back to my first dinner with Cullie on the *Marlowe* and smiled. "On second thought, Marvin, make that a Mount Gay rum and tonic."

"A what?" my mother said, looking startled.

Marvin did too, but he took the order, bowed at the waist, and left.

I'd love Cullie to see this place, I chuckled to myself. Maybe when things settled down and we got to know each other better, I'd introduce him to my mother. Then again, maybe not.

"Now tell me about this murder investigation," my mother prompted, her eyes fixed not on me but on our fellow diners, some of whom waved at her and blew her kisses.

I recounted the story of how I came to be employed by Melanie, how I discovered her body in her office, and how

I had no alibi for the night she was killed. At first, my mother, like Bethany Downs, seemed particularly interested in whether I had taken a peek at the Alistair Downs manuscript while I worked in Melanie's house. Then, when I explained that I had no idea what was in the book, she moved on to where I'd been the night of the murder and why I had no alibi.

"I was out with a man," I said. "He brought me home at about eleven o'clock and left. I spent the rest of the night alone, at Maplebark Manor."

"Who is this man?" she asked.

"His name is Cullie Harrington, Mom. He's a photographer." I knew what was coming and braced myself.

"What kind of a name is Harrington? Not a Jewish name, I can tell you that."

"No, he's not Jewish, Mom. He's Episcopalian."

My mother grew pale, but she did not faint. "And what does he do for a living? He's a photographer, you say?"

"Yup. He shot the photographs for the brochure of Maplebark Manor. That's how we met."

"So it was a business dinner? You discussed the marketing of your house?"

"No, the house never came up. It was a social evening. Cullie and I are . . . dating."

"Dating? Photographers don't have money. What's gotten into you, Alison?"

Just in the nick of time, before I was forced to explain to my mother that I had changed, that I no longer needed money to be happy, that Cullie was sweet and wonderful and talented, Marvin arrived with our drinks. I stirred mine. My mother took a long swig of hers—so long that she accidentally swallowed the twist of lemon that was wedged between the ice cube and the Dubonnet, and she began to cough violently. Within seconds, the lemon twist was lodged in her windpipe and she was choking. "Help! Help!" she wheezed, her face turning an odd shade of blue.

I admit it. For one split second, I was paralyzed to help

her. I kept trying to think of a joke. Quick! A joke! A joke!
I commanded myself, as my poor mother sat slumped over
the table gasping for breath. Fortunately for her, my daugh-
terly instinct kicked in and I bolted out of my seat, wrapped
my arms around her and applied my fist to her chest. Once,
twice, three times.

To my mother's and my great relief, the dreaded twist of
lemon finally shot out of her mouth and landed on the table
next to the sterling silver salt and pepper shakers.

"Are you okay now, Mom?" I asked. "Shouldn't we call
a doctor?" I glanced around the room, thinking there might
be a doctor in the house.

Surprisingly, none of the other diners seemed the least bit
concerned about my mother's near-death experience. They
just sat there stuffing themselves like a scene out of *Tom
Jones,* their chests draped in white plastic lobster bibs, their
fingers busily dissecting their five-pound crustaceans, their
mouths sucking meat out of claws, their chins dripping with
melted butter. They were so involved with their meal and
each other that they wouldn't have noticed if a space ship
landed in the middle of the room. Maine Lobster Night was
Maine Lobster Night, and that was all there was to it.

"Are you sure you're all right?" I asked my mother again.
"Would you like some water? Would you like to go home?
We could have Marvin ask the parking attendant to bring
the car around."

"Absolutely not," my mother said sharply, sounding like
her old self. "I'm not going anywhere. We haven't had our
lobsters yet. I paid good money for those lobsters, so we'll
just have to stay and eat them."

"I don't think you should be eating lobster right now.
You nearly choked to death. On a lemon."

"The lemon had nothing to do with it. When you told me
you were seeing a gentile photographer, I nearly died."

"Yes, Mom, you did."

I suggested that we avoid the subject of my love life and
stick to less provocative topics, like whether it would snow

over the weekend and whether "As the World Turns" would lose another actor to prime time. She was happy as a clam—or should I say lobster?—by the time Marvin brought our food to the table and dressed us in our plastic bibs, which, by the way, were imprinted with the words: GRASSY GLEN COUNTRY CLUB—#1 CHOICE OF THE CHOSEN PEOPLE.

"Very sweet and tender," my mother proclaimed after spearing a large fork-full of meat from the tail of the lobster, dipping it in melted butter, and popping it into her mouth.

"Yes, very sweet and tender," I agreed.

The tastiness of the lobster was about all we did agree on. We were miles apart on what we wanted out of life and miles apart on how to get it. The realization saddened me, but it didn't frighten me. Not anymore. Not after what I'd been through. I no longer needed my mother's approval. I no longer needed a man's approval. The only person's approval I really needed was my own, and I was doing my best to get it.

Chapter 12

My plan for Friday was to haul the Alistair Downs manuscript out of my Porsche, bring it into the house, and read the whole damn thing. But nobody would let me. First Janet Claiborne called and asked if I would show the house to a couple from Kansas. The husband's company, she explained, was relocating to Manhattan. Eager to unload Maplebark Manor before the bank took it, I agreed to interrupt my plans and show the house. The hayseeds from Kansas turned out to be a couple of producers from "A Current Affair," as I learned when I found them fishing in my underwear drawer, an act they defended by calling it "good, solid television journalism." Then Todd Bennett, Melanie's prodigal research associate, called and asked if he could come over. He had an important matter to dithcuth with me, he said. So much for settling into a comfy chair and reading all about Senator Downs.

Todd showed up at about noon. It had only been a couple of weeks since I'd last seen him, but the once-pudgy man with the Pillsbury Dough Boy body appeared to have slimmed down considerably. When I asked him if he'd been on a diet, he shook his head. "I've been worrying. I can't eat when I'm worried."

"I know you and Melanie had some kind of a disagreement before she died, but you must have been terribly upset when you heard she'd been murdered," I said, trying to comfort Todd, who refused to sit down when I invited him into the house but preferred to pace back and forth in my foyer.

"You knew about our fight? How?" He seemed alarmed.

"Melanie told me. Not what it was about, just that you hadn't come in to work and she didn't know where you were."

"Yeth, we had a fight, all right. The cunt reneged on our deal."

"You mean, the deal where she had agreed to give you credit for writing the book with her?"

"You got it. A couple of weeks ago, our publisher asked us to approve copy for the book jacket. They wanted to start selling the foreign rights, so they did a mock-up of the jacket to take to a book convention. They FedExed a C-print to Melanie and I happened to get a look at it."

"Happened to get a look at it?"

"Yeth. She wasn't planning to show it to me. I had to steal it when she was out of the office. And when I saw it, I knew why she wouldn't let me see it. I was so mad I could have killed her."

"What did the jacket have on it?"

"It read: 'CHA CHA CHA: THE ALISTAIR DOWNS STORY—A Biography by Melanie Moloney.' "

"That's the name of the book? *Cha Cha Cha?*" The manuscript stuffed under the seats of my car had no title page.

"Yeth, on account of how the Senator started out as a dance teacher. But do you believe how Melanie cheated me? She'd promised we'd be co-authors on this book. But whose name was on the jacket? Hers. Not hers *and* mine. Hers."

"But couldn't you have talked to her about it? Reminded her that you had an agreement?"

"Talk to Melanie? What are you kidding? You worked for her. You know what she was like."

"But you had an agreement. Surely an attorney would have been able to—"

"There was nothing in writing. We had a verbal agreement. A handshake."

Todd was even stupider than I thought. But then again, I'd had a written agreement with Sandy—a prenuptial agreement—and where had that gotten me?

"So you had it out with her? You told her how you felt about what she did?"

"Of course I did. She laughed in my face and called me a wimp. I hate being called a wimp."

"Anybody would."

"She said *she* was a bestselling author and *I* was a first-class wimp."

"She said that?"

"Yeth. And more."

"So you walked out on her? Quit your job?"

"I didn't quit, I just took a little sabbatical. I had every intention of coming back to work and helping Melanie with the promotion of the book."

"But how could you, after the way she reneged on your deal and called you a wimp?"

"Because I *am* a wimp. She'd been treating me like dirt for years. I'd threaten to quit, then I'd always come back. She knew I'd come back this time, too."

Did you come back to kill her this time? I wondered. Are *you* the murderer, mild-mannered, wimpy Todd? Do you have an alibi for the night Melanie was killed, or did your "little sabbatical" take you over to Melanie's office for a little pushing and shoving match?

"What did you want to see me about?" I asked Todd.

"Oh, yeth. That. I got a call from a Detective Corsini yesterday. He said he's interviewing people who were close to Melanie. He asked me to come down to police headquarters at my convenience."

"So you went down there?"

"Not yet. It hasn't been convenient."

"How can I help you?"

"I was watching 'A Current Affair' last night, and I saw

a piece about you, how you found Melanie's body, how you were questioned by the police, and all that. I just thought I'd ask your advice about how to handle this detective."

Nobody had asked my advice in years, maybe ever, but I was too suspicious to be flattered. "Just tell him the truth," I said. "Do you have an alibi for the night Melanie was murdered?"

"Not exactly. I was home reading."

"Oh? What were you reading?"

"Cha Cha Cha. I wanted to go over the finished manuscript one more time before we sent it out to be duplicated."

Todd had the original Alistair Downs manuscript? Impossible. *I* had the manuscript. The *original* manuscript. I knew it was the original because the boxes it was in were marked ORIGINAL. It had to be the genuine article.

"You mean, you had a *copy* of the manuscript at home," I said breezily, trying to keep panic out of my voice. "I assumed Melanie kept the original at her house, under lock and key."

"No, *I* have the original. She asked me to keep it for a while. She was afraid Alistair Downs's daughter or one of his other henchmen would find a way to steal it. Somebody from Downs's camp had been calling Melanie with death threats."

Todd had to be lying about the manuscript. *I* had the original. The question was, why would Todd lie?

"Did Melanie tell the police about the death threats?" I asked.

"I don't think so. She was used to them. Everybody hated her. That's what's going to make the police's job so hard. How's this Detective Corsini going to figure out who murdered her when there are so many of us who wanted her dead?"

"Hair fibers," I replied.

"What are you talking about, Alithun?"

"Our hair fibers will set us free."

* * *

That afternoon I received my own call from Detective Corsini, who asked if I'd mind coming down to headquarters to answer a few questions. I'd already told him everything I knew, but said I'd be glad to oblige.

When I got to the station, I was told to wait outside Corsini's office until he was through with the person he was interviewing. Ten minutes later, his door opened. There was the good Detective Corsini, arm in arm with the one and only, larger than life, dance-instructor-turned-actor-turned-Senator-turned-newspaper-publisher Alistair P. Downs.

A perfect couple, I thought. The celebrity and the celebrity whore.

"Splendid talking with you," I heard Alistair tell Corsini.

"My pleasure, Senator," Corsini ass-kissed back. "Oh, Mrs. Koff, go on in," he said when he saw me.

"Ms. Koff," I said militantly.

"Well, well, it's Miss Koff from the newspaper," Alistair chimed in, ignoring my stab at feminism. "Splendid to see you again. Ho ho."

Alistair looked dashing. He wore a dark blue pin-striped suit under a cashmere camel's hair topcoat whose lapels and cuffs were lined with Persian lamb. His thick reddish-brown hair was slicked back, little waves framing his face. His complexion was smooth, his green eyes clear. He had aged well, no doubt about it.

"Hello, Senator Downs," I said, extending my hand, which he shook with both of his.

"Don't be too hard on her now," Alistair chuckled as he gave Detective Corsini a playful poke in the ribs. "She's one of mine."

One of his what? "I'm happy I ran into you today, Senator," I pressed on. "I want you to know that I meant you no harm when I took the housekeeper's job at Melanie Moloney's. Your daughter Bethany seems to view my work for Ms. Moloney as an act of betrayal. But it was simply a matter of economics."

"Ah, yes. Economics. I, myself, am a big fan of Ronnie's supply-side economics. Good man, Ronnie. We worked together in the movies, and we worked together in the Party. Nancy's a splendid gal, too."

"You're friends with Ronald and Nancy Reagan?" Detective Corsini gushed.

"Why, of course. Had them on the *Aristocrat* many times. Splendid people. Ho ho."

"Did you want to talk to me, Detective?" I said, cutting this chitchat short.

"You can go on into my office," Corsini said. "I'll be spending another minute or two with the Senator here."

I went into the office and left the door open. I listened to Corsini thank Alistair profusely for taking the time out of his busy schedule to come down to police headquarters and answer all those nasty questions about where he was on the night of Melanie's murder and how he felt about the book she had written about him. Then I heard Alistair chuckle several times and tell Corsini that the Layton Police Department was the best local police force in the entire country in his opinion, that he was proud to be a Layton resident and taxpayer, and that he was planning to make a big donation to the Policemen's Benevolent Association. What a crock.

"Now, Miss Koff," said Detective Corsini when he finally managed to tear himself away from Alistair and return to his office to grill me. "I gotta ask you about some of the people who came to see Miss Moloney at her house. What do you know about the names on this list?"

He handed me a sheet of paper. I recognized a few of the names—Jason Roth, Melanie's friend at the *Star;* Arlene Malkan, her occasional gofer; Carmen Cordero, her manicurist; and of course, Todd Bennett, her long-suffering research associate.

I told Corsini what little I knew about these people. Then

he handed me another list. "How about these names?" he asked.

The second sheet of paper contained what Corsini considered to be Melanie's Enemies List. On it were, among others, the people quoted in that damning *Vanity Fair* article. There was Ron Delano, her first husband, an accountant whom she deserted for Scott Whitehurst, a perennially out-of-work actor who became her second husband and then sued her for $50,000 a month in alimony after she dumped him. There was also Mel Suskind, the literary agent whom she dumped for a big-shot agent at ICM, and Roberta Carr, Melanie's former editor who paid her $3 million a book, then got dumped when Melanie took a rival publisher's offer of $5.5 million for the Alistair Downs biography. I suggested that Corsini read the *Vanity Fair* article if he wanted to know more about these people—more than I could tell him anyway. I was just Melanie's lowly maid. What did I know? All I knew was that Todd was right: plenty of people hated Melanie. But enough to kill her? I was sure that as disgruntled as her former agent, editor, and husbands undoubtedly were, whoever offed Melanie was a lot more than disgruntled.

As I drove home from my meeting with Detective Corsini, who had ended our interview by reminding me not to leave town, I flipped on the radio. The top news story on WANE was that Alistair Downs had scheduled a press conference for four o'clock that afternoon to comment on the murder of his dreaded biographer and to respond to scurrilous allegations in the tabloid press and elsewhere that he was, in some way, responsible for Melanie Moloney's death. Oh boy, I thought. I can't wait to hear what old Alistair has to say. I prayed that the press conference would be televised so I could see that dance teacher dance with my very own eyes.

My prayers were answered. The press conference was to air on that evening's eleven o'clock news.

"Want to come watch your favorite person make an ass of himself on TV?" I asked Cullie when I reached him on his cellular phone aboard the *Marlowe*. "We can have leftover chicken cacciatore."

"I accept. Be right over."

I showered and changed into a pair of tan corduroy jeans and a chocolate brown turtleneck sweater, and ran down to the kitchen to heat up the chicken. I was amused to find myself humming. I had never been the humming type, but there I was humming the Everly Brothers' "All I Have to Do Is Dream," or a reasonable facsimile. The fact was, I was happy. My life was a complete mess, but I was happy. I didn't have a husband, a job, or a dime, and I didn't own my house anymore, the bank did. But I was happy. The thought of spending the evening with Cullie filled me with joy.

When my doorbell rang, my heart leaped. I bounded to the door and opened it for Cullie.

"Hi," he said. "For you."

He handed me a gift-wrapped box. It's candy, I guessed. A Whitman's Sampler. A somewhat mundane gift but a thoughtful one, nonetheless. I remembered how Sandy despised drug-store chocolates. For him, it was Godiva or nothing.

"Open it," Cullie urged as he entered the house and hung his ski jacket in the guest closet, then kissed the top of my head.

I tore the paper off the box and was surprised to see, not a Whitman's Sampler, but a stunning brown leather diary, complete with lock and key.

"This has been a tough time for you," he explained. "I thought that since you're a writer, you might want to scribble down all the things that are happening to you. Get a handle on them."

I was so moved that I honestly didn't know what to say.

What did I do to deserve Cullie? I wasn't good enough for him. He was much too good for me. He was much too good to be true. "Thank you so much," I said finally, then hugged him. "Thank you for making me so happy."

Cullie and I ate our leftover chicken cacciatore, washed the dinner dishes, and went upstairs to the bedroom to watch Alistair Downs do his dance on the eleven o'clock news. And what a show it was.

"Ladies and gentlemen of the media," Alistair began. "Ladies and gentlemen of Layton. Ladies and gentlemen of these United States."

"Oh, brother," Cullie and I muttered simultaneously and then laughed.

"Welcome to Evermore, my home." Alistair was standing on the front steps of his house, with Bethany at his side and a throng of reporters and photographers at his feet. Smoke billowed from his mouth in the frosty February air. "In view of the fact that my staff and I have been deluged with requests for some sort of public response to the death of Melanie Moloney, I have decided to issue the following statement: I did not know Miss Moloney personally, nor did I read any of her books, but I respected her success in the literary world and was deeply saddened by her tragic passing. I offer my sincerest, most heartfelt sympathies to her family and friends. I offer, too, the complete and thorough support of the Layton Police Department, a department that, while small, is held in high regard by the nation's law enforcement community. I feel confident that very shortly the Layton Police will learn the identity of Miss Moloney's attacker and move swiftly and expertly to bring him to justice. I thank you for your time, ladies and gentlemen of the media, and I thank God for giving us the strength to forge ahead in this time of great sorrow and mourning."

Cullie and I looked at each other and shrugged. "What

did we expect him to do, confess to killing her?" he asked.

"Do you really think he did it?" I said. The idea shocked me. Alistair was a pompous ass, but a murderer? He was a United States Senator, for God's sake. "I know you think he's immoral, Cullie, but I assumed that was just because he's a Republican."

"Shhhh. They're asking him questions. Listen."

I turned my attention back to the television. Alistair had started to walk away from the media, into his house, when reporters began firing questions at him.

"Where were you the night of the murder, sir?"

"Aren't you anxious to get a look at Moloney's book about you?"

"Do you know what's in it?"

Alistair waved off his questioners with a smile and the parting words, "Our splendid police officers have all the information you need, ladies and gentlemen. It's been a pleasure to see you all. Good afternoon. Ho ho."

Alistair went inside Evermore, Bethany following at his heels, and the eleven o'clock news moved on to other stories of the day.

"What do you think?" I asked Cullie after I flicked off the remote control and turned to face him. We were lying on the bed, our backs propped up against pillows.

"I think the guy's a bastard who's capable of just about anything."

"But why? Because he has money and power? Because he's a big shot at the Sachem Point Yacht Club where your father was the hired help?"

"Paddy Harrington was ten times the man Alistair Downs is," Cullie snapped.

"Hey. I didn't say he wasn't. I'm sure your dad was a wonderful man. I was just trying to understand your resentment toward Alistair."

"Sorry. I didn't mean to bark at you."

"If I knew more about you, maybe I'd understand better. Tell me what it was like to grow up at the yacht club."

"All right. But first, I'll tell you about my father. Coming to this country and working for people like Alistair destroyed him."

"I'm listening."

"As I told you on the boat the first time we had dinner, Paddy came from the Isle of Wight."

"I remember."

"The Isle of Wight is the sailing center of England, the launch point for all four Admiral's Cup races, including the Fastnet Race, the most prestigious of the four. Before the war, my father crewed on the biggest and fastest boats that competed in these races. He was sought after. He was respected for his skills. He was there when King George showed up. He was invited to the same parties the royals were invited to. He was making an honorable living, the same as his father had—from sailing. Then came World War II."

"What happened?"

"He enlisted in the Navy and was waiting for his orders when the English Army had their notorious brush with the Germans at Dunkirk."

"My world history is a little rusty. Refresh my memory."

"Dunkirk is a seaport on the northern coast of France, near the Belgian border. In the spring of 1940, about three hundred thousand British and French troops were trapped on the beaches by the advancing German forces. Their only escape was to cross the English Channel, but their Navy's boats and troops were otherwise engaged. With the Germans closing in, the British organized a makeshift armada of civilian crafts. Fishing boats, sailboats, small freighters— every conceivable type of boat was pressed into service. It was this makeshift armada that rescued the British troops and brought them across the Channel to safety."

"Was your father part of the evacuation?"

"He was. He was one of the organizers and he crewed one of the boats. After that, he was posted in the Navy and served until 1946."

"So he was a hero."

"Yeah, he was. Then everything went to hell. By the time he was discharged in '46, the English economy was in shambles. Sailing races had been suspended, and the outlook for sailors in Europe was bleak. He was a sailing hero *and* a war hero, but he had no way to make a living. So when people said there were opportunities for sailors in the States, he came over here."

"And started working at the yacht club?"

"Yeah, in '46. He was in his mid-thirties, and he considered himself lucky to land the position of sailing instructor at a Connecticut yacht club. Little did he know."

"It wasn't all bad, was it? Sachem Point is a beautiful club, after all."

"No, it wasn't all bad. He met my mother there, as I told you. They lived in a small cottage on the property, separated from the rest of the club by a wire fence. At first, my father enjoyed his work. Being around sailboats and sailors was like breathing for him. But the job was bullshit. The members of the club didn't need an experienced sailor to teach their spoiled, bratty kids to sail; they needed a babysitter. People who belong to the club don't really care about sailing. They don't even like it. They just like to show off their boats and throw their weight around. My father was their pet English monkey. 'Paddy, my boy,' they'd say. They actually called him 'boy,' and he was forty years old. 'Take the wife and kids out for a little sail, would you, Paddy?' Or: 'See that my boat is stocked with plenty of Tanqueray, would you, Paddy?' Or: 'Don't bother coming to the barbecue tonight, Paddy. It's a private party—for members only.' I don't know how he took it for so long. Well, actually, I do."

"How?"

"He drank too much."

"That must have been hard on you."

"It was."

"Why didn't he quit the club and take you back to England?"

"He fell in love."

"Oh."

"That's where your friend Alistair comes in. And if it's all the same to you, I'd rather let it go for another time. I'm kind of tired. Big day tomorrow. Two houses to shoot."

Cullie got up from the bed and stretched his arms.

"Mind if I check my answering machine?" he said.

"Of course not. The phone's right here."

I went downstairs to make a cup of tea, and when I returned, Cullie was undressed and in bed.

I undressed and climbed in next to him, leaving the tea on the night table.

"Is everything all right?" I asked. "You seem a little down."

"Sorry. You've got enough on your mind without me getting grouchy."

"I know a way to get you un-grouchy," I teased. I kissed him on the mouth and pressed my naked body against his. Then I reached down to touch his penis. It was soft. "Be right back," I whispered in his ear, then burrowed under the covers, placed his flaccid member in my mouth, and began to suck the living daylights out of it.

"Ummm," he moaned after a few seconds of my action. "I'm getting more un-grouchy every minute."

"Imgld," I mumbled. It's difficult to speak distinctly with a man's manhood halfway down your throat.

I continued to massage Cullie's now rock-hard dick with my mouth and caressed his balls with my hand. His breathing quickened. His pelvis began to gyrate.

"Faster, faster," he moaned suddenly.

Oh God, I thought. He wants to come in my mouth. I'd never had oral sex with my first husband. And the few times I'd gone down on Sandy he'd warned me in time to take my mouth off his cock and finish the whole business with my hand. But this was the new me. The new, open, adventurous me. I would not wimp out. I would not back down. I would not deny Cullie what was, according to everything I'd ever read or seen on TV, the ultimate pleasure for a man: to discharge his semen into the mouth of his beloved.

So faster and faster I sucked. Up and down. Up and down. I did not gag.

"Oh, God. Oh, God. Oh, baby. I'm . . . *ahhhhhhhhhhhhh!*"

At the sound of the *"ahhhhhhhhhhhh,"* Cullie fired off a volcano's worth of molten lava.

Go on, swallow it, you chicken shit, I scolded myself. It can't taste any worse than that creamy pickled herring your mother made you eat when you were a kid.

I counted to three and gulped down Cullie's essence. It wasn't nearly as bad as creamy pickled herring. As a matter of fact, it reminded me of a very tart lemon meringue.

Feeling very pleased and proud of myself, I emerged from underneath the blankets and took my place on my pillow, next to Cullie.

"Thank you," he whispered, then kissed my lips. "Is there any way I can repay you?"

"Yes, but you said you were tired, that you had two houses to shoot in the morning."

"Tomorrow will take care of itself. I'm not finished with tonight."

And he wasn't.

Chapter 13

"Want to come along on my shoot this morning?" Cullie asked as we drank coffee in my kitchen. "I'm doing a house for Prestige Properties on Layton Harbor, right next door to that mausoleum Alistair Downs calls a house."

"Next door to Evermore?"

"The very same."

"I wouldn't be in the way?"

"Nope."

"What about the TV reporters and police detectives who seem to follow me everywhere I go?"

"Fuck 'em."

We drove over to the harbor in Cullie's Jeep Cherokee. It was a crisp and sunny late-February morning, and I was in a cheerful mood; I was excited about watching Cullie work.

"See, Sonny?" Cullie said as he pointed out my window. We were cruising along the road that overlooked the picture-perfect harbor. "The house we're shooting is just past Evermore."

We were approaching Alistair's estate when a black Cadillac Seville came racing out of his driveway. "Cullie, look out! That car's going to hit us!" I screamed.

Cullie swerved to his left to avoid the onrushing car that was about to bash my side of the Jeep. We came to a screeching stop on the wrong side of the road, while the driver of the Cadillac kept right on going.

"Boy, are we lucky," Cullie said, resting his head on the steering wheel and trying to collect himself. "Are you all right?"

I was stunned, but not from nearly being hit by a car. I was reeling from the realization that the person who almost ran us down was my mother—or someone who looked very much like her. "Cullie, did you get a good look at the driver of that Cadillac?" I asked.

"Not really. I just saw it was a woman."

"Yeah, and I'm almost sure the woman was my mother."

"What would your mother be doing at Alistair Downs's house? You never mentioned that they were friends."

"They're not. That's why this is so weird."

"Does your mother drive a black Cadillac Seville?"

"Yeah."

"Fine. But that doesn't prove anything. Plenty of people drive Cadillacs. Is your mother a rotten driver?"

"No. She's a good driver."

"Well, the woman who almost hit us was a rotten driver. So it probably wasn't your mother."

"I'm telling you, it was my mother. The clincher was the smoke inside the car. My mother is a chain-smoker. She never goes anywhere without her Winstons."

"Okay, so it was your mother, and she's not as good a driver as you thought. But what was she doing at Alistair's house?"

"That, my sweet man, is a very good question."

In the eleven years that I had worked for Alistair at the newspaper, my mother had never given me the slightest impression that she knew or had ever met the Senator. In fact, she often pumped me for information about what he was like—what he looked like in person, what kind of man I thought him to be, whether he "kept company" with one special woman, that sort of thing. So what was she doing racing out of his house at ten o'clock in the morning? I was mystified, to say the least.

"Do you want to follow her home and ask her what she was doing there?" Cullie suggested.

I was tempted. But Cullie had a house to photograph, and I didn't want him to be late on my account. "I'll call her as soon as I get home," I said, wondering how long the shoot would take and how long I'd be able to contain myself until I could get some answers out of my mother.

The house Cullie was to photograph for Prestige Properties wasn't a Colonial or Georgian or Tudor-style mansion. It was of a style that could best be described as Castle Nouveau. It was a massive stucco structure of at least 25,-000 square feet, newly constructed but meant to look like it had been there since the Middle Ages.

"Who wants a house with turrets?" Cullie asked as he unloaded his equipment from the Jeep. "Don't these people know this is Connecticut? The Connecticut shore? Armed towers aren't really necessary, are they?"

I laughed. "Be nice. Not everybody has your impeccable taste."

"It has nothing to do with taste. It has to do with excess."

Cullie wasn't kidding. Even I, the former Princess of Excess, was overwhelmed by the ostentation of the place, which, by the way, the owners had named Colossus.

"How much is this baby selling for?" I asked.

"Six million."

"Are you kidding me? It doesn't look like there's more than an acre of land here."

"Yeah, but there's a lot of house. Wait till you see."

Cullie was right. The place was enormous—and about as extravagant as I'd ever seen. Everywhere I looked I saw marble, mirrors, and gold, then still more marble, mirrors, and gold. The rooms were mammoth, the ceilings nearly twenty feet high. The kitchen had, not one, but three electric ranges, dishwashers, and refrigerator/freezers. The foyer had, not one bathroom for guests, but two—a ladies' powder room and a slightly smaller men's room or "gun room"—each with its own fireplace. The second-floor master bedroom suite, reached by a marble staircase that sat beneath a huge skylight, had, not one bedroom and bath, but three—plus walk-in closets, a study, three fireplaces, and a fully equipped indoor lap pool. On the third floor, reached by an elevator, there were three bedrooms, each with fireplace and bath, and five maids' rooms and baths, along with a full-sized kitchen and sitting room.

"Whew! I'm exhausted," I said after Cullie and I had given ourselves the tour. The owners of the house were a very intense, expensively dressed, two-career couple who explained that they had to run off to a meeting but said they'd be back to check on things during their lunch break. "How come they're selling this little shack?" I asked. "Too small for them?"

"They bought it in the freewheeling eighties. Now they're hurting for money, same as you are."

"They both have careers. Didn't they say they were stock brokers?"

"Used to be. They got laid off."

"Then what about that meeting they said they had to run off to?"

"It's a meeting of Layton's walking wounded—axed white-collar workers. You know, one of those support groups for executives who lost their jobs."

"Wow. How do you know all this?"

"The listing agent told me. Real estate agents know everybody's personal business and don't mind sharing it."

"So I've learned." I shuddered to think how much mileage Janet Claiborne was getting out of my recent notoriety.

Cullie's assignment for the morning was to photograph Colossus's colossal living room—a room that contained, no joke, at least seventy-five pieces of furniture of every style and period. Chairs, tables, sofas, you name it. It also contained numerous and very large stone statues of naked women, all of whose breasts were so protuberant it was difficult not to bump into them. But the greatest challenge in photographing the room was the mirrors. They were everywhere, including a ten-foot job over the fireplace.

"How am I supposed to shoot this room when no matter where I put a light, there's a reflection," he asked.

I shrugged.

Cullie spent the next two hours moving furniture, fiddling with the light, and trying everything he knew to get a shot without a reflection. I could tell he was exasperated when he plopped down on one of the dozen sofas in the room and said, "If it weren't February, I'd say, 'Let's blow this pop stand and go sailing.' "

I kissed him. "It's noon. The sun's at the back of the house now. Will that make the shot easier?"

"Not really, but I'll keep trying. At least I don't have the homeowners breathing down my neck."

Wrong. No sooner did Cullie utter those words than Mr. and Mrs. Ex-Stockbroker showed up.

"We've been thinking," said Mr. Ex-Stockbroker as he paced back and forth in front of Cullie. His support group meeting hadn't rendered him any less hyper. "We'd like you to come back and shoot the living room later in the day."

"How much later? I've got other jobs to do," said Cullie, clearly not in the mood for interference.

"About three A.M.," said Mr. Ex-Stockbroker.

"Three o'clock in the morning? Are you people nuts?" Cullie snapped.

"We've checked the almanac," explained Mrs. Ex-Stockbroker, ignoring Cullie's outburst. "There's going to be a full moon tonight. At three A.M. it should be coming through the living room windows and cast a particularly dramatic glow all over the room, which would make an absolutely stunning photograph."

Cullie and I looked at each other with disbelief and tried our best not to laugh. I flashed back to my own, absurdly

pretentious treatment of Cullie and shook my head. No
wonder he has such a chip on his shoulder, I thought. A lot
of people with money *are* nuts.

"Look, folks," he said hotly. "I'm going to shoot your
living room now. Not at three A.M. Not at three P.M. Now.
The photograph will be fine, with or without the full moon,
and it'll make everybody want to buy your house. Okay?"

Mr. and Mrs. Ex-Stockbroker grimaced. "Photographers," I heard the husband mutter to his wife. "They're all
a bunch of fucking prima donnas."

Seconds later the doorbell rang. I peered out a living
room window and saw a huge moving van parked directly
in front of the house.

Mr. and Mrs. Ex-Stockbroker went to answer the door.
Within minutes Cullie and I heard shouting, then weeping.
Minutes after that, four men entered the living room and
began moving all seventy-five pieces of furniture out of the
house and into the truck outside. We were mystified.

"What the hell is going on here?" Cullie asked. "I've got
a shot to do. How am I supposed to shoot a room with no
furniture in it?"

"It can't be helped," Mr. Ex-Stockbroker replied, his
lower lip quivering. "The bank has chosen the day of your
shoot to repossess all our furniture."

I felt sick—sick for these people and sick for myself. For
all I knew, four men in a moving van were parked outside
Maplebark Manor right this very minute, sent by the Layton Bank & Trust Company to repossess all *my* furniture. It
was only a matter of time.

"Tell you what," Cullie told the bereft homeowner in a
much gentler tone than he'd used minutes before. "I'll come
back at three A.M. and shoot your living room—furniture or
no furniture. We'll make it an artsy kind of shot, show off
the room for the architectural masterpiece it is. It'll be great,
okay?"

Mr. Ex-Stockbroker was so touched by Cullie's offer that
he wept. "I can't tell you how much I appreciate this," he

said. "If your photograph helps sell Colossus, you'll be saving our lives."

The two men shook hands. Then Cullie and I packed up his equipment and left. When we were back in his Jeep, on our way home to Maplebark Manor, I leaned over and kissed him on his bearded right cheek.

"You're a nice man to go back there at three o'clock in the morning and shoot that poor bastard's house—turrets and all," I said.

"I'm a stupid man," he corrected me. "I'll be standing in that mirrored monstrosity, hunched over a camera at three o'clock in the morning, when I could be lying in a warm, cozy bed with you. That's stupid!"

Cullie had errands to run, clients to appease, and a friend to meet for dinner before heading over to Colossus for his three A.M. shot, so he kissed me goodbye, promised to see me the next day, and dropped me at Maplebark Manor.

I went inside, checked my answering machine, and found six messages on the tape: three from "A Current Affair," begging me to talk on camera about the "truth behind Melanie Moloney's murder"; one from Todd Bennett, asking if I'd told the police about his argument with Melanie; one from the Layton Bank & Trust Company, notifying me that foreclosure proceedings would begin within the month if I failed to make the mortgage payments on the house; and one from Detective Corsini, requesting that I come down to headquarters to answer a few more questions.

You'll all have to wait, I said out loud as I dialed my mother's number.

"Hello?" she answered.

"Hi, Mom. It's me."

"No, dear. *I.*"

"Were you at Alistair Downs's house this morning?" I thought it best to come straight to the point, but braced myself for a denial.

"Why do you ask?"

"Because I saw you coming out of his driveway. You nearly crashed into the car I was in."

"This isn't an inquisition, is it, dear?"

"Answer the question. Were you at his house this morning or not?"

"As a matter of fact, I was."

"But why? You don't even know the man."

"I did it for you."

"What are you talking about?"

"About what am I talking? About the fact that when we had dinner at the club the other night, you told me that Bethany Downs had fired you from the newspaper. I thought it was high time I interceded on your behalf."

"I don't understand."

"I went to see the Senator about hiring you back."

"You never seemed to care about my professional life before."

"You never had to take a job as a maid before. A maid! How could I stand by and allow my daughter to throw her life away? I had to do something, Alison dear. I decided it was time to become more involved in your work as a journalist. That's why I went to see Alistair Downs."

"Give me a break, Mom. You expect me to believe that you picked up the phone, called Alistair, introduced yourself as the mother of one of his reporters—a reporter he barely acknowledges—and invited yourself over to his estate for a little chat?"

"That's exactly how it happened. A mother's got to do what a mother's got to do."

"And he said, 'Why, of course, Mrs. Waxman. Come right over?' "

"Yes, indeed he did. The Senator is a kind, compassionate man, dear."

Ho ho. "What did you say to Alistair? What did he say to you?"

"I told him that you were the most talented writer on his

staff; that everyone at the club reads your interviews word for word; that the whole town would suffer if he denied us your articles."

"You really said that, Mom?" I was overwhelmed. My mother had never—I mean never—taken an interest in my work, let alone praise it. "How did Alistair react?" I asked.

"He was charming, really charming. But he didn't promise anything, dear," she said, drawing on a Winston. "He was awfully busy. He's a Senator, you know."

"Was a Senator." His current titles were Publisher of *The Layton Community Times* and Commodore of the Sachem Point Yacht Club. "So he didn't say he'd hire me back at the paper, right?"

"He didn't say he wouldn't."

"Was Bethany around?"

"I left when she arrived."

"Is that why you drove out of his estate in such a hurry? If it is, I understand completely. Take it from me—she's no picnic to be around."

"Around which to be. No, she isn't."

"Well, I don't know what to say." I paused. Should I yell at my mother for meddling or thank her for trying to help me? I was still suspicious of her real motive for paying Alistair a call, but I had to concede that if her meeting with him got me my job back, thanks were what she deserved.

"You don't have to say anything," she said. "I just want you to know that your mother is there for you always."

Perhaps she truly had my best interests at heart. Perhaps she and I were embarking on a new mother-daughter relationship built on trust, on shared responsibility, on mutual respect.

"Of course, I won't be there for you always in the literal sense," she added. "I am getting on, and my time on this earth is dwindling." She drew on her cigarette, then exhaled. "Which is why it's so important that you get that little job back at the newspaper."

That little job. My heart sank.

"You see, dear," she continued, "having a byline on the *Community Times* gives one a certain prominence in town. It's an excellent way for you to attract others of prominence—people who can support you when I'm gone."

"People? You mean, men?" I was beginning to get my mother's drift. It wasn't my career she cared about. It was the rich men my career would help me hook.

"Yes. Men of means. Men like Sandy. Let's not forget, it was he whom you met through your work at the newspaper."

"Let's not forget."

"And let's not forget what I've been telling you since you were a little girl. Money is security. Money is a buffer against all the hurts of the world. Money is . . . well, you know my philosophy of life: it's not who you are, it's what you have."

What do you do when your mother tells you her philosophy of life is: it's not who you are, it's what you have? You hang up on her, try to knock some sense into her, or come to the sad conclusion that no matter what you do, she just won't get it.

"Someone's at the door, Mom. I've got to go," was what I opted for.

After returning the messages on my answering machine (excluding the one from Detective Corsini), making myself a late lunch, and straightening up the house, I realized that the coast was finally clear to read Melanie's manuscript. I raced down to the garage, retrieved all thousand or so pages from the car, and lugged the boxes upstairs to my bedroom. I grabbed the first fifty pages, lay down on the bed, and licked my lips in anticipation. Okay, Melanie, I thought. Let's see what goodies you've got on Alistair and who might have killed you to keep them quiet.

According to the table of contents, the biography was divided into three main sections, each dealing with a significant aspect of Alistair P. Downs's life. There was a section covering his career in the movies, one focusing on his career in politics, and a final section entitled simply, "The Personal Life."

I read slowly, hungrily digesting every word, careful not to miss a single revelation or even the inference of one. By five o'clock, I had read only a quarter of the section dealing with Alistair's Hollywood years, but I was stunned by the sleaziness of the material—and its subject.

The biggest shocker, and the revelation that was certain to be discussed on talk shows across the nation, was that when Al Downey first went out to Hollywood, he forged a close friendship with a thug named Frankie Fuccato, a man who would later become one of the country's most legendary Mafia dons. According to Melanie, the friendship between Alistair and this Fuccato fellow continued to this day. It was Alistair's ties to the Mob that got him into the movies in the first place and, later, into the Senate as well.

Alistair a member of the Mafia? The Commodore of the Sachem Point Yacht Club and Layton's most beloved citizen a gangster? Could the Mafia have put a hit on Melanie to shut her up and protect their boy?

I was about to read on when the doorbell rang. Damn! I couldn't let anyone find out I had the manuscript.

I gathered it up and carried it downstairs to my exercise room, where I deposited it in the corner of the sauna. Then I closed the sauna door and ran to see who my visitor was.

"Your mail, Miss Koff," said the man who stood at my door holding assorted letters, newspapers, and magazines and looking every bit the U.S. postal worker.

"What's wrong with the mailbox?" I asked. "Why the door-to-door service?"

"Just trying to be helpful," he said. "How about letting me come inside so I can put these things down for you?"

As he started to move uninvited into my foyer, I spotted the mini–tape recorder he was wearing in the pocket of his "uniform."

"Take one more step and I'll call the police," I said, lifting the recorder out of his jacket and waving it in his face.

"Hey. Give that back," he shouted, his cheery postman demeanor giving way to the desperate manner of a tabloid TV producer who's just had his cover blown.

"Tell you what," I said. "I'll trade you. You give me my mail and get the fuck out of here, and I'll give you your tape recorder and forget about calling the police."

He dropped the mail on my flagstone landing and waited for me to hand over his recorder. I didn't. Instead, I bent down and picked up my mail, then threw the recorder into a bush of snow-covered rhododendron.

"Why you . . . you," he sputtered, shaking his fist at me. "You said you'd give it back!"

"I lied," I said, and slammed the door in his face.

I carried the mail into the house and set it down on the kitchen counter. Instinctively, forgetting I was no longer writing for the *Community Times,* I reached for the latest edition of the paper first. The headline on the front page read: NEW INFORMATION REVEALED IN MOLONEY MURDER CASE.

The article reported that the police investigation into Melanie's murder, which was being spearheaded by Detective Joseph Corsini of the Layton Police Department, was continuing at full speed. According to the article, the cause of death was now being listed as a CVA (cerebral vascular accident), also known as a brain aneurysm. The police were speculating that Melanie had suffered a blow to the back of the head while seated at her desk, a blow forceful enough to cause her to smack her forehead on the desk and fracture the front of her skull, which, in turn, produced the aneurysm. The police were currently searching for the blunt object which they believed the murderer used.

The article went on to say that nearly everyone who figured prominently in Melanie's life had been or was soon

Wish You Were Here?

You can be, every month, with Zebra
Historical Romance Novels.

AND TO GET YOU STARTED, ALLOW US TO SEND YOU

4 Historical Romances Free

A $19.96 VALUE!
With absolutely no obligation to buy anything.

YOU ARE CORDIALLY INVITED TO GET SWEPT AWAY INTO NEW WORLDS OF PASSION AND ADVENTURE.

AND IT WON'T COST YOU A PENNY!

Receive 4 Zebra Historical Romances, Absolutely <u>Free!</u>

(A $19.96 value)

Now you can have your pick of handsome, noble adventurers with romance in their hearts and you on their minds. Zebra publishes Historical Romances That Burn With The Fire Of History by the world's finest romance authors.

This very special FREE offer entitles you to 4 Zebra novels at absolutely no cost, with no obligation to buy anything, ever. It's an offer designed to excite your most vivid dreams and desires...and save you almost $20!

And that's not all you get...

Your Home Subscription Saves You Money Every Month.

After you've enjoyed your initial FREE package of 4 books, you'll begin to receive monthly shipments of new Zebra titles. These novels are delivered direct to your home as soon as they are published...sometimes even before the bookstores get them! Each monthly shipment of 4 books will be yours to examine for 10 days. Then if you decide to keep the books, you'll pay the pre-ferred subscriber's price of just $4.00 per title. That's $16 for all 4 books...a savings of almost $4 off the publisher's price!

We Also Add To Your Savings With FREE Home Delivery!
There Is No Minimum Purchase. And Your Continued Satisfaction Is Guaranteed.

We're so sure that you'll appreciate the money-saving convenience of home delivery that we guarantee your complete satisfaction. You may return any shipment...for any reason...within 10 days and pay nothing that month. And if you want us to stop sending books, just say the word. There is no mini-mum number of books you must buy.

It's a no-lose proposition, so send for your 4 FREE books today!

YOU'RE GOING TO LOVE GETTING
4 FREE BOOKS

These books worth almost $20, are yours without cost or obligation
when you fill out and mail this certificate.
*(If the certificate is missing below, write to: Zebra Home Subscription Service, Inc.,
120 Brighton Road, P.O. Box 5214, Clifton, New Jersey 07015-5214*

Complete and mail this card to receive 4 Free books!

Yes! Please send me 4 Zebra Historical Romances without cost or obligation. I understand that each month thereafter I will be able to preview 4 new Zebra Historical Romances FREE for 10 days. Then, if I should decide to keep them, I will pay the money-saving preferred publisher's price of just $4.00 each...a total of $16. That's almost $4 less than the publisher's price, and there is no additional charge for shipping and handling. I may return any shipment within 10 days and owe nothing, and I may cancel this subscription at any time. The 4 FREE books will be mine to keep in any case.

Name _____

Address _____ Apt. _____

City _____ State _____ Zip _____

Telephone ( ) _____

Signature _____ LF0695
(If under 18, parent or guardian must sign.)

Terms, offer and prices subject to change without notice. Subscription subject to acceptance by Zebra Books. Zebra Books reserves the right to reject any order or cancel any subscription.

TREAT YOURSELF TO 4 FREE BOOKS.

A $19.96
value.
FREE!

No obligation
to buy
anything, ever.

ZEBRA HOME SUBSCRIPTION SERVICE, INC.

120 BRIGHTON ROAD

P.O. BOX 5214

CLIFTON, NEW JERSEY 07015-5214

to be interviewed by the detective. "Among the Layton residents already questioned by Detective Corsini," said the article, "are Alison Koff, Ms. Moloney's housekeeper; Todd Bennett, her research associate; and *Community Times* publisher Alistair P. Downs, the subject of her forth-coming book. Of the three, only Senator Downs can pro-vide proof of his whereabouts the night of the murder. Ms. Koff and Mr. Bennett maintain that they were alone in their respective homes on the night in question, but have no one to corroborate their alibis. Senator Downs, on the other hand, asserts that he spent the evening at the home of a 'lady friend,' and the woman has come forward to confirm that the Senator was her companion that night. As a result, Senator Downs is free of suspicion in the case."

Okay, so he was with a lady friend the night Melanie was murdered. Maybe he had someone else bop his evil biogra-pher on the noggin—like a Mafia hit man? Anything was possible, I was fast discovering. Even in the suburbs.

And who was this "lady friend"? Why wasn't her name divulged? Probably because Alistair told Corsini not to di-vulge it. What Alistair wants, Alistair gets.

What really pissed me off was the tone of the article. How dare the newspaper suggest that either Todd or I had some-thing to do with the murder? Talk about biased reporting. Talk about a libel suit!

Naturally, there was no byline for the article. Bethany was too chicken to put her own name on this filth, but I knew she was responsible for it. It had her sticky donut fingers all over it.

I put the newspaper down and went to the phone to return Detective Corsini's call. The direction his investiga-tion was taking was making me nervous. I knew I should get a lawyer—a very good lawyer—but how was I supposed to pay for one? A murder case was way too demanding for the ambulance chasers at Jacoby & Meyers. And I wasn't about to settle for those court-appointed attorneys who work for free but aren't exactly top of the line. Besides, after being snookered into signing that bogus prenuptial agreement by Sandy's high-priced lawyer, lawyers weren't exactly high on my list of reputable characters. Come to think of it, I didn't know which were lower on the food chain—lawyers or the media vultures camped outside my house.

"Corsini," came the voice on the phone.

"It's Alison Koff, returning your call, Detective. Your message said you had more questions to ask me. Frankly, I've told you all I know about Melanie and the day she died."

"You gotta come down to headquarters again. For drug testing. We wanna get a urine test and some other stuff from you."

"Drugs? I've never used drugs in my life!" Well, not really. You couldn't count the marijuana and hashish I smoked in college.

"You're not obligated to take these tests, Miss Koff. It's completely up to you. But if I were you, I'd take them—if you want to clear your name, that is."

"Of course I'll take them. I'll cooperate with your investigation in any way I can."

"Good. We'll need some hair samples too."

"With or without conditioner?"

"What did you say?"

"I said, 'My hair and I will be right over.'"

My Porsche cut a swath through the throng of reporters and photographers huddled outside my house as we wound our way down Maplebark Manor's driveway and out onto the street. I wondered when these vultures would finally get the message that I wasn't going to talk to them and disappear. Then I wondered when my life would return to normal. Then I wondered what "normal" was.

When I arrived at police headquarters, there was another

throng of reporters and photographers hovering outside Detective Corsini's office.

As the good detective opened the door of his office, they hurled questions and fired flashbulbs at him. He loved every minute of it.

"Is it true forensics found drugs at the crime scene?"

"Was Melanie Moloney a crackhead?"

"Was the murderer selling her coke?"

I listened with disbelief. Melanie on cocaine? I couldn't believe what I was hearing. Sure, she was tense and irritable all the time. But I'd assumed it was either because she was constipated, menopausal, or just born that way. It had never occurred to me that drugs were to blame for her awful behavior.

Besides, she was a health nut. She didn't smoke or drink, and she worked out regularly in the exercise room in her house. Maybe her murderer was into drugs, but I was sure she wasn't. Or maybe the Mafia hit man hired by Alistair had deliberately dusted her desk with cocaine.

"What's all this about drugs?" I whispered to one of the reporters.

"The police report released to the media this morning says they think they found cocaine on Moloney's desk," he informed me.

"Why do you say they *think* they found cocaine on her desk? Don't they know?"

"They've got to send the stuff out for evaluation."

"How long does that take?"

"Maybe six weeks. It's got to go to the state forensic lab in Meriden."

"Six weeks? The killer could be in Beirut by then."

The reporter flashed me a puzzled look. "Why would the killer go to Beirut? You think he was a Lebanese terrorist?"

"No, I was just making a joke."

"Oh. I get it."

"Good." The guy clearly needed cheering up. "That reminds me of another joke," I said. "You're in a room with a mass murderer, a terrorist, and a lawyer, and you have a gun with only two bullets in it. What do you do?"

"I dunno."

"Shoot the lawyer twice."

Again, a puzzled look.

"Never mind," I told the reporter. "It wasn't that funny anyway."

I hadn't told a joke in a while. Maybe I was rusty. Maybe my timing was off. Or maybe the guy was a big fan of lawyers. I had more important things to worry about—like urinating without further implicating myself in Melanie's murder. Who said life in the suburbs was dull?

Chapter 14

"How about letting me take you out to dinner tonight?"
Cullie said. We'd been on the phone for a half hour, regaling
each other with tales of our latest nightmares—mine having
to produce a urine specimen at the police station, his having
to put up with Mr. and Mrs. Ex-Stockbroker, who, after he
had taken his three A.M. shot of their moonlit living room,
insisted that he hang around until sunrise, so he could *really*
do the room justice.

"I accept, Mr. Harrington, but I don't expect you to take
me places or buy me things. I'm not into that stuff anymore."

"I hear you. But a quick bite at McGavin's won't com-
promise your newfound independence, will it?"

"You're on. Pick me up in an hour."

I was thrilled to spend the evening with Cullie after yet
another disconcerting day with Melanie's manuscript, the
second section of which I'd found time to read that morning. Since I'd hidden the book in the sauna, I'd decided to
kill two birds with one stone and read the manuscript while
I took a sauna. Unfortunately, I found the manuscript so
irresistible that I stayed in the sauna way too long and
nearly passed out from heat exhaustion.

The eye-popping allegation in the second section of the

book, which dealt with Alistair's political career, was that in the early fifties, when he was an increasingly sought-after member of the Hollywood community, the Senator-in-waiting was a snitch for Joseph McCarthy's Government Operations Committee, tipping the Committee off to the Communists among his fellow actors and ruining the careers of some of America's foremost entertainers. Melanie also claimed that he was a secret and active supporter of various white supremacy groups, and that the real reason he decided to retire from the Senate was that his involvement with such groups was about to be revealed to the public.

I was shocked. Sure, Alistair was a conservative Republican. So were most people in Layton. But a McCarthy witch hunter *and* a white supremacist? If what Melanie alleged was true, the man was a monster! Never mind the Mafia killing Melanie; Alistair himself probably murdered her. Alibi or no alibi, he probably slugged her in the head to keep her from ruining his reputation. Maybe he wasn't with a woman the night Melanie was murdered. Maybe there was no "lady friend." Maybe Alistair wrote a big fat check to Detective Joseph Corsini, the celebrity whore, and Corsini masterminded a big fat coverup of the truth.

What a scumball that Alistair is, I thought as I lay in the sauna, weak with dehydration. To think I'd worked for the man. To think my poor, unsuspecting mother had gone over to his house to discuss *my* future at his newspaper. To think he'd fooled our entire town—hell, our entire country—into believing he was some kind of hero, some kind of role model, some kind of moral leader. Talk about giving people the cha cha cha!

Cullie and I arrived at McGavin's at seven-thirty and were seated right away at a corner table. "Would you like something to drink?" the waiter asked.

"Mount Gay rum and tonic," we answered simultaneously, then giggled.

"Hey, when did you start drinking Mount Gay?" Cullie asked.

"On Maine Lobster Night."

"On what?"

"Forget it. I've decided I like Mount Gay. I've decided I like you too."

Cullie reached across the table for my hand and squeezed it. "I'm glad," he said and smiled.

We were about to inspect the menu when I spotted Julia getting up from her stool at the bar and heading toward the door. She was alone. "Hey, Applebaum!" I called out to her. I was hoping I'd run into her. We hadn't seen each other since news of Melanie's murder and my life as a maid hit the media. "Julia!" I called again, but she kept walking as if she hadn't heard me. "Julia!" I yelled, waving my arms to catch her attention. "Over here!"

She stopped and looked in my direction, but did not smile or even acknowledge me.

"Hey, it's me. Alison. Come join us," I yelled, waving her over to our table.

Then she gave me a truly bizarre look—a deer-caught-in-the-headlights look, a look that suggested I had nabbed her at something, something she was ashamed of or frightened about. "Hello, Koff," she said quickly. "Gotta go, sorry." Then she left the restaurant.

"I don't get it," I said to Cullie. "Julia's my friend. She'd never snub me."

"It didn't really seem like a snub," he offered. "Seemed more like a duck."

"I know. It seemed like she wanted to get away from me. Is it possible that she actually believes what she's read in the paper? Is it possible that my old friend Julia thinks I killed Melanie?"

"I'm sure that's not it, Sonny. Maybe she was just late for a date and couldn't take the time to chat."

"Maybe. The last time we talked, I got the feeling that she

was seeing somebody. But I couldn't get her to tell me who her mystery man was."

"There's got to be a reasonable explanation for her behavior," said Cullie. "Let's not let it ruin our evening, okay?"

"Okay."

The good news is that Julia didn't ruin our evening. The bad news is that somebody else almost did.

Cullie and I were taking the first bites out of our cheeseburgers when Sandy and the caterer-whore showed up. They were standing by the door, waiting for a table, and they appeared to be dressed as twins in matching purple ski outfits. They looked like a couple of eggplants.

"Oh, God," I gulped. "Don't turn around. My ex-husband is here with his expectant first wife."

It's a given. Somebody tells you not to turn around, you turn around. Cullie craned his neck to get a look at Sandy and Soozie. "That's your ex-husband? The guy with the tan?" he asked.

"Yeah. I hear business is so bad at his store that he's working part-time at the Layton Health Club in exchange for free use of their tanning bed. Amazing, huh?"

Before Cullie could answer, Sandy and Soozie were approaching our table. What the hell was my erstwhile second husband doing at McGavin's, I wondered, a restaurant he'd always referred to as "a hang-out for deadbeats"? In the old days, he wouldn't have set foot in the place.

"Good evening, Alison," Sandy said. "It's nice to see you getting out and enjoying yourself in these trying times. And this must be . . ." He turned to face Cullie.

" 'This' is Cullie Harrington," I said. "Cullie, meet Sandy Koff and his friend Diane." It was such fun pissing Soozie off by calling her by her dreaded real first name.

"Pleasure," Sandy said, shaking Cullie's hand. Soozie and I did not shake hands, we nodded.

"What brings you to McGavin's?" I asked. The Sandy I knew preferred eateries known for their Crusty Edged

Mako Shark with Caramelized Shallot Vinaigrette or their Charred Lamb Medallions with Pear Chutney and Deep-Fried Celery Root Chips.

"There's a new reality out there, Alison, and it's called a recession," Sandy explained in his most patronizing voice. "McGavin's intersects very well with the new reality. It's like I was telling Soozie on the way over here: life is about personal growth, and eating at McGavin's is part of that personal growth. Personal growth is about escaping from one's boundaries, breaking out of ruts, eating at restaurants one has never eaten at . . ."

I could tell by the way Cullie was gripping his cheese-burger that he was dying to mash it into Sandy's psychobabbling mouth. He restrained himself.

"But Sandy," I said. "Recession aside, you always despised restaurants that played rock 'n' roll music." McGavin's had a jukebox from which hits from the fifties, sixties, and seventies blared nonstop, and I had a hard time imagining Sandy putting up with it. He hated rock 'n' roll, especially soul music. When we were married, he wouldn't let me play it—even in the car.

"The food's not bad here," said Sandy, further explaining his appearance at McGavin's. "I try to deal with the background music the best I can. Life is full of irritants."

"You're telling me." Two of them were standing right in front of me.

Sandy's willingness to eat at McGavin's wasn't his only nod to the recession. His shoes were another tip-off that he had undergone a radical lifestyle change. Always a Gucci, Bally, or Cole-Haan man, Sandy appeared to be wearing a pair of penny loafers of the Kinney/Florsheim/Thom McCann variety. I was shocked. The old Sandy despised such shoes. In addition to his disdain for mall shoe stores, he had absolute contempt for pennies. I'm serious. Sandy hated pennies so much that when they began to accumulate in his pocket, he'd throw them out. I'd try to reason with him. "A hundred pennies make a dollar," I'd say. But he'd

ignore me. Oddly enough, he had a much higher regard for
nickels and dimes.

"What's that you've got there, Curly?" Sandy said, star-
ing hungrily at Cullie's plate.

"It's Cullie," Cullie corrected Sandy with a scowl.

"Cullie. Forgive me. What's that you're eating tonight?
Some sort of pâté au gratin on focaccio? It looks awfully
good."

"It's called a cheeseburger. It's tonight's 'Recession Special.' "

I burst out laughing, and laughed so hard everyone in the
place turned to see what was so funny. What was so funny
was that my ex-husband was so out of touch he didn't know
a fucking cheeseburger when he saw one. New reality, my
ass.

"Sandy," I said after I'd finally stopped laughing and
caught my breath. "Don't let us keep you from your meal.
You and Diane are eating for three now. Better get started."

Sandy glared at me. Then, as if remembering that the
diners at McGavin's might be observing him, scrutinizing
his every move, he forced his mouth into a beatific smile. "I
bid you peace," he said, forming a "V" with his fingers,
giving me the sixties peace sign and marching himself and
his first wife to their table.

"You were married to that?" Cullie said with a smirk.

"Hey, let's get a look at your ex-spouse before we start
dumping on mine, shall we?" I smirked back.

"Fair enough. But I doubt Preston will be walking into
McGavin's anytime soon. I heard she's living out in California now. La Jolla, to be exact."

"Tell me about her—if it isn't too painful."

"It's not painful at all. I haven't seen her in nine years.
And it's true what they say: time does heal."

"You met her at the Sachem Point Yacht Club, where
your father worked?"

"Yup. The Parkers were members. Still are, I guess. Preston took sailing lessons from my dad, and since I helped him

out sometimes, she also took lessons from me. One thing led to another and we got involved."

"Was she beautiful?"

"Very."

I felt a stab of jealousy, knowing myself to be attractive in an energetic sort of way but hardly beautiful. "So you two started dating after you taught her how to sail?"

"I wouldn't exactly call it dating. We didn't go out in public together. Her parents would have freaked. We saw each other on the sly. She'd sneak into my cottage at the club when my dad was out. Or I'd pick her up at some out of the way place and drive us somewhere. That kind of thing."

"But her parents must have found out about you eventually. You did get married, right?"

"Oh, we got married all right. Ceremony at their church, reception at the yacht club. The whole enchilada. You probably read about the wedding in *Town & Country* or on the society page of *The New York Times*. It was big stuff. All the Parkers' friends and family were there."

"What about your friends and family? Weren't the Harringtons represented there?"

"Paddy wanted his brother and sisters to fly over from Europe, but none of them could afford it. I'm sure the Parkers were glad. As far as they were concerned, the less said about the Harringtons, the better."

"I don't understand. If Preston's parents were so dead set against your romance, why did they throw you such a fancy wedding?"

"They had no choice. Preston was pregnant."

"Oh." I looked at the remnants of the cheeseburger on my plate and lost my appetite. So Cullie and Preston had a child. The man was full of surprises. "Is that why you married her? Because she was pregnant?"

"I can't say. I might have done it anyway. She was a wild, impulsive girl with a spontaneous approach to life that I lacked. I was very taken with her."

"Where's the child now? With Preston in La Jolla?"

"No, Preston miscarried a month after we got married. That's when the relationship started to go down the tubes."

"So soon?"

"We had nothing in common, except sailing. I got into photography and started making a name for myself. She spent her days having lunch with friends, visiting with Mummy and Daddy, and thinking about what she wanted to be when she grew up. The only time we connected was on the water, when we sailed."

"Then she must have loved it when you went up to Maine to buy the *Marlowe.*"

"She did, at first. That boat was supposed to be a joint effort. We were going to rebuild it together, then live on it together. But from the minute we gave up our house and settled in on *Marlowe,* it was easy to see we weren't going to make it. If you want to find out if you're compatible with a woman, go live on a boat with her."

"So she left you?"

"As fast as you can say, 'Daddy, get me a good divorce lawyer.' "

"Sorry."

"Don't be. I'm not. I wasn't the guy for her. The guy she's married to now is not only a billionaire businessman, he owns the *Sharpshooter.*"

"What's the *Sharpshooter?*"

"It's an eighty-foot sled, a racing boat that won the Trans-Pacific Cup three consecutive times. In other words, Sonny, the guy is keeping Preston in jewelry *and* silverware."

Sort of the way Sandy used to keep me. "Sorry," I said again.

The waiter came and took our plates away, then asked us if we wanted dessert or coffee. We didn't. Cullie paid the check and drove me home. When we pulled up to the front of Maplebark Manor, we were met by an angry swarm of reporters and TV cameras—angrier and more demanding than ever.

"Tell us how you killed her, Alison."

"Were you selling Moloney cocaine?"

"Are you a cokehead?"

The barrage of questions, which now incorporated the news that cocaine had been found on Melanie's desk, would not abate. I didn't know how I would cope with them. I was so sick of the media—never mind the police—breathing down my neck that I thought I'd scream.

"Maybe I should run away," I said to Cullie as we sat in his Jeep, afraid to venture out of the car and be forced to confront the vultures. "Maybe I should dye my hair, change my name, and go south."

"Mexico?"

"Nope. Can't drink the water. Maybe Florida. Palm Beach."

Cullie laughed. "I've got a better idea. Why not let me help you out?"

"Actually, this is all *your* fault in a way."

"My fault?"

"Yeah. If you hadn't insisted on bringing me home at eleven o'clock the night Melanie was murdered, these vultures would be hovering over someone else's house. If you had let me spend the night on the *Marlowe,* I'd have an alibi for Detective Corsini and none of these assholes would be bothering me. But nooooo. You said you had an important shoot first thing in the morning and had to take me home. So you see, it is all your fault."

Cullie looked stricken.

"Hey, I was only kidding. You couldn't help it if you had an early job the next morning. I don't blame you, really I don't."

"You sure?"

"I'm sure. Come here." I pulled Cullie's face toward mine and kissed him. "There, that'll give the TV cameras something to shoot."

"Sonny, I mean it about helping you. You need a place to escape, a place where these jerks won't bother you, a place where you can hang out until the police solve Melanie's murder."

"TV cameras are very portable; they can follow me everywhere."

"Not on my boat they can't. And the marina doesn't take kindly to trespassers. There's a security guard on duty every night."

"You're inviting me to move into the *Marlowe* with you?" I was surprised. Cullie and I had only been dating a few weeks. I'd assumed that cohabitating was the last thing on his mind.

"Don't get nervous, Sonny. This isn't a marriage proposal or anything. It's just an idea for giving you a little peace and quiet, so you can get your life together. Boats are great places for that."

"I don't know what to say. After what you told me about you and Preston, I'm not sure we'd make any better berth mates than you two did."

"Worth a try, don't you think?"

I looked at Cullie, then at the media camped outside Maplebark Manor, then back at Cullie. "You're on," I said. Cullie seemed pleased. "But not tonight. Tomorrow morning."

"Why not tonight?"

"I've got to pack."

"Sonny, you saw the *Marlowe*. It's not the *QE2,* it's a forty-foot sailboat. There's no room for a lot of stuff, so pack light."

"Aye aye, skipper." I threw my arms around Cullie's neck and kissed him. "Thank you," I whispered. "For everything."

"You're welcome. Should I pick you up in the morning?"

"Not necessary. I'll drive myself over to the marina." I kissed him again. " 'Night, skipper."

" 'Night, matey."

I let myself out of the Jeep and plowed through the reporters and camera crews until I got to the front door of Maplebark Manor. I waved good night to Cullie, went inside the house, and began to prepare for life aboard the *Marlowe.*

The next morning I loaded three Louis Vuitton bags into my car—one filled with basics (underwear, socks, sneakers, jeans, sweaters, T-shirts, a couple of paperback novels, and my new diary), another with toiletries, makeup, and my blowdryer, and a third with the complete Alistair Downs manuscript. Viewing my stay on the *Marlowe* as a sort of open-ended camping trip, I left the designer stuff at home.

When I arrived at the marina, Cullie was there waiting for me with a smile and a hug. But his mood changed when he saw all the luggage I'd brought with me.

"I told you to pack light."

"This is light—for me."

"Sonny, there isn't room for all three bags. Are they really necessary?"

I nodded.

"How about this one? What's in it?" He unzipped the bag containing my makeup and hair dryer.

Before I could stop him, he dumped all my cosmetics into the trunk of my car—my astringent, my moisturizer, even my Retin-A. I was furious.

"Why'd you do that?" I cried.

"You won't need all that on the *Marlowe,*" he explained. "I've got plenty of soap, toothpaste, and shampoo. The rest is bullshit."

"What about astringent? How do you expect me to keep my face tight?"

"It's called sea air. Step outside the boat in the morning and your face will get plenty tight."

"And my hair blower?"

"You'll be living on the *Marlowe,* not Maplebark Manor.

A boat's electrical circuitry is completely different from a house's. Oh, I could run out and spend two thousand dollars on an inverter so your hair blower would be compatible with *Marlowe*'s system. But guess what—I'm not going to. You'll just have to make do."

I shot Cullie a major-league pout.

"Come on, cheer up, Sonny. You won't miss your blow dryer one bit, I promise you. Whenever your hair needs blowing, *I'll* blow on it. It'll work fine, trust me."

"Yeah, I trust you, all right. You and Captain Queeg."

"Now, let's have a look at your other suitcases," he said. "I'll just unzip this one and—"

"Oh, no you don't!" I yelled, wresting the bag out of his hands. It was the one that contained the manuscript. I hadn't told a soul I stole it, and the way Cullie was acting, I certainly wasn't going to tell him. "Keep your hands off my things," I snapped. "If you touch my property once more, I'll go home and we can forget all about our little arrangement."

"Be my guest," he scoffed. "Go on home, if that's what you want to do. I'm sure you'll have a lot of fun dealing with the bank, the police, and the media people."

"I don't *have* to go home. I have other options."

"Oh, right. I forgot. You could always check into the Plaza Hotel."

"You know I don't have the money for that. But I could go and stay with my mother." I bit my tongue when I said that. I would rather have thrown all my suitcases into the Long Island Sound than move in with my mother.

What was going on here anyway? Cullie and I had been getting along so well. Sure, in the beginning we had our sparring contests, but we were over that, I thought. Maybe things were moving too fast. Maybe we weren't ready to live together, even temporarily. We were too different, too set in our ways, too inflexible.

"Look, Sonny," Cullie said, moving toward me. "I know all this is a real adjustment for you. I'm sorry if I came on too strong. But as I tried to explain to you, living aboard the *Marlowe* means changing your lifestyle a bit."

Cullie was right, of course. "I'm sorry," I said. "You were kind enough to help me out of a tough situation and I acted like Joan Collins on 'Dynasty.' I want another chance. Let's rewind the tape and start this whole scene over again."

"You're on," he said, brightening considerably.

"Good morning, skipper. Your first mate is ready to board," I said cheerfully, pretending I had just arrived at the marina.

"Right, matey."

Cullie carried one of the two remaining suitcases and I carried the other—the one with *Cha Cha Cha* in it. As we approached the slip where the *Marlowe* was docked, my pulse quickened. The truth was, I couldn't wait for this new adventure. I'd enjoyed spending time on the boat, and I was excited about learning how to live like a sailor. Most of all, I was excited about living with Cullie. Moving in with him on his boat was the most spontaneous thing I'd ever done.

"Home, sweet home," he said as we stepped down the hatch and entered the cabin.

"Oh, Cullie, a rose!" A vase containing a single, long-stemmed red rose rested on the dining room table.

"I wanted to welcome you to the *Marlowe* in the style to which I *know* you are accustomed," he said wryly.

"You're the best. The absolute best!" I kissed him. "Now, if you'll just show me where to put my things, I'll unpack these bags and get them out of your way."

Cullie led me to the bow of the boat and pointed out the small hanging locker located between the head and the V-berth. "You can put a few things in there," he said. "The rest of the stuff can go under the mattress in the V-berth."

I wasn't about to complain. I unpacked the bags and crammed my clothes into the meager space I was allotted. I left the Alistair Downs manuscript in its suitcase and stowed it at the bottom of the hanging locker. One of these days I'll get to it, I assured myself.

"Wow. I'm really here," I sighed. Cullie and I were sitting on one of the settee berths in the main salon.

"How does it feel?"

"A little strange, but exciting."

"Not claustrophobic yet?"

"Nope," I laughed.

"Not seasick?"

"Don't be silly."

"How about something to drink? Some juice or coffee? You're not a guest. Feel free to help yourself to anything that's here."

"Thanks," I said. "But to tell you the truth, what I'd really love is a nice hot shower. I left so early this morning, I didn't have time to take one. And in this freezing weather, a hot shower is a necessity—just to get your blood circulating."

"I agree," said Cullie. "It's only a five-minute walk."

"What's a five-minute walk?"

"To the showers."

"I don't understand. The head—isn't that what you sailors call it?—is right in there," I said, pointing toward the bow of the boat.

"Yeah, the head's in there, all right, but you can't use it. I closed off the water hoses for the winter. If I didn't, the water in the lines would freeze."

I panicked. "You mean there's no bathroom on this boat? No shower? No sink? No toilet?"

"That's what I mean."

"Are you saying that every time I have to go to the bathroom, I have to leave the boat?"

"That's what I'm saying. But like I said, the marina's public bathrooms are only a five-minute walk from our dock. And they have plenty of nice hot showers." Cullie smirked. I could tell he was having a ball.

"What about the kitchen—er, galley?" I asked frantically, hoping there was some mistake, hoping that any second Cullie would say "April Fool's" and we'd both have a good laugh at his joke. "You have running water in there. You cooked dinner for me, remember?"

"The galley's a whole different story. The water in there comes from the hot water heater."

"I see," I said dejectedly, seeing nothing but weeks of showering in a public bathroom at the Jessup Marina. "I guess I'll pass on the nice hot shower."

"Then how about some nice hot coffee?" Cullie asked, putting his arm around me and trying to jolly me out of my sour mood.

"How about a nice hot *Irish* coffee—and hold everything but the whiskey," I said glumly. Getting drunk seemed like an excellent alternative to showering in a public restroom.

"I'll make an Irish coffee for you," Cullie offered. "But then I've got to get going."

"Going? Where?" I said.

"To work."

"You're going to leave me here alone? Now? What if something goes wrong? What if the boat sinks? What if a band of pirates comes to pillage and plunder me?"

Cullie laughed, then hugged me tightly. "Nothing's going to happen, Sonny. You'll be just fine. *Marlowe* will take good care of you, I promise."

I wasn't so sure.

Cullie made the Irish coffee, kissed me goodbye, and left. Suddenly, I was all alone on a sailboat. His sailboat. The sailboat he'd spent ten years rebuilding. The sailboat that meant more to him than anything in the world. What if I damaged it in some way? What if I inadvertently flicked the wrong switch or turned on the gas and set the boat on fire? What if water started pouring into the cabin and the *Marlowe* went down? What if? What if? What if?

The more "what-ifs" I imagined, the more terrified I became. I became so terrified that I polished off the Irish coffee in under five minutes. Before I knew it, I was seasick, what with the boat rocking back and forth and the Irish whiskey sloshing around in my stomach. Minutes later, a new "what-if" invaded my mind: what if I had to throw up? *Where* would I throw up? The head was off limits, I'd just learned, and the galley was totally inappropriate. What was I going to do and where was I going to do it? In the public restrooms? I didn't even know where they were.

When I became certain that my nausea was stronger than my wish not to throw up, I grabbed my coat, climbed the stairs up the hatch, stepped off the boat, and ran across the marina parking lot as fast as my sea legs could carry me to a gray clapboard building, outside of which hung a sign: BOATERS WELCOME. I assumed it was the public restrooms. I prayed it was the public restrooms.

I charged inside, found an unoccupied toilet, flipped up the seat, and waited to be sick. Quick! A joke! A joke! I thought as I sat on the floor next to the toilet with my head hanging over the bowl. Quick! A joke! Don't let this situation get the best of you. Distract yourself. Think of something funny. Okay, okay. Here's a joke, Alison. Did you hear about the bulimic bachelor party? The cake came out of the girl.

Okay, so it wasn't a great joke. What do you expect from a person whose head is hanging over a toilet bowl, superior material?

The bad news was that seconds after I delivered that lame punch line, I got sick. The good news was that now I knew where the public restrooms were.

Chapter 15

Life on the *Marlowe* improved dramatically after that first rocky day. For one thing, I never got seasick again. For another, I, Alison Waxman Koff, a lifelong landlubber who didn't know a boom from a bilge or a helm from a halyard, discovered that I loved living on a sailboat.

I was so at peace there, so content playing Robinson Crusoe, so removed from the chaos that had surrounded my life at Maplebark Manor, that it was a terrible struggle to plug myself back into the world of bank officers and police detectives and media vultures. And instead of missing my creature comforts, as I thought I would, I found that I felt liberated without them. Cullie was right: who needed astringent to keep your skin tight when you had sea air?

Best of all was how well Cullie and I got along. Once we moved past our initial bickering and awkwardness, we coexisted as if we'd been together all our lives. Never once did I feel trapped or overwhelmed or even bored. I missed Cullie when he was gone and looked forward to his return. And from the enthusiastic way he greeted me each evening, I knew he felt the same.

Over the next few weeks, I became more and more at home on the boat, more and more accepting of my daily trips to the public restrooms, more and more grateful to Cullie for allowing me to share his special place. By the middle of March, we had settled into a comfortable and thoroughly enjoyable daily routine. We'd wake up next to each other in the V-berth, make love if there was time, or head for the showers if there wasn't. Then we'd come back to the boat, cook breakfast, do the dishes, and perform whatever chores needed to be done—straightening up the boat, deciding who would do the shopping, refilling the kerosene lamps, and pumping out the bilge. Then we'd gather at Cullie's navigation station and use his cellular phone—he to confirm his photographic assignments and plan his shooting schedule, I to retrieve the messages on my answering machine and respond to ads for jobs. Yes, jobs. I was determined not to let Cullie pay my way. I'd been a kept woman long enough.

Of course, leaving the boat to go job hunting, only to have my prospective employer slam the door in my face when he realized I was The Maid Suspected Of Killing Melanie Moloney, was my least favorite part of the day. I wasn't crazy about having to keep popping over to the police station so Detective Corsini could test another one of my hair follicles either. From what I'd read in the *Community Times,* the police were no closer to nabbing Melanie's murderer than they were to establishing a motive for the killing—or should I say, *the* motive for the killing. The problem was that all the people Corsini interviewed about the murder had a motive for killing poor Melanie. The fact that everybody hated her made his job next to impossible. He kept telling the media that as soon as his drug tests and hair samples were evaluated by the state police lab in Meriden, he'd have his murderer. But that could take another month, and as I'd told that reporter, the murderer could be in Beirut by then.

Which was why I kept going back over the first two sections of Melanie's manuscript, scouring them for my own clues to her murder. I was no Miss Marple, but every time Cullie would leave me alone on the boat, I'd scurry over to the hanging locker next to the head, pull out the suitcase containing the manuscript, and read a few pages, hoping to seize on some specific aspect of Alistair's sham of a life that would confirm his role in her demise. So far, what I'd learned was that he was a mobster and a bigot. Not great entries on a résumé, but did he kill her? Did one of his cronies? I couldn't be sure. I was looking forward to reading the third section of the book, which dealt with his personal life. Unfortunately, every time I'd start to dip into it, Cullie would come home and I'd have to stuff it back in the suitcase. He had no idea that I'd stolen the manuscript from Melanie's house and that it was sitting right under his nose. There didn't seem to be any point in involving him or getting him in trouble with the police, who, according to the *Community Times,* finally realized it was missing after interviewing Todd Bennett, as well as Melanie's agent and publisher—none of whom claimed to have seen it.

That's funny, I thought when I saw the article. Todd had told me he was home reading *Cha Cha Cha* the night Melanie was murdered. Somebody was lying. What did it mean? Obviously, Melanie had known the murderer was after the manuscript, or she wouldn't have hidden it under her bed. But who was after it? And why? It was time to finish the damn book and find out.

I kept trying to get to the third section of the manuscript, but I was constantly interrupted. Take the time I had just settled onto the V-berth with the book when Cullie's phone rang. It was my fourth week aboard the *Marlowe*—a sunny Saturday morning. I thought about letting his answering machine pick it up, since he was out on a shoot, but decided to take the call myself.

"Is Alison there?" said the woman on the phone.

"This is she," I said.

"You called about our ad in the *Community Times?* For an au pair?"

"Oh, yes, I did. Last week." The ad was for an au pair who would take care of a working couple's two kids three days a week. I didn't have any experience being an au pair, but au pair, shmau pair. A babysitter was a babysitter, I figured, and called the number in the ad. So I'd be babysitting a couple of kids while their yuppie parents were at work. It wasn't brain surgery, but it had to be more challenging than scrubbing Melanie's toilets, right?

"Would you like to come and meet the children?" the woman asked.

"Oh, yes," I said, thrilled that the woman neither asked about my previous experience with children, nor expressed concern that I was Alison Koff, the murderous maid. Maybe she was too busy to watch tabloid television shows, what with a job, a husband, and two kids to worry about.

"Good," she said. "Our address is 102 Harborview Terrace. The name is on the mailbox: Silverberg."

Harborview Terrace was one of Layton's premier addresses. Obviously, the Silverbergs weren't poor. I had no idea what kind of money au pairs got away with charging, but I assumed that if I landed the job, I'd have no trouble keeping Cullie and me in chicken cacciatore. "What time would you like me to stop by?" I asked.

"Could you come now?" she said rather plaintively. "I'm in a bit of a bind today. My husband's out of town, I've got a meeting with a client in an hour and there's nobody to stay with the children. If they like you and vice versa, perhaps you could start right away."

"I'll be there in fifteen minutes," I said. What a break. All I had to do was make nice to the little kiddies and I was hired!

102 Harborview Terrace was an antique saltbox with a "winter view" of the Long Island Sound—i.e., you could see the water from the house only when there were no leaves on the trees. Often referred to as the John Hoggins Homestead, it was built in 1767 by the first minister of the Christ Episcopal Church in Layton, who had inherited the land from his father, a staunch Loyalist and supporter of the King of England during the Revolution. Despite the fact that the

British burned much of Layton in 1779, the house was spared the Redcoats' torch and remained in the Hoggins family until 1850. Subsequent owners took great care to preserve its period flavor, which brings us to the Silverbergs, who, I was dismayed to find, had given the John Hoggins Homestead a spin all their own. Oh, the wideboard flooring, chair rail moldings, exposed beams, and beehive ovens were still in place. But the Silverbergs' idea of preserving authentic period detail was to throw every cutesy thing they'd ever seen in *Country Living* magazine at the place—quilts, decoys, straw baskets, corner cabinets, rocking chairs, American flags, you get the picture. But here's where the decor got really nauseating. The Silverbergs' idea of updating the house was to install the trendiest amenities of the nineties right alongside the authentic period detail: track lights sitting atop rough-hewn beams, a Jennaire oven inside the beehive oven, wall-to-wall carpeting over the wideboard floors, and so on. But hey, it was the Silverbergs' house. Taste or no taste, they had a right to trash the place if they wanted to.

"Please come in," said Mrs. Silverberg as she opened the (what else) paneled antique front door with American flag hanging overhead.

"Thanks," I said. "I'm Alison Koff. Nice to meet you." I braced myself for a reaction, expecting her to recoil at the sound of my name, but she didn't. Maybe she was new in town.

"Let me get the children," she said quickly, appearing somewhat frazzled. She was thirtysomething, with bushy, shoulder-length auburn hair held in place by a pink velvet headband. She wore wire-rimmed glasses of the type that Gloria Steinem used to wear before she realized it was okay for America's most famous feminist to wear contact lenses. Her outfit was pure Laura Ashley—from her ruffled pink-and-green-flowered blouse to the matching pink-and-green, mid-calf-length flowered skirt, under which she wore brown leather riding boots. Oh, and let's not forget the pearls—a thin strand around her neck, tiny studs in her earlobes. It struck me that Mrs. Silverberg wanted very much to appear authentic, but authentic what I couldn't figure out.

"What are the children's names?" I asked before she could hurry out of the foyer, which was so crammed with wood-painted ducks I could practically hear their quacking.

"Tiffany and Amber," she said proudly. "Our two little angels."

Tiffany and Amber Silverberg. And I thought putting wall-to-wall carpeting over wideboard floors was a mixed metaphor.

Mrs. Silverberg ushered me into the living room and suggested I wait there while she fetched Tiffany and Amber, who, she explained, were playing upstairs with their brand-new Barbie doll, a gift from their doting father who was nowhere to be seen. Tiffany, she also explained, was six; Amber, five.

Playing upstairs with their Barbie doll? This job's gonna be a snap, I thought, imagining the two little girls taking turns combing Barbie's long, blond, dynel hair, dressing her anatomically correct body in tacky, gold-sequined evening gowns, and leaving me mercifully alone while their mother went off to her meeting.

As I waited for them to come down and meet Auntie Alison, I spotted yet another Revolutionary War artifact resting next to the stone fireplace: an honest-to-goodness musket! I hoped it wasn't loaded.

"Girls, this is Alison. Say hello," said Mrs. Silverberg as she led Tiffany and Amber into the living room to meet me.

They said hello and curtsied. No kidding. Not only that, they were dressed in the same identical outfits as their mother—right down to the pink velvet headbands that adorned their long, bushy auburn hair. They weren't wearing their mother's riding boots, however. Their feet were in black patent leather Mary Janes. But they looked enough like miniature Mrs. Silverbergs to make the whole thing a tad bizarre. Why they were so dressed up to sit around the house on a Saturday morning was beyond me. Maybe the Silverbergs were just a very formal, very civilized, very perfectionist family, I thought. And maybe their children were better behaved than most. I congratulated myself on finding this job, which I was now more certain than ever would be a piece of cake.

"Nice to meet you girls," I said, kneeling so I'd be closer to them in height. "I hear you've got a new Barbie doll. Want to take me upstairs and show me?"

"Can we, Mommy?" Tiffany said eagerly.

"Oh, please, Mommy," Amber added.

Mrs. Silverberg nodded. "I'll hang around for another ten minutes or so," she whispered to me. "Just to make sure everything's all right."

"Great," I said. Tiffany took one of my hands, Amber the other, and both sisters led me up the stairs to Tiffany's room, a large pink affair filled with enough "children's product" to rival Toys Я Us. "My, what a pretty room," I said.

"Thank you," Tiffany said politely. "Amber's room is pretty too."

"I bet it is." I couldn't get over how well mannered these girls were.

The three of us sat on the floor and bonded for several minutes. Tiffany showed me some of Barbie's clothes, while Amber let her stuffed Mutant Ninja Turtle sit on my lap. After a while, Mrs. Silverberg came upstairs and asked her daughters how they liked their new friend Alison.

"She's neat," Tiffany exulted.

"Yeah, neat," Amber echoed.

I was touched.

"Why don't we talk for a few moments, then I'll go," said Mrs. Silverberg, motioning for me to follow her downstairs.

When we got to the first floor, Mrs. Silverberg took me into the kitchen and explained that she and her family had indeed just moved to town and hadn't been in their new house long enough to find an au pair for the girls. Then she asked me for a reference. I stalled. I hedged. I tried to change the subject by asking her who sold her her house. "Janet Claiborne of Prestige Properties," she said. I was in luck. "I have a reference for you to call," I said with relief. "Janet Claiborne is my realtor too." "Oh," she said. "If you know Janet, then everything's fine. We found her to be a fine person and an excellent realtor." Maybe Mrs. Silverberg was a better mother than she was a judge of realtors.

The question of my references behind us, she showed me around the kitchen and pointed out the egg salad she had prepared for the girls' luncheon sandwiches. Then she wrote down the phone number where she could be reached for the next three hours or so.

"We'll consider today a trial run," she said. "If it works, we'll discuss a more permanent arrangement, all right?"

"Sure." I finally had a job.

At around eleven o'clock Mrs. Silverberg, who said she was an interior decorator and her absent husband was a gastroenterologist, departed for her meeting and left me to care for her little angels. I checked my watch. Three hours with a couple of well-mannered kids. Easy money.

I went back upstairs to Tiffany's room to resume our fun and games. The girls weren't there.

"Tiffany? Amber? Where are you, sweetie pies?"

No answer.

"Are we playing a little hide and seek?" I called out as I roamed the hall, sticking my head into all four bedrooms on the second floor.

No answer.

"Alison has a surprise for Tiffany and Amber," I lied, thinking I could lure the kids out of their hiding place by promising them something. I'd decide what the something was when the time came.

No answer.

"Okay then. If you girls don't want my surprise, I guess I'll just go downstairs and have a soda or something."

I started to walk down the stairs when both girls jumped

out from behind me and screamed "Boo!" in my ears. I almost fell down the stairs. I almost went deaf. I almost killed them. Instead, I smiled. "Well, well. There you are," I said sweetly. "How about going back into Tiffany's room and playing with Barbie some more?"

"We want the surprise," Tiffany, the ringleader, demanded.

"Yeah, the surprise," Amber said.

"Oh, yes," I said. "The surprise is . . . uh . . . uh . . . that I'll tell you all about the dolls I used to play with when I was your age."

"Boring," said Tiffany.

"Yeah, bor-ing," Amber copied her sister.

"I bet she never had any surprise," Tiffany scowled. "She's nothing but a big, fat liar."

"Yeah, and a big, fat turd," added Amber.

So much for their impeccable manners. "That's not very nice," I said gently, reaching out to pat Amber on the head and reestablish our previous good feelings toward each other. Bad move: Amber tried to bite my hand.

"Hey," I snapped. "Cut that out, okay?"

"You can't tell my sister what to do," Tiffany sniffed as she tried to push me down the stairs.

"What do you think you're doing?" I yelled. "Do you want me to call your mother?" Yeah, I know. The old Do You Want Me to Call Your Mother threat was pretty tired, but in this case it worked—temporarily. The girls agreed to go back to Tiffany's room if I promised to go with them. I did.

"How about a game of Chutes and Ladders," I suggested, spotting the board game on Tiffany's shelf.

"That's for babies," Amber whined. "Let's play doody bombs." Obviously, Amber had a waste-product fixation. Perhaps she'd been reading her father's medical texts.

"Yeah, doody bombs!" Tiffany cheered, then proceeded to pick her nose and wipe the result on her Laura Ashley skirt.

"Ooh, look what Tiffany did," Amber sneered. "Tiffany is a big fat booger snot. Nah-nah na-*nah*-nah."

"Come on, girls. Enough with that talk," I said impatiently. "Tiffany, please go into the bathroom and wash your hands."

"Tiffany, please go into the bathroom and wash your hands," Tiffany mimicked me.

"I mean it. Good hygiene is very important," I said.

"I mean it. Good hygiene is very important," she mimicked me again.

"I'm going downstairs," I said.

"I'm going downstairs," Tiffany said.

"Make us our egg salad sandwiches now," Amber commanded.

I was so grateful for the break in the mimicking that I agreed to make them lunch. It was only eleven-fifteen, but I hoped that stuffing the mouths of these brats would somehow shut them up.

Tiffany and Amber spun around the kitchen in circles, trying to make themselves dizzy, as I attempted to spread the egg salad their mother had made for them on the Wonder Bread she'd left out on the counter.

"Okay, girls. Here are your sandwiches. Come sit down," I said, motioning for them to sit at the authentic Shaker breakfast table that occupied a corner of the kitchen.

Tiffany and Amber scrambled to the table, each fighting for a place on the same chair.

"It's *my* seat," Tiffany screamed.

"No, *mine!*" her sister whined.

Before I could intercede, Tiffany had punched Amber in the arm and made her cry.

"She socked me," Amber wailed, rubbing her arm.

"Come on, you two. Eat your sandwiches," I said, ignoring Amber's tears.

They each took a seat at the table, as did I.

"Look-y look-y, Alison," Amber said after biting into her sandwich.

"Oh, gross," Tiffany snorted. Amber, it seemed, had opened her mouth and exposed her half-eaten egg salad sandwich in all its mushy yellow glory.

"That's not polite," I said to Amber.

"That's not polite," Tiffany mimicked me. We were back to square one.

I checked my watch. It was only eleven-forty. I wanted to go back to the boat. I wasn't the au pair type.

"Give me some soda," Tiffany ordered.

"How about saying please?" I suggested.

"Pleeeese," Tiffany said, then stuck her fingers up her nose.

I got up and walked toward the refrigerator. When I started to pull out a Pepsi, Tiffany yelled, "No. I want a Sprite."

I put the Pepsi back and fished deeper into the refrigerator for a Sprite.

"Nooo," she wailed. "I want a Pepsi."

I put the Sprite back and took out the Pepsi.

"I said I wanted a Sprite," she screamed.

That was it. I snapped, I admit it. Maybe it was my lack of experience in dealing with children or maybe it was my recent and frustrating brush with the law that had put me on a short fuse, but I opened both the Pepsi and the Sprite bottles and dumped their contents on the pink-velvet head-banded heads of Tiffany and Amber Silverberg. "You wanted some soda? You got it," I said, and began to make myself an egg salad sandwich.

"You got our clothes all dirty," Tiffany wailed after several seconds of silence. My unexpected act of retaliation seemed to have sent both girls into shock.

"Yeah, and our hair's dirty too," said Amber.

"Yeah, and the kitchen table's all sticky," Tiffany added.

"I'll make you both a deal," I said. "You promise to behave yourselves from now on and I'll let you go upstairs and change your clothes. You didn't really want to wear those fancy outfits on a Saturday, did you?"

"Noooo. Mommy made us," Tiffany said.

"She said we had to look nice for the new babysitter," Amber added.

"Well, the new babysitter says you can wear whatever you like."

"We can?" they squealed.

"Sure."

"Anything we want?" Tiffany asked.

"Yup. Now go upstairs and change your clothes while I clean up the kitchen, okay?"

"Yeah! Let's go," said Tiffany.

"I'm coming," said Amber.

And off they went. Alone at last. I finished my sandwich and wiped the soda off the table. Then I listened. The monsters were quiet. I commended myself for my handling of the situation. No, Dr. Spock wouldn't have approved, but I had found a way to shut the brats up and keep them busy for at least another hour or so.

At one o'clock I went upstairs to check on the girls. They weren't in either of their rooms. From the wet towels strewn across the floor of their bathroom, I guessed that they had attempted to wash their hair. But what they had done with themselves after that, I couldn't guess.

"Tiffany? Amber? Where are you?" I called out.

"In here! In Mommy's closet!" one of them yelled back.

I followed the voice and walked to the end of the hallway, into the master bedroom.

"In here, Alison!" Tiffany said. "Look at us!"

I found the girls. They had indeed changed their clothes. They were now decked out in their mother's evening gowns, complete with long, white gloves, high-heeled shoes, and glittery purses. They had painted themselves with their mother's makeup too—red lipstick, blue eyeshadow, black eyebrow pencil. I was sure Mrs. Silverberg would have a fit if she saw them, but I laughed so hard I could barely breathe. They looked adorable.

"Dahlings," I said, batting my eyelashes and playing the

grand society lady. "How mahvelous to see you both again. You do look ravishing."

The girls grinned and played along.

"Have you seen Barbie yet?" Tiffany asked.

"No, but I heard she was at the pahty," I said. "Shall we check the other rooms?"

"Yeah, let's find Barbie," Amber said.

I led the way to Tiffany's bedroom, where I had last seen the new Barbie doll. "Here she is, ladies. Barbie? Is that you, dahling?"

Tiffany and Amber chatted with Barbie and me. Then I started singing "The Itsy Bitsy Spider"—the only children's song I could think of—and invited both girls to dance with me. They accepted with delight. We took turns on the dance floor. I'd waltz Tiffany around the room, while Amber danced with Barbie. Then we'd switch partners. We were having so much fun that none of us heard Mrs. Silverberg come home. As I guessed, she didn't find her daughters' attire as amusing as I did. Apparently, her closets were off limits.

"But Alison told us to change our clothes," Tiffany wailed after her mother scolded her and forbade her from playing Nintendo for a month.

"Yeah. She said we could put on whatever we wanted after she dumped soda on our heads," Amber added.

"Dumped soda on your heads?" Mrs. Silverberg said.

"That's right," I admitted. "But you see—"

"Dumping soda on children is abuse, pure and simple," she said.

"I think punishing children for playing dress-up is abuse, pure and simple," I countered.

"Here," she said and handed me a fifty-dollar bill. "I'm afraid I'll have to make other arrangements for the girls. You can show yourself out."

So I was out of a job. What else was new?

* * *

The next morning, Cullie was up and dressed before I was.

"Hey, Sonny girl. It's seven o'clock," he said, tousling my hair as I lay in the berth. "It's gorgeous out. I had the VHF radio on, and they say it's going to be ten knots and sixty degrees—a perfect day for a sail."

"Sixty degrees? Can't be. It's only the end of March. Too cold to go sailing," I said, still half asleep.

"I'm telling you, babe. It's one of those freakish winter days out there—fifty degrees already. I've got one house to shoot and then we're out of here."

"Really? We're going sailing? Today?" I was wide awake now. The thought of finally taking the *Marlowe* sailing after weeks of talking about it was exhilarating.

"Yup. You get dressed and I'll be back in a couple of hours. I'll stop on the way home and pick up some provisions. Then you'll help me get the boat ready and off we'll go."

"Aye aye, skipper."

"Bye, matey." Cullie kissed me goodbye and left.

I bolted out of the berth, threw on a sweatshirt and sweatpants, and headed for the restrooms. By eight o'clock, I was showered, dressed, and ready for my first sailing adventure. But Cullie wasn't due back for another hour.

I decided to kill time by reading more of Melanie's manuscript.

I reached down into the hanging locker and pulled out the suitcase. Then I unzipped it and lifted out the manuscript. I settled into my usual reading position on the berth and began the third section of the book, the one entitled "The Personal Life."

The first couple of chapters chronicled Alistair's childhood as a somewhat rebellious Irish kid in Queens, who spent more time in the street than he did in school. The book went on to describe his teenage years, his interest in movies, his talent for dancing, and his stint as a teacher at the local Arthur Murray Dance Studio. No big revelations there. But then Melanie really let the sleaze fly. According to her, young Al Downey wasn't just a dance instructor; he was a gigolo, who was paid to do a lot more than dance with the ladies from Queens. As if that piece of dirt wasn't sleazy enough, Melanie also claimed he had an affair with a male dance instructor at the studio—and also with the male dance instructor's sister!

God, how do people stand books like this? I muttered. The whole exposé concept revolted me. And to think I had aspirations of becoming Melanie's collaborator, of seeing my name appear beside hers on the cover of a book like this. What could I have been thinking? I *know* what I was thinking: of money. People get rich writing sleazy biographies. But not me. I'd get rich some other way. Or maybe I wouldn't get rich at all. Maybe getting rich wasn't all it was cracked up to be.

I got up to get a glass of orange juice, then went back to the berth and picked up the manuscript. Okay, I told myself. Keep slogging through this thing. There may be a clue to Melanie's murder in here somewhere.

I was about to read on when I realized I couldn't: the rest of the section was missing! All that remained were about fifty pages of Melanie's bibliography, her notes and sources, and her acknowledgments. That left over a hundred pages of section three unaccounted for—a hundred pages that presumably would have dissected Alistair's marriage to Annette Dowling, the birth of their darling daughter Bethany, Annette's tragic death, and juicy details about the women he'd bedded after she died. Where were these pages?

I thumbed through the whole manuscript to make sure the missing pages hadn't gotten mixed up in the previous sections of the book. They hadn't. They were gone. But where?

Okay, calm down, I told myself. Maybe Melanie never finished the book. Just because Todd *said* it was finished didn't mean it was. After the way he lied about having the original manuscript at his house the night Melanie was murdered, I didn't believe anything he said. Maybe the missing pages had somehow gotten separated from the rest of the manuscript. Maybe they were still in my sauna at Maplebark Manor, or under the seats of my Porsche, or under Melanie's bed at Bluefish Cove. Or maybe they were right here on the boat.

I raced over to the hanging locker and checked to see if there were any stray pages on the floor. Nothing. Then I checked my suitcase. Empty. I was about to thumb through the manuscript one more time when I heard Cullie step onto the deck of the *Marlowe*. I shoved the manuscript back into the suitcase and returned it to the floor of the hanging locker, just in time to greet Cullie as he came down the hatch.

"Ready for your first sail, matey?" he said cheerfully. "I've got turkey sandwiches and potato chips and plenty of ice cold Heineken. We're going to have ourselves a good time!"

I hugged him around the waist. "I can't wait. When do we leave?"

"As soon as we prepare the boat. Poor *Marlowe* hasn't been out all winter."

I helped Cullie remove the boat's canvas cover, then watched carefully as he put the three sails on.

"Schooners have two masts and three sails," he explained. "This sail's called the jib, this one's the staysail, and this one's the mainsail. Got that?"

"Yup."

"Now I'll turn on the engine and let it warm up awhile," he continued. "Diesels take warming up."

"What should I do?" I asked as we stood in the cockpit. I was eager to be more than a spectator.

"You're going to steer us out of here, while I take in the dock lines," Cullie said, putting both my hands on the teak steering wheel.

"I am?" I said with alarm. "But I've never steered a boat before."

"Great. Then this will be a new experience for you."

"But what if I put a dent in the boat?"

"Tell you what," Cullie said, sensing my panic. "I'll back us out of the slip. Then you can take over."

Cullie put the engine in reverse and backed the boat out of the slip away from the dock. When we were out in the Long Island Sound, a safe distance from the marina, he placed my hands back on the steering wheel. "Your turn," he said.

"Tell me what to do."

"See those red and green buoys out there? Just stay between them. We're only going about four miles per hour, so you shouldn't have any problem. Just take us through the buoys while I go up on deck and hoist the sails."

With the sun on my face and the wind in my hair, I clutched the steering wheel and felt a surge of excitement. I, Alison Waxman Koff, the least adventurous, most predictable person I knew, was at the helm of an Alden schooner. I was out on the Long Island Sound on an unseasonably warm March day, guiding the very vessel that had been my home for weeks. The thrill was indescribable. But what really captivated me was the sight of Cullie hoisting all three sails. There they were—the jib, the staysail, and the mainsail, flapping in the wind, crackling and snapping against the brilliant blue sky. Their majesty took my breath away.

Cullie came into the cockpit and shut off the engine. Then he showed me how to trim the sails and taught me all about winches and sheets. "We're under sail," he exulted, gazing out at the sea. "Is this the most fantastic experience you've ever had, or what?"

"It is. It really is."

"The first sail of the season is always special. I'm so glad you're here to share it with me, Sonny." He kissed me. "If anybody told me I'd be out for a late-winter sail with the mistress of Maplebark Manor, I would have said they were crazy."

I elbowed him in the ribs. "We've come a long way, haven't we?"

"Yup. And we're going to keep going."

A profound sense of quiet surrounded us as the wind filled the sails and the *Marlowe* surged forth upon the waters of the Long Island Sound. As we sailed along, the boat began to tip over on its side. The motion scared me.

"We're going overboard," I cried, tugging on the sleeve of Cullie's windbreaker.

"It's called heeling," he explained. "The wind pushes on the sails and makes it *seem* like the boat's going to tip over but it won't, I promise you."

"How do you know? It sure feels like we're going overboard."

"The ten thousand pounds of lead in the bottom of the keel will keep us upright. Trust me."

"I do. I do." The truth was, I did. I trusted Cullie in a way I hadn't allowed myself to trust any man before. The realization surprised and excited me.

We sailed along the Connecticut coastline as sounds of Jimmy Buffett, James Taylor, and the Everly Brothers serenaded us from the stereo in the cabin. At about one o'clock, we ate our lunch in the cockpit and toasted our first sail together with a cold beer.

"Life doesn't get much better than this," Cullie said.

"I don't ever want to go back," I said. "Being out on the boat makes me feel so . . . so . . ."

"So free?" Cullie volunteered.

"Yeah, and so powerful. Out here, I feel like I could accomplish anything."

Cullie nodded in assent. "Come here," he said, motioning for me to come into his arms.

I let him wrap me in his arms and hold me for several seconds. This feels so good, so right, I thought. "Cullie," I said haltingly. "I . . . I . . ."

"Me too," he whispered.

Was it love we were feeling but afraid to verbalize? Or just the intoxication of a March sail, or the newness of our relationship? Time would hold the answer, I knew. Time would hold the answer to a lot of my questions.

"Whoah," I said, clinging to Cullie for dear life as the boat heeled. "I trust you, really I do, but are you sure this thing isn't going to tip over?"

"I'm sure," he laughed.

"Where are we anyway?" I asked, shielding my eyes from the sun as I peered out over the horizon.

"About midway between the Connecticut and Long Island coastlines."

"How can you tell? I can't see anything."

"If you go down into the cabin, to my navigation station, you'll find a chart that'll tell you exactly where we are. Bring it up and I'll show you."

"You have a lot of charts. Which one do you want me to get?"

"The one marked 'Western Long Island Sound.' "

I climbed down the hatch into the cabin and rummaged around in Cullie's navigation station but couldn't locate the chart he mentioned.

"Can't find it," I called up to him.

"It's there somewhere. Try lifting the top of the desk and seeing if it's in there. The drawer's a mess, but you should be able to find it."

I went back down into the cabin, into the navigation station, and lifted the top of the desk, as Cullie had instructed me to do. He was right, the drawer was a mess. Papers and charts were scattered everywhere.

As I fished around in the drawer, my hand rested on a small stack of papers held together by a rubber band. Thinking the stack might contain the chart I was looking for, I pulled it out. To my utter shock, it wasn't a pile of navigation charts at all—it was the missing pages of Melanie's manuscript!

What on earth were they doing in Cullie's desk? I asked myself. What possible interest could he have in Melanie's

book about Alistair? And why was it the third section of the
book that he was hiding in his desk? Why had Cullie stolen
these particular pages out of my suitcase?

I was dizzy with questions. As the boat heeled, I fell
across the cabin, nearly hitting my head against the pantry
in the galley. Easy, Alison baby, I told myself. Don't jump
to conclusions. There's got to be a reasonable explanation
for all this. You love Cullie. You trust him. He wouldn't lie
to you. He wouldn't hurt you. So what was he doing with
a section of Melanie's manuscript, a manuscript that would
undoubtedly damage Alistair Downs's reputation?

Did Cullie plan to leak the pages to the media in an effort
to ruin Alistair? Did he hate the man that much? Or did he
mean to hide something from me—something in the manuscript he desperately didn't want *me* to read? But what?

I sat on the settee berth and tried to steady myself. I began
to reflect on the months I'd known Cullie. I flashed back to
the day he came to photograph my house . . . to the night
we ran into each other at McGavin's when I was with Julia
and he was with Hadley Kittredge, the dockmaster's daughter . . . to the afternoon he showed up at Melanie's when I
answered the door in my maid's uniform . . . to our first
dinner together on the *Marlowe* when he voiced his contempt for Alistair and bombarded me with questions about
Melanie's book . . . to the night Melanie was murdered
when he brought me home instead of letting me sleep with
him on the boat . . . to the night he invited me to move in
with him on the *Marlowe* when I was being hounded by the
media.

Something about Cullie's interest in me just didn't play.
When we met, he was openly antagonistic toward me. Then
he found out I worked for Melanie and invited me to have
dinner on his boat. Then he showed up at Maplebark
Manor bearing gifts and take-out dinners. Then he asked
me to move in with him. Why? I asked myself. Why the
sudden interest?

And why had Cullie really come to Melanie's house the

day he found me dressed as a maid? He'd said he was there to shoot her house for a real estate brochure. But where was his equipment? He'd come empty handed. And why didn't the security guard at the Bluefish Cove gatehouse phone ahead to let us know Cullie was coming? Nobody was allowed into Bluefish Cove without a pass or a phone call. What's more, Melanie had never mentioned anything about a photo shoot. If she'd been expecting a photographer, she would have had me Windexing up a storm. What was Cullie really doing there that day? Did he know Melanie? Were they friends?

Come on, Alison. Get a grip. Your imagination is getting the best of you as usual. Fine, but what was he doing at her house that day?

Had he come to steal the manuscript, the very manuscript he'd now stolen from *me?* Did he go back to Melanie's house to steal it the night she was killed? Was *he* the one who killed Melanie?

I gasped when I remembered that he had no alibi for the night she was murdered. He claimed that after he dropped me off at Maplebark Manor at eleven o'clock, he drove straight back to the boat and went to sleep. But did he? Or did he drive over to Bluefish Cove, sneak into Melanie's office to steal the manuscript, surprise her at her desk, and then hit her over the head and kill her? With what? And why? And what would make him want to get his hands on the manuscript so badly he'd commit murder for it? So he could ruin Alistair, the man he says ruined his father? Was that why he invited me to live with him on his boat? Because he knew I had the manuscript?

I couldn't think straight. I only knew I wanted desperately to get off the boat, to go back to Maplebark Manor where I could think clearly, try to figure it all out. But I wasn't going anywhere—I was stuck in the middle of the Long Island Sound.

Clutching the pages of Melanie's manuscript, I ventured

up the stairs to the deck and entered *Marlowe*'s cockpit.
Cullie was standing at the steering wheel, whistling along
with the Everly Brothers' rendition of "Bye Bye Love." I
prayed the title of the song wasn't some kind of an omen.

Chapter 16

"Did you find the chart?" Cullie asked in a cheery voice when he saw that I had returned to the cockpit.

"No," I said defiantly. "But I found these." I held the missing manuscript pages in front of his face so he couldn't possibly miss them. The ends of the pages flapped in the wind.

"So you did," Cullie said matter of factly.

"I want to know why you stole this manuscript."

"*I* stole the manuscript? You're the one who stole it."

"Yeah, but you stole it from me, and I want to know why. What were you looking for? Why did you steal *these* pages and not the rest of the book?"

"Would you believe they made better reading than the rest of the book?"

"Turn this boat around right now," I insisted. "If you're not going to give *me* a straight answer, maybe you'll give the police one."

"Why would I want to talk to the police?" he said, appearing puzzled. "I'd much rather stay here and talk to you."

"All right then. Answer my question: Why did you steal Melanie's manuscript?"

"Same reason you did. I wanted to know what was in it."

"*I* stole it because I thought it might contain clues to Melanie's murder—clues that might come in handy if the police decided to make me a suspect. What's *your* excuse? Were you worried the police might make *you* a suspect?"

"Me? What the hell are you talking about?"

"Lies, that's what I'm talking about. What were you doing at Melanie's house the day you came over and found out I was her maid? And don't tell me you came over to shoot her house for a real estate brochure. I happen to know that line was bullshit."

"Fair enough. It *was* bullshit. I didn't come over to shoot her house. I came over to talk to her."

"Aha! So you did lie."

"Sure, I lied. I didn't know you from Adam back then. I had no reason to trust you with my personal business."

"So you admit it! You and Melanie had *personal business*. You knew each other!"

"I had things I wanted to discuss with her."

"Things you'd rather not tell the police?"

"Look, Sonny," Cullie said, moving toward the main halyard. "Let's give this a rest for a while. The wind's picking up. If I don't shorten sail, we'll be blown to South America."

South America? "All right," I said. "Do whatever you have to do to this boat. Just get us back to the marina."

"Yez, ma'am. Yez, Miz Koff." Cullie bowed at the waist.

I hurried down to the cabin and stayed there. For the next two hours I sat rigidly at the navigation station next to the cellular phone, poised and ready to call the police if the need arose. At four o'clock, Cullie came down the hatch to inform me that we were about to dock at the marina.

"We'll talk as soon as we're back in the slip, okay?" he said, finally showing a modicum of concern.

"Fine." The least I could do was hear him out.

"Why don't we have a drink," he suggested once we were back at the dock.

"I don't want a drink. I want the truth."

"Suit yourself. *I'll* have a drink. Then I'll tell you the truth."

Cullie poured himself a Mount Gay rum and tonic, then stood beside me at the navigation station.

"The reason I went to see Melanie that day was to talk to her about my father," he said softly.

"Did Paddy know Melanie?"

"No, but he knew Alistair."

"So?"

"As I've told you, Alistair ruined my father's life. I was afraid Melanie's book would go into all that."

"Why would you care? I would think you'd be ecstatic if the book made Alistair look like a scumbag. You hate the guy."

"I hate the guy, all right, but I loved my father and I didn't want him linked with one of Alistair's slimy scandals."

"I don't understand any of this," I said. "Why would your father show up in Melanie's biography of Alistair?"

"Remember I told you that Paddy was fed up with his job at the yacht club and wanted to take the two of us back to Europe to live?"

"I remember. You said he ended up staying in Connecticut, because he fell in love with somebody here."

"Right. Guess who he fell in love with?"

I thought for a second. "Alistair P. Downs," I said with as much sarcasm as I could muster. Didn't Melanie's book say that young Al Downey had an affair with a male dance instructor?

"Close. He fell in love with Annette Dowling, *Mrs.* Alistair P. Downs."

I was speechless—momentarily. "Your father was in love with Alistair's *wife?* No wonder the Senator wasn't too fond of your dad."

"The Senator wasn't too fond of his wife either. He didn't love her. He treated her like shit, traveling all the time and sleeping with other women. Annette gave up her acting career and her life in Hollywood to marry Alistair, but when she moved to Connecticut she had no friends, no career, no way to fill her time—except to raise Bethany, and there was a nanny to do that. So while Alistair made movies, played politics and screwed around with other women, she was a neglected suburban housewife—a very beautiful neglected suburban housewife."

"So beautiful your father fell for her?"

"Yup, but it was more than just her looks. He took her sailing. They made each other happy."

"Then what happened?"

"They planned to run away together. My father was going to take Annette and me back to England."

"What about Bethany?"

"Annette thought she'd be better off with Alistair. The girl adored her father. Still does."

"Don't I know it. So let me get this straight. Annette asked Alistair for a divorce, so she could marry your father?"

"Are you kidding? Do you think Alistair Downs would allow his wife to divorce him for the sailing instructor at the yacht club? Do you think he would allow himself to be humiliated that way?"

I shook my head.

"Here's what Senator Downs, that paragon of virtue, did when he found out Annette and my father were planning to run off together: he threatened to deport my father if he didn't break it off with her."

"But that's bribery."

"Yup. Alistair's specialty. He summoned my father to Evermore, sat him down in that library of his, and said, 'Paddy, my boy, I'm going to give you a choice: either you end your little fling with my wife or I get my pals in Immigration to send you back to England.' Alistair had my father by the balls."

"Why, if the three of you were planning to move back to England anyway?"

"My father was a British citizen. I'm an American citizen. If he were deported, he would have to leave me behind. I would have become a ward of the state. He wasn't about to let that happen."

"Of course not. I'm sure he loved you very much. But it sounds like he loved Annette too. And Alistair made him choose between you?"

"Bingo."

"Obviously, he chose you."

"Yup, and he paid a pretty price for his choice. When Alistair gave him his little ultimatum, my father punched the good Senator right in the jaw, then walked out. Little did he know that Annette saw him leave."

"What happened?"

"She confronted her husband and asked him what Paddy Harrington was doing in the house. Alistair gleefully delivered the news that her precious sailing instructor had taken his bribe and wouldn't be seeing her again."

"The bastard! No wonder you despise him. How could he do something so slimy?" I said, shaking my head. "Annette must have been devastated when she found out your father was leaving her."

"Devastated is exactly what she was. Faced with the prospect of spending the rest of her life with a husband who didn't love her and a daughter who didn't need her, she took her XKE for a drive—right into a guard rail off the Merritt Parkway. Alistair conned the police and the media into reporting her death as a tragic accident. But it wasn't an accident. It was a suicide. Alistair knew it and my father knew it."

"I can't believe all this. How did your father react to Annette's death?"

"He got drunk. And he stayed drunk a lot of the time. He was a broken man, Sonny. His years at the club were pure torture for him after Annette was gone."

"You don't mean he continued to work there after all that happened."

"He sure did. He had to support me, don't forget. There weren't exactly hundreds of employment opportunities for a middle-aged sailing teacher who liked his whiskey *and* had a young son to tote around. So he stayed at the club and drank his days away."

"Alistair didn't try to run your father out of the club?"

"You don't understand the sick mind of Alistair Downs. Whenever the members would complain about my father's drinking or his surly attitude or the fact that he wasn't getting any younger, it was Alistair who insisted that the club keep him on. He loved watching my father suffer. He enjoyed watching the members order him around. Most of all, he enjoyed telling the tale of the uppity sailing instructor who made a pass at his wife and then fell into a whiskey bottle when she rejected him. He actually told the other members that story. And they all believed him. My father became a joke. A poor old English rummy. It was painful for him and painful for me. If it hadn't been for me, he could have quit the club and lived a happy life in England. With Annette."

"I don't know what to say. Why didn't you tell me all this before?"

"Before what? Before we fell in love? Are you ashamed to be seen with me, now that you know my father was the laughingstock of the illustrious Sachem Point Yacht Club?"

"Cullie, I didn't mean . . ." I started to put my hand on his cheek, then pulled it back. There were still too many questions to be answered. "You haven't told me what you were doing at Melanie's house that day," I said.

"I loved my father, and I didn't want his sordid history showing up in a book. So I went to see Melanie to talk to her about leaving it out. When you told me she wasn't home, I went back later that night."

"Did you get to talk to her then?"

"I tried to. She listened to everything I had to say, then thanked me for giving her such 'usable material' about Alistair. What an idiot I was! Instead of telling her my father's story as a way of convincing her not to use it, I actually volunteered information she hadn't known about. I pleaded with her not to include it in the book. I said, 'My father's dead. Let him rest in peace. Why drag him down just so you can write a bestseller about Alistair?' She laughed at me, Sonny. She laughed and told me to stop bothering her. I was fighting for my father's dignity and she told me I was bothering her. But that didn't stop me. I tried to bargain with her. I said, 'Okay. Tell my father's story if you have to. But don't use his name. At least have the decency not to use his name.' You know what she said? She said, 'Of course, I'll use his name. He's dead. He can't sue me. It's the live ones I have second thoughts about. Live ones have lawyers, and lawyers make my publisher nervous.' 'What about Alistair?' I said. 'He's a live one and he's probably got an army of lawyers.' She laughed. 'Don't be naive,' she said. 'Alistair Downs won't sue me. He's much too high and mighty to dirty his hands with a lawsuit that'll bring him so much unwanted publicity he won't be able to stand it. No, he won't sue me. He may kill me, but he won't sue me.' "

Maybe Cullie was telling the truth. But how could I be sure? I wasn't sure of anything anymore. "This is all very well and good, Cullie, but what made you think Melanie even knew the story of your father and Annette? What gave you the idea she'd write about it in her book?"

"Remember Hadley Kittredge?"

"Vaguely." I remembered. She was the one with the humungous tits and the miniature brain.

"One of the reasons we got together that night I ran into you was so she could tell me what she knew about Melanie."

"How would Hadley Kittredge know Melanie? Didn't you tell me she was the dockmaster's daughter?"

"Right. And people who work at marinas talk to each other. Anyway, Hadley said Melanie and some guy that worked for her were snooping around at the yacht club, asking about my father's relationship with Annette Downs. She wanted to warn me. That's why I went to see Melanie."

"So you went to see Melanie and became furious with her when she wouldn't take you seriously," I said, prodding Cullie the way I'd seen courtroom lawyers prod witnesses on TV. "You were so furious with her that you went back to her house, tried to steal the manuscript from her, and killed her."

"What?" Cullie started laughing. "Run this by me again? You think *I* killed Melanie?"

"You did try to steal the manuscript from her house, admit it."

"I did no such thing. After that horrible meeting with the woman, I never went back to her house again. I figured, if she's insensitive enough to put the stuff I told her about my father in her book, there's nothing I can do about it. I wasn't happy about it, but I was helpless."

"So you didn't go back to Melanie's house, try to steal her manuscript, and kill her? Then explain why you stole these pages from my suitcase." I held the missing pages in front of his face and shook them at him.

"Curiosity. I knew you had the manuscript the day you moved in on the *Marlowe*. Remember when I told you you brought one too many bags onto the boat?"

"How could I forget?"

"Well, I thought maybe the other bags were just as unnecessary, so I checked to see what was in them. I saw the manuscript on the floor of the hanging locker. I read bits and pieces of the book when you were out. I was crazy to find out if Melanie had used the material I was stupid enough to hand her."

"Fine, but why didn't you tell me you knew about the manuscript? Why did you have to read it behind my back?"

"I didn't want you to know what happened to my father. I didn't want anybody to know."

I felt for Cullie. I really did. But was he telling me the truth? How did I know he wasn't conning me, pretending to be something he wasn't, giving me the old cha cha cha, as his father would say?

I let go of the manuscript pages and slumped in my chair. I didn't know what to believe—about Cullie, about Alistair, about Melanie's murder.

"How do I know all this isn't one big lie?" I asked Cullie. "I was really starting to believe in you, to believe in us. I was actually starting to believe we were in love. I've just been through the most traumatic few months of my life, but I was happy. I was happy with you. I was happy trusting you. Please, tell me how I can trust you now."

Cullie moved closer to me and took me in his arms.

"The answer is in these pages," he said softly, looking down at the section of the manuscript that lay on top of his desk. "I've read them. It's all there. Melanie didn't miss a trick. The only thing I care about now is that you read these pages and satisfy yourself that I'm telling the truth. Please, Sonny. I want us back where we were."

"I will read these pages," I told him. "And I hope they'll give me the answers I need."

"Good," he said. "Now, it's getting late. How about dinner? Should I pick us up some chicken cacciatore, your favorite?"

"No, Cullie. I'm going back to Maplebark Manor. I need some time to take all this in. I really think it's best if I go home."

He looked disappointed, then assumed the I-don't-care-if-you-don't posture he often affected when he was hurt. "Home," he scoffed. "That place was *never* your home. It was your prize acquisition, your way of showing the world you were somebody. But you were somebody even in that maid's uniform, Sonny. You brought me a kind of joy I'd never experienced, do you know that?" Tears welled up in his eyes, but he wiped them away quickly, hoping I wouldn't notice. "Hey, if you want to go home, go home. It's up to you."

It *was* up to me, and I needed a break from the intense atmosphere on the boat.

* * *

I packed my suitcases and Cullie helped me load them
into the trunk of my car. It was dark and cold as we stood
next to my Porsche and fumbled with a goodbye.

"Should I call you or do you want 'space'?" he asked.

"You remind me of Sandy," I laughed. "He always
talked about people needing their 'space.'"

"I'm nothing like Sandy," he said solemnly. "Sandy left
you just when you needed him most. I'm not the one who's
doing the leaving."

"I know," I whispered, a giant lump forming in my
throat. "I really do know."

Cullie put his arms around me and held me for several
seconds. Then he let go of me and opened my car door.
"Give my best to Maplebarf Manor," he said, trying unsuc-
cessfully to smile. He helped me into the car, closed the
door, and walked away. I didn't turn on the ignition. I just
watched him go, across the parking lot, over to Arnie's All
Clammed Up, up the stairs of the restaurant and inside the
crowded bar. I imagined him pulling up a stool and asking
for a Mount Gay rum and tonic. I imagined him taking a sip
of his drink, gazing out over the crowded bar and hurting
as much as I hurt. When it hurt so much I could no longer
stand to imagine him, I started the car, flipped on the lights,
and began the long drive home.

Chapter 17

After spending so much time on a forty-foot sailboat, Maplebark Manor seemed bigger than ever as I entered the house and turned on the lights. "Hello?" I called out to the empty rooms and hallways. "Anybody home?"

I carried my suitcases upstairs and dropped them beside the bed in the master bedroom. Then I turned on the television and let it blare. I needed noise. I had never felt so alone.

I unpacked my bag—not the one containing the manuscript—and lay down on my bed. I closed my eyes and let the sound of the TV wash over me. I was too tired to sleep.

I thought of Cullie. I tried to imagine where he was, what he was doing, whether he was thinking of me. I thought of how I had come to depend on him, how I had held him in such high esteem, how I had envied his values. I thought of how I had trusted him, and wondered how I would trust him now. I trusted my first husband and he left me. I trusted Sandy and he left me. I trusted Cullie and he lied to me. And if he could lie about why he was at Melanie's house, he could lie about other things, more important things. Like saying he loved me and then leaving me, the way the others had.

I believed he didn't kill Melanie, but could I believe his story about Paddy and Annette? There was one way to find out: I could read Melanie's book. "The truth is in these pages," Cullie had said.

I got up from the bed, retrieved the suitcase containing the manuscript, and pulled out the pages Cullie had hidden from me. I carried them over to the bed, sat with my back propped against two pillows, and began to read. I didn't have to read long before I came to the chapter called, "Alistair/Annette/Paddy: The Love Triangle That Turned to Tragedy." It was all there, just as Cullie said it was, the whole sorry saga recounted in excruciatingly florid prose. I shuddered to think what Alistair's reaction to the book would be. I thought of Bethany too, and wondered how she would take Melanie's assault on her father's character. Not well, I was sure. Would either of them be angry enough to kill Melanie if they knew the damage the book could cause?

I should call Cullie and tell him I believe him, I thought. I was foolish to leave the boat. I could have read the missing pages of the manuscript on the *Marlowe,* with Cullie next to me. I should have stayed. I should have had more faith in the man I loved. Stupid, I scolded myself. Stupid, stupid.

I put the manuscript aside and reached for the phone to call Cullie. I checked my watch. It was ten-thirty. I dialed his number and waited.

"Hi, this is Cullie Harrington," said his answering machine.

"Cullie, it's me," I managed, after hearing the beep. I felt the lump rising in my throat. "I read the manuscript. Do you think we could talk?" I paused. "Please call me back, no matter what time it is. I miss you."

I hung up and took a deep breath. Please call me back, I prayed. Please give me another chance. I love you.

I went down to the kitchen, made some coffee, and brought it upstairs. Then I climbed back on the bed and stared at Melanie's manuscript. There were about twenty pages remaining in the section Cullie had hidden, but I'd read enough for one night. I was about to put the pages aside in favor of one of the magazines on my night table when the next chapter in the section on Alistair's personal life caught my eye. It was entitled, "Alistair's Jewish Princess: The Woman He Couldn't Marry." I was intrigued, to say the least—intrigued enough to keep reading. Melanie did have a knack for keeping the reader hooked, I'll give her that.

The chapter began with Melanie's allegation that, during his dance instructor days in Queens, Al Downey had a steady girlfriend, a Jewish girl who used to take lessons at the local Arthur Murray Dance Studio. According to Melanie, Al had promised to marry the girl but claimed he didn't make enough money to support her. When he was discovered by a Hollywood talent scout, he told the girl that he'd go out to California, make a name for himself in the movies, and send for her. He went out to California, made a name for himself in the movies, but didn't send for her. Instead, he broke up with her—first, according to Melanie, because he thought a Jewish wife would be a liability; second, because he got out to Hollywood and found that, as the newly christened movie star Alistair Downs, he had his pick of beautiful women; and third, because he ended up marrying glamorous show girl Annette Dowling. The poor girl from Queens was heartbroken and married a young businessman from Manhattan on the rebound. But she continued to pine for Alistair. When she read that he had purchased an estate in Layton, Connecticut, and planned to settle there with his new wife, the woman convinced her husband to buy a house there too. Before long, Alistair and his old flame rekindled their romance, unbeknownst to their respective spouses. Thinking he might marry her this time, the woman waited for Alistair to divorce Annette. It never happened. Alistair had political aspirations, and a divorce was out of the question. Alistair dumped her for the second time. Years later, though they both continue to live in Layton, Alistair and the woman remain estranged.

Ah, Melanie, you've done it again, I sighed. You've dug up yet another sad episode in the Alistair Downs saga. Poor, pathetic woman, I said out loud, thinking of the Queens woman Alistair spurned. Get out the violins for the old girl. From Melanie's description, she sounded like one of those pitiful, long-suffering heroines on my mother's soap opera—the ones who endure year after year of mistreatment at the hands of some cad. I wondered who she was. I wondered if she belonged to my mother's country club. I wondered how any woman could love a guy like Alistair. He was a complete fraud.

My musings were interrupted by the sound of the phone ringing. I jumped when I heard it.

"Cullie?"

"How did you know it was me?" he said, slurring his words, the result, I guessed, of one too many rum and tonics.

"I was hoping it was you. Cullie, I read the manuscript and I wanted you to know that I—"

"Is this the mistress of Maplebarf Manor?" he mumbled. I could barely understand him.

"Cullie, listen to me. I want to tell you how sorry—"

"Is your house the one with all the turrets?"

"No. Cullie, please let me—"

"Oh. Then it must be the one with the indoor swimming pool and squash court."

"No. Would you please stop—"

"I got it. I got it. It's the one with the movie theatre in the basement."

"Why don't we talk when you're feeling better," I said gently.

"I'm feeling fine. Just great. How about you?"

"Fine. I'm fine. It's you I'm worried about."

"Sonny?"

"Yes?"

"I love you."

"I love you, too. That's what I was calling you about."

"Then why aren't we together tonight? Why am I here and why are you there?"

"Because I was too quick to believe the worst about you," I admitted.

"Would you have been less quick to believe the worst about me if I had a lot of money and came from the kind of family you did?"

"Of course not." Well, maybe not. Would I have been more trusting of Cullie if his parents had belonged to my mother's country club? Would I have believed the worst about him if he'd been "in the Mold"—a rich doctor or lawyer or president of a department store, someone my mother would approve of? I hated to think so.

"Do you think we can make this right?" he said, garbling his words terribly.

"Yes, I do. But first, you need to get some sleep. So do I."

"You don't want me to come over there now?"

"I'm not letting you drive in your condition. I love you, remember?"

"Yeah, I remember. It feels good that you love me, Sonny . . ." His voice trailed off.

"I'll see you tomorrow, okay?"

"Your berth or mine?"

"Mine. I've got to stay here and take care of a few things. Like Connecticut Light and Power. Like the gas company. Like the phone company. They're all threatening to cut off service unless I pay them."

"How're you gonna do that? You're broke."

"I'm gonna make like Scarlett O'Hara: I'm gonna think about it tomorrow. And speaking of tomorrow, will you come over here when you're finished with work?"

"You got it. Is yours the house with all the turrets?"

"Oh, shut up and go to sleep," I laughed.

"Good night, Sonny girl. Sleep tight."

"That reminds me of the advertising slogan of my father's mattress company: 'Sleep Rite. Sleep Tight.' "

"Catchy. I wish I could meet your father. I'd tell him I love his daughter."

"You're sweet. He would have loved you, I know it." My mother was another story.

"Would he have accepted me as the man in your life? Even though I'm just the sailing teacher's boy?"

"You're not *just* the sailing teacher's boy. You're lots of other things. Lots of other wonderful things. Now say good night to me and hang up."

"Good night to me and hang up."

"I'm serious. Go to sleep. I'll see you tomorrow."

"Yes, Sonny girl, you will."

I spent the next day trying to appease my creditors, all of whom were not amused that I owed them so much money. I promised them I'd come up with some cash by holding a county-wide tag sale, unloading all my clothes, furniture, and tableware, as well as whatever jewelry I hadn't already sold. They seemed to like the idea.

I called the woman who ran all the tag sales in my area.

"Hello?" I said. "Is this Second Hand Rose?"

"Yes, it is. How may I help you?"

"I'd like to sell my things at one of your tag sales. How soon could you arrange it?"

"In about two months." My creditors would never wait that long! "Everybody in Layton's having a tag sale, it seems. I've never been so busy."

"And you can't handle one more? The items for sale will be the entire contents of my estate on Woodland Way." I thought I'd get her to change her mind by dazzling her with the big commission she'd earn by taking me on as a client.

"Ah, Woodland Way. Good address." She was impressed. My strategy was working. "It just so happens I have three other clients on Woodland Way, all of whom are having tag sales this weekend."

"Really? I didn't know any of my neighbors were moving."

"Who said anything about moving? They're all on the verge of bankruptcy and have to raise cash. It's that nasty recession, you know. Awful for the economy. Wonderful for me."

It was gratifying to know that somebody was getting rich from the recession. "So there's no way you can have my tag sale right away?" I tried again.

"Absolutely not. There are people ahead of you. As I said, I'm very busy."

I wasn't giving up. "Could you have my tag sale right away if we made a deal?"

"What kind of a deal?"

"Instead of your usual twenty percent of the profits from my sale, I'll give you thirty percent of the take."

She paused. "Forty percent."

"Thirty-five percent."

"I'll run the sale next week."

"I appreciate it."

Cullie arrived at my house at six o'clock that evening. I flew into his arms and draped mine around his neck.

"Whoa. I'm happy to see you too," he laughed after I almost knocked him over.

We'd only been apart for a day, but I felt as if I hadn't seen him in months. "You look so handsome," I cooed, stroking his beard. He was wearing jeans and a golden yellow sweater that played nicely off his wheat-blond hair.

"We should separate more often," he smiled. "This is quite a reception." Then his expression darkened. "On second thought, we shouldn't separate at all. It's bad for my liver."

"Are you hung over?" I asked.

"Let's put it this way. When I looked into my camera lens to shoot the exterior of a house today, I saw two houses instead of one. Everything took just a little longer than it needed to. I came straight here from my last job."

"I'm so glad you did. Let's go upstairs and get reacquainted," I said suggestively.

"Love to. Oh, but first, I've got something for you."
Cullie handed me a gift-wrapped package that looked and
felt like it might contain a magazine.

"Another present? You're going to spoil me."

"It's not exactly a present, Sonny. Why don't we go into
the kitchen and sit down."

I followed him down the hall into the kitchen and sat next
to him at the breakfast table. "What's in here?" I asked,
shaking the package like a kid at Christmas.

"In view of our new policy of full disclosure, I wanted you
to have these. They're part of the missing pages of Melanie's
manuscript. You didn't find them in the navigation desk
yesterday, because they must have come loose from the pile
and ended up on the floor. I wrapped them up with the same
gift paper I bought when I got that diary for you. I wanted
to make a present of them. You know, like a symbolic
gesture. I didn't want you to think I was holding out on you
again."

"I told you last night. I was wrong to doubt you. Now
let's see what new indignity Melanie planned to inflict on
some poor, unsuspecting soul."

I unwrapped the package and lifted out a small stack of
what appeared to be photocopied photographs.

"They must be the ones that were going into the book,"
Cullie explained. "Melanie must have copied them to give
the publishers an idea of what she was planning to include."

"Let's look," I said mischievously. Each 8 × 11 copy
featured a black-and-white photograph and a short, typewritten caption. "You take some and I'll take some."

"You go ahead. I've already looked at them," he said,
waving me off. "I wanted to see if Melanie wangled a picture
of my father out of the yacht club and used it in the book."

"Did she?" I asked.

"No. At least it's not in this group of photographs."

I began to leaf through the photos. They were in no
particular order or chronology, just random glimpses of
Alistair Downs's life. There was one of him standing beside

his Mafia pal, Frankie Fuccato, outside a Beverly Hills restaurant. There was a shot of him sitting with Annette in her brand new XKE. There was a picture of young Al Downey attending elementary school in Queens, and another one of him watching the Giants play baseball at the old Polo Grounds.

"Hey, look at this one," Cullie said, handing it to me. "It's a shot of Alistair in his Al Downey/Arthur Murray period. Looks like he and the woman with him won some kind of dance contest in the forties."

"Lemme see," I said, swiping the photo out of Cullie's hand. First, I looked at the caption, which read: *Al Downey and girlfriend win swing jitterbug contest at Forest Hills Dance Studio.* Then I peered at the grainy old photo and felt a stab of recognition—a stab so jolting I nearly stopped breathing. There, in black and white, on the dance floor of the Arthur Murray Dance Studio in Queens, was a handsome young man with his arm draped around an attractive young blonde. The man was unmistakably Alistair; the woman looked like my mother.

"Cullie?" I said nervously. "You mentioned that you came straight over here from your last job. Does that mean you have your equipment with you?"

"Sure. It's in the car."

"Do you by any chance have one of those things that magnifies a picture?"

"You mean a loupe? Yeah, I've got one."

"Would you go get it, please?"

"Now?"

"Right now, if you don't mind." Cullie jumped out of his chair and made it out to his Jeep and back before I even realized he was gone. I was so mesmerized by the photograph in my hand that everything else became a blur.

"Know how to use this?" he asked.

"Yeah. You just put it down on the photograph and look into it, right?"

"Right."

I placed the loupe on top of the face of the woman in the photograph and bent over to examine the magnification. There was no mistaking the fact that the woman was a very young Doris Waxman. She looked just like she did in our old family photo album—the clothes, the hair, the makeup all vintage 1940s. What was different from the old photos I'd seen of her was her smile. I'd never seen her smile the way she smiled at the man in that picture—not at me, not at my father, not ever. That look of pure, unadulterated adoration was apparently reserved for Alistair Downs. A chill ran through my body.

"Hey, what is it, babe? You look like you've seen a ghost." Cullie put his arm around me, much as Alistair was putting his arm around my mother in the photo that now rested on the kitchen table.

"I haven't seen a ghost, Cullie. I've seen my mother."

"What are you talking about?"

"The woman in that picture—the woman the caption calls Al Downey's *girlfriend*—is my mother." My mouth was dry with panic and my throat was closing.

"Your mother? I sink you've got vhat vee call a mother complex," Cullie intoned. "You keep seeing your mother everywhere, Sonny. Remember when you thought she was the one whose Cadillac raced out of Alistair's driveway and almost hit us?"

"She *was* the one who almost hit us. I asked her. She admitted it."

"You're kidding? What did she say she was doing at Evermore? You told me she'd never met Alistair."

"That's what I thought. Obviously, I was wrong." I glanced down at the photograph on the table and shuddered. "She told me she went to see him to convince him to hire me back at the newspaper."

"Maybe she was telling the truth."

"Look at this picture, Cullie. The caption says the woman in the picture was Alistair's girlfriend. His *girlfriend*. This is all so bizarre I don't know what to think."

I began to shiver uncontrollably. Cullie went to the closet, brought me his jacket, and draped it over my shoulders.

"Look, maybe Alistair and your mother did have something going when they were young," he said. "So what? It's not as if they've been lovers all these . . ."

Cullie stopped himself and looked at me with a mixture of horror and compassion. He'd read the final missing pages of Melanie's manuscript, and he knew I had too. We'd both seen the chapter called "Alistair's Jewish Princess: The Woman He Couldn't Marry." Suddenly, we both realized the all too chilling implications of that chapter and the photo in front of us.

"Oh my God," I screamed, grabbing onto the table for support. "My mother was the woman Melanie was writing about. But how? How could she have loved Alistair all these years? She loved my father. They were blissfully happy. She said so. She would never have carried on an affair behind his back. Never! And never with Alistair! It can't be, it just can't be!"

Cullie tried to calm me down, but I ignored his attempts.

"All those years," I cried. "All those years of lecturing and pontificating and trying to run my life. All those years of making her marriage out to be so perfect I couldn't possibly measure up to it. What a fucking hypocrite! My mother spent her whole life running after a man who didn't give two shits about her. If what Melanie writes is true, my mother's marriage was a lie."

"And that's a big 'if,' " Cullie reminded me. "Maybe Melanie was embellishing the truth, just to sell books."

"She told the truth about your father and Annette, didn't she? She didn't embellish that story one bit, according to you."

"True. But I just don't want you to—"

"To what? To uncover a secret like this about my own mother and not go crazy?"

The thought suddenly crossed my mind that I might as well add my mother's name to the list of murder suspects.

She had turned out to be an adulteress. Maybe she was a killer too. Maybe she, of all people, couldn't afford to stand by and watch Melanie publish her book. Maybe she was the intruder who smacked Melanie over the head and offed her.

The idea was so gruesome I couldn't look Cullie in the eye. What must he think of me now? I wondered. And he was so worried about not measuring up to my family. What a joke.

Quick! A joke! A joke! Don't let yourself feel this pain, Alison. Tell Cullie a joke about Doris Waxman, his mother-in-law-to-be. You must have a mother-in-law joke in your repertoire, right? Quick! A joke!

"Cullie," I said. "What's the definition of mixed emotions?"

He looked at me helplessly, as if he wanted to ease my pain but didn't know how.

"Seeing your mother-in-law driving off a cliff in your brand-new Porsche. Get it?" I began to laugh hysterically. I was a basket case. Poor Cullie didn't know what to do or how to help me.

"Let's get you upstairs," he offered. "Maybe if you lie down for a while . . ."

"Lie down? *Lie down?*" I said, getting up from the table and walking toward the back door. "I'm going over to Mommy Dearest's house. I'm going to get the story straight from the whore's mouth."

"Not without me you're not. I'm going with you."

"You sure? It's not going to be pretty."

"Who needs pretty?"

"Some men do. Some men only want things to be nice and neat and pretty. Take Sandy. The minute things got rough, he split."

"I told you yesterday. I'm not Sandy. I'm here for all of it. Pretty or not."

"I don't deserve you," I said, my eyes welling with tears.

"You don't deserve to be lied to," Cullie responded, grabbing my hand and leading me toward the door. "Let's pay your mother a visit. My Jeep awaits."

Part Three

Chapter 18

We pulled up to 89 Pink Cloud Lane at eight o'clock. As I raced up the stone walkway toward the front door of my mother's house, Cullie grabbed my arm and stopped me.

"I think you should slow down," he coached. "Try to stay calm. No point in storming in there and putting your mother on the defensive—not if you want to get the truth out of her."

"You're probably right," I said, then took a deep breath.

I rang the doorbell and waited anxiously for my mother to let us in, but it was Nora Small, her live-in housekeeper, who answered the door.

"Hi, Nora," I said, entering the house without being invited in. "My mother around?"

"No, Miss Alison," she said in her Jamaican lilt. "Mrs. Waxman has gone out."

"Gone out? Where?" I hadn't thought to call ahead to make sure my mother would be home.

"With a gentleman."

"A gentleman? Do you happen to know this gentleman's name?"

"No, miss. Your mom didn't say."

"Did you see what he looked like when he came to pick her up?" I asked Nora.

"No, miss. It was the gentleman's chauffeur who came to pick your mother up."

"His chauffeur?" I sneered. "It's got to be Alistair. He's got a driver for that Corniche of his."

"Is there something wrong, Miss Alison?"

"Oh, no. Sorry, Nora. Would it be all right if my friend and I waited for my mother to come home?"

"No problem. I'll be in the kitchen if you need anything."

Cullie and I sat in silence in my mother's living room for several minutes. Then, I rose from the sofa and pulled him up with me. "Come," I said taking his hand. "Let me show you the Seymour Waxman Memorial."

"What are you talking about?"

"Follow me."

I led him into the master bedroom. "There. That's what I'm talking about," I said, pointing to the array of photos, tennis trophies, and other memorabilia that decorated the walls, bookshelves, and dresser tops. "Welcome to the shrine to my father—the room designed to ease the conscience of the grieving widow Waxman."

"Amazing," he said, shaking his head. "There must be a hundred pictures of your father. I'll say one thing for your parents: they gave the appearance of a happy couple," he said, holding up a photograph of Sy and Doris honeymooning at the Fontainebleau Hotel in Miami Beach.

"I can't bear to look at these now," I said. "They're all a lie. My mother's big, fat lie. Imagine carrying on an affair with Alistair Downs when she had a wonderful man like my father to love."

"Let's wait to hear what she has to say," Cullie advised. "Come on, we'll make ourselves a drink."

At about nine-thirty, I heard the front door open. Then I heard my mother's husky smoker's voice wheeze, "Thank you for a divine evening. You're a kind and generous man. Good night."

There were muffled sounds, then the sound of a car driving off, and finally my mother's footsteps on the marble floor of the foyer. Kind and generous, my ass. I didn't make out the man's voice, but it had to belong to Alistair, the swine. He was probably kissing her good night, with those seventy-five-year-old liver lips of his. Gross. The whole thing was gross.

Like two loyal subjects who'd been granted an audience with the Queen of England instead of the Queen of Pretension, Cullie and I stood as my mother entered the living room.

"Alison, dear. What a nice surprise. I didn't recognize that truck outside the house," she said, walking toward me with her arms outstretched. I kept mine at my sides but permitted her to bestow one of her phantom kisses on my cheek—the air kisses she resorted to when she didn't want to smudge her lipstick.

"It's not a truck, it's a Jeep," I said curtly. "The same Jeep you almost hit as you were coming out of Alistair Downs's house the other morning."

"I see. And who is this?" she said, meaning Cullie but not deigning to look at him. Instead, she peered down at her Perry Ellis plaid skirt and picked off a speck of lint.

"This is Cullie Harrington. Cullie, meet my mother, Doris Waxman," I said.

"Hello," Cullie said, extending his hand without smiling. My mother did not take it.

"Harrington . . . Harrington," she mused. "Do we know any Harringtons?" she asked me.

"Yes, one. And he's standing right in front of you," I snapped.

"Still, there must be others. The name is familiar somehow," she said.

"That's because I mentioned Cullie's name the night you took me to the club for Maine Lobster Night. You nearly choked to death when you heard it, remember?"

"Yes, I suppose I do." There was a pause. "Please, sit

down," she instructed Cullie and me. We took our places on the sofa, while she sat in a nearby wing chair. "So, young man," she said, lifting a Winston from her gold cigarette case and lighting it. "Tell me about yourself, your people."

His people. God, my mother was a piece of work. I remembered an afternoon from my elementary school days when I'd brought home a boy named Chuck, whose father was a dishwasher at the local deli. I'd felt sorry for him because he said his family had only one television set, while we had four—three color and a black and white, for the maid. I'd invited Chuck over to watch "American Bandstand" after school one day, when all of a sudden my mother stormed into the TV room where Chuck and I were dancing. She stopped dead in her tracks and said in her deepest, most intimidating, most disapproving voice, "Whom are you entertaining, Alison?" "Oh, hi, Mom," I said. "This is Chuck. He's in my class at school." "From where does Chuck come?" she asked with a puss that made her look like she'd just stepped in dog shit. "I don't know. What road do you live on, Chuck?" I asked him. "Hitchcock Avenue," Chuck replied, sensing that he'd just given the wrong answer. "I've never heard of Hitchcock Avenue," my mother said, speaking directly to Chuck for the first time. "What is your last name and who are your people?" That did it. I remember wanting to strangle her. I always wanted to strangle her when she asked about people's people, as if she were saying, "What tribe are you from?" or "What cave did you crawl out of?" or "How dare you pollute my air with your presence." Who did she think *she* was anyway? She was a Jewish girl from Queens whose "people" were Hungarian immigrants who worked so hard to give their daughter the finer things in life that they forgot to teach her a little humility. Boy, I thought. She and Alistair deserved each other.

"My people?" Cullie asked with a puzzled look on his face. "You mean, my parents?"

My mother nodded.

"My dad was a sailor."

"A delightful hobby. What did he do for employment?"

"He taught sailing at the Sachem Point Yacht Club."

"How intriguing," she said, drawing on her cigarette. "Is he retired now?"

"No, he passed away nine years ago."

"So sorry. And your mother?"

"She was a waitress at the club. She's gone too."

"My my. How tragic for you." I could tell she was crushed. "You and Alison have that in common, I suppose."

"You mean, the loss of a parent?" Cullie asked.

"Exactly. Alison's father, my beloved husband Seymour, passed away when she was only a girl. I miss him terribly." My mother blew smoke out of her nose in a long, downward stream.

"Speaking of my father," I interrupted, itching to get to the point of our visit, "who was the gentleman you were out with tonight?"

"The gentleman with whom I was out?"

"Right."

"I'm not sure I should tell you," my mother said coquettishly, batting her eyelashes for dramatic emphasis.

"Oh, come on, Mom. You and I don't have secrets from each other. Fess up. Who's the guy? A new beau? An old beau? A beau so old you won the swing jitterbug contest with him in the forties?"

"Of course not," she said. "There hasn't been anyone since your father."

"Really? Then who were you out with tonight?"

"If you must know, I had dinner with Louis Obermeyer. From the club. You went to school with his daughter, Betsy, remember?"

Was this another of my mother's cha cha chas? "What were you doing with Mr. Obermeyer?"

"I wanted to talk to him about you, dear."

"About me?"

"Yes. But I'm not sure we should discuss this in front of
. . ."

"Cullie? He and I share everything."

"Oh?"

"That's right, Mrs. Waxman," Cullie said. "Your daughter and I are very close."

"Oh?" My mother grew pale, just as she had on Maine Lobster Night when I'd first told her about Cullie. Thank God there were no lemon twists around.

"What did you talk to Mr. Obermeyer about?" I pressed on.

"I don't want you to be angry, Alison dear. But I've been so worried about this murder investigation in which you're involved. Louis is a lawyer, a very successful trial lawyer. He defended Edith Eisner's son Fred when he was arrested for insider trading, remember? Fred's a free man now, thanks to Louis. Not only is he a free man, he's a very *wealthy* man. He's made a fortune in the stock market, Edith tells me."

"Bully for Fred," I said.

"I consulted Louis," she went on, "because I wanted to make absolutely certain that if the police accuse you of murdering that Melanie Moloney, you will have the best representation money can buy. If anyone can get you out of the mess you've made for yourself, it's Louis."

"I'm touched by your confidence in me," I said, dripping sarcasm. "I'll get myself out of my own messes, thank you. Which reminds me, Mother. Tell me more about your meeting with Alistair Downs the other day. It was swell of you to go over to Evermore to plead my case the way you did."

"That's for what mothers are," my mother said in her absurd version of grammatically correct English.

"Did you find the Senator charming? Cordial? Sexually arousing?"

"Alison! What's gotten into you? You never used to speak to me that way. When you were married to Sandy, you were respectful of your mother. Now, I simply don't know you." She glared at Cullie, as if he were the cause of the breakdown of my morals.

"What's gotten into me?" I said, my voice rising an octave. "The truth. That's what's gotten into me."

"What truth?"

"About you and Alistair. Tell me how you met."

"I told you. I went over to his estate to discuss your employment at the newspaper. I—"

"Tell me how you met the first time, when he was teaching ballroom dancing at the Arthur Murray Studio in Queens." So much for Cullie's suggestion that I not put my mother on the defensive.

My mother's complexion became as white as the lies she'd been telling me all my life. Her lower lip began to quiver and her left cheek developed a twitch.

"What . . . what . . . gives you the right to . . . to speak to me . . . this way?" she sputtered, looking back and forth between Cullie and me.

"I'm your daughter, that's what gives me the right. That and the fact that you've made yourself out to be something you're not. You pretended to be the poor, depressed widow after Daddy died. And all the while, you were having an affair with our United States Senator from Connecticut."

"That's a lie!" my mother wheezed. "Al and I haven't been—"

"Al?" I sneered. "Tell me all about you and Al. Go on, mother. You might as well get it off your chest."

"Get what off my chest? I have nothing to be guilty about, Alison."

"Holy shit! My mother just made a grammatical mistake! You *did* mean, 'I have nothing *about which* to be guilty,' didn't you, Mom?" I admit it. I was enjoying this. Making my mother squirm after a lifetime of being her squirmee was too delicious to describe.

"Where are you getting your information?" my mother asked, glaring at Cullie.

"From Melanie Moloney's biography of your boyfriend," I said.

"You read that book? She talks about me? She actually mentions me by name?" My mother looked horror-stricken. I did not feel sorry for her.

"She doesn't use your name, but she devotes an entire chapter of the book to your star-crossed romance with Alistair—sorry—*Al.*"

"If she doesn't mention me by name, why do you assume it's I about whom she's writing?"

"Take a look at this, mother." I handed her the copy of the photograph of her and Alistair.

"Oh my God! I don't believe this. Where on earth did you get this old picture?"

"Obviously, not from *your* personal collection," I said wryly. "It was with the manuscript. Melanie must have dug it up from somewhere."

"I just don't believe this," my mother said again, lighting up another Winston.

"Believe it, Mom. I do. Cullie does."

"Cullie? Who is this Cullie person and what does he have to do with *my* life?"

"I wouldn't be so quick to judge Cullie, if I were you," I said as calmly as I could. "He wasn't the one who cheated on his husband. You were." I paused, letting my mother feel the sting of my words. "Now why don't you tell us the truth, Mom. We're listening."

My mother slumped in her wing chair and sighed. "All riiiiight," she said in a long, drawn-out whine. She reminded me of the Wicked Witch of the West in *The Wizard of Oz* who, when her power had finally been diminished by Dorothy's pail of water, cried weakly, "I'm *mellllting . . .*"

"I met Al when I was sixteen," she began, dragging on her cigarette. "I was an impressionable young girl. I had never been with a man. I had no experience with that sort of thing." She paused. "My friends wanted to learn the latest dances. They said they were going to take lessons at the

Arthur Murray Dance Studio in Forest Hills. I went with them. You should only know how I wish I'd never gone."

There seemed to be genuine pain in my mother's expression, but who could tell what was genuine anymore?

"Al was one of the teachers there," she continued. "He terrified me. He was handsome and charming, and flirted with me mercilessly. Why me, I'll never know."

"Oh, don't be modest, Mother," I snapped. "You were quite the stunner, if the picture from Melanie's book is any indication."

"Oh, I looked all right, I suppose. It was Al who made me feel beautiful." Her lip quivered. "He took quite an interest in me, and I was quite taken with him. He was so different from the boys at school, so smooth, so worldly, so . . . forbidden."

"So gentile," I added, then winked at Cullie, who was sitting so rigidly on the sofa that he looked like an exhibit at a wax museum. It occurred to me that this little scenario probably wasn't the best backdrop for introducing one's boyfriend to one's mother.

"Yes, so gentile," my mother conceded. "My parents were opposed to my dating gentile boys, so I had to see Al on the sly. It was terribly upsetting to me."

"Tell me about it." When I was in high school, my mother was so dead set against my dating gentile boys that if she suspected I was even thinking of going out with Mike Methodist or Eddie Episcopalian, she'd hire a private detective and have me followed.

"Al had big plans," my mother went on. "He was going to take all the money he earned from giving dancing lessons and go to California, to Hollywood. A talent scout had discovered him and offered to help him break into the movies. I was so proud. I knew, even then, that he would be an important man someday. He had a certain something—a certain something that made him shine brighter than the rest."

"Yeah, he had a certain something that made him shine, all right. A set of brass balls."

My mother gave me a disgusted look. "What he had, Alison, was ambition. A little ambition never hurt a man." She glared at poor Cullie again. "He promised that as soon as he got settled in Hollywood, he would send for me and we would be married."

"You were really going to marry the guy?" Sleeping with him was one thing, marrying the asshole was another.

"Oh, yes. I would gladly have married him. I was so mad for the man I would have done almost anything for him."

My stomach turned. My mother mad for Alistair Downs? The same woman who warned me never to wear my heart on my sleeve? The same woman who acted as if it was against the law to really love a man? My stomach turned again. I wished I'd eaten something.

"Six months I waited. Six months without so much as a phone call or a postcard. My only news of Al was reading about him in the newspaper. I couldn't understand it. We had planned to be married."

"So he dumped you when he got famous, is that it?"

"That's not the way it happened at all," my mother scolded me. "Al decided that the life out in Hollywood was inappropriate for me. He wrote me a letter telling me I was too much of a lady to be subjected to the depraved and decadent lifestyle those movie people enjoyed. He said he wanted to shield me from all that. He said it would be better if we went our separate ways. He said that giving me up was the most difficult and unselfish thing he'd ever done."

My mother wiped a tear away from her left eye. I, on the other hand, was unmoved. As for Cullie, he remained in his state of near catatonia.

"You bought his act?" I asked her. "You believed him?" I'd never before regarded my mother as stupid. Out of touch, maybe, but not stupid.

"Of course I believed him. When you truly love a man, you believe him." I felt a pang of guilt as I remembered how quick I had been to believe that Cullie, the man I loved, was a murderer. "When I found out he had married Annette Dowling, I was more certain than ever that he had told me the truth. Annette was in show business, just as Al was. He knew she would be better suited to the life out there than I would have been."

"Fine. So then you met ambitious, man-on-the-way-up Sy Waxman, a nice Jewish guy perfectly suited to the life your parents wanted you to lead. He treated you like a queen. He bought you everything your heart desired. He loved you. He didn't mind that you didn't love him. You figured, why not marry this man? If I can't have Al, I might as well have money. Am I getting warm, Mother?"

"I loved Sy. Not the way I loved Al, I admit, but I cared for him. He did treat me like a queen. He was very good to me, to you too, Alison."

"Yes, he was. He was so good to me that I hate to think of how you cheated on him, how you talked your nice, sweet husband into buying you a house in Layton, how you resumed your relationship with Alistair and continue to see him to this day."

"That's not true. Al and I broke it off just after Sy's heart attack."

"So you admit you resumed your affair. Behind your husband's back."

"Yes, I admit it." She took a long drag on her cigarette and blew the smoke up toward the ceiling. "But the fact that Al lived in Layton wasn't the only reason I wanted us to move here. I had read about the town in several magazines. It seemed to me that the people here had quality. Their houses were architecturally significant. Their schools had an excellent reputation. I wanted the best for my family."

"Sure, plus a little nookie for Doris."

"Alison, don't be cruel."

"Sorry, Mother. Cruelty comes easily when you've had a good teacher."

"Perhaps I deserve that. I don't know."

"Tell us what happened when you and Daddy bought a house here. How soon was it before you took up with Alistair again?"

"I don't remember exactly. I went to see him at Evermore. He was surprised and delighted to see me. We felt that old excitement, that old electricity between us. We fell into each other's arms. We couldn't help ourselves. There was no denying the power of our love."

Oh, brother. Years of listening to dialogue from "As the World Turns" had addled my mother's brain. "If your love was so powerful, why didn't you and Alistair divorce your spouses and get married?"

"Al had political aspirations, let's not forget. A divorce would have been out of the question. And I had no desire to hurt Sy. He was such a kind man."

"So you and Alistair thought it would be better all around if you committed adultery over a thirty-year period."

"It didn't last that long, Alison. I told you. We broke it off after Sy's heart attack."

"Why? Because you felt too guilty to keep it going?"

"No, guilt had nothing to do with it. I was devastated when Sy passed away. I cared deeply for him. I was grief-stricken."

"So it was grief, not guilt, that made you break it off with Alistair?"

"No, not exactly. Shortly after Sy died, I discovered that Al was seeing other women. I was furious."

"Let me get this straight. You were cheating on Daddy, but you were furious because Alistair was cheating on you?"

"Yes. I thought what Al and I had was sacred. Apparently, he didn't share my view."

"What did you expect? He dumped you once. Why wouldn't he dump you again? The man is scum."

"Stop that, Alison. I won't have you talking about Al that way. Not in my house."

"Okay. I'll confine myself to talking about him that way in *my* house. Please continue."

"I told him to make a choice. It was they or I."

"Don't tell me: he chose they."

"Them, yes."

"How did you learn of his dalliances in the first place?"

"It was Bethany who told me about them."

"Bethany?" Now that was a surprise. "She couldn't have been more than a teenager then. How did she know about you and her father?"

"I don't know. I just know that my doorbell rang one afternoon and there was Bethany Downs, standing on my front steps. She introduced herself and asked if she could come inside. She said she had an important matter to discuss with me. I remember being quite taken aback by her precociousness. She seemed much older, much more in command than most children her age."

"Oh, she's in command, all right. Especially when she's running an errand for her dear old daddy. What did she say?"

"First, she asked me if I had any sweets in the house—cookies, doughnuts, that sort of thing. I said I didn't usually keep sweets in the house as I didn't want *my* daughter to lose her teeth when she got older. She told me to forget the sweets and reached into her purse for a sucking candy. All that sugar, poor girl. I hate to think what her teeth must be like. But that's what happens when a girl has no mother to teach her what's right and wrong."

I tried not to laugh hysterically when my adulterous mother said that, but I was unsuccessful.

"If this is all so funny, Alison, I'll just stop talking right now."

"Oh, no, Mom. Don't do that. Cullie and I are dying to know what Bethany told you. Aren't we, Cullie?"

He nodded.

My mother continued. "I asked Bethany the purpose of her visit. She looked straight at me with those ice blue eyes of hers and said, 'Mrs. Waxman. I've come to give you some advice.' The girl had come to give *me* some advice! 'My father will never marry you. You might as well give up and find some other man.' I was so shocked I nearly fainted! Imagine the nerve of the girl. 'What makes you so sure of that, young lady?' I asked her. 'Because you're only one of six women he goes out with,' she said. 'I don't believe you,' I said. 'Then take a look at this,' she said and handed me a half-dozen pages from Al's appointment book. There were women's names penciled in throughout each day, often for times Al had promised to see me but later said he couldn't because a more pressing engagement had come up. I was desolate.''

"What made you think Bethany was telling you the truth?" I asked. "How do you know she didn't pencil in those women's names herself? She's so possessive of her father's love, she'd probably do anything to keep him all to herself. Did you confront Alistair? Did you ask him if he was cheating on you?"

"No. I just stopped seeing him."

"What happened to that powerful love you both couldn't deny?"

"If you must know, I didn't go to Alistair with the information because Bethany threatened me not to."

"She threatened you?"

"She said if I didn't stop seeing her father, she'd tell *you* about our affair. I couldn't risk that."

"Me? Bethany was going to tell *me* about you and Alistair?"

"That's what she said. I believe the girl has mental problems, dear."

"Don't we all." I couldn't get over all this. "You're not going to insult me by telling me you gave Alistair up because of me."

"I gave him up partly because of you and partly because he was unfaithful to me. His faithlessness wounded me more than you'll ever know."

"So you and Alistair haven't been carrying on with each other these past twenty years? What were you doing at his house the other day?"

"I told you. I went there to convince him to take you back at the newspaper. Al and I are finished. I still love him, of course, but we weren't meant to be."

"Cullie, get a violin," I said mockingly. He shook his head. He was probably trying to figure out how he got lucky enough to have a front-row seat for this mother-daughter psychodrama. "What I don't understand, Mother," I continued, "is your utter hypocrisy. Why, for example, have you been so opposed to my dating gentile men all these years, when you're in love with one yourself?"

"Because Al hurt me deeply. I didn't want you to be hurt by one of them."

"One of them? You think Alistair hurt you because he's not Jewish? Get a grip, Mother. He hurt you because he's pond scum."

"I warned you, Alison. Don't talk about him that way."

"Why not? Why shouldn't I talk about him that way? He *is* pond scum, and if you weren't so dazzled by his fancy dance steps, you'd see it."

"Stop it right now!" my mother shouted, getting up from her chair. "It's downright disrespectful the way you talk about him. You're his namesake, for God's sake. His namesake!"

"I'm what?"

"After whom do you think you were named, Alison?"

I was speechless. My mother named me after Alistair Downs? I was that bastard's namesake? What else was I? Was I his daughter too? Was it possible that I was actually the man's daughter? Oh, God, please no. Life wasn't *that* unfair, was it? A wave of nausea washed over me. Quick! A joke! A joke! Don't let yourself feel, Alison. Crack yourself up so you won't have to endure this pain. Quick! A joke!

"Sonny, are you all right?" Cullie asked, finally getting in on the action.

"No, I'm not all right. I can't think of a joke."

"Maybe that's good. Nobody here is in much of a joking mood," he said.

I looked over at my mother, who had returned to her wing chair. "Mom, please tell me the truth," I implored her. "For once. Just this once. Is Alistair Downs my real father?"

She drew on her Winston, then exhaled slowly. "No, Alison. He's not your real father. Sy Waxman was your real father."

I sighed with relief. There was a God.

"I wanted to name you after Al because I loved him. That's all there was to it. Your father thought Alison was a lovely name for a girl, so we went ahead with it."

Hell, I didn't look a thing like Alistair Downs anyway. I had Sy Waxman's hair and eye color, not to mention his tendency to gain weight in the old gut. "What would you have named me if I'd been a boy, Mother? Alistair? Al Junior? Or maybe just Junior?"

"That's enough, Alison. I've told you everything you wanted to know. I don't have to put up with any more of this." She got up from her chair again and started to move toward the foyer.

"Oh, yes you do," I said, following her. "Just one more question. Where were you the night Melanie Moloney was murdered?"

"What?"

"You didn't hear me or you didn't understand the question?"

"I can't believe you would ask your mother such a thing."

"Believe it. You had a very good reason not to want Melanie's book published. Where were you the night she was killed?"

"I was right here. Sleeping."

"Was Nora here too?"

"No, I don't believe she was. She stayed with her sister in Brooklyn that night."

"Did you hear that, Cullie? My mother's alibi isn't any better than the rest of ours. She was home alone. I was home alone. You were home alone. Todd Bennett was home alone. Only Senator Downs, that devil, has an airtight alibi. He told the police he was with a lady friend that night. But then that little story could be as phony as Alistair's whole life." I paused to recall what else I knew about Detective Corsini's investigation—the fact that Melanie was killed by a blow to the head, a fractured skull, and a subsequent aneurysm, and the fact that the police found white powder on her desk. "I've got one more question for you," I said to my mother.

"You already asked me your 'one more question.' "

"I know. But just one more. I promise."

"One more. Then I'd like you and your friend to go. This interrogation of yours has left me very weak."

"Okay. We'll go. But first, I was wondering about something you said earlier. Remember when you explained that Alistair didn't send for you when he got to California because he didn't want to expose you to the decadent Hollywood lifestyle?"

"Yes."

"Did he ever get specific about that decadence?"

"No. Not really."

"Did he ever mention any involvement with drugs? Cocaine, in particular?"

"Of course not. Al isn't that kind of person."

I regarded my mother with pity. She didn't have a clue what kind of person Alistair Downs was, and what's more she didn't want to. "Good night, Mother," I said, opening her front door.

"No kiss?" she said, as she always did when I tried to leave without giving her a peck on the cheek. Talk about denial. The woman had just confessed to lying to me all her life, yet she acted as if things were hunky-dory between us.

"No, Mom," I said. "No kiss." I took Cullie's hand. We walked out of my mother's house and headed for home.

Chapter 19

Cullie and I went straight back to Maplebark Manor. He had suggested we stop for a bite to eat, but I had no appetite. I was dying to crawl into bed, pull the covers over my head, and escape into sleep with my man's arms tight around me.

As we drove up to the house, we were met by the usual horde of media vultures. But it was the police car—a white Chevy Caprice with the words LAYTON POLICE emblazoned on the sides in large purple letters—that sent my heart palpitating.

"What are *they* doing here?" I said to Cullie when I saw that the car's occupants were Detectives Corsini and Michaels. "The last person I want to deal with tonight is that media hound and his partner in crime prevention."

"Maybe they're here to arrest the media," Cullie offered.

"For what?"

"I don't know. Trespassing. Disorderly conduct. Something like that. Maybe one of your neighbors complained."

"I doubt it. Here comes one of the good detectives now."

Joseph Corsini approached Cullie's Jeep on the passenger's side of the car. *My* side of the car.

" 'Evening, Miss Koff. Quite a crowd you got here," he said, looking out over my front lawn and running his fingers through his hair. "There are crews from all the top tabloid shows."

The top tabloid shows. What an oxymoron. "What can I do for you, Detective?" I asked politely.

"We got a tip earlier this evening," Corsini said. "How about letting us come in for a few minutes so we can talk about it?"

"Now?" I said. "This couldn't wait until tomorrow? My boyfriend and I are eager to get to bed."

"I'll bet," he smirked.

"What's that supposed to mean?" said Cullie.

"Not a thing, Mr. Harrington. Not a thing," Corsini said.

"How do you know my name?" Cullie asked.

"It's my job to know your name. Now, Miss Koff. How about letting me and Detective Michaels come inside for a while? We've got something we want to talk to you about. No need to do it in front of these TV cameras, right?"

"Sure," I said resignedly, wondering about the tip Corsini mentioned. Maybe it had to do with the missing manuscript, which I had stashed in my sauna before going over to my mother's house. Maybe the police got a tip that I was the one who'd stolen it. But how? Nobody knew I had it except my mother and Cullie, and they both wanted the book buried as badly as I did.

I opened the front door of the house, stepped inside the foyer, and was about to punch in the security code on the burglar alarm panel on the guest closet wall when I realized the system was already disarmed. Figures, I said to myself. I must have been so upset about the revelation of my mother's affair with Alistair that I ran out of the house without setting the alarm. Oh, well. No harm done. The place hadn't been robbed, as far as I could tell.

"Come on in," I said to the detectives, waving them inside my house. "We can talk in the living room."

"Pardon me, Miss Koff," said Detective Corsini. "Would you mind if we stopped in the kitchen first? I've got a thirst that won't quit, and a cold glass of milk would really do the trick."

"Oh, sure. No problem." Somehow, I hadn't figured Corsini for a milk drinker, but I led everybody into the kitchen.

"Skim all right?" I asked.

He nodded. "You women. Always dieting."

I opened the door of the refrigerator and was about to reach for the carton of skim milk when I felt Corsini's hand on mine, removing it from the milk carton.

"What are you doing?" I asked. "I thought you said you wanted some—"

"What I wanted was this." He pushed the milk carton aside, reached behind it on the shelf of the refrigerator, and pulled out what appeared to be a plastic Ziploc sandwich bag filled, not with a sandwich, but with fine, white powder. "Well, well. What have we got here, little lady?" he said as he held the bag in front of my face and shook it. "A sweet stash of coke—about an ounce, I'd say. And it was right there behind the skim milk, exactly where our informant said it would be." He winked at Detective Michaels, who winked back.

"Coke?" Cullie and I said simultaneously.

"Pure, premium cocaine," Detective Michaels said as he fingered the bag Corsini had handed to him.

"Cocaine? How on earth did cocaine get into *my* refrigerator?" I asked, horrified.

"I guess you put it there," Detective Corsini smirked. "Remember the tip I told you we got?"

"Yes, I remember."

"Our informant told us to look inside your refrigerator, behind the skim milk, if we wanted to know who killed Melanie Moloney."

"What? What is this? What informant?" I couldn't believe what was happening.

"We can't tell you that," Detective Michaels said, removing the pair of handcuffs that hung from his belt.

"I'll tell you what else you can't do," Cullie said angrily. "You can't come barging into a private citizen's home looking for drugs or anything else. Not without a search warrant."

"You're right," said Detective Corsini. "But we didn't barge in. We were invited in. And we didn't search the premises for drugs. We didn't have to. Miss Koff opened the refrigerator door of her own volition. The coke was sittin' right there in front of our eyes. You don't need a search warrant for somethin' that's in plain view."

Detectives Corsini and Michaels exchanged smug and self-congratulatory looks. Then Detective Michaels moved toward me with the handcuffs.

"You want to read her her rights while I cuff her?" he asked Corsini.

"Cuff me?" I screamed. "Is everybody crazy? I didn't do anything wrong. I don't know where that cocaine came from. I've been set up! I've been set up, I tell you!" Yeah, I know. I sounded like every crook you've ever seen on a TV cop show. But I figured I was better off going with hackneyed, warmed-over TV dialogue than with original and potentially incriminating material.

"What do you think you're doing?" Cullie snapped as Detective Michaels pulled my arms behind my back and placed the handcuffs on my wrists. "This woman is innocent. You're making a big mistake. Take those handcuffs off her now!"

"Sorry, Mr. Harrington," said Detective Corsini, who appeared not the least bit sorry. "We can't transport criminals without handcuffs. Departmental procedure."

"I don't care about departmental procedure. Alison Koff is not a criminal."

"Alison Koff, you are under arrest for possession of cocaine with intent to sell," Detective Corsini said, ignoring Cullie. "You have the right to remain silent. Anything you say can and will be used for or against you in court. You have the right to—"

"You're charging me with cocaine possession?" I said, starting to sob. "With intent to sell?"

"You have the right to stop answering questions at any time," he continued, ignoring me, too. "You have the right to have an attorney present during questioning. If you can't afford an attorney, one will be provided for you."

"Why are you arresting her?" Cullie yelled. "She wasn't dealing cocaine and she didn't kill Melanie Moloney."

"We gotta disagree with you, fella," said Detective Michaels. "We've had our eye on your girlfriend for a while now. We think she did it. Now that we've got her on the cocaine charge, she can cool her heels in the Women's Correctional Facility in Niantic while we nail down the murder charge."

"But why would you think *I* killed Melanie?" I asked. "There are so many people who hated her."

"You had the opportunity, seeing as you were her maid and all," said Detective Michaels. "What we couldn't figure out was the motive. Now we've got that too."

"What motive?" I cried. "I had no reason to kill Melanie. I was broke. She paid me well. Why would I murder my meal ticket?"

"Sure you were broke. Coke's an expensive habit," Detective Corsini said, holding up the bag of cocaine. "We happen to think you're a heavy user. We think you went to work all coked up one day and Miss Moloney caught you with the stuff. She threatened to fire you, have you arrested. You panicked. You went back to Bluefish Cove the night of the twentieth, after Mr. Harrington here brought you home. You walked in on Miss Moloney as she sat in her office. She had your stash of coke right there on her desk. You snuck up on her from behind, smacked her on the back of the head, and killed her. When you went to grab your coke, the bag broke and the stuff spilled out onto the desk. You thought you cleaned it all up, but some of it stayed there. You left the house and returned the next morning for work. Later that afternoon, you called 911 and reported the murder. Open and shut, huh?"

Detective Michaels smiled at his partner, then said, "Like I said before, we had a hunch it was you, Miss Koff. But we couldn't prove it. Then we got the tip about the coke in your refrigerator. It was the coke that tied you to the crime scene."

"But you aren't even sure the white powder on Melanie's desk was cocaine," I cried. "You aren't even sure the white powder in my refrigerator is cocaine. Don't you have to wait for the lab reports before you can accuse me of murder?"

"Nah. We know what we're doin'. The lab reports will only confirm what we already know."

"I'd like to know more about this tip you got," Cullie said. "Who was the informant? And how do you know it wasn't the *real* murderer who planted the coke in Alison's refrigerator?"

"We just know, that's all," said Corsini. "This case is open and shut, I'm tellin' ya."

"What about the murder weapon?" I asked. "What am I supposed to have hit Melanie over the head with? My vacuum cleaner? My dust mop? My Windex bottle?"

"Always making jokes, aren't you, Miss Koff?" said Detective Michaels. "You even made jokes at the crime scene, right in front of the corpse. That's what made me suspicious of you from the very beginning. Most people don't make jokes when somebody they know has just been murdered."

He looked at Detective Corsini, who nodded in agreement.

Great, I thought. I'm being arrested because I make jokes. Sandy always said my jokes would get me into trouble someday, but I never imagined he meant *this* kind of trouble.

"Let's go," Detective Michaels said, leading me out of the kitchen by my right arm, which was pulled behind my back and fastened to my left arm by the handcuffs, which, if they'd been sterling silver instead of cheap steel, would have looked just like the ones Sandy ordered from Tiffany's 1988 Christmas catalog.

"Where do you think you're taking her?" Cullie barked at both cops.

"Down to the station," Corsini replied. "Your girlfriend here is gonna spend the night in a cozy little jail cell."

"Don't worry, Sonny," Cullie said, looking much more frantic than he sounded. "You won't have to spend a second in jail. They'll let you out on bail."

"Not tonight," said Detective Michaels. "Judges don't set bail at this time of night. And even if they did, your girlfriend's bail would be so high she'd have a tough time comin' up with the money. Possession with intent to sell is big-time."

I was so dizzy I nearly fainted. "Help me, Cullie. Help me," I cried. Tears streamed down my cheeks as I was led out of the house in handcuffs, into the waiting camera lenses of America's tabloid media.

"Don't worry, baby. Don't worry," Cullie called out to me as he stood helplessly on my front lawn, watching me being stuffed into the back seat of the police car. "I'm going to get you some help."

"How?" I wailed.

"I'm going over to your mother's," he said.

"Oh, gee. I feel much better now," I muttered.

"I'm going to ask her to call that lawyer she had dinner with tonight," he said.

"Louis Obermeyer?"

"Yeah, that's the guy. We'll get you out of this, Sonny. I promise. I love you."

"I love you too," I sobbed as the police car pulled away.

When we arrived at the station, I was taken into Detective Corsini's office and freed from my handcuffs. Then I was booked, fingerprinted, and photographed. A few minutes later, a middle-aged policewoman named Officer Nancy Dancy instructed me to follow her into the ladies' room, where she told me to take off my clothes and raise my arms. I'd done everything else I'd been asked to do—without complaint—but when it came to Officer Dancy's request, I demurred.

"Do I have to?" was the way I put it.

"Yeah. Off with the clothes—now."

"But it's so cold in here," I said. I was terrified. I'd heard about so-called "strip searches" but never thought I'd be the searchee.

"Let's go," said Officer Dancy, clearly losing patience with me.

"All right," I said, fighting back tears.

First I pulled my sweater over my head. Then I took off my T-shirt. Then I stepped out of my boots. Then I peeled off my blue jeans, then my socks. When I was standing in front of Officer Dancy wearing nothing but my bra and panties, I demurred again. "I can keep these on, right?" I asked with as much respect for Officer Dancy's authority as I could manifest, while trying to establish a sort of slumber-party, just-us-girls rapport with her.

"No. Take 'em off—now," she grumbled, then added, "you better get over the modesty bit, honey. Once you get to the state facility at Niantic, the women there will be on you like flies on shit."

I froze. "How do you mean?" I asked tentatively.

"It's guaranteed—especially if you're a first timer. There'll be thirty other women on your cell block. If they don't get you in the day room, they'll get you in the showers. And if *they* don't get you, the guards will."

I didn't have to ask what "get you" meant, but I was not about to be intimidated by Officer Dancy or anybody else. I was Alison Waxman Koff, mistress of Maplebark Manor. I was innocent of all crimes of which I'd been accused. I would go free. It was The American Way.

I took off my underwear and stood stark naked and perfectly still (well, almost perfectly still) while Officer Dancy checked me for drugs and weapons. I say "almost" because when she felt under my arms, in the center of my armpits, I had an attack of the giggles.

"I'm sorry," I said, trying to squelch my laughter. "I'm ticklish there. Always have been. You too?"

Officer Dancy ignored my question, reached into the left pocket of her uniform, and pulled out a pair of rubber gloves.

"What are those for?" I gulped.

"They booked you on possession of cocaine, right? I gotta check your body cavity for drugs."

My body cavity? I was horrified.

"Bend over," said Officer Dancy.

Quick! A joke! A joke! Don't let this situation traumatize you. Crack yourself up so you won't feel the pain and humiliation of what's about to happen to you. Pretend you're at your gynecologist's office having a checkup. Quick! A joke!

"Hey, Officer Dancy," I said as I bent over and allowed her to insert her gloved fingers into my body cavity. "An eighty-year-old woman goes to the gynecologist and finds out, much to her great surprise, that she's pregnant. She immediately calls her husband on the telephone. 'You old coot,' she says. 'You got me pregnant.' The husband pauses for a second, then asks, 'Who's this?' "

Officer Dancy was not amused. "All finished," she said. "You can get dressed now."

Officer Dancy brought me back to Detective Corsini's office, where I was interrogated yet again—about both the cocaine that had been seized from my refrigerator and the cocaine that had been detected on Melanie's desk. I refused to comment on anything I was asked, and wondered when Cullie would show up with my lawyer.

At midnight, I stopped wondering. Just as I was about to be taken down to the basement, where the female jail cells were located and where, Detective Corsini had explained, I would be spending the night, Louis Obermeyer, the Alan Dershowitz of Grassy Glen Country Club, strode into the station trailed by Cullie and my mother, both of whom looked weak with worry.

"Thank you so much for coming," I said to Mr. Obermeyer as I pumped his hand enthusiastically. I don't remember ever being so glad to see anyone. I'd only met him once, at his daughter Betsy's Bas Mitzvah when I was thirteen, but I recognized him instantly from his picture, which was frequently in *The New York Times* business section. He was tall, had a big gut which he made no effort to conceal, and wore his kinky white hair in what Sandy used to call a "Jewish Afro." His opponents in the courtroom often referred to him as Louis Ogremeyer, because of his cantankerous, curmudgeonly manner. But I didn't care how crabby he was, as long as he got me out of jail. "Sorry you had to come out so late, Mr. Obermeyer," I offered. "I sure do appreciate it."

"Damn right, it's late. I'm tired and I want to go home," he said, then belched.

I embraced Cullie and air-kissed my mother. No, I hadn't forgotten our set-to earlier in the evening, but I had more important things on my mind than her tangled love life.

"Where's the arresting officer?" Mr. Obermeyer barked.

"Right here," Detective Corsini replied, then ran his fingers through his hair and buffed his nails against his pant leg.

"What in the hell makes you think you can search this woman's house for drugs without a search and seizure warrant?"

"Who says we searched her house?" Corsini said smugly.

"According to this young man here," Mr. Obermeyer said, nodding at Cullie, "you and your partner conducted an unlawful search and seizure."

"That's right. They did," I chimed in.

"Shut up, Alison. Don't tell them anything," my lawyer snapped at me. "Keep your damn mouth shut until I tell you otherwise."

Okay, so his jail-side manner was nothing to write home about.

"We didn't do a search," Corsini said. "Didn't have to. Miss Koff let us into her house *voluntarily*. She also opened her refrigerator door *voluntarily*. The cocaine was in plain view. We didn't have to search at all."

"Boloney," said Mr. Obermeyer. "She didn't open the refrigerator door voluntarily. She was deceived into opening it."

"Exactly!" I said. "Detective Corsini pretended he wanted a glass of milk so he could—"

"I thought I told you to shut up, Alison," Mr. Obermeyer snapped again.

"Sorry," I whispered.

"You detectives arrested my client falsely because you had no warrant, and you violated her reasonable expectation of privacy because you deceived her into opening that refrigerator door," he continued.

"You got your opinion of how it went, and we got ours," Corsini said. He was as cocky as my lawyer was cranky. "Now, if there's nothin' else, we're gonna take your client down to the basement to beddy-bye."

I looked at Mr. Obermeyer with pleading eyes. "You're going to let them take me? They can do that? I have to spend the night in jail?"

"I'm afraid so," he said. "It's too late to do anything about bail. But you're a tough cookie, your boyfriend tells me. You'll be just fine down there. You'll see."

"But Louis," my mother said, tugging on his arm. "Surely, there's something you can do about this."

"Yes, Doris. There's something I can do. I can go home, get a decent night's sleep, and be wide awake when I represent her in court tomorrow morning. Now if you people will excuse me . . ."

Louis Obermeyer strode out of the police station. A few minutes later, I said a tearful goodbye to Cullie and my mother, who appeared to have become fast friends. As they walked out together, she hooked her arm through his.

Out of every evil comes good, my father the mattress king always said. In this case, the evil was that I was in jail for cocaine possession and suspicion of murder. The good was that my Jewish mother seemed to approve of my gentile boyfriend. I hoped they'd be a comfort to each other when I was serving my time at the state correctional facility in Lesbian Land.

Officer Dancy escorted me down to the basement and showed me to my cell. It wasn't a suite at the Helmsley Palace, but at least I didn't have to share it with anyone else. It had a bed, a blanket, a Bible, and its own little toilet— without a seat, I was quick to notice.

"Is there another cell available?" I asked Officer Dancy. "The toilet in this one is missing its seat."

"They're all like that," she sniffed, not believing my ignorance. "We gotta make sure you don't kill yourself."

"With my toilet seat?" A razor blade, okay. But a toilet seat?

"People hang themselves with it," she explained. Then, sensing my skepticism, she added, "People do strange things when they're incarcerated."

"Yes, I bet they do. What's that for?" I asked, pointing to the camera in the corner of the cell. I was hoping she'd tell me that I was on "Candid Camera" and that the whole business about my being arrested and thrown in jail was just part of the gag.

"It's a suicide camera," she said. "Like I told you, we gotta watch the inmates. Can't afford to lose one of ya, huh?" She smiled for the first time since we met. I was surprised to see that she wore braces on her teeth. Had she decided to have orthodontia in middle age because she wanted to improve her appearance or because the s edges of braces offered her a secret weapon against recalcitrant prisoners?

"I understand about your not wanting us to commit suicide," I said. "But what about our privacy? We can't even go to the bathroom without that camera recording the action."

"You got it. That's why most people would rather stay out of jail than deal drugs or commit murder. Jail's no picnic."

"No, I suppose not." I never thought it would be a picnic. More to the point, I never thought I'd have to think about it. "Speaking of picnics, do they serve meals here? Or should I ask my family to bring in some take-out?"

Officer Dancy looked at me as if she wished she'd taken another career path. "You'll get breakfast in the morning," she muttered. "Nighty night."

She walked out of my cell, locked me in, and turned to go back upstairs.

"Good night," I called after her. "Thanks for . . . well, for whatever."

God, I was really in jail. I stared at my little cot with its thread-bare, scratchy green wool blanket and felt a catch in my throat. I flashed back to my luxurious master bedroom at Maplebark Manor—its sleigh bed and matching night tables, its chintz drapes and matching upholstered club chairs, its random-width cherry wood floor, its needlepoint area rug, its linen-pleated swing lamps.

Stop it, Alison. Just stop it right now, I scolded myself as tears streamed down my cheeks. It won't do any good to think about your "abundant life" at Maplebark Manor. Even if you hadn't been arrested and sent to jail, you'd have been forced to give up that life anyway. Sandy is gone. Your marriage is over. The bank is going to foreclose on your unless Janet Claiborne finds a buyer for it. The from Second Hand Rose is going to run a tag sale your worldly goods to complete strangers.

I considered the question, then sat gingerly on the bed. I wondered if the inmate who had the cell before me had crab lice and if I'd catch it. I wondered if the camera in the corner of the cell was shooting me on my good side. I wondered if Detectives Corsini and Michaels were watching my every move on a big-screen TV monitor. I wondered if they would get bored and change the channel.

I lay down on the bed and pulled the blanket over me. I clutched the Bible to my chest and prayed.

Please, God, I whispered. Please get me out of here. Or please help Mr. Obermeyer get me out of here. And when you get me out of here, God, please help me find out who planted that cocaine in my refrigerator, who killed Melanie Moloney, and who wants me to take the rap for it. Please give Cullie and me a real chance to be together when this is all over, God. He's a special person, don't you think? Oh, and one more thing, God. Please find a buyer for my house—someone who doesn't mind that Maplebark Manor has no family room. Thanks a million. Amen.

Chapter 20

Sleeping in jail, I discovered, was next to impossible. For one thing, the guards left the lights on all night. For another, they spoke in ridiculously loud voices, just the way nurses in hospitals do. And for a third, the mattress on my cot was so thin the bed springs practically bored a hole into my back. But I must have dozed off at some point, because I was awakened with a start by the sound of clanking against the bars of my cell.

"Breakfast," boomed a policewoman named Rita Zenk. She had a mop of curly, dyed-red hair and wore a thick layer of clownish white makeup, the result of which was that she looked more like Ronald McDonald than a police officer.

"What time is it?" I asked.

"About seven," she said as she slid a tray of food through the narrow slot in the bars.

"Thank you," I said, getting out of bed to receive my breakfast. "I wasn't expecting room service. Nice touch."

"Yeah, and you don't have to pay for it. The taxpayers do."

Breakfast consisted of powdered eggs, stringy bacon, toast that was burned beyond recognition, and black coffee.

"They forgot to give me a knife and fork," I told Officer Zenk when I saw that the only utensil on the tray was a plastic spoon.

"Oh, sorry. You can't have a knife and fork," she explained in a much gentler tone than her colleague, Officer Dancy, would have used. "You aren't allowed to have anything in the cell that might be used for self-mutilation."

"I see," I said, digging into the eggs with my plastic spoon. I hadn't eaten since yesterday's lunch and I was famished.

"People don't realize it but those plastic knives and forks are sharp," Officer Zenk continued. She was chattier than Officer Dancy too. "Last year a guy used one of those knives to cut off both his ears. There was blood everywhere. Every time I go in that cell now, I can still see the stains."

So much for breakfast. I set the tray down on the bed, closed my eyes, and tried to transport myself out of that jail cell, onto an American Airlines DC-10 bound for Saint Martin, onto the little eight-seater that gets you from Saint Martin to Anguilla in six minutes, into the taxi that navigates Anguilla's narrow roads, up to the lushly landscaped entrance of the Malliouhana, the scene of my most memorable Caribbean vacations with Sandy. I tried to imagine us eating breakfast on the patio of our favorite deluxe villa at the hotel, munching on croissants and muffins, mangoes and papayas, omelets and smoked fish, admiring the hibiscus and bougainvillea below, soaking up the sun, inhaling the sea breezes, discussing which of the island's many activities we would take advantage of that day. Ah, bliss, I sighed. Sheer bliss. No matter how bitter I was about Sandy and the way things turned out between us, we did live well. The money was great, while it lasted. Freedom was great, while it lasted.

"Not gonna eat that?" Officer Zenk asked. I was so caught up in my reverie I'd forgotten she was still there.

"No. Thanks anyway though." I hoped she wouldn't take my rejection of her breakfast tray personally.

"You're probably too nervous," she said. "I hear they're settin' your bail this morning."

"I guess so. If I can make bail, I won't have to go to the state facility in Niantic, right?"

"Right. But from what everybody upstairs is sayin', they're goin' for a high bail."

"Because of the cocaine?"

"No. Because they think you murdered that celebrity author. They don't want you skippin' town while they're gettin' their case together."

"But I didn't murder anybody," I wailed. "I'm not a cocaine dealer either. I've been set up. I haven't done anything wrong. This is all one great big miscarriage of justice."

Officer Zenk looked at me sympathetically. "You got a good lawyer?" she asked.

"Louis Obermeyer," I said proudly. "He's very famous."

"I didn't ask you if he was famous. I asked you if he was good."

I thought for a second. "Yes, I believe he is. He's had tremendous success defending insider traders."

"You were arrested on a drug charge. What's that got to do with insider trading?"

"Well," I said, "lawyers are lawyers. And besides, Mr. Obermeyer is a member of my mother's country club. That makes him practically one of the family."

"Has he ever handled a murder case?"

"You really think I'm going to be arrested for murder?"

"Corsini's pretty close to gettin' a warrant. He's just waitin' for some lab reports."

"That's insane," I said, louder than I meant to. "All Corsini has on me is the fact that I was Melanie Moloney's maid, so I had access to her house. And he thinks he's got his motive after seeing cocaine in my refrigerator—cocaine that was planted there. I've never used or sold cocaine in my life."

"You forgot one other thing Corsini's got on you."

"What's that?"

"The murder weapon."

"He does?" I was about to make a joke about how dangerous the family-size Windex bottles were, but thought better of it. These cops were a tough audience.

"Yeah. The lady you worked for, Miss Moloney, was killed with one of her books. The hardback kind."

One of her books? Now that was interesting. I let Officer Zenk's little tidbit sink in for a second or two.

Melanie killed with a book? Smacked on the back of the head with one of her exploitative biographies? Bludgeoned to death with one of her filthy, sleazy, reputation-sullying bestsellers? The irony did not escape me.

"Which of Melanie's books was it?" I asked Officer Zenk, the Layton Police Department's very own Liz Smith. Was it the book on Ann-Margret that sent Melanie's head crashing into the desk? Or was it the Charlton Heston tome? Or maybe the 700-page monster about Merv Griffin? Either way, the answer was sure to wind up in a future edition of Trivial Pursuit.

"I can't tell you exactly which book it was," she said. "But I can tell you that somebody in forensics saw it lying on the floor next to the corpse the day after the homicide. The book jacket had a grease smudge on it, where it made contact with the head of the deceased."

"A grease smudge?"

"Well, not grease. Gel. Mousse. Stuff you put on your hair. Miss Moloney must have been into gels and mousses."

Sure, Melanie was into gels and mousses. How else do you put a sheen in hair that has been bleached so many times it's drier than the brushes of a broom?

"Forensics checked out the smudge, and it was consistent with whatever hair product Miss Moloney had used that day. They also sprayed the book jacket with ninhydrin."

"Sounds like a new nasal decongestant. What is it?"

"It's a toxic chemical you spray on paper materials to detect fingerprints. Several prints turned up on the book jacket, most of them yours. That clinched it for Corsini. He's sure you killed your boss."

"What is he, nuts? Of course my fingerprints are on that book jacket. I was the woman's housekeeper. I cleaned her office. I touched her things all the time. So did Todd Bennett, the guy who wrote the books with her."

"Yeah, I know. His prints are on the book too."

"Why doesn't Corsini arrest Todd then?" I asked. "He hated Melanie as much as I . . . as much as I *loved* her." That was close. You never could tell if Corsini and Michaels were taking all this in on their little suicide camera.

"Mr. Bennett didn't have an ounce of cocaine in his refrigerator. You did."

"I was set up. I already told everybody that." Stay calm, Alison. This cop is trying to be helpful. Get as much out of her as you can. Don't blow it. "You mentioned that there were several fingerprints on the book. Who else's were on it?"

"Your boss's, for starters. Then there were some that haven't been identified."

"Haven't been identified? Isn't it possible that *that* person's the real killer? Instead of locking me up, why don't you guys go out and find the person with the mystery fingerprints and arrest *him?* Or better yet, arrest Todd Bennett. He has no alibi for the night she was murdered."

Okay, I was a snake to throw suspicion on poor, wimpy Todd, but for all I knew, poor, wimpy Todd killed Melanie *and* planted cocaine in my refrigerator. If he was so good at getting the inside scoop about celebrities, maybe he was also good at getting inside someone's house, planting drugs, and tipping off the police.

"Look, I know this is tough on you, your first offense and all," said Officer Zenk. "But try to cheer up. The state of Connecticut has a death penalty, but they haven't executed anybody in years."

My bail hearing was scheduled for ten o'clock that morning. At nine-thirty, I was put in the Department of Corrections van and driven to the state courthouse in Jessup. When I arrived, I was taken to something with the quaint name of a "holding pen," a large area where women from every town in the county were incarcerated while awaiting their turn with the judge. There were prostitutes and drug dealers, an arsonist, a shoplifter, even a woman accused of slicing her husband to death with a Veg-o-matic.

There I was, Alison Waxman Koff, Mistress of Maplebark Manor, locked up with the dregs of society. What had I done in a past life to deserve this? I wondered. What had I done in *this* life to deserve this? Spend a lot of money? Rack up a lot of debt on my credit cards? Buy a house that was obscenely expensive and way too large for two people? Was I getting my just desserts for my excesses? Was it pay-back time for the greed-is-good eighties?

After an hour or so in the holding pen, an officer came to escort me to my appointment with the judge. I bid farewell to my fellow prisoners by telling them to have a nice day. One of them reciprocated by telling me to go fuck myself.

I walked into the courtroom and took my seat at a table next to my lawyer, who seemed even more out of sorts than he'd been the night before.

"My indigestion. It's killing me," he said, taking a swig of Maalox.

I waved to my mother and Cullie, who sat in the first row of the courtroom. They smiled. Cullie gave me the thumbs-up sign. My mother did too.

"All rise," a voice boomed as the judge entered the room.

We rose, we sat. Then the judge addressed us. His name was the Honorable Judge Wilson Pickett. He was black and bald and stern-looking. I wondered if he was named after my favorite soul singer or if my favorite soul singer was named after him. I tried to imagine him singing "Midnight Hour." I could not.

I spotted Detectives Corsini and Michaels sitting at a table with another man, who turned out to be a prosecutor by the name of Fred Goralnik. It was Mr. Goralnik who spoke to the judge first. He explained that his detectives had found an ounce of cocaine in my refrigerator and were recommending that the judge ensure my future court appearances by setting a bail of—get this—$50,000!

"Can they do that?" I asked Mr. Obermeyer. "I won't be able to come up with $50,000. Maybe my mother can, but I don't want to ask her for it."

"Keep quiet," my lawyer snapped. "I'll take care of everything."

I took a deep breath and prayed that Louis Obermeyer knew what he was doing.

"Your honor," he said. "I'd like to see the bail reduced for the following reasons. First, my client was arrested falsely. The police had no warrant. They forced their way into her home, acting, they claim, on a tip from an informant. They deceived her into opening her refrigerator door, where the cocaine was found. Their conduct and the circumstances surrounding the arrest were questionable at best."

Mr. Obermeyer clutched his stomach, belched, muttered an "Excuse me," and took another swig of Maalox.

"Furthermore, your honor," he continued, "my client has no prior record of criminal behavior. Not an arrest. Not a parking ticket. Nothing." He paused to check his notes. "She has never failed to appear in court because she has never *had* to appear in court. She's an upstanding citizen. She has an unblemished record of service to her community. She pays her taxes. She's gainfully employed."

I cleared my throat to get Mr. Obermeyer's attention. He leaned over and I whispered in his ear. "I don't want you to perjure yourself or anything," I said. "So I think I should tell you: I'm not gainfully employed. And I'm not sure I can pay my taxes either. Not this year."

He scowled at me. "Sorry for the interruption, your honor. As I said, my client is a fine citizen with no criminal record whatsoever. While she is no longer employed, due to the recent death of her employer, she has ties to the community. Her mother is a longstanding member of Grassy Glen Country Club, as am I, and I can assure you that she will not fail to appear in court, thereby invalidating the need for an extraordinarily high bail."

"Good work," I told Mr. Obermeyer when he had finished his little speech.

It *was* good work. The judge decided to reduce my bail from $50,000 to $1,000.

"Alison, dear. You're free!" my mother wheezed after she wrote a check for $1,000 and gave it to Mr. Obermeyer to give to the appropriate law enforcement official. I hugged her tightly. All was forgiven. She had just kept me out of the State Correctional Facility in Niantic. I was so grateful, I was willing to put aside all my gripes against her, for the time being anyway.

"Oh, Sonny. I'm so happy," Cullie said, kissing my cheeks, my forehead, my lips. "It won't be long before this whole nightmare is over."

"Don't be so sure," barked Mr. Obermeyer. "We've got a trial to prepare for. Then there's the murder charge they want to pin on you."

"Now Louis," my mother scolded my lawyer as if he were a little boy. "Let Alison and her beau have a few moments of happiness, can't you? They've had so much with which to deal. Give them some peace."

"Thanks, Doris," Cullie said, patting my mother's arm. "You've been great. Sonny and I appreciate it." He kissed her on the cheek.

I was flabbergasted. Cullie and my mother genuinely seemed to like each other.

"Your mom just kept you out of jail," he whispered when he saw my reaction. "That counts for something, doesn't it?"

"Yes, I guess it does. You came through for me too, Cullie. I'd like to show my appreciation as soon as they let me out of here, okay?"

"Your berth or mine?"

"Yours. It's closer."

* * *

Cullie and I spent the night on the *Marlowe*. I felt as if I were home—really home.

"Will you take me sailing again?" I asked as we undressed and climbed into the V-berth. "Our last trip didn't exactly cut it."

"No, it sure didn't," he laughed. "If I remember correctly, everything was going just fine until you accused me of murder."

"Please forgive me," I said, snuggling up against him. "I'll never doubt you again. I promise."

"Promises, promises. You did enjoy the sailing, though, didn't you? You seemed to."

"Oh, I loved it. When can we go again?"

"Maybe next week. It's April—finally. Great sailing weather."

"Cullie?"

"Yeah?"

"I love you."

"I love you too."

"Then make love to me. Make me forget all the terrible things that have happened. Make me forget everything except your taste, your smell, your touch. Make me for—"

Cullie pressed his lips on mine and plunged his tongue into my mouth. I felt a stirring in my groin and surrendered to the sensation. Within minutes, any thoughts of Melanie's murder and my impending arrest melted away, and I slipped into the kind of sweet oblivion only a woman in the arms of the man she loves can know.

Chapter 21

Cullie brought me back to Maplebark Manor early the next morning. He said he was taking the day off to help me with whatever I needed help with. I needed help with everything, I told him. He said our first order of business was to find out who planted the coke in my refrigerator and how the person who did it got into my house—a mystery that was partially solved by a telephone call from Janet Claiborne.

"Mrs. Koff, I'm so terribly soddy about last night," she said.

"Thank you," I said, assuming she meant my unfortunate arrest and even more unfortunate stay in jail.

"It really was all my fault," she went on.

"My getting arrested was your fault?"

"Arrested? I was speaking of your burglar alarm, dear."

"I don't understand."

"I forgot to reset it after I showed the house last evening. I disarmed it when I arrived, but completely forgot to arm it again when I left. Forgive me."

"You were here last night? You showed my house?" Janet hadn't showed my house once in all the months she'd had the listing.

"Indeed I did show your house. And to a very significant member of our community."

"Really? Who?"

"I'm afraid I'm not at liberty to say. You know how these

people like to maintain their anonymity. Let's just hope we get an offer."

Hope was beside the point. Desperation was the point. "So let me get this straight. You forgot to arm the security system when you and this significant member of the community left the house?" I had given Janet the code for the alarm as well as a key to the house when we'd signed the listing agreement.

"Yes, dear. And I am truly soddy. The customer was in quite a hurry—you know how impossible people of consequence can be—and I must have been a trifle scattered."

The customer was a person of consequence? I was dying to know who had come and looked at Maplebark Manor while I was at my mother's house sorting out her love life. Figures, I thought. Janet finally produces a live one and I'm not around to see it.

At least now I knew how the cocaine planter got into my house. He broke in after Janet and her consequential customer left. It was easy enough to break into a person's house, I supposed, but not so easy to disarm a security system—unless, of course, the system wasn't armed in the first place.

"Well," I said. "I'm very encouraged about the showing. Let me know if your customer wants to come back and see the house again."

"Oh, absolutely. As I told you, this customer is a veddy important person in our little town," Janet said proudly. "That's why I was willing to show the house at such an odd hour. I don't believe that houses show best at night, but a showing is a showing. At Prestige Properties, we do our veddy best to bring buyers and sellers together."

Yeah, right. The woman was in the twilight zone. "Oh, Janet," I said. "There's something you should know. I'm planning to have a tag sale. I've asked the woman from Second Hand Rose to sell all my furniture, fixtures, everything. The house probably won't show as well when it's empty."

There was silence on Janet's end of the phone. Then a deep sigh. "If you must, you must," she said finally. "Everyone in town knows of your difficulties, so there's no surprise there. As a matter of fact, all that business about your being Melanie Moloney's housekeeper should work to our advantage."

"How?"

"You're a professional maid, Mrs. Koff. Prospective buyers will assume your house is spotless."

Somehow, between consultations with my lawyer about my impending drug trial, visits to the Layton Bank & Trust Company about their threatened foreclosure of Maplebark Manor, and brainstorming sessions with Cullie about the identity of Melanie's murderer, I managed to schedule the dreaded tag sale. It was held on a rainy, dreary Friday. The weather was so depressing I feared that nobody would show up, despite Second Hand Rose's impressive, full-page ads in the *Community Times*. I also feared that lots of people would show up and track mud all over my spotless house.

My fears (the latter ones) were realized—everyone in the state of Connecticut came to my tag sale. By the end of the day, my floors, which were the only things left in the house after virtually every piece of furniture except my bed was carted off, were covered with sludge. But at least I had raised enough cash to satisfy my creditors and keep my Porsche filled with gas.

"I've never seen such a turnout," raved Second Hand Rose after the last item had been sold.

"People have admired this house for years," I explained. "I guess they thought there would be some valuable pieces for sale."

"Valuable, yes. But not in the way you mean," she said. "They didn't come because of the house. They came because of you."

"Me? Why?"

"They wanted to be able to tell their friends they bought a lamp that was once owned by Alison Koff, the woman who murdered Melanie Moloney."

I was livid. "I didn't murder anyone," I snapped.

"That's not what they're reporting in the *Community Times*. That newspaper has you tried and convicted."

Enough was enough. I was sick and tired of being portrayed as Jill the Ripper in Alistair Downs's pathetic excuse for a newspaper. It was time I had a little chat with its managing editor. I dismissed Second Hand Rose, changed my clothes, and drove over to the paper.

Once inside the building, I headed straight for Bethany's office, but found it empty when I got there. Fine, I thought. I'll wait.

I sat on the sofa and fidgeted. Then I looked up at the portrait of Alistair and Bethany that hung on the wall. What evil deeds have you two been up to? I asked myself. Did either of you kill Melanie? Did either of you plant cocaine in my house and try to implicate me in her murder?

I checked my watch. Where the hell was Bethany? I knew she was in the building, because I'd seen her ice-blue Mercedes in the parking lot.

I got up and paced. I walked over to her pigsty of a desk, which was piled high with papers and littered with doughnut crumbs, and began to snoop—the perfect way to kill time when you're waiting in somebody's office. I was about to sneak a look at a memo written on stationery that read, "From the Office Of Senator Alistair P. Downs," when I heard someone enter the room.

"Koff! What are you doing here?"

I was relieved to find Julia Applebaum, not Bethany Downs, standing before me.

"Oh, hi," I said. "It's nice to see a friendly face. I'd shake your hand, but mine is sticky from all the sugar on Bethany's desk."

"That's what you get for sticking it where it doesn't belong," she laughed. It was great to see her smile. The last time we met, she'd acted like I was a murderer. But then so did everyone else in town.

"How have you been?" I asked. She looked wonderful. Slimmer and more fashionable. Perhaps it was the haircut. The long braid had been chopped off in favor of a stylish, shoulder-length perm.

"Pretty good. Can't complain. How about you, Koff? You surviving your ordeal?"

"Barely."

"Sorry about that," she said sheepishly.

"If you're so sorry, why haven't you called me? It's been months since we got together. You never struck me as one of those women who dumps her girlfriends the minute a man turns up."

"I'm not—usually. Look, we really need to talk about this."

"So you admit you've been seeing someone."

"Sure, she's been seeing someone," Bethany interjected. Neither Julia nor I had heard her come in. She was wearing jodhpurs, riding boots, and a white shirt unbuttoned down to her cleavage, and her blond hair was pulled back in a tight ponytail bound with a perky red ribbon. She wasn't dressed for success in the board room; she was dressed for a tryst at the Hunt Club.

"Hello, Bethany," I said. "I came to talk to you."

"So I see. You don't look so good, Alison. Bad cocaine trip?"

Okay, so Bethany was going the bitch route. Two could play that game. "No, Bethany. No bad trips. Just bad newspaper coverage. There's this local rag that keeps churning out articles implicating me in Melanie Moloney's murder. Know anything about that?"

She shrugged. "We get all our information from the police reports. What can I tell you?"

"Bullshit." I paused to appraise Bethany's riding habit. "Or should I say horse manure?"

"Get to the point, Alison."

"The point is, you've been out to get me ever since you found out I went to work for Melanie Moloney, your father's intrepid biographer."

"That's ridiculous."

"Is it? Julia, remember when Bethany gathered us all together in her office and told us if we didn't stay away from Melanie she'd spank us with her riding crop?"

"Yeah, I remember, Koff. What's that got to do with the murder?"

"Guess who fired me when she found out I was Melanie's maid? And guess who told me she'd rehire me if I told her what was in Melanie's book about Alistair?"

"I did no such thing," Bethany said.

"Don't try to deny it. You told me you'd take me back at the paper in a second—for twice the money I was getting before—if I'd hand over the manuscript or tell you exactly what was in it. You were desperate to know what Melanie wrote about your dear old dad and you assumed I could help you."

"You must be as drugged out as they say," Bethany sneered. "You're not making the least bit of sense. Now if you'll excuse me, I've got a newspaper to put to bed." She pushed her way past me to get to her desk.

"A newspaper to put to bed?" I said, not budging. "Don't make me laugh. Your only experience with beds is sleeping with every married man in town."

"Now just a minute, you, you . . ."

"Hey, take it easy, you two," Julia refereed. "Try to act like adults, would you?"

"Speaking of sleeping with men," Bethany said, curling her lip and drawing her face close to mine. "How's that mother of yours, Alison? Still pining for my father?"

"Your mother knows Alistair?" Julia asked.

"Yeah, they were an item for years, and it drives Bethany crazy," I said. "She likes to have her daddy all to herself."

"Don't listen to her, Julia," Bethany said. "She's got a screw loose."

"Beds. Screws. Did anyone ever tell you you had a one-track mind, Bethany?"

"Why don't you both stop this?" Julia said. "Koff, get a grip, for God's sake. I know you've had a hard time lately, but none of it is Bethany's fault."

"What's gotten into you, Julia?" I was amazed that she was sticking up for Bethany. She always thought Alistair's daughter was as insufferable as I did.

"Nothing's gotten into Julia," Bethany said. "It's just that blood is thicker than water. She and I are practically blood now."

"What's she babbling about, Julia?" I asked.

"Daddy. That's what," Bethany replied. "Didn't Julia tell you, Alison? She and Daddy have been seeing each other."

I stared at Julia, who refused to look me in the eye. "Is it true?" I asked her. "Is Alistair the man you've been so reluctant to tell me about?"

Julia nodded. "I thought it was a good idea to keep our relationship quiet, Koff. Alistair does own the newspaper I work for. I didn't want anybody to cry favoritism. And then there was the matter of my politics. He didn't want it to get out that he was dating a Democrat."

Jesus. Was there a woman's brain Alistair Downs couldn't turn to mush? But Julia? Solid, no-nonsense, Republican-hating Julia? I couldn't believe it.

"Surprised, Alison?" Bethany asked.

I ignored her. "Be careful, Julia," I said to my old friend. "I've read Melanie's manuscript—every last word. Trust me when I tell you, Alistair Downs is not what you think. He's not a man to be toyed with."

"You read the book?" Bethany cried. "You said you didn't have access to it."

"I lied. I not only have access to it, I *have* it. Period." I know, I know. I just admitted to stealing the manuscript from Melanie's house, but I couldn't help it. I had to warn Julia about Alistair. Let the police arrest me. I was getting used to it. "I have the manuscript and I've read it," I said again. "Julia, watch out for the guy. It wouldn't surprise me if he killed Melanie to keep the book and its author out of circulation—permanently."

"You're totally out of it, Alison," Bethany said. "Daddy has an alibi for the night of the murder. He was with somebody."

"Yeah, a 'lady friend,' " I scoffed. "Some alibi. He's got the police so bamboozled, they'd buy anything he told them."

"It's true, Koff," Julia said. *"I* was with Alistair that night. There's no way he could have murdered Melanie Moloney."

So Julia was the lady friend. "Maybe he hired someone to murder her for him," I said. "Or maybe he had his faithful daughter do it."

"You really are depraved, Alison," Bethany said, shaking her head. "Must be all those drug dealers you hang out with."

"I wouldn't talk about the company *I* keep, if I were you," I smiled. "I'm the one who's read Melanie's book, remember? I know all about your father's Mafia pals, his buddies in the KKK, you name it. There isn't a closet in the country that could hold that man's skeletons." I paused for effect and waited for a reaction. There was none. "I wonder what would happen if some of Melanie's little anecdotes about the Downs family found their way into the press?" I paused again. "What do you think, Bethany?" Silence. "Here's what I think," I said, walking toward the door. "I think that if *The Layton Community Times* continues to run stories linking me to Melanie's murder, I'm gonna have to slip a few excerpts from the manuscript to the tabloid reporters, who are camped outside my house as we speak." I stopped and looked at Bethany and Julia. They were stunned. "No comment?" I waited. "Well then, I guess I'll be going, kids. Julia, have a nice day. And Bethany . . ." I paused as I gave her riding outfit the once-over. "Have a great time mounting those stallions."

* * *

"You told them you had the manuscript?" Cullie asked when I recounted the story of my trip to the newspaper. He'd come to the house to help me pack. As Maplebark Manor was now devoid of any furniture except my bed, we both thought it would be less depressing for me if I moved back to the *Marlowe*.

"I guess it wasn't the smartest thing I could have done," I conceded. "But when I heard that Julia, Ms. Feminist, Ms. Politically Correct, Ms. Champion of the People, was keeping company with Alistair, the elitist chauvinist bigot, I snapped. I had to warn her. And I didn't mind giving Bethany something to chew on either. Now that she knows I know what's in that manuscript, I've got her right where I want her. She wouldn't dare write about me in that newspaper of hers now."

"I hope you're right," Cullie said. "Where is the manuscript, by the way?"

"It's still in the sauna."

"Let's take it with us. You never know who might come looking for it."

"Right."

I went downstairs, opened the door to the sauna, and retrieved the manuscript. Then I brought it upstairs and stuffed it in a Bloomingdale's shopping bag.

"Ready," I said when I had packed two bags and called both my mother and Mr. Obermeyer to let them know where I'd be if they needed me.

We spent a soothing, restorative night on the *Marlowe*. The air was balmy and sweet, and the moonlight shimmered on the water. Cullie made us dinner—the same aromatic seafood stew he'd prepared for our first date—and we bundled up and ate our meal in the cockpit instead of inside the cabin.

"Is there anything you love more than this boat?" I asked him as we sipped our wine and inhaled the sea air.

"Fishing, are we?" he smiled.

"No, I'm not. Honest. I know you love me. You've more than proven it these last few weeks. But I think you love the *Marlowe* in a way that transcends romantic love."

He thought for a minute. "I love the boat, sure." He fingered the steering wheel affectionately, then looked dreamily out to sea. "You get attached to a boat when you rebuild it from the keel up. But it's living on the boat that I really love."

"You mean, living on a boat as opposed to in a house?"

"I mean, living in harmony with the elements instead of trying to master them. When you live on a boat, with the sea as your backyard, you're not competing with nature, you're respecting it. You learn your place in the scheme of things." He paused to take a sip of wine. "Living on a boat teaches you self-reliance. It teaches you how to savor the little things, the things that really matter. It teaches you to survive with less, without excess. It reduces life down to its bare essentials: getting warm, getting dry, getting fed, getting sleep." He took another sip of wine. "The fact is, Sonny girl, the sea doesn't care how many corporate takeovers you've engineered, how many Porsches you've got in your garage, or how many brands of balsamic vinegar you can cook with. Living on a boat, away from all that, helps to put stuff in perspective, see?"

I kissed Cullie's cheek, put my arms around him, and stared up into the starlit sky. "I see," I said and breathed in the sights and sounds of the marina.

We stayed up on deck, in the cockpit, for another hour or so, then climbed down the hatch into the cabin and got ready for bed.

"You working tomorrow?" I asked.

"Probably. The guy on the radio said it's supposed to be sunny, and I've got some exterior shots to do."

"Rats. I was hoping you'd take me sailing. But I guess I

should spend tomorrow trying to get a job—if anyone in this town will hire me."

"Somebody will hire you, my sweet," Cullie said tenderly. "What's more, Mr. Obermeyer will get that cocaine charge off your back, and the police will find out who really killed Melanie. Everything will work out, I know it will."

"It's got to, Cullie. It's just got to."

We climbed into the V-berth and held each other. A few minutes passed, and I could tell by Cullie's heavy, open-mouth breathing that he was about to drift off to sleep. I, on the other hand, was wired—and aching to be made love to.

"Cullie? Are you awake?"

"Sort of. Anything the matter?"

"Remember when we were up on deck and you were telling me how living on a boat reduces life down to its bare essentials?"

"Umm."

"Remember how you said those bare essentials were getting warm, getting dry, getting fed, and getting sleep?"

"Umm."

"Didn't you forget something?"

"Good point. Come 'ere."

The next morning we woke up early, went over to the marina's restrooms to shower (the *Marlowe*'s head was finally operational but Cullie said we should continue using the public bathrooms and save the head for sailing trips), and came back to the boat for coffee and cereal. I knew Cullie had several houses to shoot before the morning sun was gone, so I encouraged him to get going. He'd sacrificed enough of his work time for me and my dramas. But he seemed hesitant to leave, despite my not-so-subtle attempts to usher him out the door.

"If you're worrying about me, don't," I said. "I'll be just fine."

"I know." He kissed me. "But I keep thinking about your conversation with Bethany Downs yesterday. I really wish you hadn't admitted you had the manuscript."

"Why? Bethany's not going to tell anybody. She wants the book buried. If people find out what's in the manuscript, her daddy's reputation will be so badly damaged he won't be able to get arrested in this town."

"It's *your* getting arrested that worries me. How do you know she or Julia won't go to Corsini? Finding out that you were the one who stole the manuscript from Melanie's house could be the key to his nailing you for the murder."

"Hey, buddy? Weren't you the one who told me everything was going to work out?" I put my arms around Cullie and hugged him.

"Yeah, but humor me. Let me put the damn manuscript someplace where Corsini won't find it—just in case he comes snooping around here."

"Okay, but where?"

"I'm thinking."

Cullie paced back and forth inside the cabin.

"You said you rebuilt this baby from the keel up," I said. "You must know its every nook and cranny. Is there a secret space somewhere?"

He stroked his beard and pondered the question. "As a matter of fact, there is," he said finally. "When I replanked the topsides, I built a secret storage area under the anchor locker, just forward of the V-berths."

"Don't tell me, let me guess: you had a premonition there'd be a missing manuscript you'd have to hide from the cops someday."

"No, actually a lot of sailors like to have a secret locker when they travel to foreign ports. It's great for storing valuables."

"Terrific. Is this secret locker big enough to hold the manuscript?"

"Should be. You get the manuscript. I'll get everything ready."

I retrieved the Bloomingdale's bag from the hanging locker and brought it into the V-berth, where Cullie was pulling up the mattresses.

"Better get something to wrap it in so it doesn't get wet down here," he said as he crawled down into the tiny compartment between the anchor locker and the V-berth.

I scurried into the galley and found a large plastic garbage bag, then went back into the V-berth and wrapped the manuscript in it, then taped it securely.

"Okay. Now hand it to me," Cullie said, his voice muffled.

I lowered the manuscript down to Cullie, who was burrowing beneath the secret subfloor.

Seconds later, he emerged. "Mission accomplished," he said proudly.

"You don't think Corsini and his boys would look down there?" I asked.

"They wouldn't know to look there. And even if they did, they'd have to move two hundred feet of mud-encrusted anchor chain to find it."

We both breathed a sigh of relief.

"Feel better now?" I asked after Cullie had restored the mattresses to their normal place in the V-berth and returned to the galley for a last sip of coffee.

"A little."

"Good. Now go. I'm planning to be very busy today," I said, holding up the classified advertising section of the *Community Times.*

"I'm going. I'm going," he smiled. "Knock 'em dead."

I winced. "Do you have to use that expression? I'm a murder suspect, remember?"

"Sorry. How about: give 'em hell."

"Better. Much better."

*   *   *

Jane Heller

At about one o'clock, as I was sitting by the phone at
Cullie's navigation desk, eating a tuna fish sandwich and
trying to swallow the fact that all four jobs I'd called about
had already been filled, I heard footsteps on the deck of the
boat, then pounding on the hatch.

"Who's there?" I called out.

"Detective Joseph Corsini, Layton Police Department.
Open up."

I nearly choked on my sandwich. Oh, God. Maybe Cullie
was right. Maybe Bethany did tell Corsini I took the manuscript and now he had come to get it. I glanced over in the
direction of the secret storage area under the anchor locker
and sighed with relief that the manuscript was safely hidden
there. No manuscript, no evidence.

I opened the hatch. Corsini was not alone. Detective
Michaels was along for the ride.

"What's up, boys?" I asked, trying to sound nonchalant.

"This," Detective Corsini said, and handed me an offi-
cial-looking, four-page document.

I scanned the first page and gasped. "It's a warrant for my
arrest," I cried. "But for what? There's no cocaine on this
boat. You can check the refrigerator."

"Read the last paragraph," said Detective Michaels with
a self-important smirk on his face.

I flipped to the last page of the document and read the
final paragraph. "Based upon the facts and circumstances
contained herein," it said, "a warrant is requested for the
arrest of Alison Waxman Koff, of 33 Woodland Way, Layton, Connecticut, charging her with one count of murder in
violation of Section 53a–54a of the Connecticut General
Statutes for her participation in the crime described herein."
Murder!

"Alison Koff, you have the right to remain silent . . ."
Detective Michaels began, unhooking the handcuffs from
the back of his belt and fastening them around my wrists.

"But wait," I screamed as he continued to read me my
Miranda rights. "You can't arrest me for Melanie's murder.

I didn't kill her! I didn't kill anybody! Somebody help me!"

"We *can* arrest you and we just did," said Detective Corsini. "That's what this document is about. A judge signed it, see?" He waved the warrant in front of my face.

"On what grounds? My fingerprints on the book? The cocaine in my refrigerator? That's not enough to—"

"A little birdie told us you stole the manuscript Miss Moloney was workin' on," said Detective Corsini. "Stole it right from the crime scene, eh, Miss Koff?"

Bethany. Cullie was right.

"Our informant claims to have seen the manuscript in your possession, Miss Koff," Detective Michaels explained. "The informant also said you were hidin' it somewhere. One of these days, we'll find out exactly where."

"That's a lie." Well, the part about Bethany having actually seen me with the manuscript was.

"We'll let the judge decide," said Detective Corsini. "But I guarantee you, he'll see it our way." He chuckled and buffed his fingernails against his pant leg. "This news about the manuscript really sews up the case for us."

"But I'm innocent, I tell you. I didn't do it."

"If you're innocent, why'd you steal the manuscript?"

"I was all out of bedtime stories," I said.

"There she goes again with the jokes," said Detective Michaels.

"She won't be jokin' for long," Detective Corsini said, running his fingers through his slicked-back hair. "Will you, Miss Koff?"

I stuck my tongue out at him. I would have given him the finger but mine were handcuffed behind my back.

"Stealin' that manuscript was a greedy, greedy thing to do," said Detective Corsini. "It was bad enough that you killed your boss to stop her from turnin' you in for cocaine dealin'. But to steal her book so you could extort money from honest, reputable, hardworkin' people like the Downs family? Tsk tsk. Shame on you."

"The Downs family? Reputable? Don't make me puke."

I made gagging noises. "What's this about extortion? I didn't extort money from the Downs family or anyone else. What are you talking about, Corsini?"

"Our informant told us there are some nasty allegations about the Senator in that book," Detective Michaels said. "Our informant also told us you were playin' the blackmail game. Blackmail isn't very nice. Is it, Miss Koff?"

"Let me get this straight. First, you accuse me of cocaine possession. Then you accuse me of murder. Now you're accusing me of blackmail. What's next, child abuse?"

"Well?" said Detective Corsini. "You got something you want to get off your chest?"

"No!" I suddenly remembered Mrs. Silverberg. The way my luck was going, she'd probably come forward and tell Corsini about my dumping soda on her daughters' heads. "I'm not going to say another word without talking to my lawyer. I *am* allowed to call my lawyer, aren't I?"

"You know the routine, Miss Koff," he said. "You're gettin' to be an old hand at this arrest stuff. You can call your lawyer when we get down to headquarters. Let's go."

Chapter 22

By four o'clock that afternoon, I was back in my old cell in the basement of the Layton Police Station—my home away from home. No, it didn't boast all the amenities of Maplebark Manor, but at least *this* home wasn't on the verge of foreclosure.

"Well, hello. Look who's here," said Officer Zenk as she slid a tray of food through the narrow slot in the bars of my cell.

"Hello yourself," I said, trying to be friendly. Officer Zenk had been a fount of information about my case the last time I was in the slammer. I was counting on her to be just as forthcoming this time around. "I hope you don't mind my asking, but is this a late lunch or an early dinner?" Judging by the food on the tray—chipped beef on toast, mashed potatoes, and raspberry Jell-O—it could have been either.

"It's dinner. Enjoy."

"Thanks, but I think I'll pass." Shit on a shingle wasn't my idea of dinner. Besides, I'd had that tuna sandwich a few hours before, and in all the excitement, it was beginning to repeat on me.

"I ran into your boyfriend upstairs," she said.

"Cullie?" I'd left a message on his answering machine, explaining what had happened.

"I didn't catch his name. He was talkin' to your lawyer."

"Mr. Obermeyer. Do you know if he's still here?"

"Your lawyer or your boyfriend?"

"My lawyer."

"Yeah. I heard him yellin' at Corsini."

"About what?"

"He was yellin' about how you were arrested wrongfully, how Corsini had no proof that you stole Miss Moloney's manuscript, how the police were takin' an informant's word over yours, how they were only goin' on hearsay, how they hadn't handled a murder case in forty years and were so inept they were an embarrassment to the law enforcement community."

"Wow. I told you I had a good lawyer."

"If he's so good, let's see him get your bail reduced again."

"Why? How much will it be this time?"

"They're talkin' about half a million dollars."

"Are you serious? Last time, it was only fifty thousand."

"Last time you were up on drug charges. This time, it's murder. Big difference."

I fought back my tuna sandwich. I wished Mr. Obermeyer were around. I'd mooch some of his Maalox. "I didn't do it, Officer Zenk. I didn't kill Melanie Moloney. Honest, I didn't."

"Corsini thinks you did," she said. "He says it's an open-and-shut case now. He's got the motive: your boss caught you doin' coke on the job. He's got the proximity: you had access to the house since you were the maid. He's got your fingerprints on the murder weapon. And now he's got the fact that you stole the deceased's manuscript from the crime scene."

"This is incredible," I said, shaking my head. "I'm completely innocent."

"It's not me you have to convince," said Officer Zenk. "But if I were you, I'd get my lawyer to cut a deal."

"A deal?"

"Yeah, a plea bargain. It goes like this: they let you off the murder charge, you plead guilty to manslaughter."

"Why would I do that? I didn't kill anybody."

"Honey, do you know what the sentence for murder is in the state of Connecticut?"

"No," I said tentatively.

"Twenty-five years to life. Like I said, if I were you, I'd tell my lawyer to cut a deal, especially if I didn't want to eat chipped beef on toast for the rest of my life."

After Officer Zenk left, I paced back and forth in my cell, feverish with worry over my bail hearing the next morning. Obviously, I would never be able to come up with $500,000. And I knew my mother wouldn't be able to either.

After I wore myself out pacing, I sat down on my cot and contemplated my future. What if Mr. Obermeyer couldn't persuade the judge to reduce my bail? What if he couldn't persuade a jury that I was innocent of murdering Melanie? What if I were found guilty and sentenced to life imprisonment in the State Correctional Facility in Niantic?

I decided that my future was too awful to contemplate, so instead I contemplated my past. I wondered if God were punishing me for my fur coats, my Porsche, my big house. Were we all being punished? Was the stock market crash God's way of telling us that we had overstepped, overspent, overdrawn? Was the recession His idea of a spanking?

I put my head in my hands and cried. Please help me, God, I prayed. I swear I will cut wastefulness and gluttony out of my life forever. I will never covet my neighbor's house, his pool and tennis court, or even his professionally landscaped grounds. I will never utter the words, "Charge and send." I will never order merchandise from a TV infomercial, no matter how many movie stars endorse the product. I will repent, Lord. I swear I will. Amen.

*   *   *

"Rise and shine," said Officer Zenk as she deposited the breakfast tray into my cell the next morning. The meal consisted of coffee, burnt toast, and a waffle that was so flat and lifeless it looked like it had been run over by a fleet of Mack trucks.

"Thanks, Officer," I said, groggy from lack of sleep. "But I'm not very hungry. Bail hearings don't do much for the appetite." I sent my breakfast tray back through its shoot.

"You mean you haven't heard?" she said.

"Heard what?"

"They're sayin' the judge is gonna throw the murder charge right out the window. Lieutenant Graves is flippin' out."

"My murder charge?"

"You got it."

"Who's Lieutenant Graves?"

"The big cheese. Corsini's boss. He's madder than hell over the way Corsini and Michaels have botched your case so far."

"Wait a minute, Officer Zenk. Rita. May I call you Rita?"

"It's okay, I guess."

"Good, Rita. Now let's start from the beginning. Why is the judge going to throw out the murder charge and why is Lieutenant Graves so angry at the detectives handling my case?"

" 'Cause they screwed up. They never field-tested the white powder that was found on the deceased's desk."

"You mean the cocaine?"

"Right."

"What do you mean by 'field-tested'?"

"Detectives have these little kits that come with chemical ampules," Rita explained. "When they find powder at a crime scene and want to know if it's cocaine, they take a little dash of the powder, put it in a plastic tube, break an ampule into it, and shake it up real good. If the stuff tests positive for cocaine, it'll turn purple. Then they send the rest of it to the lab for confirmation."

"I assume the stuff turned purple, right?"

"That's just it. Corsini never field-tested the powder on Miss Moloney's desk. Neither did Michaels. They tested the stuff in your refrigerator, but they didn't test the stuff at the crime scene. And oh, man, are they in for it."

"I'll bet." I still didn't understand how the Layton Police Department's latest display of ineptitude would provoke a judge to set me free, but I trusted that Rita would get to the point eventually.

"Yeah, you should have seen Lieutenant Graves chew 'em out last night. He comes stormin' into Corsini's office, wavin' the lab reports, and yellin' so loud I'm surprised you didn't hear him down here in the basement."

"The lab reports? They came back from Meriden?"

"Yeah, they came back. That's why the lieutenant went bat-shit. He walks in and says to Corsini and Michaels, 'Didn't either of you assholes field-test the powder found on the deceased's desk?' They look at each other like they've been caught, right? Corsini says to Michaels, 'Didn't you field-test the powder?' Michaels says, 'No. I thought *you* were going to.' Corsini says, 'Well, I thought *you* were going to.' Then the lieutenant says, 'How can you fuckin' assholes send the stuff to the lab without field-testing it first?' The whole thing was bad news. If you ask me, I'd say your lawyer was right: this police force hasn't had a murder case in forty years and they don't know what they're doin'. And that Corsini." She shook her head. "He's so celebrity-crazed that when he heard it was a famous author who got murdered, he kind of lost it."

"If he ever had it to begin with."

Officer Zenk laughed.

"So let me get this straight, Rita. The powder on Melanie's desk was never field-tested. Therefore, the judge is gonna let me go?"

"No, honey. The lab reports from Meriden came back negative. Therefore, the judge is gonna let you go."

"Negative? You mean, the powder on Melanie's desk wasn't cocaine after all?"

"You got it. Corsini's goin' berserk because he's got no case against you now. No cocaine, no motive. Of course, he's not finished with you yet. He still thinks you murdered your boss. But he's got to find another way to prove it—and he's not givin' up till he does. His job is on the line."

Who cared about Corsini's job? I was about to go free! No cocaine, no motive for the murder. That's what Rita said. So what if my fingerprints were on the book that somebody used to bash Melanie over the head. There were other fingerprints on that book. Maybe I'd find out whose.

"I'll be back to get you in a couple of hours or so," Rita said. "The hearing's at ten."

"Thanks, Rita. You've been great to me. Really, you've saved my life in this place. I'll never forget you."

"Don't mention it. I mean, don't mention to anybody that I told you all this stuff. The guys upstairs are always sayin' what a big mouth I have. I could get in trouble if they find out I blabbed."

Rita moved away from my cell and was starting to walk back upstairs when I called out to her.

"Rita?"

"Yeah?"

"About the lab reports."

"What about 'em?"

"You said they came back negative, that the powder on Melanie's desk wasn't cocaine."

"Right. It wasn't."

"So what kind of powder was it?"

"In police lab language, the report said: 'Polysaccharide conjoined by a disaccharide with traces of a cellulosic cinnamaldehyde.' "

"How about in plain English?"

"Sugar. Powdered sugar. With a touch of cinnamon."

Powdered fucking sugar? I was arrested for murder because of a few measly granules of confectioner's sugar?

"Hey, cheer up," said Rita. "In a couple of hours you'll be out of here."

"Thank you, God," I whispered to the ceiling of my cell after Rita had departed for the great upstairs. "It looks like you kept your end of the deal. Now it's up to me to keep mine."

My bail hearing turned out to be a thrilling example of the American Justice System at work.

"Your Honor," my lawyer addressed the judge. "The police arrested my client on the basis of pure hearsay. Hearsay! They never found a missing manuscript in her possession. They never even searched her house. So they have her fingerprints on the murder weapon. So what? They have no motive for the murder. The cocaine on the deceased's desk turned out to be sugar. Now what are they gonna do? Accuse my client of killing her employer over a spoonful of sugar?"

I laughed. Mr. Obermeyer gave me a dirty look and shushed me. Then he took a swig of Maalox and belched.

"Under the circumstances, your honor," he continued, "I move that all charges be dropped against my client—the cocaine possession with intent to sell and the murder charge. Thank you."

Judge Pickett threw the case out. Then he threw us out—but not before inflicting a punishing tongue-lashing at the prosecution for arresting me on the basis of such flimsy evidence and for embarrassing the court with its astonishing ineptitude. It was fun watching Corsini flinch every time Judge Pickett used words like "dimwitted," "idiotic," and the old standby "stupid" to describe the way the police had bungled the investigation thus far. I could only imagine Corsini's relief that Court TV wasn't videotaping the proceedings.

"This isn't over," he whispered as we left the courtroom.

"The judge seems to think it is," I smiled.

"The judge isn't out to nail you. I am."

"Is that a threat?" I asked Corsini. "If it is, I'll have to inform His Honor."

"Go ahead and inform him. It'll be your word against mine."

"Exactly. I may be a murder suspect, but my credibility with Judge Pickett is a lot better than yours right now."

Corsini scowled, ran his fingers through his hair, and slid out of the courtroom.

"What's his problem?" Cullie asked, nodding in Corsini's direction.

"Bad hair day," I shrugged.

"What do you say we go out for dinner to celebrate your freedom?" Cullie suggested when we were back on the *Marlowe*. I had showered and changed and was relaxing on the settee berth.

"You mean, McGavin's or Arnie's or someplace like that?"

"No. I'm talking about Les Fruits de Mer or one of the other la-de-da places."

"But they're so expensive."

"Yeah, but you don't get murder charges dropped against you every day. We should celebrate in style, don't you think?"

"You know I don't have any money. And I can't ask you to pay for it."

"I just did a four-page brochure for Prestige Properties. I can certainly handle one dinner out—especially for such a momentous occasion."

"But the dress code's jacket and tie. Do you even own a tie?"

"Yeah, one. Fortunately, it goes very nicely with the one sport jacket I also own."

"Great. You can change here, then we'll stop by Maplebark Manor and I'll put on the one nice dress I didn't unload during my tag sale."

"We'll be quite the fashionable couple."

"Oh, quite. The sailing instructor's son and the murderous, cocaine-sniffing scullery maid."

Les Fruits de Mer had been one of Sandy's favorite restaurants during the early part of our marriage, those glory days of the eighties when nobody minded spending 200 bucks for a little Tuesday night supper. And I do mean *little*. The portions at Les Fruits de Mer were so tiny you had to eat again when you got home.

Overlooking Layton Harbor, Les Fruits de Mer served "Continental" food as opposed to strictly French fare. In other words, its menu, which had the look of a leather-bound literary classic and was printed in gold script, featured Cuisses de Grenouilles Provençale right up there along with the Wiener Schnitzel. As I mentioned, the actual meal was a lot more Schnitzel than Wiener. But hey, the place wasn't a total rip-off. They did give you a complimentary dish of lemon sorbet so you could cleanse your pallet between courses.

"Bon soir," said the maître d' as we entered the restaurant. He was dressed in the obligatory tuxedo and tried very hard to make his Brooklyn accent sound French.

"Reservation for two at seven-thirty. The name is Harrington," Cullie said.

"Oui, Monsieur Harrington. Right this way."

The maître d' showed us to a lovely table by the window. I was surprised we were granted such an important table, seeing as Cullie was not exactly a regular at the place. Then again, the regulars weren't in evidence. The restaurant was empty, except for a party of three seated at the other end of the room.

"Looks like business isn't so good," Cullie said. "I'm

disappointed. This is my first time here and I was expecting to see some of Layton's big shots."

"It's the recession, I guess," I said. "Nobody can afford to come here anymore, except extremely talented architectural photographers, of course."

"Of course." He smiled. "How about a toast?"

I picked up my champagne glass. "Here's to Janet Claiborne," I said gaily.

"Why on earth would you want to toast her?" Cullie asked. "Because the brochure I did for her is paying for this meal?"

"No, silly. Because she brought *you* into my life."

Cullie raised his glass and clinked mine. "To Janet Claiborne," he said. "With my deepest gratitude."

We ordered dinner, both of us opting for some fruits de mer—Cullie, the Lobster Newburg, me, the Dover Sole.

"Where's the rest of it?" Cullie said after the waiter had brought our entrées and departed.

"Oh, you mean the portions?" I said. "Small, aren't they?"

"You're not kidding," he said, looking down at the thimble-full of Lobster Newburg that rested on his plate.

"Try the bread," I suggested. "It'll fill you up. If not, you can always munch on the Pansies."

"Gee, thanks."

"Hey, this place was your idea, remember?" I kidded him. *"Bon appetit."*

"Bon appetit yourself," he said, then took a bite of his lobster and smiled. "There may not be much of it, but what's here is pretty damn good."

"Here's to 'pretty damn good,' " I said, raising my champagne glass for another toast.

We toasted and ate and enjoyed ourselves for another hour or so. Then I excused myself and went to the ladies' room, which was at the far end of the restaurant. I was about to pass the table of three—the only other diners in the place besides Cullie and me—when I saw that the gruesome threesome was none other than Alistair, Bethany, and Julia. What a way to spoil a pleasant evening.

I debated whether to pretend I didn't see them or to walk over to their table and say hello. Why shouldn't I say hello? Why should I let Bethany think she got the best of me when she told Corsini I had Melanie's manuscript? Why should I let her think I was rotting in a jail cell eating chipped beef on toast? Why shouldn't I walk right over to her table and shove my freedom right up her miserable ass? Besides, Julia was at the table too, and she was my friend. At least she used to be. There was no point in snubbing her, just because she had lousy taste in dinner companions.

As I approached the table Alistair and Julia were sipping cognac, while Bethany was diving into a mile-high chocolate soufflé.

"Good evening, everyone," I said.

Alistair stood. Julia smiled. Bethany looked up momentarily, then resumed eating.

"Oh, please don't get up," I told the senator. "I just stopped by to say hello."

"Splendid of you," Alistair chortled, his face ruddy with drink. "You know everybody, I presume?"

Of course I know everybody, you big phony. "Yes, Senator. I know everybody."

"Well, then," Alistair said, clearing his throat. "Won't you sit down?"

"Yeah, Koff. Why don't you join us?" Julia said.

"No, thanks. I'm with somebody," I said, nodding in Cullie's direction.

"The photographer?" Julia asked after glancing over at Cullie.

"Yup," I said. "As a matter of fact, I've moved in with him. On his sailboat, the *Marlowe.*"

That seemed to get Bethany's attention. She actually stopped chewing. "You can't mean Cullie Harrington, Paddy Harrington's son?" she said.

"I can and I do," I said, then watched to see if Paddy's name would produce a reaction in Alistair. It didn't.

"Where's his boat docked these days? I haven't seen him around the yacht club since Preston left him," Bethany said.

I ignored her little reference to Cullie's ex-wife. "The *Marlowe* is docked at the Jessup Marina," I said.

"The Jessup Marina? That must be quite a comedown for you, Alison, after living at 33 Woodland Way."

How did Bethany know my address? I wondered. She'd never set foot inside Maplebark Manor—certainly not at my invitation.

"Any luck selling the house?" Julia asked.

"Not yet. But my broker says we're close. She was encouraged by our last showing," I replied, thinking of Janet's "customer of consequence."

"That's great, Koff," said Julia. "It's great about you and Cullie too."

"What fun to live on his sailboat, just the two of you," Bethany cooed as she shoveled a huge helping of soufflé into her mouth. She was every bit the big phony her father was. She wanted me to have fun on Cullie's sailboat about as much as I wanted her to enjoy her dessert. "You may not know this, Alison, but your boyfriend's father gave me sailing lessons at the yacht club years ago. He taught me everything I know about boats. Unfortunately, the old man had a booze problem. I certainly hope his son doesn't have the same problem. It could be hazardous to your health."

"I didn't know you cared," I said wryly. "But you needn't worry about me, Bethany. Cullie's a very competent sailor. I don't anticipate any problems."

"Just warning you," Bethany smiled. Her improbably white teeth were smeared with chocolate. "You never know what could happen if he were to take you out for a sail and something went wrong with the boat and he'd be too drunk to handle the situation, especially since you're not much of a sailor, are you, Alison?"

"No, but then Cullie isn't much of a drunk," I said.

Bethany smiled again. She put down her spoon and placed her hand across her mouth while she let forth a loud yawn. Then she tapped her father on the arm. "How about getting the check," she said to Alistair. "I've got a busy day tomorrow."

"I guess that's my cue to take off," I laughed. Bethany had such tact. " 'Night, everyone." I strolled toward the ladies' room.

"Who were you talking to over there?" Cullie said when I returned.

"Would you believe, Alistair, Bethany, and Julia, the three musketeers?"

"You went over to their table and talked to them? After what Bethany did to you?"

"Yup. I wanted to show her that she can't hurt me," I said. "None of them can."

"I'm not so sure," Cullie said solemnly. "Every time you tangle with Bethany, something terrible happens. Look what happened after you told her you had the manuscript. She got you thrown in jail and charged with murder."

"I know, but what could she do to me tonight? Besides, she seemed much more interested in her chocolate soufflé than in me."

"Chocolate soufflé? Ummm. Why didn't we order one of those?"

"We should have. The one Bethany was eating looked really scrumptious. I couldn't take my eyes off it. It had this rich, gooey chocolate inside and this flaky, cakey stuff outside, and the whole thing was dusted with confectioner's . . ." I stopped.

"Sonny, what is it?" Cullie asked.

"I know who killed Melanie," I announced. In one split second, one random moment in time, I knew beyond a shadow of a doubt who the murderer was. "It was the confectioner's sugar that sealed it."

"What are you talking about?" Cullie said.

"Confectioner's sugar. That's what the powder the police

found on Melanie's desk turned out to be—not cocaine, but powdered sugar with traces of cinnamon."

"I know. You told me. What does that have to do with Bethany's soufflé?"

"Bethany is a sugar-holic. She's addicted to the jelly doughnuts they sell in the lunch room at the newspaper. Her own desk has that powdered shit all over it."

"So you think the powder on Bethany's desk is the same powder that was found on Melanie's desk?"

"Yup. I'm sure of it. She had a motive for killing Melanie, wouldn't you agree?"

"Sure, but why on earth would she have eaten a doughnut at the scene of the murder?"

"Maybe she was hungry. You've heard of these sickos who get sexually aroused after they commit murder? Well, maybe Bethany's the sort of sicko who gets ravenously hungry after a good kill."

"Jesus."

"If I could just prove that the sugar on Bethany's desk is the same as the sugar the police found on Melanie's desk . . ."

"And prove that Bethany's fingerprints were the ones the police found on the murder weapon . . ."

"And prove that Bethany was the one who left that nice little bag of cocaine in my refrigerator."

"I think we ought to get her favorite donuts analyzed by a lab," Cullie suggested.

"We will, we will. But first, I've got a plan for getting her fingerprints."

"How?"

"Look." I nodded in the direction of the Downs table. "They're getting up to leave. The minute they walk out the door, I'm going over to their table and swiping Bethany's wineglass, before the busboy clears the dishes away."

"What'll you do with the glass when you get it?"

"I'll figure that out later. What I'm *not* going to do is give it to Corsini. I don't trust that bastard. He won't go after a member of the Downs family unless there's conclusive evidence."

"You're probably right. Oh, look, Sonny. They're gone."

Alistair, Bethany, and Julia had just left the restaurant. The coast was clear.

"You pay the check and I'll scoot over there," I whispered.

I walked nonchalantly past the Downs table, pretending I was on my way to the ladies' room. I stopped when I got to Bethany's chair, grabbed her linen napkin off the table, and picked up her wineglass by its stem, making sure it was the napkin and not my hand that touched the glass. Clutching my booty for dear life, I hurried back to the table.

"Mission accomplished," I smiled.

"Tell you what," Cullie said. "You slip outside and wait for me. I'll pay the check, get our coats, and meet you in a few minutes."

"Done."

Instead of going straight back to the boat, we stopped at a pay phone so I could call my lawyer. He'd know what to do with the glass and any other evidence I came up with.

"Do you have any idea what time it is?" Mr. Obermeyer barked after answering the phone. It was ten-thirty.

"Yes, Mr. Obermeyer," I said, "but this is important. I found a way to remove all suspicion of murder against me: I know who killed Melanie Moloney."

"Can't this wait until tomorrow?" he asked, then belched.

"No, really it can't. Cullie and I would like to come right over. We need to give you something, something too valuable to keep on the boat."

Mr. Obermeyer grudgingly agreed, and off we went. When we arrived at his house, which, ironically, was in Bluefish Cove, where Melanie had met her tragic end, he showed us into his kitchen and demanded to know what was so important. I explained how I came to believe that Bethany had murdered Melanie, and produced the wineglass with the prints all over it.

"I've got a private investigator who'll lift the prints off the glass," he said.

"I hoped you might," I said. "What happens after that? Can we compare these prints with the ones on the murder weapon?"

"We'll have to petition the court to allow us to examine the evidence," he explained. "The police have jurisdiction over the murder weapon. They don't have to let us near it, now that the judge has thrown out all charges against you."

"Okay, let's petition the court. And while you're getting that process going, I'll check out the donut powder on Bethany's desk to see if it matches the powder at the crime scene," I said.

"Oh, I'll get the process going all right," said Mr. Obermeyer. "But it's gonna cost you—plenty."

"You know, Mr. Obermeyer, your mentioning your fee at a difficult and delicate time like this reminds me of a riddle." I paused. "Why do you bury lawyers a thousand feet under the ground?" I paused again. "Because down deep, they're probably all right."

"I'll show you out," Mr. Obermeyer said, and then he did.

Chapter 23

With Mr. Obermeyer working on the business of the finger-prints, I turned my attention to the business of the donuts. My plan was to sneak into Bethany's office, get a sample of the powder on her desk, and have it evaluated.

But first, I had to find out when Bethany would be out of her office. Remembering the riding habit she wore during my last visit to the paper, I took a chance and called the Layton Hunt Club, where Bethany boarded her horses and bedded her trainers.

"Good morning. I wonder if you might help me," I said, holding my nose so my voice would have a nasal quality and sound just like all the other horsey types at the Hunt Club. "I'm supposed to meet Bethany Downs there today, and—oh, this is terribly embarrassing—I seem to have misplaced my appointment book, and I haven't a clue what time I'm scheduled to ride with Bethany. Can you tell me when she's due to arrive?"

"We're expecting her within the hour," said the receptionist.

"Oh, my," I said. "Well then. I must be off. Tell Bethany she simply must wait for me. Ta ta."

I grabbed my purse and left the boat. Twenty minutes later, I was sneaking into Bethany's office at the *Community Times,* praying no one would see me. I scurried over to her desk, checked for telltale sugar granules, and found some, right next to a box containing a half-dozen jelly donuts. Working quickly and carefully, I tore a sheet of paper from a legal pad on the desk and used the corner of the paper to shovel the sugar into the little plastic sandwich bag I'd brought along. Then I hid the bag in my purse and fled the building. I drove straight over to Jessup Community College and found my way to the chemistry department.

"I'm writing a novel and I was wondering if you could help me with my research," I said sweetly to the clean-cut man sitting at the desk near the door. He had neatly trimmed brown hair, wore red suspenders and a matching bow tie, and said his name was Professor Ed Dudley.

"A novel, eh?" he said, appraising me. "Come to think of it, you do look familiar. Have you been on TV?"

"Why, yes. I have." For being a murderous maid, not a famous novelist.

"Gee, that's interesting. What can I do for you?"

"Would there be any way that you or someone in the chemistry department could analyze the contents of this plastic bag?" I pulled the bag out of my purse and handed it to him.

"Is your novel one of those sex, drugs, and rock 'n' roll things?" he asked, arching an eyebrow.

"No. Why?"

" 'Cause this stuff looks like cocaine. I figured that's what your book must be about."

I laughed. "No, my book's sort of about life in the suburbs. That powder isn't cocaine. It's a type of sugar, but I'm trying to find out exactly what the breakdown of elements is. You know, get the right chemical name for the stuff?" He looked skeptical. "The main character in the book is a chemistry professor who likes to use chemical terms for everything, even food," I explained, hoping to involve him in the game. "Personally, I've had it with books that make heroes out of lawyers and policemen and movie stars. I think it's about time we had a chemistry professor as the main character of a novel, don't you?"

He nodded enthusiastically. "Give me twenty-four hours," he said, placing the bag in a large envelope and marking it "Priority."

When I got home, I called Janet Claiborne. As long as I was playing detective, I thought I'd try to confirm my suspicions that Janet's "customer of consequence" was Bethany, that it was Bethany to whom she had showed Maplebark Manor the night of my arrest on cocaine possession, and that it was Bethany who had placed the cocaine in my refrigerator when Janet wasn't looking.

"Oh, hello dear. Calling about the house?" she said.

No, I'm calling about the weather, you dope. "Yes," I said. "About that big customer you brought over the other night. I know it was Bethany Downs who looked at the house." Bluff, bluff. "She and I are old friends. We worked together at her father's newspaper, remember?"

"Of course you did. I'd forgotten that." I was right! The fucking bitch tried to frame me for Melanie's murder—twice! "When Miss Downs asked to view the property when you weren't home, I naturally assumed you didn't know each other. Forgive me, dear."

"I forgive you, Janet."

"Well, since you two are colleagues, I urge you to discuss the house with her. Maybe a little nudging from you will produce that offer we're looking for."

"A fine idea," I said. "Nudging Bethany, I mean."

"Veddy good, dear. Let me know what happens."

"Thanks, Janet. You've been a big help." For once.

When Cullie came home that night, we caught each other up on our days while we made dinner. He told me about the houses he shot and the homeowners he tolerated. I told him all about my trips to the *Community Times* and Jessup

Community College, as well as my telephone conversation with Janet. He was impressed with my sleuthing.

"Sounds like you've got Bethany Downs cornered, Sonny girl," he smiled.

"I think I do," I said proudly. "Now, what would you say to my cornering you?"

I pinned Cullie against the ice box, wrapped my arms around his waist, and hugged him. "Have I told you lately how much confidence living with you on this boat has given me?" I said.

"Nope. Tell me."

"I don't know whether it's living on the boat or loving you or surviving all the horrible things I've survived lately, but I don't feel as frail as I used to. When I was married to Sandy and living at Maplebark Manor, I felt as if a little breeze could blow me down. Now I don't think even a stiff wind could do the job. I may teeter, but I don't fall down."

Cullie kissed me. Then suddenly he gathered me up in his arms and carried me almost the entire length of the boat, from the galley to the V-berth. After laying me down on the berth, he undressed me, shed his own clothes, and came into my outstretched arms, our naked bodies as at home with each other as the *Marlowe* was with the sea.

"Let's make waves," he whispered, turning his body around so his head was at my crotch and my head was at his.

"I was never any good at math, but I still can't figure out why they call this 'sixty-nine,' " I said after a few minutes of playing popsicle with Cullie's penis.

"Call it forty-two, fifty-four, whatever number you want, only don't stop what you're doing," Cullie groaned.

Numbers, shmumbers. After a while, we were so tangled up in each other I couldn't tell who was who or what was what.

"Whoa, baby." Cullie shuddered. "Did anyone ever tell you you have some kind of mouth?"

"My mother always told me I had some kind of mouth, only I'm positive she didn't mean it the way you do."

The next morning, I called Ed Dudley at the Jessup Community College chemistry lab.

"I hate to seem pushy," I said, "but do you have the results of that analysis we talked about yesterday?"

"Oh, yes," he said. "You want me to tell you what I found?"

"Please."

"Okay. Your sample breaks down as a polysaccharide conjoined by a disaccharide with traces of a cellulosic cinnamaldehyde."

Bingo. Professor Dudley's results were exactly the same as the police lab's, which meant that the donut sugar on Bethany's desk was the same as the donut sugar on Melanie's desk, which meant that the donuts were made from the same recipe and purchased at the same location. The only difference between the police lab's test and Ed Dudley's was that Ed's took one day and the police lab's took six weeks.

"Professor, you're a life saver," I said, imagining Corsini's face when I demanded a public apology from the Layton Police Department for having arrested me instead of Bethany.

"Are you going to stop by and pick up your bag of sugar?" Ed asked.

"You better believe it," I said. "I wonder if I could impose on you for one more favor though."

"Sure, if I could impose one on you."

"Okay. You go first."

"No, ladies first."

"All right. I wonder if you could give me a written report of your lab analysis—something I could refer to from time to time." Something I could make Corsini read and weep.

"No problem at all," said Ed. "It'll be waiting for you."

"Great. Now what was the favor you wanted to ask me?"

"Well," he began. "Since you're an author and all, I was hoping you'd read *my* book, maybe help me get a publisher."

"Your book?"

"Yes. I've been working on it for three years."

"What kind of a book is it? A scientific treatise of some sort?" I figured Ed for a Stephen Hawking wannabe.

"No, it's a comprehensive biography of Ed McMahon."

"You're kidding."

"No, honest I'm not. I've followed his career from his early days on 'The Tonight Show' to his recent stints as host of 'Star Search.' And then, of course, there's his fine work with the American Family Sweepstakes."

Has everybody in this fucking country gone celebrity crazy? I asked myself.

"I don't have much experience getting celebrity books published, but I'd be happy to give you the name of someone who does," I said.

I wrote down Todd Bennett's name and address. Ed thanked me profusely, and said that if Hollywood ever bought the movie rights to my novel about the chemistry professor and wanted to hire him as their technical advisor, he was available.

I hurried to a pay phone and called Mr. Obermeyer at his office to tell him about the lab report on the sugar as well as my conversation with Janet Claiborne. In his own crabby way, he seemed pleased with the results of my investigation and suggested I drop the report off at his house.

The noose around Bethany's neck was tightening. Corsini's investigation may have slowed to a crawl, but mine was really hopping. It would just be a matter of days before Alistair P. Downs's daughter—a member of one of Layton's "Founding Families"—would be cooling her riding boots in the State Correctional Facility in Niantic.

Of course, there was one aspect of the murder investigation I hadn't quite come to terms with: before putting Bethany away for life, the prosecution would need a thoroughly convincing motive for the killing, a motive that I alone could provide by handing over the manuscript in which Bethany's daddy dearest was defamed beyond even her worst nightmares. But if I handed over the manuscript, then the world would learn the truth about my mother and Alistair, about Cullie's father and Alistair's wife, about the rotten, disgusting way Alistair had cha cha cha-ed the entire country. Telling the American people the truth about their leaders was one thing; making them feel so duped they couldn't face themselves in the mirror was another. That's the real bummer about the cha cha cha—the person who gets cha cha cha-ed comes out looking just as dopey as the person who does the cha cha cha-ing. Or to put a Yiddish spin on things, it's like the difference between the shlemiel and the shlimazl. The shlemiel is the waiter who's always spilling hot soup on his customer, and the shlimazl is the customer the waiter is always spilling hot soup on, but both of them come out looking like shnooks.

The next morning, I was getting ready to leave the boat to go grocery shopping when someone pounded on the hatch. It was Julia.

"What are you doing here?" I asked, more than a little surprised to see her.

"I came to warn you, Koff. Can I come in?"

I led Julia down the hatch and into the main cabin.

"Coffee?" I asked.

"Sure. Hey, this is really nice," she said, surveying the interior of the boat.

I poured some coffee and handed her a mug. "What did you want to warn me about?"

"Bethany. You're playing around with her and, trust me, Koff, she's not someone to play around with."

"Why tell *me*, Julia? You're the one who's buddy-buddy

with her. But then, you have to be. She's practically your stepdaughter, right?"

"Hardly. Look, Koff. I admit it. I got caught up in the Alistair Downs thing, the mystique, the charisma, whatever you want to call it."

"You don't want to hear what I'd call it," I said dryly.

"Your own mother fell under the man's spell, for God's sake, even while she was married to your father. Doesn't that tell you something?"

"Yeah. It tells me that my mother has no taste *and* no scruples. But you." I paused. "I thought you had your act together, Julia. You championed the underdog and espoused all the right causes and I looked up to you. At the very least, I thought you were above falling under the spell of a man like Alistair."

"Then you were naive."

"Apparently."

"Anyway, the spell's been broken."

"Oh? What happened? A spat with the senator?"

"You could say that. After all my years chairing civic groups, I've finally been asked to run for state representative—on the Democratic ticket, of course."

"Let me guess. Alistair's reaction was, 'No woman of mine is going to run for anything—and certainly not on the Democratic ticket! Ho ho!' Am I warm?"

"Very. I told him I'd run for whatever I damned well pleased on any ticket I damned well pleased. That put a damper on the romance."

"So now that you and Alistair have split up and you've convinced yourself I didn't kill Melanie, it's all right to resume our friendship, is that it?"

"I know it may seem like I distanced myself from you for a while there," she conceded. "But truthfully, when I found out you'd been working as Melanie Moloney's maid—and that she'd been murdered—I didn't know what to think. Now I'm here to warn you."

"About what?"

"I was leaving Evermore last night, after my argument with Alistair, when I heard Bethany yelling at someone on the phone. Normally, I'm not much of an eavesdropper, but when I heard your name mentioned, I—"

"My name?"

"Yeah. Bethany was talking to someone named Janet and saying, 'You real estate brokers are incapable of keeping your mouths shut. I asked you not to tell Alison Koff you showed me her house. And what did you do? You told her anyway.' Then there was more yelling. Then Bethany said, 'I don't care what Alison said. She and I are not friends. She's a murderer and a thief, and I plan to see to it that she doesn't make any more trouble for anyone in this town.' It sounded to me like Bethany's out to get you."

"She's been out to get me for a long time. Now I'm out to get her, and I will—very soon, I suspect."

"Do me a favor, would ya?"

"Sure."

"Don't push Bethany. You seem happy living on this boat with your photographer-boyfriend and much more in control of your life than when you were married to Sandy. You're your own woman now, Koff. I'm impressed."

"It's funny, Julia. Months ago, impressing you was important to me. Back then, you'd put me down for my princessy ways, and I'd keep trying to be as independent and right-thinking as you were. All I wanted was to be worthy of your friendship. Now look at us." I paused. "You fell under the spell of a man who's about as wrong-thinking as they come, and I'm the one who's taken charge of her life—so much so that Julia Applebaum is impressed. How's that for irony?"

"What can I say?" Julia shrugged as she got up to leave.

"There's nothing to say." I grabbed my keys and purse. "I've got to go grocery shopping. Cullie and I are planning a little sailing trip tomorrow if the weather holds."

"Sounds nice. I don't know how to sail."

"I don't exactly know how to sail either, but I'm learning. Cullie's a great teacher."

"Well, take care of yourself, Koff."

"Thanks, Julia. I intend to."

Chapter 24

"Rise and shine, Sonny girl. We're outta here." Cullie shook me as we lay in the V-berth. It was seven A.M. and I was barely awake. "The wind is from the southwest at twelve knots, the temperature's going up to seventy-five degrees, and you and I are taking the *Marlowe* for an overnighter."

"I thought we'd decided on a quickie day sail."

"Yeah, but the weather's so nice we should take advantage of it. We'll be back by midafternoon tomorrow."

"What about work? Our trip won't screw up your shooting schedule, will it?"

"Haven't you learned anything from living on this boat for the last couple of months? The *Marlowe*'s motto is: When in doubt, go sailing—preferably overnight."

"That's a lovely motto." I kissed Cullie. "An overnighter it is, as long as we're back by midday tomorrow. Mr. Obermeyer said he'd have some information for me by then."

"About Bethany's fingerprints?"

"Yup. I want to be there when he confronts Corsini with all the stuff we've come up with."

"The stuff *you've* come up with. You're the one who figured out who killed Melanie—and how to prove it."

"Enough about Melanie. We're going sailing, and there'll be no talk of Melanie or murder or manuscripts today. Deal?"

"Deal."

"By the way, where are we sailing to?"

"How do the Thimble Islands grab you? If we leave by eight, we'll make it up to the Thimbles by midafternoon. Then we'll find a nice quiet anchorage, drop anchor, and spend the night. How 'bout it, sweet thing?"

"You're on."

"Tell me about the Thimble Islands," I prodded as Cullie and I got dressed. "I've lived near the Connecticut coast all my life and never been to the Thimbles."

"Okay. Here's a quick lesson. There are about thirty islands. Half of them are inhabited."

"Do any of them have names?"

"Yeah, and two of them have great names."

"What are they?"

"Pot and High."

"You're not serious."

"Look on my navigation chart. You'll see Pot Island and High Island."

"Sure, and there's a third one called Busted Island."

"Cute. Legend has it that Captain Kidd used the Thimbles as one of his hideouts."

"Wow. So Captain Kidd got stoned right in our backyard."

"The Thimbles aren't exactly in our backyard. They're halfway between Branford and Guilford, about an hour up the coast by car and ferry."

"Are they pretty?"

"They're interesting. They look as if a piece of the Maine coastline broke off from the mainland, floated into the Long Island Sound, and ran aground off Branford. If you've ever seen the Maine coastline, you'll know what I mean."

* * *

We ate a hearty breakfast, straightened up the galley, and readied the boat for departure. It was just after eight when Cullie fired up the diesel.

"I'm gonna do the safety and maintenance checks while the engine's warming up," he said. "Want to help me? It's the best way to learn."

"Absolutely."

I followed Cullie around the boat while he checked the exhaust pipe to make sure the engine's cooling system was working properly, rigged the anchor and stowed it on the bowsprit, and inspected the bilge to make sure there wasn't more than an inch or two of water there.

"I'll take the sail covers off and rig the halyards while you go back to the cockpit, rig the dinghy for towing, and get ready to steer us out of here, okay?" he said.

"Aye, aye, Captain," I said.

After a few more chores, we were under way.

"Okay, Sonny girl. Put her in gear," Cullie instructed after he had taken in the dock lines and stowed them in the storage compartment. Then he went below to put a tape in the cassette player. Seconds later, he and sounds of Bob Marley's "Get Up, Stand Up" emerged, which made me feel as if I were en route to the Caribbean, not the Thimble Islands.

"Should I steer us out the channel?" I asked as we motored out of the marina.

"Sure. Just watch for the buoys. Like last time, remember?"

"Yup. All I have to do is stay between the red and green ones, right?"

"Right. Then once we're out the channel, I want you to head us into the wind so I can raise the mainsail. Just keep the bow pointed southwest, in the direction of the Northport stacks. See 'em?"

I took one hand off the steering wheel and shielded my eyes from the sun. Squinting, I looked across the Sound and spotted the stacks from the Long Island power plant that had become a familiar navigation point for sailors. "Yup, I see 'em."

Cullie hoisted the mainsail, then the staysail and the jib. "Okay, Sonny girl. Fall off," he called out from the deck.

"The hell I will," I said. "The water's freezing."

"No, matey. That's a sailing term. I want you to *fall off* to port. Turn the wheel toward the east."

"Why didn't you say so?" I laughed, and did as I was told.

Suddenly, the wind filled the sails. My pulse quickened just as it had the last time I'd seen them in all their majesty.

"Turn off the engine," Cullie cried, as excited as a kid at Christmas. "We're under sail!"

I shut off the diesel and waited to be enveloped by the eerie quiet that comes over a boat when its engine gives way to the power of the sails—a quiet that was punctuated, this time, by Bob Marley's reggae melodies.

Cullie kissed me as we stood together in the cockpit. "Let's go below and we'll plot our course," he suggested.

Once at the navigation station, we pored over Cullie's charts. He showed me the latitudes and longitudes of the buoys and reefs we'd encounter along the way, and explained the route he had planned for us to take.

"We're about here," he said, using his index finger to indicate our position on the chart. "We're heading east out of the Jessup Harbor. Then we'll pass the Stratford Shoal Lighthouse, sail outside the Branford Reef, and approach the Thimble Islands from the backside. There's a channel that leads to a great anchorage between the four main islands. That's where we'll spend the night, okay?"

"How could it *not* be okay? It sounds like a dream voyage, my Captain oh Captain."

Cullie turned on the Loran, his electronic, high-tech radio navigation system that allows sailors to determine their position at sea. He punched in the latitudes and longitudes of our waypoints—as well as our destination—on the Loran's keypad, and showed me how the system calculated and displayed the distances between points.

"Pretty fancy equipment for a purist," I teased. "Didn't you say wooden boaters eschew modern technology?"

"Yeah, but I'm the kind of purist that isn't crazy about getting lost at sea. That's why this Alden schooner's got a Loran. If we were to veer too far off our course, the Loran's alarm would go off. It's a good little toy."

"I'll say. Let's hope we don't hear any alarms. I don't need any more excitement today. Just being on the *Marlowe* with you on our first overnighter is excitement enough."

We were about three-and-a-half hours into our trip and had just passed the Stratford Shoal Lighthouse en route to the Branford Reef when hunger pangs began to overwhelm me.

"It's nearly noon," I said, linking my arm through Cullie's as we sat in the cockpit taking in the sights. "How about some lunch?"

"What a brilliant idea," he replied, and smiled. "Want some help?"

"Naw. I think I can handle a couple of tuna sandwiches. While I'm down there, I'll change the tape. What's your pleasure?"

"How about Peter, Paul and Mary? I'm a sucker for 'Blowin' in the Wind.' "

"Your wish is my command, you old folkie. One more question: what do you want to drink with your sandwich? We've got beer, soda . . ."

"Oh, say no more. Beer it is. What could be better than a nice cold Heineken on a day like this? Come to think of it, what could be better than a day like this?" He let out a war whoop that went something like, "Wa-hooo!" He was in ecstasy, that much was clear.

I climbed down the hatch, my eyes trying to make the adjustment from the bright sunshine of the cockpit to the cozy darkness of the main cabin. When I stepped onto the teak floor and realized what I had stepped in, I screamed. I was up to my shins in water!

I ran back up the hatch to tell Cullie.

"There's at least six inches of water in the main cabin," I said breathlessly, trying not to panic. "I think the *Marlowe* is sinking."

"There you go again, Sonny girl. Miss Disaster of 1990," he said. He was stretched out in the cockpit, enjoying the sun and sea. "The last time we went sailing, you accused me of murdering Melanie. Now you're telling me my boat is sinking. You've got to learn not to imagine worst-case scenarios all the time. You gotta chill out, as they say."

"Yeah? Well I don't know how to break it to you, mister, but *you're* gonna chill out when you go below and find yourself in a boat-full of cold water. I'm telling you, Cullie. It's bad. You'd better come look."

"Sonny, I know my boat. I rebuilt it myself, remember? There's no way anything could—"

"This is not about your boat or your expertise as a boat builder or your manhood," I cut him off. "This is about water in the main cabin. Just come. Now."

Cullie sighed, got up, and followed me down the hatch. He didn't scream the way I did when he saw the water that had accumulated in the main cabin. He did the macho equivalent: he said nothing. He just started *doing,* without so much as a word to me about *what* he was doing or *why.*

"What's happening?" I said as I followed him up to the cockpit.

"Nothing's happening. I'm just turning the engine on. I want to get the automatic bilge pump going."

"Oh," I said. I was relieved. I assumed that the automatic bilge pump would pump the water out of the main cabin in no time and that Cullie and I would have our tuna sandwiches and beer and laugh about the whole episode.

Wrong.

"Shit," Cullie said. "The engine's not working."

"What do you mean, 'The engine's not working'?"

"Just what I said. You saw me turn on the ignition. Nothing happened. The water in the boat must have disabled the engine."

"What about the automatic bilge pump?" I asked with growing dread.

"No engine, no automatic bilge pump."

"Oh, God. Now what are we going to do?"

"Alison, let me take care of this, okay?" I could tell he was just as worried as I was. "The first priority is to stabilize the situation and get the water out of the boat. Then I'll try to figure out how the water got into the boat in the first place."

He grabbed the handle for the manual bilge pump and started pumping furiously. And pumping. And pumping.

"I can't fucking believe this," he said finally. "The thing isn't working. There's no suction. Nothing."

To say I had a sinking feeling about the boat was too corny a pun even for me. But a sinking feeling was exactly what I had.

"I don't understand what's happening," Cullie said more to himself than to me. "The water's coming in and my two pumps are disabled."

"Maybe you didn't check everything thoroughly enough before we left the marina," I said.

"And maybe you don't understand that what's happening here has nothing to do with maintenance. This boat was in perfect shape when we left the marina. Someone tampered with it."

"This isn't the time to be defensive," I said as gently as possible. I didn't want to wound the man's macho pride in his boat, God forbid. You know men and their machines. But he had to face reality sometime. People weren't perfect. Boats weren't perfect either. "Maybe you missed something," I said.

"Alison, I'm gonna say this once more. My boat has been

sabotaged. I don't know how. I don't know when. All I know is that I've got to fix it. Now."

Cullie went down below. I followed him. He found a flashlight and opened the engine compartment.

"Shit," he said. "There's water coming up through the stuffing box."

I didn't know what a stuffing box was, but I was sure the fact that water was coming up through it wasn't good.

"Now where are you going?" I asked.

"To check the sea cocks."

He disappeared, then returned to explain that the sea cocks, too, had apparently been disabled. The result was that water was pouring in through the valves. The wood plugs he was going to plug them with would stop some of the water from coming into the boat, but not all of it.

"Shouldn't I call 911 or something?" I asked.

Cullie gave me a what-are-you-kidding look, then said, "Tell you what you *can* do. Get Channel 16 on the VHF radio and call the Coast Guard."

"Oh, my God. The Coast Guard. You wouldn't tell me to call *them* unless you thought we were in danger. Are we, Cullie? Are we in danger? I can handle it, really I can."

"Yeah, we're in danger. Someone played with the *Marlowe*—big time. Someone who knows his way around a boat."

"But why would anyone want to—"

I didn't have to finish the question. It had suddenly dawned on me that Cullie was right. Someone did play around with the *Marlowe*. Someone who knew *her* way around a boat. Didn't Bethany say, just the other night at Les Fruits de Mer, that Paddy Harrington had taught her everything she knew about boats?

"It was Bethany," I said aloud. "She did this."

"Jesus."

"She probably monkeyed with the boat while I was out grocery shopping yesterday."

"Maybe she also figured we had the manuscript and that the damn thing would go down right along with us."

"The manuscript! It's in the compartment below the anchor locker!"

"Yeah, well we don't have time to worry about Melanie's masterpiece right now. We're gonna sink if we don't get some help. You call the Coast Guard while I go and try to do something about this water."

Cullie ran off and left me alone with the VHF radio.

"Hello, Coast Guard? This is Alison," I said, not sure how to begin. I had never called the Coast Guard before, nor any other branch of our military, for that matter.

"Coast Guard. Petty Officer Dunne speaking," said a gruff male voice. There was nothing petty about our situation. I hoped the officer's title in no way reflected his ability to rescue us.

"We're sinking," I said. "There's water coming in everywhere, and we need help—badly."

"Name?"

"Alison Waxman Koff."

"No, the name of the vessel."

"Oh, sorry. The *Marlowe.*"

"Type of vessel?"

"A forty-three-foot, hunter-green John Alden schooner."

"What is your position?"

"My position?"

"What is the position of your *boat?*"

"Oh. It's sinking. Why else would I be calling the Coast Guard?"

"No, no," said Petty Officer Dunne. "The location. What is the *location* of your boat?"

The location of the boat? Now I was really stumped. We were somewhere in the middle of the Long Island Sound, but I had no idea where.

"Hold on a second," I said and yelled for Cullie.

"Tell him we're about five miles east of Branford Reef," he yelled back.

"We're about five miles east of Branford Reef," I told Petty Officer Dunne. There was so much crackling and static on the radio that I wasn't sure if he heard me, so I said it again.

"Did not copy, yacht *Marlowe*. You're breaking up," said Petty Officer Dunne, confirming my suspicions. "Switch to Channel 22."

"Sure, if you think Channel 22 gets better reception," I said. I used to have the same problem with my cable TV. HBO came in great, while the Weather Channel was a mess.

I switched to Channel 22 and proceeded to report the location of the boat for the third time. Then Cullie came running over to the navigation station and grabbed the microphone out of my hand.

"This is the captain of the *Marlowe*. MAYDAY. MAYDAY. MAYDAY," he shouted.

MAYDAY? Oh, God. We were going down. We were fucking going down. And I wasted all that energy worrying about spending the rest of my life eating chipped beef on toast at the State Correctional Facility in Niantic. Eating chipped beef on toast wasn't so bad when you compared it with drowning. Boy, did being on the verge of going down in the Long Island Sound put things in perspective.

"MAYDAY. MAYDAY. MAYDAY," Cullie said again into the microphone. There was no reply. "MAYDAY. MAYDAY. MAYDAY." No reply. Not even any crackling or static. "Shit. The radio has shorted out. Must be all that water."

"What are we gonna do?" I cried.

"Get in the dinghy and abandon ship. The water's coming in too fast to stay here."

"But Cullie. How can we abandon ship? This boat is your baby, your pride and joy. It's your home, your—"

"There's an emergency kit in a canvas bag in the cockpit, next to the life preservers. Go get it," he said, ignoring my words. "I'm gonna rig a marker buoy so the Coast Guard can find the boat if it sinks."

"But how will they—"

"Just get the life preservers and the emergency kit, Sonny. Please."

We stared at each other for a second or two.

Whoever came up with the observation "Silence speaks volumes" was right. Cullie's silence said, "My beloved boat is sinking and so is my heart, but I refuse to go to pieces because I'm a Big Strong Man." My silence, on the other hand, said, "I know how much you love this boat, Cullie, and I'd give anything in the world to save it for you, but there's a part of me that wishes I had never laid eyes on you or your fucking boat."

I ran up to the cockpit and retrieved the emergency equipment. Inside the kit was a whistle, some flares, a space blanket, a signaling mirror, some canned foods (B&M Baked Beans, Chef Boyardee Ravioli, and Campbell's Split Pea Soup with Ham), and a bottle of Demerol.

"What are you doing now?" I asked Cullie when I turned around in the cockpit and saw him up on deck.

"I'm dropping the sails," he said quickly. "No point in pretending anymore. This boat's going down and there's nothing I can do about it."

I could feel his resignation as he negotiated the slippery deck, trying to maintain his balance and his composure as he dropped the mainsail, then the staysail.

He was about to drop the jib when he slipped on the staysail sheet, fell onto the deck, and howled in pain.

"Cullie!" I cried and ran up on deck.

"Jesus," he moaned, clutching his leg. "I've broken it."

"Your leg?"

"No, my cherry."

I stared at him. He scowled at me. Then he began to laugh. I couldn't believe it. His boat was sinking and his leg was broken, but the man was laughing. He had made a joke in a time of terrible crisis. He had tried to mitigate his awful pain and suffering with a good line.

"Cullie, my boy, I see I've rubbed off on you."

He smiled, albeit weakly.

"Where does it hurt?" I asked, touching his leg gingerly.

"Here," he grimaced, pointing to his shin.

I didn't know a tibia from a fibula, so I didn't even attempt to diagnose the situation. All I knew was that the boat was going down, its captain had a broken leg, and I was suddenly in charge of the rescue operation.

"Okay, graceful. Now what do we do?" I asked.

"Put a life preserver on. Then put one on me," he instructed, then winced from the pain in his leg.

I ran back to the cockpit for the life preservers and the emergency kit and carried them onto the deck, where Cullie lay on his side.

I put on a life preserver, then rummaged around in the kit for the Demerol.

"Here. Take some of these," I said and handed Cullie a couple of pills.

He swallowed the Demerol and reached for his life preserver, which I helped him put on and fasten.

"Okay," he said. "Now pull the dinghy close to the boat and cleat it."

I followed his orders and drew the eight-foot Nutshell Pram that we'd been towing behind the *Marlowe* as close to the schooner as possible. Then I tied it securely to the boat.

"Are you feeling up to moving?" I asked.

"No choice," he said. "Just drag me along the deck and help me into the dinghy."

"Drag you? You weigh a hundred and sixty-five pounds."

"Okay, don't drag me. Help me drag myself."

I dragged Cullie along the deck of the boat, grateful for its slipperiness as I was able to slide him as well as drag him.

I tossed the emergency kit into the dinghy, then lowered myself into the small wooden lifeboat.

"Okay, Captain Harrington. Your turn," I called up to him as I opened my arms to receive him. "Let's go very slowly, very carefully. Take your time. Easy does it."

Cullie eased his way down into the dinghy, grimacing

from the pain, but all in all maintaining an amazingly stiff upper lip. I had to hand it to these WASPs. They weren't complainers, no sir. If I'd been the one with the broken leg and the sinking ship, I'd have been kvetching so loud every petty officer in the Coast Guard would have heard me, VHF radio or no VHF radio.

"Should I untie the dinghy and start rowing?" I asked, once Cullie had settled into the lifeboat.

"In a second. I need to take one last look at the *Marlowe.*" He swallowed and gave the boat a long, hard look. His eyes filled with tears, which he made no attempt to hide. "I put every dollar I had into that boat," he managed, choking back sobs. "And a whole lot of love."

"I know. I know." I felt his sorrow. I identified with it. I had put plenty of dollars—and love—into Maplebark Manor, and it, too, had sunk. "We'll be okay," I said, trying to reassure myself as well as Cullie. "We'll make it. We will."

"We will," he echoed.

"Is the Demerol starting to work?" I asked.

"A little."

"Then what do you say we shove off?"

"Okay, but first, there's a red flare in the emergency kit. I want you to launch it."

I found the flare, but had no idea what to do with it.

"Just shoot it into the air, like a gun," he explained. "If the Coast Guard's out looking for us, they'll see it."

I fired the flare and watched it shoot into the sky like a rocket.

"That's about all we can do from here, Sonny girl," Cullie said. "Time to go."

He looked longingly at the *Marlowe* one last time, then turned his attention to me.

"Okay, matey. Start rowing," he said.

"Where to?" I asked, grabbing the oars.

"Branford."

"I've never been to Branford. How will I know when I get there?"

"Just keep rowing till you see land."

"Well, here goes nothing," I said and began to row. And row. And row.

A half-hour into my rowing, my stomach muscles were aching and my hands were sore with blisters. My back didn't feel so hot either. What's more, I was shivering.

I looked over at Cullie, who was slumped in the stern of the boat, his eyes closed, his body limp from the combination of the painkiller and his ordeal. I felt a surge of love wash over me. I stopped rowing, opened the emergency kit, took out the space blanket, and covered him with it. Then I resumed rowing. And rowing. And rowing.

I tried to amuse myself as I rowed. I told myself jokes, asked myself riddles, and made up a slew of limericks, some saltier than others.

Another way I tried to amuse myself was by pretending I was at the Layton Health Club, working out on one of their rowing machines. I imagined how flat my stomach would be after all the rowing, how firm the crepe-y skin under my arms would become.

I also thought of all the wonderful things Cullie and I would do together after we were rescued—from going to the movies and stopping on the way home for a hot fudge sundae, to getting the state of Connecticut to enforce its death penalty and watching Bethany Downs fry in the electric chair.

Yet another way I amused myself was by thanking God. I thanked Him for the dinghy that was carrying Cullie and me to safety. I thanked Him for the Demerol that seemed to be easing Cullie's pain. I thanked Him for all those summers at sleepaway camp, without which I would not have learned how to row a boat. I even made a game out of thanking Him by thanking Him alphabetically ("Thank you for the *azure* blue sky above us," "Thank you for the *b*oat I'm rowing," "Thank you for *C*ullie," etc.).

And I sang to amuse myself. Boy, did I sing. Rock songs. Show tunes. Themes from TV sit-coms. You name it. I do not have a good voice, but Cullie, who was out cold, didn't seem to mind.

"Row, row, row your boat gently down the stream," I sang, wondering if the person who'd written that little ditty had ever been forced to row a dinghy all the way to Branford after abandoning ship in the Long Island Sound. "Merrily, merrily, merrily, merrily life is but a dream."

Some dream.

Chapter 25

I'd been singing and rowing in the bone-chilling Long Island Sound for two hours when I saw a motor boat racing toward us.

"Cullie! Cullie, wake up!" I cried, tugging on his blanket.

He stirred, opened his eyes, winced from the pain in his leg, and closed his eyes again.

"Cullie, come on. Listen to me." I tugged on the blanket once more.

"Huh? What? Where are we?" he mumbled. He seemed very groggy from the medication. Either that or he was in shock.

"I think we're about to be rescued," I said, trying not to get my hopes up if it turned out that the boat I heard and saw was one of those hallucinations sailors have when they've been out at sea too long.

Fortunately, the United States Coast Guard cutter that was headed in our direction was no hallucination.

"Oh, thank God," I cried, a seasoned thanker of God by this time. "You found us. You really found us."

There were six men aboard the Coast Guard boat—two petty officers and four seamen—and they were so helpful and caring I wanted to take them home with me.

They gave us blankets and hot coffee, tied our dinghy to the rear of their boat, and took it and us to a dock in New

Haven, where there was an ambulance waiting to transport us to the hospital.

When we got to Yale–New Haven Hospital, I was treated for hypothermia, an aching back, and some really mean-looking blisters on my hands, then released. Cullie, poor boy, was taken into surgery so his broken bone could be set.

"Will he have to stay here overnight?" I asked the emergency room nurse.

"I'm afraid so," she said.

I waited around until Cullie came out of surgery. Then I watched him being wheeled to the hospital room they'd found for him. It was on the seventh floor, and its walls, curtains, and bed linens were vomit-green. I will never understand why hospitals can't see the light on the subject of decor: does vomit-green strike you as a color that promotes a sense of health and well-being?

"Hey, Sonny girl," Cullie said weakly when he opened his eyes and saw me.

"Hey, yourself," I whispered. "How are you feeling?"

"Pretty awful. How 'bout you? You did all that rowing."

"Yeah, but think how much bigger my tits will be now. Rowing bulks up the chest muscles."

He smiled. "I love your tits. I don't want them bulked up."

"Thank you. I love yours too."

I blushed when I suddenly remembered that we weren't alone: Cullie had a roommate on the other side of the vomit-green curtain.

I pulled the curtain back and sneaked a look at the man in the next bed. He was fast asleep, but I recognized him right away.

"Cullie!" I whispered. "You'll never guess who your roommate is."

"You're right," he said. "Who?"

"Dr. Weinstein. Sandy's shrink."

What was Dr. "Whine-stein," as I used to call him, doing at Yale–New Haven Hospital? I wondered. Then I remembered he had a weekend place in Guilford and was probably vacationing there when whatever happened happened.

"What's wrong with Dr. Weinstein?" I asked one of the nurses.

"One of his patients tried to kill him," she said. "Threw a Molotov cocktail in his bedroom window."

"Was he badly hurt?" I never thought Dr. Weinstein was much of a shrink—look at Sandy, for God's sake—but I certainly didn't wish him any harm.

"No. Just some cuts and bruises. It's the depression we're concerned about. He says he feels like a failure, a fraud, and an imposter. He's being transferred to the psychiatric ward as soon as there's a bed available."

"How sad." And it was. Everybody felt like a failure, a fraud, and an imposter now and then. It was one of those feelings you just had to grin and bear.

I tiptoed back into Cullie's room. "I guess I'll go," I said softly, kissing the tip of his nose. "You must be pretty out of it."

"I am. Sorry."

"Don't be sorry. Just rest."

"Sonny?"

"Yeah?"

"The *Marlowe*'s gone, isn't she?" His eyes filled with tears.

"She went down, yes," I told him. "But that doesn't mean she's gone. You rigged a marker buoy, remember? The Coast Guard will help us find her, if they haven't found her already."

His expression brightened. "I forgot about that buoy. Maybe there's hope," he said.

"No 'maybe' about it. Now get some sleep. I'll be back in the morning to take you home."

"Home?" His face clouded over again.

"That's right. *My* home. I've still got one, sort of."

"I guess so," he mumbled.

"Hey, perk up," I said, hoping Cullie would snap out of

his depression so he wouldn't have to be moved to the psychiatric ward like Dr. Weinstein. "Maplebark Manor's not so bad when you get used to it." Of course, it wouldn't be wise for Cullie to get used to it, seeing as the bank would be foreclosing on it any day. "Let's look on the bright side. We didn't drown in the Long Island Sound. We're alive. We have all our body parts. We have enough evidence to put Bethany away for life. This is where the good times begin. This is where we get to love each other and support each other and watch Little Miss Downs get what's coming to her. What's to be depressed about?"

I left Cullie at the hospital and waited in the lobby for my mother. I had telephoned her from the Coast Guard cutter when I realized I didn't have a dime, my money and credit cards having gone down with the ship.

"Are you all right, dear?" she'd asked on the phone.

"Sure, Mom. Cullie's got a broken leg, but there's nothing to worry about."

"Nothing about which to worry."

"Exactly. Just meet me at Yale–New Haven Hospital, okay? I hate to put you out, but I'll need some cash and a change of clothes. Something warm."

"We'll be right there," she said.

"Who's 'we'?"

"Louis and I."

"Mr. Obermeyer?" He and my mother seemed to be getting awfully chummy lately, what with their dinners at the Club and telephone conversations about my case.

"Yes, dear. But don't read anything into it. Louis and I are not having sex. We're just friends."

I laughed hysterically. One of the petty officers from the Coast Guard cutter asked me what was so funny. I told him I was just happy to be alive.

Mr. Obermeyer got rooms for us in a motel near the hospital—three separate rooms. We checked in and I changed into the clothes my mother brought me: a black gabardine suit (Chanel), black silk blouse (Anne Klein), and black leather pumps (Ferragamo). I looked like I was dressed for a funeral, but hey, dry funeral wear was better than wet sailing clothes any day, particularly in this case, since nobody had died.

We had dinner at the small, family-owned restaurant adjoining the motel, where the menu featured only two entrées: baked scrod and broiled sirloin steak. No contest, obviously. But before I could give the waiter my order, my mother ordered for me.

"She'll have the scrod," she said.

"I'll have the steak," I told the waiter. "Medium rare."

"Steak is high in cholesterol," she said.

"It's also high in protein," I countered. "I've just spent the past several hours fighting for my life. I deserve a steak. Screw the cholesterol."

"Watch your language," my mother scolded.

"Let her have the steak, Doris," Mr. Obermeyer jumped in. "What does she want with scrod? She's probably seen enough fish today."

"You're right, Louis. Of course," said my mother, then addressed the waiter. "She'll have the steak."

Mr. Obermeyer, my hero.

Over dinner, I told Mr. Obermeyer how Cullie and I suspected Bethany of disabling the boat in an attempt to silence me and the manuscript.

"Did you hear that, Louis? She said the manuscript was on that boat." My mother looked as if an enormous weight had been lifted from her bony shoulders. "That means no one will ever find out about Al and me."

Apparently, my mother had told Mr. Obermeyer all about her long, sordid past with the senator.

"What's happening with the murder investigation?" I asked my lawyer.

"Here's the good news. The fingerprints on the wineglass were a match with the prints on the murder weapon," he said. "The police have a case against Bethany Downs now, what with the prints, the donut sugar, and the fact that she was at your house the night the cocaine was planted."

"So what are they waiting for?" I said. "Why doesn't Corsini arrest her?"

"Here's the bad news. Corsini's a star fucker," Mr. Obermeyer replied, then belched.

"Louis, your language is as bad as Alison's," my mother scolded, then handed Mr. Obermeyer a roll of antacid tablets from her purse.

"Thanks, Doris. You're a sweetie." He smiled and patted my mother's cheek. Then she patted his. Just friends, my ass.

"You mean Corsini isn't going to arrest Bethany? Because she's Alistair Downs's daughter?" I was flabbergasted. I thought police cover-ups only happened in the movies, or when one of the Kennedys committed a crime.

"It isn't just Corsini," Mr. Obermeyer explained. "The whole department kisses Alistair Downs's butt."

"Louis, please," my mother scolded again.

"Well, if all the evidence we've gathered against Bethany isn't enough for Corsini," I said, "wait until the Coast Guard finds the *Marlowe* and confirms the boat was tampered with. That'll be the nail in her coffin, won't it?"

"Maybe. If someone at the marina saw her tamper with the boat," Mr. Obermeyer said. "If not, there's no way to prove she did it."

"Then I'll find someone who saw her," I said. "In the meantime, there's another way to put pressure on the Layton Police: get the media to do it for us."

Why not? If the vultures smelled a cover-up, they'd be all over Corsini like a cheap suit. Maybe I'd just have to tell "A Current Affair" and the other tabloids everything I knew about Bethany.

*   *   *

We brought Cullie home from the hospital the next morning. As the bed in the master bedroom was Maplebark Manor's only remaining piece of furniture, I settled him in there. I made him some lunch, brought him the phone, and told him I loved him.

"You must feel pretty lost without the boat," I said.

"I do, but I'm gonna get her back. I'm calling the Coast Guard right now to see if they've had any luck in locating her."

"Great. You do that while I have a little chat with some of the reporters outside."

"Yeah, I noticed they were still out there."

"More than ever, thanks to our excellent adventure on the high seas. We've even got reporters from 'Wide World of Sports' out there now."

"What are you going to do?"

"I've decided it's time I addressed the troops, made a statement. Justice moves a tad too slowly around here for my taste."

"You're gonna go before all those TV cameras and tell them about Bethany?"

"Yeah. I'm also gonna tell them about Corsini's—how shall I put it?—ineffectuality."

"Wow. My very own media star. Can I get your autograph before you become so famous you forget your old friend Cullie?"

I pulled the blanket off Cullie, exposing the virgin white cast that enveloped his broken leg. Then I fished around in the night table for a pen.

"You want my autograph?" I said. "You got it."

"To my old friend Cullie," I wrote on the cast, which extended from his toes to his groin. "Get well soon so I can suck your popsicle without cracking my jaw on this thing. Cheers, Sonny."

* * *

"Ladies and gentlemen of the media," I said. I was standing on the steps of Maplebark Manor, about to address twenty-five reporters, photographers, and cameramen, including a crew from "A Current Affair."

I proceeded to go into detail about Melanie's murder, Corsini's botched investigation, and most of all, Bethany's evil deeds and the evidence the police had against her but refused to acknowledge. The vultures loved it. So did all the assholes in town when they caught my act on the eleven o'clock news that night. One minute I was a murderer in their eyes, the next minute I was a heroine who had single-handedly saved Layton from dethroning Miami as the nation's hot bed of murder and mayhem. Only Sandy, who had recently remarried the very pregnant caterer-whore, felt I'd made a fool of myself. It wasn't what I told the media that bothered him; it was the fact that I told them for nothing.

"You did it for free?" he asked when he called the next night, minutes after seeing me on "A Current Affair."

"Of course," I said.

"They would have paid you big bucks, Alison. Maybe fifty thousand dollars. They do it all the time."

"I don't think people should be paid to tell the truth," I asserted. "Money isn't everything. Besides, seeing that justice is done is reward enough."

Pretty high-minded stuff for a recovering member of the money obsessed. Sure, I could have used fifty thousand dollars. I had no home, no job, and no prospects of either, but I was not about to be subsidized by "A Current Affair," thank you.

Two days went by, and despite the fact that the media vultures had departed Maplebark Manor and were now camped outside Evermore, demanding a statement from either Bethany or Alistair, the Layton Police still did not make an arrest.

Then came several significant breaks for the Good Guys.

First, the Coast Guard located the *Marlowe*. Cullie was ecstatic when he heard. He whooped and hollered and played the drums on his cast. So much for depression.

Then the marine contractors that Cullie's insurance company had hired to salvage the boat pulled it out of the water and hauled it back to the Jessup Marina. It was pretty beat up, but all in one piece—so much so that Cullie figured it would only take three or four months to restore it to its former glory.

Then the boat was examined by the authorities, who found that the stuffing box had been tampered with, the sea cocks had been disabled, and the diaphragm seals on the bilge pumps had been broken. "Whoever messed with this boat left no stone unturned," said the Coast Guard's chief investigator.

Then came the best break of all: Hadley Kittredge, the dockmaster's daughter, told Cullie that she had seen Bethany Downs at the marina the day before our sailing trip from hell and would be glad to testify to that effect.

"We did it, we did it," I exclaimed, hugging Cullie as he lay on his back on my bed. It was nearly midnight and we were too excited about the day's turn of events to sleep. "Now the cops *have* to put Bethany away. Before we know it, this whole nightmare will be over!"

"Let's celebrate," Cullie suggested.

"How? You're lying here with a cast on your leg."

"Yeah, but there's no cast on my dick. Wanna mess around? We could have intercast instead of intercourse. What do you say?"

I considered the question. I wasn't exactly Nadia Comaneci, and I wondered how I would mount Cullie without putting pressure on his cast. But hey, if you don't try, you don't get.

I took off my clothes and pulled down his pants. Then I straddled him, making sure I kept my thigh off his cast, which wasn't easy. I ended up doing a little straddling, a little squatting and a whole lot of squirming. My various contortions reminded me of some of the routines on Jane Fonda's workout video. The key thing was that I got the job done.

For the next hour or so, I lay awake next to Cullie, imagining what path our lives would take next, wondering how the events of the past few months would finally shake out.

Suddenly, I heard a noise. I listened more intently. There it was again. A distant creaking? A suggestion of movement downstairs? I couldn't be sure. Maplebark Manor was an old house, and old houses make lots of noises.

I turned over and closed my eyes. Try to relax, I told myself. It's nothing.

Then another noise. A bump in the night? A fallen object? Someone knocking something over? But it couldn't be. Nobody could have gotten inside the house without the burglar alarm going off. I'd armed it before I came upstairs for the night.

I glanced over at the keypad on the wall. The system was unarmed! The red light was off! But I distinctly remembered arming it. Could I have forgotten to arm it in all the excitement over Hadley Kittredge's identifying Bethany as the one who had tampered with the *Marlowe?*

That was it, I decided. I had forgotten. And the noise from downstairs was probably my imagination. Or maybe I had mice.

I turned over on my other side and tried again to relax. I'll call the exterminator first thing in the morning, I decided. Can't have Janet Claiborne showing the house with mice running around.

There it was again! The sound of someone tiptoeing? A rustling of a coat?

I sat up in bed.

"Cullie! Wake up!" I said, shaking him. "There's someone in the house!"

He didn't move a muscle. He was dead to the world, which is what I was afraid I'd be if he didn't wake up.

"Cullie! Come on. Wake up!" I said again.

He didn't budge, as I feared he wouldn't. When Cullie has a big, explosive orgasm he's out for the night.

Okay, Alison. Call the police, I told myself. What good is Cullie anyway, with his leg in a cast?

I pulled the phone toward me and was about to dial 911 when I suddenly thought better of it. Who wanted to deal with the Layton Police again? The last time I called 911, I stumbled in on Melanie's dead body and the next thing I knew I was a murder suspect.

I took a deep breath and got out of bed, pulled a robe over me, crept out of the bedroom, and tiptoed down the stairs to the first floor. I hoped I'd see a mouse. I prayed I'd see a mouse. What I saw, when I walked into the kitchen and found the lights on, was a rat.

"Hello, Alison," said the rat.

She was sitting at my kitchen table munching on the Mrs. Fields chocolate chip cookies I'd bought that day. She was making crumbs, but I had bigger things to worry about.

"Hello, Bethany," I smiled. "What brings you to my kitchen at this ungodly hour? Out of jelly donuts?"

My heart was thumping so loud I was sure they could hear it in Burkina Faso. But I tried desperately to act nonchalant so Bethany wouldn't freak out and do something rash—rasher than breaking into my house.

"I couldn't sleep," she said. "So I came over here."

She was wearing lime green slacks and a pink Polo shirt under a khaki trench coat. Her blond hair was pulled back in a ponytail with a pink ribbon. Her lips were painted with frosted pink gloss. She looked very preppie, very Layton. All except her eyes. They looked very crazed, very State Facility at Niantic.

"How did you get in, may I ask?" I said. "Janet Claiborne didn't bring you, did she?"

"Not this time. But she let me steal the code to your

urglar alarm. I took it out of her purse, the day she gave
ne a tour of your house."

"Very clever." Well, that explained *how* she got into the
ouse. What worried me more was *why*. "What do you
vant, Bethany? If it's the manuscript about your father, it
vent down with Cullie's boat, just as you planned. They
alvaged the boat, but they couldn't salvage the book. It was
o wet they dumped it in the garbage at the marina."

"Gosh. That is a shame."

I could tell she was crushed. "I'll try again. What is it you
vant, Bethany?"

"There's something you can help me with," she said, then
eached into her coat pocket and pulled out a gun—a .25
aliber automatic, one of those convenient little weapons
hat fits in the palm of your hand. Before I could stop her,
he pointed it at me.

"Don't, Bethany," I said, feeling my chest tighten and my
hroat close. "Don't kill me. If you kill me, you'll be ar-
ested for two murders. How will *that* look on your ré-
umé?"

She smiled. "I'm not going to kill you, Alison."

I allowed myself to breathe. "Well, that's a relief," I said,
valking over to the phone and picking it up. "Why don't we
all that nice Detective Corsini and—"

"I'm not going to kill you. I'm going to have *you* kill *me.*"

"What are you talking about?" She was even crazier than
thought.

"Put the phone down, Alison."

I put the phone down.

"I tried to make them think *you* killed Melanie," she said.
That didn't work. Now I'm going to make them think you
illed *me.*" She paused. "I have no intention of going to
rison. I'm going to kill myself instead. I'm going to kill
nyself and it's going to look like you did it. They'll arrest
ou and you'll be the one to go to prison. Understand?"

I was stunned. "No, Bethany. I don't understand. Why
lo you hate me so much? What did I ever do to you?"

"You mean, besides telling the whole world I killed Melanie?"

"But you *did* kill Melanie. We both know that." I was trying to be logical, which in itself made no sense, seeing as the woman was clearly off her rocker.

"Of course I killed Melanie. Her book was going to ruin my father."

I was going to tell her her father deserved ruining, but thought better of it. "Then why punish me? What did I ever do to you, Bethany?"

"You really don't know, do you?" she said as she continued to point the gun at me.

"No, I don't," I said, trying frantically to think of a way out of the situation. "How about another cookie?" I ventured.

"You really don't know?" she asked again.

"No, Bethany. Repeat after me: 'Alison really doesn't know why Bethany hates her so much, so why doesn't Bethany tell Alison?' "

"All right. I hate you because when they send me to prison, you'll try to take my place with Daddy."

"You mean, take your place at the newspaper?" I was confused.

"No. Take my place in his life."

Whoa. Bethany really was a sickie. "Now why would I want to take your place in your father's life?" I said.

"Because he's your father too."

I stared at Bethany. My heart stopped. "What are you saying?" I asked.

"That Alistair Downs is your father. When the police lock me up, you'll have him all to yourself."

Alistair Downs was my father? That was impossible. My mother said he wasn't. I believed her. Bethany was a raving lunatic.

"Alistair isn't my father," I said with assurance. "I don't know where you got that idea, but it isn't true. Please believe me."

Bethany ignored my attempt at reasoning with her. She was beyond being reasoned with.

For what seemed like an eternity, we went back and forth about Alistair being my father. She said he was, I said he wasn't, and around and around we went.

"It's time for you to kill me now," she said finally, as calmly as if she'd told me it was time to take a batch of cookies out of the oven.

"Bethany, I have no desire whatsoever to kill you." Well, all right. A teeny-weeny desire. "Why don't you give me the gun and we'll—"

"Stay where you are," she commanded, pointing the gun in my face.

I stood still.

"Now, go over to the sink, pick up the dish towel, and drop it on the floor in front of me."

I followed her instructions.

"Now, walk away from me and stand over in the corner."

I obeyed.

"Now, I'm going to use this dish towel to wipe my finger-prints off the gun."

I considered screaming for Cullie, but remembered his state of post-coital catatonia. I considered screaming for the neighbors, but remembered the house's secluded four acres. I considered screaming for the media, but remembered that they had abandoned Maplebark Manor for Evermore. Evermore! Maybe one of the tabloid reporters followed Bethany to my house, I thought. Maybe the reporters and TV cameras would burst in on us any second, wrestle Bethany to the ground, and save me. Then again, maybe not.

"Now, I'm going to wrap the gun in the dish towel."

"Bethany, what are you doing?" I asked with growing dread. If my dread grew any more, it would strangle me.

"I already told you, Alison. I want them to think you killed me, so they'll put you away for life. Just wait until they find you standing over my dead body—especially after they go back to Evermore and see the note I left."

"What note?"

"It said, 'Dear Daddy. In case you're looking for me, I got this urgent call from Alison Koff insisting that I go over to her house. She made terrible threats, so I thought I'd better go.' That ought to do it, don't you think?"

Oh, God. Please tell me this isn't happening. Tell me this is a bad dream. An off-the-charts bad dream.

"Now, stay right where you are and don't move a muscle," she commanded as she shifted the gun from her right hand to her left, pointed it at her chest, and faced me.

"Bethany! Bethany!" I cried. "Don't do it! Don't pull that trigger! I beg you!" She was going to shoot herself right in front of my eyes, not to mention bleed to death all over my nice clean kitchen floor. "Bethany! Bethany! Please!"

Before she could pull the trigger, somebody pounded on the kitchen door.

"Bethany! Open up! It's your father," the voice bellowed.

Good God. It was Alistair! At Maplebark Manor! And he was using the service entrance!

"Daddy!" Bethany cried.

Clutching the gun to her chest, she ran to the door and let her father in. He was not alone. Detective Star Fucker and a posse of Layton Police officers were along for the ride.

"It's all right, dear. Give me the gun," Alistair said as he moved toward his daughter.

Bethany did not budge. Nobody did.

"Come on, Bethany dear. I want you to give me the gun," Alistair tried again, more sternly this time.

She eyed us all warily and continued to hold on to her weapon.

"If you won't give yourself up for me, Bethany dear, give yourself up for America," Alistair actually said. "For our splendid country. For the country you have helped me serve during my wonderful years in the Senate. Imagine how disappointed in us the American people will be if they think we must resort to bloodshed to solve our little difficulties."

Bloodshed. Little difficulties. I was riveted. The senator

was pleading with his nutty daughter to turn herself in on behalf of our splendid country. He had a great act, I had to admit it.

"Come, dear. Do it for our nation. Please. Please. That's a girl," said Alistair as he gently coaxed the gun from her hand. "There we go. There. There now. Good."

Bethany surrendered the gun at last. I was saved. I would live to tell about this.

"You can take her away now, Detective," Alistair told Corsini.

Corsini. What a joke he was. The whole time he was in my kitchen, I tried to make eye contact with him, but he wouldn't play. He was too embarrassed about the way he'd bungled the case, I guessed.

"Bethany Downs," Corsini said as he handcuffed Bethany. "You have the right to remain silent . . ."

He recited the rest of the Miranda rights and led Bethany out the door. "We'll need your statement, Miss Koff," he called out without looking at me.

"Gladly," I said, grateful that the ordeal was finally over. "Your place or mine?"

"One of the officers will take your statement here. Then you'll have to—"

"Yeah, I know the routine, Detective. I'll be down to the station as soon as I finish here," I said. "But first, I'd like to have a little chat with Senator Downs."

Alistair arched an eyebrow at me, then smiled. "What can I do for you, dear?" he asked breezily, as if nothing very consequential had just happened.

"Would you mind sitting down for a moment?" I said.

"Well, dear, I really must go with my—"

"You wouldn't want me to tell the media what was in Melanie Moloney's book, would you, Senator?"

He blinked. "Well, I—"

"Sit down, Senator."

He pulled up a chair and sat down. I remained standing.

"Splendid house you've got here," he said, eyeing the room.

"I'm not interested in discussing my house," I began. "I'm interested in discussing your daughter. You found her note, I assume?"

"Note? What note?"

"The note she left at Evermore, saying she was coming to see me. I assumed that was why you came here."

"No," he said. "I never saw any note. I came here because Detective Corsini and I followed Bethany here."

"You followed her here?"

"Yes."

"But why follow her? Why tonight? If Corsini was going to arrest Bethany, why didn't he do it sooner? The evidence has been piling up for days."

"Yes, well . . . I had asked the police to hold off their . . . to give my daughter one more . . ."

"One more what? One more chance to skip town? Or one more chance to do someone harm?"

"My goodness. What questions!"

"How about some answers, Senator Downs? Why don't you cut the shit and admit how you've been manipulating the investigation all along, how you got the police to busy themselves with me so you could figure out how to protect your daughter, send her out of the country, do whatever you big shots do to wriggle out of sticky situations? Why don't you admit how you made it impossible for the police to arrest Bethany, how they wouldn't make a move in the case unless you gave them the okay, huh, Senator?"

"That's laughable. You don't know what you're saying, dear. Perhaps you're overtired after all the—"

"Laughable? I'll tell you what's laughable. What's laughable is how you've been pulling Corsini's strings from Day One. Then, when you realized how wacko Bethany was, you got scared that she might commit yet another murder. That's when you had the brilliant idea that you could turn poor Bethany into an asset instead of a liability. You figured out that if you were the one to have her followed, the one to help the police arrest her, you'd be applauded for your selflessness, your devotion to the American justice system, your willingness to do the right thing, even if it meant locking up your own daughter. You said to yourself, 'Alistair, you'll be a hero if you're the one who leads the police to Bethany. Think of it, Al old boy. They'll eat it up out there in the hinterlands.' So you turned her in. Your own daughter. I can see the press conference now. There won't be a dry eye in the place."

"You're a misguided young woman, very much like your mother," Alistair said with disgust.

"I'm glad you brought her up," I said, standing over him. "Bethany seems to think your affair with my mother produced a child—me."

He swallowed, but otherwise showed little reaction. "That's rubbish," he said dismissively. "Bethany's not well, obviously. There isn't a shred of truth to what she told you."

"That's what my mother says—that you're not my father. I guess I'll never know though. You've both done your share of cha cha cha-ing me over the years."

"Done our share of what?"

"Never mind."

Suddenly I didn't want to pursue the subject any further. Even if Alistair was my father, he'd never admit it. Neither would my mother. So what was the point of asking?

Sure, there were blood tests to determine parentage. But did I really want to know the truth? What for? Couldn't I allow myself to be cha cha cha-ed just this once?

I watched out the kitchen window as the Senator disappeared down the path to the driveway, where his daughter was waiting in the back seat of one of the police cars. A few minutes later, a police officer named Patrolman White took my statement.

"You're going to want me to come down to headquarters now, right?" I asked wearily.

"Naw," said Patrolman White. "Corsini said you can come down at your convenience. Tomorrow. The next day. Whenever."

"At my convenience, eh?" Well, well. I was finally being treated like a citizen instead of a criminal.

I showed Patrolman White out, straightened up the kitchen, and trudged upstairs to bed.

Cullie was still asleep. After all that had happened, the man was still asleep!

I took off my robe and climbed into bed next to him.

"Cullie," I said. "There's this joke." I cleared my throat. He was still sound asleep.

"A man goes to the doctor. 'Doc,' he says. 'Every time I sneeze I have an orgasm.' 'My goodness,' replies the doctor. 'What are you taking for it?' 'Pepper,' the man says. 'Pepper.'"

I snuggled up next to Cullie, took his hand, and squeezed it.

"Get it?" I whispered. "'Pepper.'"

I smiled and closed my eyes. Within minutes, I fell into a deep and uncomplicated sleep.

Epilogue

"*I have absolutely no comment on Bethany Downs' sentencing yesterday or on Senator Downs' role in her conviction or on anything to do with the Downs family, but I'd be happy to answer your questions about my new business venture,*" said Sonny Waxman, founder and co-owner of Maid to Order, an employment agency specializing in providing area residents with quality domestic help. The former wife of Sanford J. Koff, president of the recently bankrupt Koff's Department Store, Waxman received nationwide media attention in connection with the February slaying of Layton resident and bestselling author Melanie Moloney, for whom she worked as a domestic. The formation of her new company, whose headquarters are at 142 White Birch Place in Layton, was an attempt, she said, to put the Moloney case behind her, not to capitalize on her fifteen minutes of fame. 'The minute Rose Horowitz proposed that we go into business together,' Waxman explained, referring to the proprietor of Second Hand Rose, the county's most successful tag sale organizer, 'I jumped at the chance to work with such a proven professional. Sure, people will say I'm exploiting the fact that I was Melanie Moloney's maid, but why should that bother me? I was a damn good maid. And that's exactly what we're offering with Maid to Order—damn good maids at damn good prices. In this depressed economy, homeowners are so busy trying to hang on to their jobs, they don't have time to clean their *homes. Maid to Order is here to help.' Following the sale of her home last month to PsychSpas, Ltd., the national chain whose luxurious retreats offer around-the-clock psychotherapy plus state-of-the-art health spa facilities, Waxman has relocated to Jessup, where she lives with architectural photographer Charles C. Harrington on their recently refurbished sailboat, the* Marlowe.*"*

—The Layton Community Times, *July 20, 1990*

* * *

LOST & FOUND

"Found: book manuscript in vicinity of Jessup Marina. Badly damaged but salvageable. Let's talk $$$$. Confidentiality guaranteed. PO Box HK, Jessup, CT 06213."

—The Layton Community Times Classifieds,
July 27, 1990

Coming next month from Kensington Books—

THE CLUB

Jane Heller's new hardcover novel of comedy, mystery and romance.

A member of her country club is murdered—and the police want Judy Mills to help them find out who did it!

Please turn the page for an exciting sneak preview of

THE CLUB

The phone rang at about nine-thirty.

"Mrs. Price?" said a male voice.

"I'm not interested," I said. God, those telephone salesmen were a pain, interrupting you in the middle of dinner or bugging you first thing in the morning, never selling anything you were remotely interested in buying.

I was about to hang up when the caller introduced himself as Thomas Cunningham—*Detective* Thomas Cunningham of the Belford Police Department.

"Oh," I said. "I thought you were trying to sell me a Discover card."

"No," he said gruffly. "I'm the guy that's trying to solve Claire Cox's murder."

"Oh," I said again. "Please excuse me. You see, the only people who call me Mrs. Price are telephone salesmen, my husband's parents, and members of my country club."

"What does everyone else call you?" he asked.

"Judy. Judy Mills."

"Mills is your maiden name?"

"Yes. I was never big on hyphenated last names. I've always felt that you either take your husband's name or you don't—and I didn't."

Silence, then: "So your full name is Judy Mills?"

"No. My full name is Judith Rifka Mills."

"I didn't catch the one after Judith."

"Rifka. It's Hebrew for Rebecca. You know, like Becky?"

More silence. I had a hunch that Detective Cunningham was really sorry he'd started this. "Look, Ms. Mills," he said. "I'd like to talk to you about Ms. Cox."

"You mean, because I was one of the people who found her body?" I asked.

"Yes," he said, "and because one of the women who was having dinner with her last night told us that you and Ms. Cox were writing a book together."

"Yes," I said sadly. "A cookbook."

"Could you come down to headquarters this morning? Say around ten-thirty?"

I thought for a minute. I didn't have anything scheduled for ten-thirty. As a matter of fact, I didn't have anything scheduled for the foreseeable future, except a gynecologist appointment two weeks from Wednesday and a periodontal checkup three weeks after that. I was jobless and appointmentless and directionless, and going down to police headquarters and talking to a cop sounded like a welcome change from sitting at home and waiting for the phone to ring. "Ten-thirty will be fine," I said. "Just fine."

I arrived at the police station and was directed to the cubicle-size office of Detective Thomas Cunningham and his partner, Detective Jake Creamer, who was not present at the time of my visit.

"Sit there," said Detective Cunningham as he pointed to the chair next to his desk.

I sat and stared at the detective as he went through a pile of pink "While You Were Out" message slips and tossed most of them in the garbage.

Gee, I thought. He's not bad-looking. Not bad at all. Thirty-five-ish and ruggedly handsome, he had a lean, sinewy build, a cleft in his chin, gleaming brown eyes, and hair that was so dark it was almost comic-book blue-black.

And then there was his nose, which, judging from the right turn it took at the bridge, had been on the receiving end of one too many fists. I'm embarrassed to admit I checked out his left hand: no wedding band. I guessed he had a girl-friend, a manicurist he'd met in the bar of the local Pizza & Brew, and that they often spent the night at his house, having rough sex and watching professional wrestling matches on Pay Per View.

"Thanks for coming, Ms. Mills," he said, finally looking up at me.

"You're welcome," I said, transfixed by the way the cleft in his chin moved as he talked.

"I'll need your address and date of birth," he said as he pulled out a notebook and pen.

"I live at 42 Beaverbrook Road. Belford."

"Date of birth?"

"Is that absolutely necessary?"

Okay, so I was being a little sensitive about my age. It's not easy to admit you're forty when you're sitting with a very attractive younger man.

"Yes, it's absolutely necessary," he said, revealing a hint of a smile.

"May thirtieth, 1955."

"Now, tell me about your relationship with Ms. Cox."

I gave Detective Cunningham the whole sad story—how I was fired from my job at Charlton House, how I hadn't been able to find another job, how my husband had sug-gested I start networking at our country club, how I had previously avoided the club like the plague but took his advice anyway, how I met Claire there, how we decided to write a cookbook together, how I spoke to her at the party the previous evening and how I was one of the group who found her body.

"How long have you and your husband been members of The Oaks?"

"About two years."

"You said you avoided the club. You don't like it there?"

"In a word: no."

"Why not?"

"There's no valet parking."

Detective Cunningham looked up from his notepad.

"Well," I said, "that's not the main reason."

"What's the main reason?"

"The people are a bunch of phonies. The food's not so hot either."

"Is there anything you *like* about The Oaks?"

"Yes. The facilities are very well maintained. If I brushed my teeth as often as they brush those tennis courts, I wouldn't have any enamel left."

"Did Ms. Cox have many friends at The Oaks?"

"No, except for the new women members. She wanted to change things at the club. She thought women should be allowed to eat in the Men's Grill and things like that."

"The what grill?"

"The Men's Grill. It used to be the club's men-only restaurant."

"Oh, yeah. My father's club has one of those." He paused. "Did Ms. Cox have any enemies at The Oaks? Anyone who might want to harm her?"

I thought for a minute. "Well, a lot of people were against her joining the club," I said. "She was the first single woman to get in. Even her great-uncle didn't want her there."

"Would that be Duncan Tewksbury?" he asked.

I nodded.

"So no enemies that you can think of?"

"Enemies? It's hard to say," I said. "At country clubs you can't really tell your enemies from your friends. The guy who plays golf with you one day could be the guy who hits you over the head with a pitching wedge the next."

Detective Cunningham stopped writing and looked up. "What do you know about that pitching wedge, Ms. Mills?"

"You mean the one we found near Claire's body?"

"Yeah."

"Nothing, except that it belonged to Henry, the golf pro. It was one of his teaching clubs."

"Did you ever see any of the members playing with that club?"

"No, but then I make it a point never to see the members playing with *any* club. I hate watching golf. It's a really boring sport, if you ask me. Right up there with fly fishing."

Thomas Cunningham stared at me. Clearly, I was not his run-of-the-mill interviewee.

"I think we're just about finished here," he said.

"Oh?" I was disappointed. I had enjoyed having Detective Cunningham ask me questions, listen to my answers, ask for my opinions.

Detective Cunningham gave the notes he'd taken during our interview to a secretary, asked her to type them up, and when she did, he handed me the pages and told me to read them over.

"If everything's correct, sign here," he said.

I signed.

"Thanks for coming in." He shook my hand and allowed himself a smile.

My eyes went straight to the cleft in his chin, and the oddest thing happened. I began to imagine myself inserting my tongue in that cleft, in and out, in and out, in and out. Yes, I was horny, and yes, my marriage was stale, and yes, I'd always thought men with cleft chins exuded a certain animal magnetism, but to have fantasies right there in the police station—during a murder interrogation, no less—was humiliating and not a little disrespectful to the murder victim.

You need to get a job, I told myself as I left police headquarters. You need to get a job and you need to get laid.

About ten days after Claire died, I was moping around the house one morning, trying not to think about the torrid sex Detective Cunningham and I would have if we were both free, when the detective himself called me.

"Yes, Detective. Of course I remember you," I said, my heart doing little pirouettes as I wound the telephone cord around my finger.

"I'd like to see you," he said.

Did I sense a certain urgency, a certain huskiness in his voice, or was it just wish fulfillment on my part?

"When?" I said, trying not to pant.

"How about in twenty minutes?" he said.

"That would be fine," I said. "You have the address."

"Yeah. See ya."

He hung up. I hung up. Then I caught a glimpse of my reflection in the hall mirror. Brother, I was still wearing my ratty bathrobe *and* the plastic bite plate that was supposed to prevent me from grinding my teeth at night.

I hurried upstairs to freshen up and change, and tried to stay calm. But I was nervous. I jumped when the doorbell rang.

I let Detective Cunningham in and suggested we sit in the living room. I offered him coffee. He said he'd rather just talk.

"Now, Ms. Mills," he began. "I hope you won't be shocked by what I came to ask you to do."

Now, I was really nervous. I'd been fantasizing about the man for days. Had he been thinking about me too? Was that why he had come? "Ask me," I said.

He cleared his throat. "I'd like to make you a proposition."

I was stunned. He was propositioning me. Be careful what you wish for, my mother always said.

Okay, so he was sexy. And sure, I was aching for a little action. But as I said earlier, I wasn't the adulterous type, not really. I wasn't clever enough for adultery. Adultery takes cunning. You've got to plan ahead. You've got to find a trysting place. You've got to remember to shave your legs.

I didn't have the time or energy for all that. I had to throw everything I had into finding a job.

"As I said, Ms. Mills, I'd like to make you a proposition."

"The answer is no," I said firmly.

"But you haven't even heard what I want you to do."

"All right," I said, "say what you came to say." How awful could it be to have to sit and listen to a handsome hunk confess his passion for me?

"We'd like to offer you a job with the Belford Police Department."

I was confused. "The police department wants to do a cookbook?"

I had once edited a cookbook that was put together by the New York City Fire Department. It had recipes for things like Firehouse Chili and Smoky Barbecued Chicken, and raised money for some charity or other. But a local police department's cookbook? It didn't sound like a huge seller.

"Are you thinking of a book that's sort of a cross between Joseph Wambaugh and Julia Child?" I asked.

"No, no. You don't understand," he said. "While we're exploring all aspects of this case and following up on each and every lead, we think it's possible that a member of your country club was responsible for Claire Cox's death."

"Oh?"

"We want you to help us find out if the killer *was* one of the members, and if so, *which* member." He paused. "We want you to be our informant."

I was dumbfounded. "You want *me* to help you solve Claire's murder?"

"That's right. Ms. Cox was a big celebrity, and the federal boys would love to get their hands on the case. But it's *our* jurisdiction, *our* case to solve. Well, actually it's *my* case to solve. Mine and my partner's. And our boss wants us to solve it yesterday. You understand?"

"Not really."

"Okay, let me try again. The Belford Police Department isn't a huge force. We're a small-town force, 'small' being the operative word here. We can't put every single guy on this one case, so my partner and I are handling it the best we can. We've got hundreds of interviews to do, hundreds of leads to follow up on, leads that have nothing to do with The Oaks. At the same time, we—or should I say I?—am interested in getting information about some of the members of The Oaks, but I don't want to go in there and upset everybody. You know how bent out of shape they get, right?"

"Do I ever. I hear some of them gave you a hard time when you asked them to come down to headquarters."

He rolled his eyes. "That wasn't the half of it. You should have seen what happened when we asked for a list of all the members."

"Nobody would give you one?"

"Oh, they gave us one, but only after we got a subpoena for it. Then we started calling the members on the list and found out that a quarter of them were dead. No, I wouldn't say the people at your club have been especially forthcoming."

"I'm not surprised."

"So, what we need right now—and I know this is a little out of the ordinary—is information about The Oaks' members and their relationship with the deceased. We need someone who's an insider, someone who could hang out there without arousing suspicion. We think *you'd* make a perfect informant."

"Me? Why?"

"Because you're a member of the club but you hate the place."

"What exactly would you want me to do?"

"The same thing you've been doing. Go to the club. Play golf—"

"I don't play golf."

"Sorry. I forgot." He smiled. The hole in his chin danced.

"Then play tennis, swim, whatever. The important thing is to just *be* there, keep your eyes and ears open, tell us if you see or hear anything suspicious."

"I see and hear suspicious things all the time at The Oaks."

"Like what?"

"The members cheat—at everything. The golfers doctor their score cards, and the tennis players call every close ball in their favor. There's no such thing as sportsmanship at The Oaks."

He laughed. "It's not their lack of sportsmanship I'm concerned about. It's their possible connection to Claire Cox's murder."

"So you're saying you want me to spy on my friends at The Oaks?"

"You said you didn't have any friends at The Oaks."

"Good point." My mind was racing. "But my husband does. He's Mr. Popularity at the club. He'd be furious if he found out I was doing anything to jeopardize his membership. He uses the club to network. He's trying to make partner at Fitzgerald & Franklin, the investment banking firm. He's—"

"Then don't tell him," said Detective Cunningham.

"Don't tell him?" What an idea. I told Hunt everything, or at least I used to. How could I possibly be a police informant and not tell him?

"Look, Ms. Mills."

"Judy, remember?"

"Sorry. Judy. And I'm Tom."

"Tom."

"It's up to you whether or not you tell your husband. I just want to know if you'll do it."

"Be an informant, you mean."

"Yeah."

"How would it work exactly?"

"First, you'd come down to headquarters so we could run your prints, that kind of stuff."

"Run my prints?"

"Yeah, the lieutenant is pretty strict about prints. He says if I'm going to go out on a limb and hire you, I've got to get you fingerprinted, make sure you are who you say you are. Then I'd give you a beeper so we could always be in touch."

Always be in touch. That had a nice ring to it.

"So I'd be working directly with you?" I asked.

"Only with me," he said. "You have a problem with that?"

"No, no problem," I said.

"As far as money goes, you'll be paid about $200 a week for as long as we need you."

Paid? That did it. I took a deep breath. "Tom," I said. "Meet your new informant."

"So you're taking the job?"

"Yes."

"Good."

"I hope so."

YOU WON'T WANT TO READ
JUST ONE—KATHERINE STONE

ROOMMATES   (3355-9, $4.95)
No one could have prepared Carrie for the monumental
changes she would face when she met her new circle of
friends at Stanford University. Once their lives intertwined
and became woven into the tapestry of the times, they would
never be the same.

TWINS   (3492-X, $4.95)
Brook and Melanie Chandler were so different, it was hard
to believe they were sisters. One was a dark, serious, ambitious New York attorney; the other, a golden, glamourous,
sophisticated supermodel. But they were more than sisters—they were twins and more alike than even they knew
. . .

THE CARLTON CLUB   (3614-0, $4.95)
It was the place to see and be seen, the only place to be. And
for those who frequented the playground of the very rich, it
was a way of life. Mark, Kathleen, Leslie and Janet—they
worked together, played together, and loved together, all behind exclusive gates of the *Carlton Club*.

*Available wherever paperbacks are sold, or order direct from the
Publisher. Send cover price plus 50¢ per copy for mailing and handling to Penguin USA, P.O. Box 999, c/o Dept. 17109, Bergen-
field, NJ 07621. Residents of New York and Tennessee must
include sales tax. DO NOT SEND CASH.*